In the Shadow of Evil

In the

Shadow of Evil

In the Shadow of Evil

BEATRICE CULLETON MOSIONIER

THEYTUS BOOKS

PENTICTON

CANADIAN CATALOGUING IN PUBLICATION DATA

Mosionier, Beatrice, 1949–
    In the shadow of evil

    ISBN 0-919441-98-X

    I. Title.
PS8576.0783I53 2000   C813'.54   C00-911027-5
PR9199.3.M659I53 2000

Editorial: Rosemary Shipton, Florene Belmore, Ursula Vaira
Design: Val Speidel

Theytus Books Ltd.
Lot 45 Green Mountain Rd.
RR#2, Site 50, Comp. 8
Penticton, BC
V2A 6J7

The publisher acknowledges the support of The Canada Council for the Arts,
The Department of Canadian Heritage and The British Columbia Arts Council.

For my families

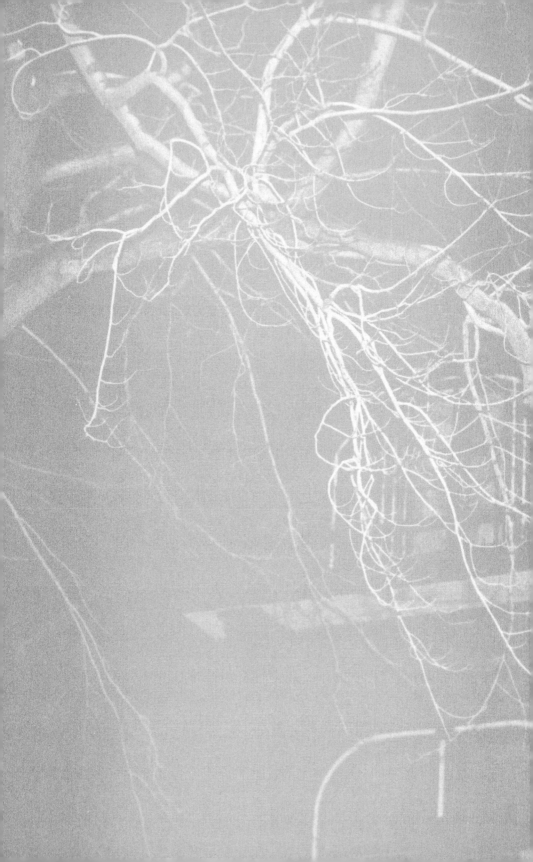

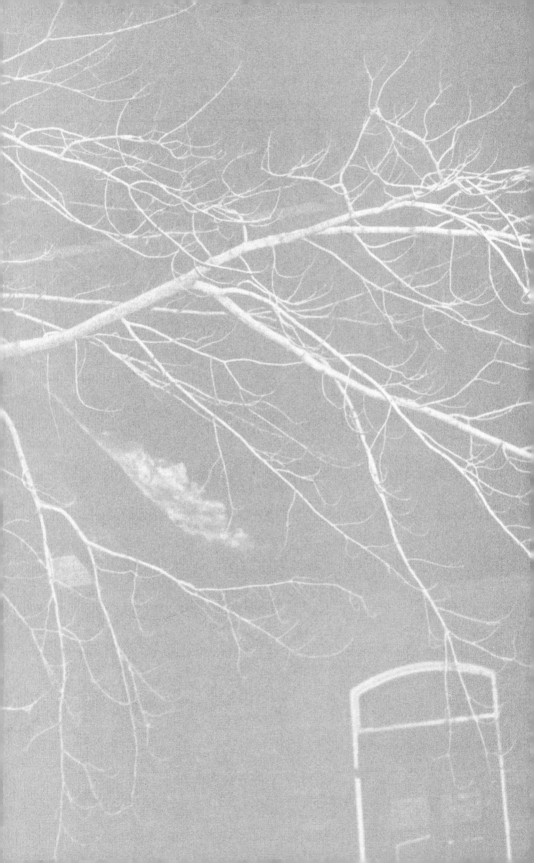

He eyed the television monitors mounted against the wall in his study, which also served as the security headquarters, before shutting them off with the remote control. He had spotted the local paper, *The Peace Valley Voice*, tossed carelessly on one of the chairs near the entrance on his way in, and the picture at the top right-hand corner had shattered his smug complacency. He sat at his desk, staring at her picture. As the memories flared up, he trembled with a rage he hadn't felt in a long time. She was within his reach at last and deserved to die. He would see to it. He thought of all the things he would do to her, and his fist, clinging to the paper, shot out as if to smash her face in right that minute. The edge of the paper caught the desk lamp and sent it crashing to the floor, but it didn't break.

A delicious new thought came to mind. Instead of killing her outright, why not play a little game with her, a game of cat and mouse? On the wall behind him, the lamplight from below froze his image in a long and eerie shadow.

*M*oonlight cast its silvery light across the quiet of the forest. High up in a black spruce a lynx lazily blinked, ever watchful for movement of prey. Its eyes widened, its head lifted, its nose quivered. In the distance, some of the surrealistic shadows created by the moonlight moved in and out, among the trees. Gentle air currents brought the low sounds of anxious whines and the soft falls of padded feet racing over fallen leaves to the twitching ears of the lynx. Its short tail switched back and forth nervously as the wolves came into view.

Neka, the black female and mother of two pups, was in the lead, followed closely by Okimaw, her mate and the leader of the nine-member wolf clan. Behind and off to the sides were seven more wolves of various ages. Of the three adult males, only Otakosin came from a previous litter and had the same markings as his father, Okimaw. The other two males, Oskinikiw and Kanatan, were older, but not quite as large or as formidable as Okimaw. Nimis, now also an adult, was of charcoal colouring, not the deep black of her mother, Neka, and she bore a white spot on her chest. Kisikaw and Wapan, the six-month-old female pups that had survived from a litter of five, were excitedly keeping up. Kehte-aya, the oldest of the wolves and once the matriarch, brought up the rear.

They were playing a game of tag. Oskinikiw shot by Okimaw to sideswipe Neka and bowl her over. She took it good-naturedly with a brief wag of her tail. Then she and the pack chased Oskinikiw. Okimaw brought the game to Shadow Lake. They lapped up water and, while five of the adults rested, Kanatan, the clown, and Kehte-aya, the old one, were drawn into more games with the exuberant youngsters.

Neka stood up and stretched, wagged her tail and nuzzled Okimaw affectionately. He, too, stood up to stretch and then he looked around. Curious, Oskinikiw raised his head. Neka pointed her nose towards the sky and gave a few low tentative howls. Okimaw immediately raised his head and blended his lower-pitched voice with hers. This duet brought the rest of the wolves racing back in delight. With tails wagging, they greeted each other as if they had been apart for weeks. The pups threw their higher-pitched, almost squeaky voices into the symphony. By then the rest of the adults joined in, all seeming to give the moon a disjointed serenade.

As abruptly as it started, it ended. In the intervening silence the wolves listened intently. They heard answering calls that carried over the mist of the night air from perhaps twenty kilometres to the west. Wapan whined impatiently and approached her father to nip at his muzzle. Kisikaw followed suit by nipping at Kehte-aya's mouth. Tails wagging, they were all soon nipping and licking at Okimaw and the rest of the pack joined in, all looking like pups begging for food to be regurgitated. In fact, the young ones did want to be fed. It was time for the hunt.

Okimaw pointed his nose in different directions, sorting out the many scents drifting by on the placid air currents. Then he set out with a deliberate wolf-trot, followed by Neka. All playfulness was now gone. The wolves were on full alert. They had an oblong summer route that they had marked out as their territory. But now they were able to leave the den and the rendezvous area; they could expand into their winter territory, an area that covered roughly 200 square kilometres. In some areas their runway overlapped the territories of neighbouring wolf packs. Elk, deer, moose, and caribou were their main large prey. From denning season to autumn, the wolf pack spent much of its time in the valley containing Shadow Lake.

In the past, they had been a pack deep in the wilderness with little contact with humans, and they had remained healthy as traditional teachings had passed from generation to generation. Among the most important teachings was the warning to avoid humans: "Awasis, watch them if you like, but do not be seen."

Now it was the season for the hunters from the south, the ones with the telescopic, high-powered, automatic rifles. In the foothills of the Rockies, reports of rifle shots cracked like thunderclaps, reverberating back and forth across mountainsides. In the lower forested regions, the sounds were more like muffled snaps. The smell of gunpowder in the air meant the days were dangerous times, and most of the wildlife took deeper cover.

That night, Okimaw led the pack away from the south shores of Shadow Lake towards the north. He soon scented an elk nearby and stopped to sniff the air. He circled, trying to get a visual fix on the prey. When he saw the young animal casually browsing on the sweet sapwood of a black spruce, then turning its head to scan its surroundings, the wolf froze. The others behind froze likewise. Lowering himself close to the ground, the wolf stalked forward to close the distance to the prey. Whenever the elk raised its head, Okimaw would freeze. Neka was just to his rear. When they saw the elk twitch its ears and look in their direction more alertly, the whole pack sprung forward.

The elk merely turned its body so it was facing them, stopping the wolves in their tracks. Oskinikiw circled to the elk's right side. Without moving his head, the elk eyed Oskinikiw, Okimaw, and Kanata, as they moved up one by one. So far he still had some lead time. Escape to the left seemed like the best choice. With a sideways leap he was off and running. The chase had begun. The elk was young and strong. The distance between predators and prey began to increase. When the elk sensed that the pursuers were giving up the chase, he turned and watched the wolves trot off to a resting place, then browsed on the vegetation around him. It was useful for both prey and predator to conserve their energy. The elk would live to see his first rutting season, if a hunter's bullet didn't get him first.

The wolves rested after the fruitless chase, then, one by one, the adults left in different directions. The youngsters with Neka and Kehte-aya made up a smaller unit. It was another way of hunting. The wolves could cover more ground by spreading out. At this time of the year when the smell of gunpowder was released into the air, chances of finding wounded prey were possible. More than once, the wolves had seen and heard the two-legged predators stumbling through the woods.

The next day, when the wolves regrouped, it was Nimis who returned carrying the scent that she had been successful. She had found and fed on the fresh carcass of a mule deer. Whenever they met, the wolves greeted each other by nuzzling and sniffing. The wolves backtracked over her trail, Okimaw in the lead, and soon they joined the ravens already feeding on the carcass.

Ravens, crows, and jays, all members of the crow family, kept company with the wolves, sometimes leading the wolves to carcasses and sometimes following the pack on their hunts. Crows were quite daring around wolves, settling down in their midst, regardless of whether the wolves were feeding or resting. Only the young inexperienced wolves would try to pounce on the birds, but they soon learned it was an exercise in futility.

One afternoon after gorging on a moose carcass, the wolves with their bloated stomachs were napping. With his muzzle resting on his front paws, Kanatan was sleepily watching one of the crows hop among the other wolves. The crow approached Otakosin's head, deliberately pecking at the ground in front. Sensing some fun, Kanatan raised his head to watch more closely. Now the crow was pecking closer and closer to Otakosin. With one swift movement it pecked the sleeping wolf right on the nose. Otakosin jumped straight up in the air, yelping, but the crow easily managed to avoid Otakosin's pounce. Otakosin spotted the amused Kanatan and, since he couldn't vent his indignation on the agile crow, he went after Kanatan. Kanatan took his licking, showing his subordination to Otakosin by rolling onto his back with his tail tucked between his legs, and pleaded for mercy. When Otakosin had satisfied himself, he returned to his resting spot, circled to settle down, and gave Kanatan another icy stare. Kanatan immediately turned his eyes away from Otakosin's. Some wolves had no sense of humour.

Until the mating season, when a change in leadership might occur, Okimaw was the alpha male. He was also a breeding male. Later, he might still retain the leadership, but the breeding male might be one of the *lower-ranking males. He was from Kehte-aya's second litter and was now in his eighth year. Okimaw decided when, where, and how a hunt would proceed. He always ate from the kills. All the members of the pack were submissive to him. Neka was the alpha female and was submissive only to Okimaw, but, as his mate, she could be more persuasive than submissive, and sometimes Okimaw allowed her to lead the pack. They were quite affectionate with each other all year round. If a female wolf were the largest, strongest wolf of a pack, it was possible for her to be the alpha wolf. But Neka was a docile, gentle wolf for most of the year.*

Oskinikiw was the beta male. If Okimaw were killed or seriously incapacitated, Oskinikiw would assume the leadership and could take Neka as his mate, or he might choose Nimis or even a wandering female. He had been adopted by Neka and Okimaw when his mother was killed by a grizzly.

Four years earlier, Oskinikiw's mother had detected the presence of a marauding grizzly bear. She had already moved two pups to a new den a kilometre away and was on her third trip. There was one pup still in the den when the grizzly located the entrance. Panicked at being alone, the pup had disobeyed his mother and wandered out of the den to look for his litter mates. His whimpering immediately attracted the bear. The mother wolf tried in vain to save her pup, but the grizzly turned on her and, with one swipe of his large paw, caught her across her head and broke her neck. When the rest of the wolves returned at the end of a long hunt and discovered the remains, they moved out of the area.

Neka and Okimaw had been on a romp while Kehte-aya remained with Neka's litter. The romp became a hunt and the hunt took them into the overlap of their runway, where markings had already become aged and where the new den was located. Neka heard the cries of the pups and began sniffing the area until she found the den. Deep inside, she found the two three-week-old pups, still alive, but barely. She nursed them both and then, picking one up by its belly, she brought it out and Okimaw followed her back to her own den. For some reason she did not go back for the other pup. Perhaps it was too sick or weak, or perhaps she didn't have enough milk, or perhaps she simply forgot about it.

Otakosin was a year younger than Oskinikiw and had begun to challenge Oskinikiw for beta position. This past summer, Otakosin had left the pack for a few weeks and, on his return, he reassumed his standing in the pack hierarchy. Any of the subordinates could leave to start their own families or join another pack. Occasionally, a wolf from another pack stayed days before rejoining its own pack. It was a way of overcoming inbreeding and, possibly, it was also a way of exchanging information from distant places. However, a strange pack of wolves could just as easily turn an intruder away or even kill it.

One cool sunny afternoon in the late fall, as the wolves were sleeping after eating their fill of a bull moose, the sound of a rifle shot snapped. They were immediately up, scattering in different directions into the surrounding stands of black spruce and jack pine. One wolf did not get up. Oskinikiw had flipped to his side with his legs splayed in a sudden tense spasm. He shuddered a few times, then his body went limp and he died. That evening, back near the south end of Shadow Lake, Okimaw raised his voice to call his wolves to him. They all eventually returned, except for Oskinikiw. When they howled the next time, it was a mournful song. Afterwards, Okimaw led the wolves further to the northwest. It was time to travel deeper into their winter territory.

In December the wolf pack was again marking its winter range and they were now hunting more often during the day. In their hunts, they attempted to get as close to the quarry as possible, hoping for a quick rush and a kill, their strong jaws ripping and slashing. Today they would split up and some of them would feed on hare. Many times they made their rushes and chased elk, deer, and moose, and many times they settled for beaver, hare, and marmot. For some of them, long periods without food were not unusual. Their stomachs were made for the feast-and-famine way of the wild.

Between September and January the days and nights in the lives of wolves were spent with hunting, resting, playing, and marking out their expanded territory. By January the pups, Kisikaw and Wapan, born in the previous March or April, had now taken part in actual kills of larger game. Only a discerning human eye could pick them out as youngsters. They would be fully mature at about twenty-two months, after which they might wander off to form new packs or join others, or they would establish a place for themselves in this pack.

The mating season began in January and the normally tolerant dispositions of Neka and Okimaw changed dramatically. Okimaw became testy, mostly towards his son, Otakosin, taking every opportunity to show his brute strength. And Neka enforced her dominance over Nimis, over every real or imagined transgression. This show of dominance passed down the line, and the wolves went around avoiding eye contact and keeping their tails well tucked between their legs. Only the alpha pair went around with their tails raised high.

Neka and Okimaw finally left the pack after three weeks to carry out the remainder of their courtship in private. After they had successfully completed their mating ritual, life among the wolves returned to normal.

In March the pack returned to Shadow Lake, where they had their denning area. Shadow Lake was seven kilometres long and, in some places, three kilometres wide. If seen from the air, it was shaped like a tight S, and it supported a family of common loons. The lake at the southeast end became marshland, an attraction to moose and fowl. On the opposite side where the lake was indented by land, the wolves had their den.

Neka prepared the den, making some slight renovations. It was located about one hundred yards from the water, and high banks provided views of the surrounding clearings and of the entrance. Stands of trembling aspen, black spruce, jack pine and hemlock protected three sides, and thickets of willow shrubs along the lake hid the den's entrance. The interior was a narrow twenty-foot tunnel, winding through the root system of the trees above, and it widened slightly at the end, where Neka would give birth to the pups.

At the beginning of spring, about two months after conception, Neka crawled in to give birth to a new generation. Six pups were born. Of these, two might survive to adulthood. The wilderness can be a harsh environment. For now, the whole pack celebrated the birth of the pups. With tails wagging, they danced around outside, whining and licking each other. Then, remembering that Neka might be hungry, they performed their pre-hunting ritual, nipping and licking at Okimaw's jaws, and he led them off to the hunt. He and other members brought food back, either swallowing it so they could regurgitate it on their return or, if portable, bringing back chunks of meat.

By the third week, all the puppies' eyes had opened and most of them were no longer deaf. Some of them were already crawling towards the entrance. Neka decided it was time to introduce them to the rest of the family. On that day, all the wolves gathered at the entrance, watching with anticipation. Each pup was greeted with much fuss. Neka, proud mother, watched her grunting, squealing pups.

Wapan, now thirteen months, was especially intrigued with the pups. Kehte-aya, Nimis, and Kanatan often took turns staying at the den while the others were away hunting. When Wapan was allowed to stay with the pups, she was quite pleased. She would settle down and allow the pups to climb all over her. If she went on the hunt, she made sure she brought back partially digested food to be regurgitated for the pups. But she preferred to be the one to stay with the little ones, although, more and more, it was Kehte-aya who remained at the den.

Kehta-aya was still agile, but she had become slower and stiffer with age. One day, she joined the hunt while Wapan remained behind. The pack came upon a mule deer, chased it, cornered it, and closed in on it. Kehte-aya was at the front while Okimaw and the others were tearing at its flanks. One of its sharp front hoofs caught Kehte-aya in the shoulder. It wasn't unusual for wolves to be struck. They healed well, and quickly, from such injuries. When the deer was down and the feeding frenzy began, Kehte-aya limped up to the carcass, but Okimaw chased her away and would not allow her to feed. She limped off to a thicket of willows to watch the feeding wolves and lick at her wound. Kehte-aya would not heal from this wound.

When the wolves had fed, Okimaw and Neka returned to the den to feed Wapan and the pups. Otakosin was the one who prevented Kehte-aya from feasting on the remains. She was driven further away into the bush and she could not feed until what was left was mostly hair and bones. Her time of usefulness to the pack had come to an end.

The pack could afford to raise a healthy new litter to continue a generation of wolves. But when food was hard to come by, when each adult member had to carry its own weight to stay strong and sustain the pack, the pack could not carry the injured and the weak. Kehte-aya would not recover, and instinct dictated that she be excluded from the pack. Even if she had not been wounded, her age and condition would have guaranteed her exile some time in the coming year.

That night, the howls of the wolves seemed to have an intensely lonely sound, almost as if they were in mourning once again. Kehte-aya, now feeding on what was left, raised her head to listen, knew her fate, and accepted it. She sighed and lowered her head to resume her meagre feeding. From now on, when Neka was away, it would be Wapan who watched over the pups.

I

The Chinook winds had blown by, teasing us with the higher temperatures they brought, but soon it really would be spring, and then summer—and that's as far as I cared to think about. Looking ahead was a jinx for me, so I stopped. The morning had been warm, but the temperature had dropped drastically and the wind that had brought the cold was now howling intermittently. Buffered from those winds inside our small log cabin, Peter had set up the chess game; Todd, our three year old, was asleep in his bed; and Lady, our collie, was lying at my feet. All the elements to ensure contentment were mine, but I was miserable.

A few months back I had accepted an invitation to a school in Norway House, in northern Manitoba, and the date of departure was closing in. No matter how reassuring Peter tried to be, I had a strong feeling that one of the flights was going to crash. I tried to remember if I had felt so certain before, but while I hated flying, once it was done, I never remembered the details of my anxieties, only that I had them.

"Let the games begin," Peter said cheerfully, holding a pawn in each hand behind his back. I picked the white pawn and made my usual opening move. After the initial play, each successive move took longer and longer. Peter loved playing chess. His first mystery book, *Check and Mate*, was about a deadly game based on chess moves between an old man, Gregory M. Thomas, the protagonist in all his subsequent books, and an elusive stalker obsessed with a young lady. Of all the books he had written since, that one remained my favourite.

Since moving up here to the foothills of the Rockies, we had a routine of ending our days with a chess game, or sometimes two, skipping the games only if Peter was into his writing. When my ever-so-perfect sister, Leona, and her son, Michael, had come to visit last summer, Peter had taught Michael the game, and Michael had taken my place.

As I responded to a move and lost my bishop, I studied Peter's face, wondering what he thought about when we weren't talking. Probably plots. Because he wrote novels, Peter had to leave home more often than I did, to do his research, maintain his contacts, and do speaking engagements, earning extra income. In contrast to him, I spent my time trying not to think of the secrets of my past—evil secrets— beginning when I was three years old.

Lady stood up, shook herself, and trotted to the door, looking back at us expectantly. As I rose to let her out, Peter shushed me: "Listen."

At first I could hear only the snaps of wet wood burning in the stove. Then I heard them, distinctly, above the howling wind. The wolves were somewhere in our vicinity. Peter and I exchanged smiles and we rushed out to the screened porch. Lady's nose quivered as she sniffed the night air and let out a soft high-pitched whine. I crouched down to pet her while we listened intently, revelling in the primeval excitement that the wolves awakened. The howling never seemed to last long enough and, tonight, there was an especially mournful quality.

"They sound how I feel," I said.

"There's no answer," Peter noted, after a few minutes of silence. Sometimes there were answering calls in the distance, but not tonight, or they were beyond our hearing. Once, when Peter was away and I had let Lady out around five in the morning, I heard them, young ones and older ones, and it seemed they were just around the bend. They reminded me of people at a cocktail party, some excited voices rising above others. Unable to resist, I let out a howling sound, which silenced them immediately. Back in my bed I pictured them rolling around on the ground, laughing at my effort. Or maybe I had insulted them in wolf language.

"Yeah, they sound so forlorn tonight," I said. We walked back in, Lady following us, and she settled again at my feet. "Or maybe it's just me."

Peter moved his black rook into place. "Check."

"Are you sure you want to do that?" I asked coyly.

"What?" Peter studied the board again. "Oh, I see. Yeah, well, it's too late. I already moved. So we're feeling forlorn, are we?"

"Well, I am. I'll miss you and Todd. And I have a really bad feeling about this trip. You can take it back," I said, as I rubbed Lady with my foot.

"I can't. Rules are you can't take a move back."

"Like this is a championship game?" My queen was at the kitty corner from his rook. Was it a setup? If I took his rook, would I lose my queen? I should have insisted that the school at Norway House wait until May, when I imagined the snow would be all gone, but no, I had let my publisher tell them I'd come at the beginning of April. Without caring too much, I made my move. If I lost my queen, I deserved it.

Closing in for the kill, Peter made another move. In doing so, he had left me an opening. He had once said I had a wicked mind, in that I pretended to play defensively, yet I was the one who pulled him in. Smiling wickedly, I made my own final move and said, "Check and mate." I sat back, with exaggerated satisfaction. Inside, I was like two people. One wore the mask of a normal person. The other was always thinking, dwelling on comments like the one Peter had made about my wicked mind. He'd been joking, but maybe he sensed that I had more than just a wicked mind. Maybe he instinctively sensed that I had a wicked soul.

Peter looked at the board, seeing only now what he had missed. "Okay, okay, what if I had taken that move back?"

"You mean rules are made to be broken?"

"Let's just try it. You still win."

"I know," I said in jest. We put the pieces back in their positions before my queen had taken his rook and he returned the rook to its original place. We played from there for another fifteen minutes, when I once again put him into checkmate.

"Another one?" Peter asked, refusing to retire as the loser.

"Oh Peter, I hate killing your men," I said jokingly.

We grinned at each other. He leaned forward and said in a lower voice, "One more."

"Okay. You set them up. I'll go check on Todd." Before I left, I put the kettle on the wood stove.

Todd was sleeping peacefully, a corner of his blanket tucked into his mouth. He was my angel, who roused feelings of gratitude in me, though at times he also roused feelings of guilt. Lady had followed me in and she now settled herself on the rug beside his bed, almost as if it was her job to keep watch over him. Later during the night she would end up on the rug on my side of the bed. I returned to the table with two cups of hot chocolate and picked a black pawn from Peter's right hand.

"Too bad," he said, smiling gleefully. He knew I wasn't as good when I played black and that he would probably win. "Remember, we can't take back any moves."

"Yeah, right," I agreed.

"What you need is a killer instinct," he said, trying to psych me out in advance.

"Okay." I picked off a pawn, unable to resist, even though I knew I was leaving myself vulnerable.

"Are you sure you want to do that?" he mimicked.

"Yup." Only two more nights at home—I squirmed at the thought. "I have a real bad feeling this time."

"You already said that, and you always have bad feelings about flying. Flying is safer than driving."

"That's because pilots are well trained and there's not as many planes in the air as there are cars on the ground. But that doesn't make me feel any better. The man who owned this place before us, he died in a plane crash."

"Yeah, but they say he mixed drugs with alcohol," Peter recalled.

"Whatever, but this time, I have an extra, extra bad feeling."

"Why don't you cancel?"

"Can't do that now. I committed myself. I should be committed for committing myself." *I should have been committed just for being me.*

"You could have said no. You should have said no."

"I know, and from now on, I vow this is the last trip—unless I can drive or take a train."

"That's what you said after the last trip. We always go through this."

"Before I only promised. This is a vow, and a vow is more serious than a promise. You can take that move back if you want."

"Okay."

The next morning, Colin Sayers dropped by, saying he was in the area on business. Colin was Leona's latest love of her life. They had met last August when she was visiting us, and then she had moved in with him in Fort St. John, instead of returning to Winnipeg as she should have.

We hadn't seen them since before Christmas and, to be polite, I asked how Leona and Michael were doing. Fortunately, Colin didn't seem to want to talk about them and, after saying they were okay, he turned the conversation back to us. Over coffee, Peter mentioned that Todd and he would have to "bach it" for a week because I was going on a trip. Surprisingly, Colin was very curious about it, to the point of asking about details. Then again, perhaps he was overdoing the pretence of being interested for Leona's sake. He seemed to have something else on his mind, but, whatever it was, he kept to himself and left after a second cup of coffee.

By the middle of that afternoon, anxiety had me pacing back and forth. Peter, who was revising another chapter before sending his manuscript off to his agent, told me to go outside to split some wood and work off my excess energy. Soon he and Todd came outside and we went for a walk. I gathered he had reluctantly abandoned his type-writer because hearing me split wood by myself had made him feel guilty. As we walked, I reviewed my inconsequential past as a writer of children's books to plan the talks I would give in Norway House.

"Loon!" Todd suddenly exclaimed, breaking into my reverie. We were at the edge of the lake. Most of the ice had broken up, but not enough for the loons to return.

"No." Peter said. "The loons aren't back from Florida, yet. It's a duck."

"Duck," Todd repeated. That set him off on a rhyming spree. "Duck. Muck. Suck. Luck …"

Peter and I looked at each other, waiting for the "F" word to come. We smiled.

"The loon will be here soon," Peter said, in an attempt to ward him off.

Todd merely looked up at him and continued, "Duck. Muck. Buck. Guck …"

"The ice is nice," I said helpfully.

Peter looked at me. "The ice is nice?"

I shrugged. "Look in his eyes. He's toying with us."

Peter studied our son and Todd seemed to know his game was up because he giggled gleefully. He knew that the "F" word, which came from movie tapes we rented, was a no-no. Peter picked him up and swung him around in the air. Todd laughed all the more with delight.

My son's eyes, shining with pure joy, looked down into his father's eyes and the wonderful sound of his laughter echoed out across the lake. The pleasure in their faces was evident as they enjoyed life as it was meant to be. The memory of them at this moment would return to either haunt me or sustain me.

Once we returned to the cabin, I began to pack a bag while Peter put the fire on. When he was done, I heard him take Todd in for his afternoon nap. Then he joined me in our bedroom, tried a few jokes to make me laugh, and went back to his editing.

I always pack light when I travel by plane so I won't have to wait for baggage to be unloaded. Unfortunately, my winter clothing was too bulky, so I had to bring out one of the larger suitcases. Later, I looked everything over and made sure I had my plane ticket. Tomorrow I would leave extra early for Fort St. John, in case the roads were icy, fly from there to Edmonton, and wait for the flight to Winnipeg. I'd stay overnight in Winnipeg, for I had to get to the airport by six-thirty next morning for the seven o'clock flight to Norway House. Besides flying, staying alone in hotel rooms was also scary. Then there were all the small worries, such as not being able to get my morning cups of coffee with real milk. When I was satisfied that all was in order, I went to Todd's bedroom.

Lady raised her head and wagged a greeting. Not wanting to disturb my sleeping son, I sat on the rug and Lady rested her head on my lap. She liked me to stroke her head. Todd's mouth moved a few times as if he were sucking on his blanket. Unable to resist, I moved his thick dark-brown hair, thinking I'd have to give him a haircut when I got back. His clear skin still had a rosy pink glow from being outside.

Although I never told Peter, I was glad that Todd had fair skin. He wouldn't get the name-calling I took as a kid. Already I knew I was going to miss him so much. Now when I saw other kids his age, I thought none of them were as perfect as he was—not as good-natured, not as eager to smile and to please, not as funny. I had only been guessing he had been toying with us out at the lake and was surprised I had been right. He was smarter than the average bear. He must have sensed he was being watched because he woke up and immediately held his arms out to me to be hugged. I obliged, then took him to wash up before supper.

F-day was upon me, F for flights. Peter, knowing my silence was due to distress and not to anger, paid cheerful attention to Todd during breakfast. I'd woken up with a feeling of dread, and now, over my third cup of coffee, I was actually feeling terror. Six different planes— and I knew one of them wasn't going to make its destination.

Premonitions were silly, I chided myself. My fear of flying was just getting worse, that's all this was. I looked at my watch and I was five minutes behind schedule. "I guess I should leave now. Do you think the roads will be icy?"

"No, they should be dry. And don't worry so much. Before you know it, you'll be back accepting another invitation to fly to another school."

"Yeah, right." I kissed him, then gave him and Todd an extra tight hug. Carrying Todd, he saw me out to the truck, where we said more goodbyes.

"You always say goodbye like you'll never see us again," Peter remonstrated.

I shrugged and said lightly, "Well, the plane could crash or something. It happens."

"You'll be fine." He gave me one last kiss, and he and Todd waved to me as I drove out of the yard. In the woods to the far north, I thought I saw a flash of light, as when the sun's rays bounce off chrome or glass. It was quickly forgotten as I watched, in the rear-view mirror, Lady following me for a ways. Then she gave up and sat to watch me drive away.

I followed our road, a cantankerous, sparsely gravelled road, six kilometres down to Kit's place. A winding road, it sometimes went east, sometimes south, and I'm sure at times it headed back west. Kit's real name was Martin Kitsewasis, and he and Mona were our closest neighbours and friends. Mona had come from Halfway River and had inherited a traditional trap line that included our two sections of land. When we first moved up here from Vancouver, Kit had come and asked Peter if they could continue trapping on our land. Catching cute little animals and skinning them was something I found distasteful, but since it was their way and they had been here first, I was pleased that Peter had given permission. Besides, they were pretty old and I didn't think they did much trapping. I passed by their driveway on my right and, even in winter, evergreens, young and old, hid their house from view.

Here, at Kit's, the road widened. It was the turnaround for the school bus, and the village of Dodging maintained it year-round only to this point. About two kilometres past Kit's place a private road went north. NAK-WAN INC. had large "Keep Out" signs posted at the entrance. Mrs. Martens, owner of the Dodging grocery store, had once grumbled that it was a biological laboratory that got all its supplies from Fort St. John. On one of his hikes, Peter had come across a high, seemingly endless chain-link fence topped with razor wire. Whatever the place was, they had invested a lot of money to prevent trespassing.

About twenty kilometres east from us I passed through the village of Dodging. Except for the gas station on my left, the sprinkling of newer buildings visible from the main road, and the paved road I was driving on, the village had a western frontier feel to it. The facing of most of the buildings was constructed from jackpine poles, and in many places the wooden sidewalks were protected with overhangs.

As in the old frontier settlements in Indian country, white people controlled all the amenities of the town. Dodging had a Presbyterian Church, a school, Mrs. Martens' general store with the gas station, and the two-storey Castaway Motel and Restaurant, which featured the only pool table in the area and housed the local drinking hole, the Palomino Saloon. At the post office on my right I exchanged glances with Mrs. Springer, the local reporter for the *Peace Valley Voice*, which came out of Fort St. John. She was getting out of her car, no doubt to get her latest piece of gossip from the lady who ran the post office.

Whenever Peter and I stopped for our mail, she seemed to be there, and she'd always gush over Peter. She adored him and Todd, and she probably wondered how come he had married a Native woman like me. A year ago Peter must have talked her into doing a piece on me, and my picture had appeared in the paper. Ever since, I'd never know whether people who stared at me were being hostile or were just thinking that they recognized me from somewhere.

Leaving Dodging behind, I entered what I thought of as the portent of destruction to come. Bulldozing equipment bullied its way into the wilderness, cutting open ugly wounds for the heavy trucks that followed. Chain saws buzzed as tall trees toppled and crashed to the ground, their silent screams unheard. Unlike our road, where towering old-growth evergreens spread their boughs overhead, herbicides were sprayed along these new roads to subdue vegetation and, consequently, the animals that grazed on them. Something about these roads reminded me of the desolation of the prairies, where nothing impeded the winds. All of this frenzied activity took place to feed man's hunger for oil, lumber, and other commodities. When we first moved up north and I looked at our road map, I thought the whole area was untouched wilderness. Even when we saw what was happening, we mostly observed those bulldozers with simple curiosity and amazement.

Three hours after leaving our cabin, I settled myself on the first plane. Though I appeared to be concentrating on a book, I was braced for takeoff. Trying to think of good things only, I pictured Todd, Peter, and Lady back at our cabin, imagining what they'd be doing right now. If I gave up writing children's books, I would never be tempted to travel like this again. When I felt the plane speed up for its ascent, I closed my eyes and held my breath until we were high in the sky. Then I spent the rest of the time listening for changes in the droning sound of the engines.

When I finally reached Norway House without incident, I was able to relax enough to enjoy the classroom visits. As planned, Peter called me during the lunch hour at the school, to assure himself I had made the trip safely. Over the next few days, I spoke or read to students, and I had a tour of the local sights. In the evenings I had supper in the company of my host and different people, and spent the balance of my nights restlessly watching TV and reading. These were the times I wished we had a phone at Shadow Lake. Kit had a phone, but we had agreed that only emergency phone calls would go through them. When my loneliness for Peter and Todd got to be too much, I tried to think of an urgent message, but I couldn't come up with one.

My weeklong visit came to an end and, while I had enjoyed it, I was happy to be heading home. When my plane taxied in at Fort St. John, I got the urge to jump and yell for joy. Instead, I chided myself for all the dumb feelings I had expressed earlier. From now on, I vowed to myself again, no more airplane trips—that's it, no more!

A perfect day with a clear blue sky kept me company on my drive home, but freezing rain must have hit the area earlier because there were still shaded stretches with black ice. As I was driving by Kit's yard, a muddy but happy Lady came bounding out to greet me. I backed up the truck and pulled into their driveway. Mona must have heard me because she came out on her porch right away and, after we exchanged greetings, she said, "Some man, he called for Leona. That was about an hour ago, maybe two. He said that Leona wanted youse to come to Fort St. John, that it was very urgent. This man, he didn't give a name, like who he was. He hung up, eh." She pulled her cardigan tighter around herself and added, "Kit went right away to tell Peter about it. I think I heard him go by not long after that, but I'm not sure."

Flip-flop, my stomach turned over. Leona had beckoned and Peter had run to her side, even though he must have remembered I'd be home soon. Why else would Lady be here, instead of at Shadow Lake? Hiding my feelings from Mona, I thanked her and turned to leave.

Lady was going down the driveway already, so I called her to the truck. She sat and barked back at me. In no mood to play games, I got in the truck and drove slowly after her. As soon as she saw me coming, she started down the driveway again, and when she got to the road, she looked over her shoulder at me as if she wanted me to follow her into the woods on the north side of the road. I wanted to get home, half hoping that Peter was there and half hoping he wasn't, because that would justify the anger I had for him right now and for all those previous suspicions I'd had about him and Leona. At the road I stopped, opened the door on the passenger side, and called again to Lady to come. She was sitting at the edge of the woods and she barked at me, so I barked right back, "Lady, get in this damned truck. Now!"

With a direct order like that, she didn't know what to do. For some crazy reason known only to her, she wanted to go traipsing off into the woods, but she wanted me to go along with her. She stood, lowered her head, looked over her shoulder towards the north, then, very slowly, came to the truck and jumped in, whining all the while.

Ice still clung to the deeply shaded spots on our road and, as I drove carefully, I reasoned that if Peter had gone to Fort St. John and I had just come from there, surely one of us would have seen the other. It was a calming thought, and my trembling subsided. He would have waited for me because he knew I'd be here about now. Lady, sporting a rank swampy smell that permeated the whole inside of the truck, continued whining. Distracted from my thoughts, I said, "Lady, where have you been, you stink so much."

As soon as I drove around the last bend, my trembling started up again. Peter's truck was nowhere in sight. Inside, a typed note sat on the table: "Had to go to Fort St. John. Be back as soon as I can. Peter."

I sat heavily at the table staring at the card, pulled from his Rolodex. It was so unlike him. He must have been in a real rush to type out a greeting like this. A rage filled me, and it was not so much directed at him but mostly at myself, because I had spent all these years trusting him. I should have known better: trust no one. And then Leona had come back into the picture and I was back to being a loser.

Adding wood to the still-burning embers in the wood stove, I put the kettle on for coffee and returned to look at the "kiss off" that lay on the table. Once I had my coffee, I settled on the couch to wait. Plans of what to do came to mind. I'd pack for Todd and myself so that when Peter returned, I'd be all ready to leave. I'd move back to Winnipeg because living in Vancouver as a single parent would be too expensive and Vancouver was Peter's hometown. Smiling wryly to myself, I thought I was like a yo-yo. Leona and Nick had driven me to Vancouver, and now Leona and Peter would drive me back to Winnipeg.

Leona!

Before I left for good, I'd go to her place and give her a piece of my mind. Then again, I couldn't really spare a piece of my mind. Well, I was going to do something to get back at her. This sudden bout of depression brought on fatigue so intense I couldn't think clearly enough to figure out how I was going to get back at her. Gulping back the last of my coffee, I leaned sideways to rest on the arm of the couch ... and that was all I remembered.

When I woke, I found that I had my jacket on, but still I was cold. In the darkness, I found that I was sitting behind the wheel of the truck. I got out and made my way to the porch, totally disoriented. When I finally made it to the side porch, I noted that the truck was not parked in my usual spot.

Inside the cabin, it was pitch black, though I vaguely remembered that the TV had been on when I went to sleep. At the couch, I removed only my tuque and, in spite of feeling that something was drastically different, I lay down and fell asleep again.

When I woke up, I was still on the couch, still in my clothes, and it was seven in the morning, my usual wakeup time. My first thought was, if Peter had come home and seen me asleep on the couch, he would have woken me to go to bed. Stiffly, I stood up, stretched, and had that same sensation to do with my head. Touching my hand to my hair, I was shocked. What had happened to my hair? I rushed to the bathroom, where I saw long strands of coal-black hair coiled on the floor before I glimpsed the strange image reflected back in the mirror. Some time in the night I had driven the truck. Some time in the night I had cut off my waist-length hair. Some time in the night my mind had snapped.

Closing my mouth, I went to check the bedrooms, but they were empty. That meant that Peter had spent the night in Fort St. John—with Leona. The fact that Michael and Todd were with them wouldn't have mattered. Another wave of depression hit me and zapped any energy I might have had. All I could do was light a fire for coffee, put food and fresh water down for Lady, and prop both the kitchen and porch doors open so she could come and go as she pleased. The odour she carried reminded me that before I took off for Winnipeg, I would have to give her a bath. Then I sat on the couch drinking the coffee, pondering my bleak future. My last thoughts were that I was going to raise hell with Peter when he did come home. Then I'd leave.

When I next awoke, the clock on the wall said it was close to 4:00 p.m. Time for another coffee. I was going to forget electricity bills and buy myself another electric kettle, even though Peter opposed the idea. Cheap bastard! Oh, but I wouldn't need an electric kettle now that I was leaving. While I waited for the kettle to boil, I returned to take another look in the mirror, trying to call up even a flash of memory of having cut my hair. Nothing came. For me, this shearing off of my hair was a form of self-mutilation, one that I'd done before. What was really weird was that I didn't have the emotions that I had back then. Right now I was angry-angry, a little bit jealous—okay, a whole lot jealous—and I was very hurt. But if I could recognize these feelings, then how could I possibly be crazy?

I must have hacked off my hair in my sleep. That was it, I'd been sleepwalking. The water in the kettle boiled over and I went to make my coffee. The thoughts that filled my mind brought on another wave of grogginess, so I abandoned the idea of eating and returned to the couch to finish off my coffee. This time I knew I was drifting back to sleep, but couldn't stop myself.

When I woke again, I felt as groggy as I had when I went to sleep. Still, I managed to tend to Lady's needs, after I put more wood in the stove. She seemed to want me to come outside with her, but, being too tired, I just propped the doors open a bit again—I must have closed them during my sleep—and headed back for the couch.

The next time I woke I looked at the clock first thing and was amazed that the hands were in a perfect vertical position, with the short hand on the six. My next thoughts were that I'd force some cereal down, tidy myself up, then make that drive to Fort St. John and reclaim my son from that bitch and bastard. But with my coffee in hand, I found myself gravitating towards the couch once more, to sit for just a minute.

Next thing, Lady woke me with the barking she used when strangers approached. It was now a little after nine. Although I was sleepy, I knew it wasn't Peter and Todd because she would be excited for them. I had just enough time to add wood to the stove and water to the kettle. If I was going to manage talking to visitors, I would need a coffee. I contemplated going to the washroom to clean up, but then I heard heavy footsteps on the porch steps, the porch door squeaking open, and loud knocking at the door. When I opened the door, Kit was standing there and behind him was a uniformed RCMP officer.

My hands went to my hair to pat what was left of it into order, and I knew I must look a mess. Kit's eyes widened in surprise when he saw me and he said, "Christine, I've got some bad news."

As they ushered me back in to sit at the kitchen table, the officer introduced himself as Sergeant Trolley. The essence of what he told me was that Peter's truck had been found in the Peace River and that the currents had carried away his body.

2

My mind grasped what he didn't say—*both* Peter and Todd had died in an accident—and my body began making erratic movements. My hands twitched, my arms moved upwards, then down, and an involuntary smile flashed across my face. Shaking my head, no, I denied the possibility that Peter and Todd could have died in an accident.

"What about Todd?" I asked, dreading the answer. My words came out sounding slurred and my mouth was dry. Even though it was warm inside the cabin, I was shivering.

"I'm sorry?" Sergeant Trolley asked, not understanding my question.

"Todd. That's her son. He's three years old," Kit explained.

"We didn't find either one, then. They were working at getting the truck out when I left but there was no one in it. I'm very sorry, Mrs. Webster," Sergeant Trolley said, sympathetically. "Was your husband in good health? Was he on any medications?"

Listlessly, I replied, "Peter's health was good, so he wasn't on any medications. All we ever took, if we had to, were aspirins."

"What about his doctor? He had a regular doctor?"

"In Fort St. John."

"Do you have his name and address?"

Zombie-like, I crossed the room to the Rolodex on Peter's desk and copied down the information on a scratch pad. When I returned to the table, I noticed that the officer's eyes now seemed more alert than sympathetic.

"Are you all right, Mrs. Webster?" he asked.

"No." With Todd and Peter gone, I'd never be all right, again. Tears rimmed my eyes, but I didn't want to break down in front of this stranger.

"I mean, you seem ... sluggish," he explained.

"Oh that. Since I got back from a trip I made, I just feel so tired. I don't understand it, I've never been like this before." His stare was so intense that I went on: "I had to go to Norway House and I have a phobia about flying."

A hissing noise came from the woodstove as boiling water sloshed out of the kettle. "I was just going to make coffee. You want some?"

Both Kit and the officer nodded, so I got up, went to the counter, spooned instant coffee into three cups, and brought them back to the table. My eyelids were so heavy. I went back for the sugar bowl and milk. Lady quietly followed me and lay down as I counted out spoons. Turning to go back to the table, I tripped over her. She yelped and got out from under me. The sugar went flying everywhere as I concentrated on holding the milk container upright. Under my breath, I swore at Lady. She tried to make up by licking my face, but I just sat on the floor, forcing myself not to cry. Kit came over to soothe me and help me up to the table. He went back for more sugar from the cupboard and returned to the table.

Eyeing me impassively, Sergeant Trolley said, "I'm so sorry, Mrs. Webster. I know how you must be feeling, but I have to ask these questions. I couldn't help see this note here. Was this the last note you got from your husband?"

As I wiped at my eyes, I looked at the note, wishing I had put it away. In all his previous notes to me, Peter had always hand-written them and signed off with "Love you, Peter." This typewritten one was so cold and aloof, as if he had no feelings for me. To answer the officer's question, I nodded.

He asked, "Why'd he go to Fort St. John? Do you know?"

I looked at Kit for him to explain. "The phone call."

Kit understood and said, "Sunday afternoon, we got a call from a man. He was calling for Leona—that's Christine's sister—and she wanted them to go there. He told Mona it was urgent."

To me, Sergeant Trolley said, "So you weren't here when he left."

"No, I got back around four-thirty. From my trip." To hide the anger and the jealousy that began on Sunday afternoon, I speculated out loud: "What's strange is that we didn't pass each other anywhere. But then, he could have pulled off somewhere for gas or a snack."

"But he knew you'd be home soon. He was expecting you, is that right?"

"Yeah, if he remembered," I said in a way that would imply Peter was forgetful. Peter would never have forgotten, unless he had something much more meaningful on his mind.

He directed his next few questions to Kit. "So you got the phone call at what time?"

"I don't know. We don't watch clocks. I came here right after Mona told me."

"How did he react when you told him?"

"He just said thanks and invited me to stay for a coffee, but I had to get back, so I left."

Kit's words sparked a hope in me that Peter didn't just race off to Leona's side, that maybe he hoped to intercept me on the road. He knew I'd be tired from the flying and the drive home, so he just wanted to save time for me, that was it.

Sergeant Trolley caught my drift and asked, "You thought of something?"

"No." The lie must have registered on my face because I saw suspicion in his eyes.

"Were you getting along?" he asked quietly and as gently as he could.

"Yes, we got along fine." From the corner of my eye I saw Kit nodding his head and I was grateful. "Why do you ask something like that?"

"We just have to consider all possibilities, and those who are closest know the most. They can help us more than anyone."

"Well, Peter was happy. He's a writer and he's got a manuscript there that's probably finished now. He was doing what he wanted to do and he had everything he wanted." Perhaps not, I thought to myself. Perhaps he wanted Leona instead of me. That was pure speculation on my part and I told myself that would not be at all helpful to a police investigation. Besides, it wasn't something I wanted to share with anyone else. So I continued, "He's the one who wanted to come up here in the first place."

"From where?" he asked.

"Vancouver," I said, yawning. Strangely, the exhaustion I'd felt for the past few days began to lift. "When did this happen, do you know?"

"At this point, we don't know, exactly. But it had to be between Sunday and last night."

"I have to go to where Peter's truck is," I said. "Are you going back there? I could follow you."

"In your condition, you shouldn't do any driving."

"I'll drive you, Chris," Kit said. His kindness touched me.

Before we left, Sergeant Trolley asked me a few more questions about my own whereabouts and time frames. He also wanted Leona's address, so I returned to Peter's Rolodex, copied her address for the officer, and put her card in my pocket. Sergeant Trolley must have thought it strange I didn't know my own sister's address, but I had refused to memorize it. In turn, Sergeant Trolley gave me his card, in case I thought of anything else or had further questions. *Or, wanted to come clean with what I knew.*

Excusing myself, I went to the bathroom, wiped my face with cold water, and ripped a comb through what was left of my hair. Then we were all on our way to the Peace River, with me in Kit's truck. Along the way, I told him I had been sleeping almost constantly since I got back on Sunday. We drove on in silence. That this was Tuesday morning was a shock to me. The last time I had succumbed to sleep like this was when I had taken Valium, prescribed by a doctor, and, before that, when Dr. Coran had put some kind of drug into my warm milk—and both of those events had happened a lifetime ago. What I did not mention was that I had woken up during the night behind the wheel of my truck and that I must have driven it somewhere.

In Peter's novels, Gregory M. Thomas, a former police detective and now the owner of a large detective agency, could always sense when someone was lying to him. Maybe Sergeant Trolley was like him and had sensed I was holding back information.

When we turned left onto the highway towards Fort St. John, Kit surprised me by saying, "We thought we heard you drive by our place on Sunday night. We thought you were going to your sister's place."

"Couldn't have been me 'cause, like I said, I've been sleeping. I can't understand why I've been sleeping so much." One thing I knew for sure was that I could not have driven anywhere and still remained on the road. All I had to do now was to convince myself of that.

"Thought we did. Didn't want to tell the police, though. He might jump to all sorts of conclusions."

"Sounds like he already has. The questions he asked, it's like he doesn't believe Peter really had an accident." But it wasn't really so much the questions as the suspicion I'd seen in his eyes.

Kit didn't answer at first, but as we drew closer to the accident site and saw many vehicles parked on both sides of the highway, he added, "I'm sure Peter and Todd are okay." This we both knew was a lie, but he had said it to give me comfort. In that moment he seemed more like a father than a neighbour.

Sergeant Trolley's police car rolled to a stop behind the last car parked on the south side and Kit pulled up behind it. He waited for us and we followed him along the shoulder of the highway. The officer explained that Peter's truck must have been coming from the east, gone out of control, and crossed the eastbound lanes. Trees were sparsely scattered along this side of the highway, but they would have prevented a vehicle from going all the way down to the river. Where we stopped, the incline down to the river was bare of trees and, looking straight down the steep path, I saw Peter's truck on a narrow shoreline, water dripping from it.

There were signs of activity. One of the men down below saw us and called out that they had found something. He retrieved a small bag and began climbing up towards us. Sergeant Trolley moved forward to meet the other officer and take the bag from him.

Meanwhile, Kit surveyed the scene. "How did you know of the accident?" he asked. "Nothing's really visible from the highway."

"We got a call early this morning," Sergeant Trolley responded. "The fellow wouldn't give his name, just told us he'd had a flat and saw what he thought was a truck in the river last night." He held up the plastic bag, asking, "Do you recognize this?"

I had been staring at the activity down below. When I turned to see what was in the bag, I almost choked on the words, "It looks like Todd's running shoe." It had maroon spots on it, which could only have been blood, and I steeled myself against tears that threatened to flow. Until this moment I had been able to stop myself from thinking that Peter and Todd were dead, but now here was proof. "Is it okay if I leave?" I mumbled.

Sergeant Trolley nodded, but said, "We'll be by later today, or tomorrow."

Kit led me back to his pickup and I saw Mrs. Springer pull into our spot as we drove away. I couldn't give in to my grief, just yet. "Could you take me to Fort St. John, first?" I asked Kit. "I should tell Leona what happened."

What I really wanted to do was find out whether Peter had gone there before the accident and, if so, whether he had spent the night with them. The police didn't know when the accident had happened and, if they hadn't received the anonymous call, Peter's truck might not have been discovered for quite some time. The other thing I needed to know was what had been so urgent to Leona.

In Fort St. John, no one answered the door at Colin's house. An elderly neighbour was outside doing some spring yard work, so I asked him if he knew where the occupants were. The man took off his hat, scratched his chin, and said, "Well, I imagine he went to work. Who are you?"

"Christine Webster. I'm Leona's sister and there's been an accident. I need to find Leona. Do you know her?"

The man smiled. "Oh yeah. Saw her leave, must have been, hmm, a couple of months back."

"You mean they moved away?"

"Yeah, her and Michael, they got in a taxi one morning and they had their bags with them. Haven't seen them since. Mikey used to clear the snow for me sometimes. And Colin, he must be at work right now. That's all I know."

Stunned by this news, I got back into Kit's truck. "That man who made the call for Leona, what exactly did he say?" I asked. "Did he leave an address of where we were supposed to meet her?"

"No, Mona would have taken it down. Just asked for us to pass on a message that you should come to Fort St. John and that it was urgent. Why? They're not home?"

"Apparently they moved out a couple of months ago."

"Maybe they came back and they're just not home right now."

That must have been the answer. Otherwise, the man would have given an address on Sunday. On Colin's visit to us the day before I left for my trip he had not mentioned that he and Leona had split up. Maybe his visit was to see if Leona was staying with us.

My confusion would have to wait because, right now, I had a lump in my throat, my grieving could no longer wait, and I had to get back to Shadow Lake where I could be alone. Todd and Peter—gone! It couldn't be, and yet it was. The sight of Todd's running shoe confirmed it. All the way back I wanted to let go, but I didn't. Except for patting my hand before he started driving, Kit did not make any more vain attempts to comfort me.

We were already in my driveway before I thought of Peter's parents.

They had to be notified, but I couldn't bring myself to return to Kit's place right now. As soon as I was inside, I went into Todd's bedroom and threw myself across his bed. I writhed in pain, wanting to get out of my skin, wishing for relief through tears at least, but the tears wouldn't come. Lady had followed me inside and showed her concern by nuzzling at me and whining anxiously. What was I going to do without them? That they would never again be in my life was just not possible.

That night I gathered Todd's blanket and pillow, along with Peter's favourite sweater, and, bunching them up as a kind of pillow, lay down on the couch, waiting for sleep to take me, comforted a little by their vague scents. The next day, after washing up, I tidied the cabin, sweeping up the hair on the bathroom floor and taking it outside to spread behind the house. Mona had told me once that birds and mice used hair for their nests. Afterwards, I headed for Kit's, dreading the phone call I had to make. Peter's mother answered the phone and, as strong and capable as she was, I asked to speak to his father. He took the news quietly, then asked, "Are you okay? Why don't you come down here?"

"No, I want to be here in case they have more news," I said. "Tell your wife that I'm very sorry. I just couldn't tell her directly."

"I understand," he said.

I gave him Sergeant Trolley's phone number at the RCMP detachment in Fort St. John. After asking me a few more questions, he concluded: "You take care and call us when you hear something new."

Declining an offer of lunch, I left Mona and Kit's place to go back to that spot on the highway. Another vehicle was already parked there and, not wanting to talk to anyone, I passed by until I found a place where I could turn back. I would return here later tonight.

Back at my cabin, I made coffee and sat with it on Todd's bed. At times, I remembered something funny he did and I smiled. The clock in the living room was ticking away and the more time passed, the more guilt I felt. The more guilt I felt, the more I hated myself. How ironic that it took such a loss to think about all the reasons for the guilt, now, when nothing could be done.

When it got dark I roused enough energy to head back to the spot where Peter's truck went off, almost to the halfway point to Fort St. John. In the dark I groped my way down the embankment, slip-sliding part of the way, not much caring whether I hurt myself. Sitting there on a cold rock, I wished I knew what had happened, wished it could be undone. If only I had burned Leona's very first letter, but I had been curious. And I had allowed Peter to see it, then talk me into inviting her back into my life. And now I was sitting alone on a rock, hopelessly wishing for the impossible.

Once Leona had been my best friend. A long time ago she had rescued me from Mount Ste. Marie, a reform school for girls, and she had talked Children's Aid into letting me live with her, although I was not quite seventeen. According to the Catholic religion, we're all born with an original sin, but it gets wiped clean if we're baptized as Catholics. So I guess it was my second sin that dictated that everything that started out good would end up badly for me—just like the last time that I lived with Leona, when she stopped being my best friend.

*

Living with Leona was liberating. I'd just spent time in the reform school, I wanted to live with her, and finally, here I was. I regretted my jealousy over a newspaper article that exposed Dr. Coran, making her the heroine. In November that year I dropped out of Grade 12, having lost the motivation to finish. Because I thought I had a criminal record, there was no sense in even trying to go on to university or college— not that I had the brains for that, anyways. I happily settled for a boring job in a factory, checking watch bands for flaws. When Leona wasn't doing part-time modelling jobs, she worked as a hostess in an expensive steakhouse and devoted her free time to sewing clothes for us. In return, I cooked and cleaned. Weekends would have been boring, except that Leona had so many friends and there were always parties somewhere.

One Friday morning in early April, 1968, Leona had her radio on and I was numbed to hear that Dr. Martin Luther King Jr. had been assassinated the day before. I hadn't thought about black people, the KKK, or equality for a long time, but hearing of his death reminded me of the hope he had planted in so many minds. Two months later I was shocked again when Robert F. Kennedy was also assassinated. Since both were involved in the fight for civil rights, I figured right away that the KKK had plotted the murders. Even after the many witnesses identified Sirhan Sirhan as the lone gunman, I was convinced he was somehow manipulated. Kill the messengers and the messages would die. For me, the messages did die, and news of the civil rights movement no longer interested me.

When I turned eighteen I was officially discharged from Children's Aid. Losing the label of being a foster kid meant I would be the only boss in my life. From now on, I would live wherever I wanted to live. At Mount Ste. Marie, most of the girls had been foster kids or adopted kids and, from now on, I would think that any adults who had been former foster kids might somehow be mental cases. This theory did not include Leona, because she had grown up in one good foster home, but me, I was suspect. Whatever I was, I would never again go back to a place like Mount Ste. Marie.

Leona and I had plans, and I was enthusiastic about making them work. After I got a car, we would buy some land on the Red River, then have a house built. The idea of just owning land was so exciting, and I spent hours drawing plans of a simple house, large enough for both of us but not too large, because we both hated cleaning up. We both got our driver's licences and, through the YWCA, I got some babysitting jobs for evenings and weekends and saved to buy a car. Sometimes when I was walking home I'd get the feeling that I was being watched. Naturally, I thought of Dr. Coran right away, but he could not possibly know where we lived and, besides, nothing bad ever happened. In January I finally had enough to buy a used car and I quit babysitting. After Leona turned twenty-one, she and her friends began going to pubs every Friday and Saturday night and, because I didn't drink at all, I went to pick them up. That was how I met the love of my life.

On Friday nights I watched TV until it was time to get Leona. On Saturday nights there was nothing on and, rather than stay home alone and read, I went out to the twenty-four-hour coffee shop nearest to the hotel where Leona and her friends spent their evenings, and treated myself to fries and a hamburger. While I ate and drank coffee, I read. One night someone sat on the stool next to mine, even though hardly anyone was in the coffee shop when I first came in. I was too engrossed in my book to pay attention to anything else.

"Could you pass me the salt?" a male voice asked.

I took no notice until I was tapped on the arm. Realizing that the question had been asked of me, I quickly reached out to pass the salt.

"Here you are." The person was handing me back the salt shaker. Putting it in its place, I resumed reading.

"Could you pass me the vinegar, please?" This time I knew the person on my right was talking to me, so I passed it to him. He used it and gave it back to me. I went on reading. Then he asked for the ketchup. I paused to fulfil his wish, then returned to my book. Pepper was the next item he requested.

"Hmm, I wonder what else I can ask for. Must be a good book, huh?" the voice came again. Slightly annoyed, I finally looked over to my right and, holy shit, this cute guy was sitting right next to me, grinning.

"A napkin. You must need a napkin," I said to cover my sudden interest.

My tone must have sounded sarcastic because he said, contritely, "I'm sorry, but I was only trying to get your attention."

"Oh," was my great comeback, so I added, "Well, it's this book. I'm almost finished, see? I got caught up in it."

"Yeah, I saw you reading last Saturday. It's hard to compete with a book." He spoke in a serious tone of voice, but he had an amused look in his eyes.

That he might be interested dawned on me and a wonderful feeling washed over me. He had noticed me last Saturday? Wow.

"You were here last Saturday?" I asked.

"Yup. Every Saturday night. I'm Nick," he said, then waited briefly before asking, "What's your name?"

"Chris. Christine for short." The ending of my book was forgotten.

"Okay, Christine for short. Want to have a coffee with me? My treat." Without waiting for my answer, he ordered two coffees and took them to a booth. I followed him.

When we sat down, I brilliantly said, "It's really Christine for long and Chris for short."

"Oh, and you were just testing me."

"That's right."

"Okay. So why does a pretty girl like you end up in a restaurant on a Saturday night, reading?"

"Well the same question goes for you. Except you're not a girl and you weren't reading."

"Oh? But I am pretty? Anyhow, I asked first."

"Okay. It's simple. I go pick up my sister and her friends at one."

"She works till one?"

"No, she drinks till one. I mean, she doesn't just drink. She and her friends, they get together and they just go out together."

"And how come you aren't with them?"

"I'm too young. You have to be twenty-one. If they have house parties, I go."

"And then you drink?"

"Well, orange crush and coffee, I do. Now you."

"Now me?" he asked before remembering. "Oh, you mean why do I come here? I finish work at nine, so I come here for supper."

"Supper. How come? I mean, I guess, I guess I should have asked about a wife before." I regretted the words the minute I was saying them.

He grinned again and, to ease my obvious discomfort, said, "That's why I dropped the hint. No one cooks for me, except my mother, and only on Sundays."

"I didn't mean to get that personal. It's just that I wouldn't want to—well, you know." The right words wouldn't come and I tried to put myself in Leona's place. What would she say? How would she act? I certainly didn't want to be sounding like a good little Catholic girl.

We talked for the rest of the time I had and it just wasn't long enough. By the time we walked out, I thought Nick was the coolest guy I had ever met. He made me feel desirable for the first time in my life. He must have thought I was exotic looking, like a Hawaiian girl or something, mostly because of my long, straight, black, shiny hair.

In the following week I walked on air. People at work commented that it was great to see a smile on my face: it made me wonder if I had always worn only a frown before. On Friday night I went back to the same restaurant, hoping he would be there, but he wasn't. He had probably gotten off work and gone out on a date. Come to think of it, he may not have been married, but a guy like that would definitely have a girlfriend. By the end of that evening I convinced myself he did have a girlfriend and, if I ever saw him again, I would be cool and distant. On Saturday night, though, I made sure to take a booth. He walked in and came straight to my table. Butterflies started fluttering inside me as soon as I saw him.

"Hi, Christine for short," he said, as he took off his jacket and sat down.

"Hello, Nicholas for long, I presume," I joked back. Okay, I wouldn't be cool and distant. I would joke around and be like a little sister.

We spent a couple of hours being nonsensical and eating and then he said, "You've still got a couple of hours, right? Want to come to my place? Watch some TV?"

That put a stop to my merriment. I had never before been alone with a man in his place. I couldn't start now, but I didn't know how to explain that.

Nick reached over and tilted my head so my eyes met his. "Hey, I'm not going to try anything funny, if that's what you're worried about."

"It's not the funny stuff I'm worried about. It's the serious stuff."

That made him laugh. "Okay, then I'll only do funny stuff."

I smiled and he made up my mind for me by putting on his jacket, saying, "Come on, Christine for short."

As we went out to the car, he took my keys and led me to the passenger side. Apprehensively, I got in, wondering if I should be allowing a "semi-complete" stranger to drive my car. That evening he was a perfect gentleman. I learned his last name was Scarlos, he was twenty-four years old, and he worked at the CN. When I asked why he didn't go to bars afterwards, he said he didn't like that scene.

For weeks, we met that way and I never told Leona about him. One night Nick and I were on his couch and he suddenly turned and kissed me, long and hard. Startled, I drew back and said, "That borders on serious stuff."

"I know. I'm seriously attracted to you."

During the week, I tried to keep my feelings in check by telling myself he had one or more girlfriends for the rest of the week. Quite possibly, I was his Saturday night girl. About a month after we first met, we ended up in his bed. When he put his arms around me or we just talked and smoked, a wonderful lazy, carefree feeling engulfed me. That aura of being warm, cosy, and protected remained with me for the rest of the week, no matter what else happened. But then, too soon, he wanted to go all the way and I just couldn't.

One Sunday afternoon Leona was working on a blouse for me and, as I was trying it on inside out so she could pin it, she asked, "So who is he?" She said this with pins between her lips.

I answered with a question, knowing very well what she was asking about. "Who is who?"

"Come on, Chrissy, you get this dreamy look on your face, you smile a lot to yourself, you hum, you're glowing. So who is he?"

"Just a guy."

"Yeah, right, just a guy."

"His name's Nick. Nicholas Scarlos."

"And when are you going to bring this Nicholas Scarlos home to meet me?"

The dreamy smile on my face vanished. I hadn't really thought of it before, but if Nick met Leona, he'd fall in love with her immediately. They were both irresistible, so how could they not be attracted to each other? I was glad that Leona was now working behind me because I didn't want her to see the insecurity written all over my face.

"He doesn't like the bar scene," was all I could think of saying.

"So? I didn't say at a bar. Bring him here for supper. There. You can take it off now." Leona moved some things off the table so she could sew the blouse together.

"He works till late," I said, tossing the blouse over to her and pulling my old sweatshirt back on. "I don't know why you keep making me these fancy clothes. You know I just like my old jeans and sweatshirts." I said this mostly to change the subject. Leona always dressed up and we would always be opposites. To my relief, we didn't talk about Nick again that night, and I was left wondering how I was going to keep them apart for the rest of our lives.

When Nick asked me to stay over one night, I told him I would the next time so I could let my sister know. That was a little white lie and I told it to delay the inevitable. I didn't really have to tell Leona anything because she herself stayed overnight at different boyfriends' places. The first times I'd been shocked by her promiscuity, but now I just silently disapproved. We had a one-bedroom apartment and she, of course, had the bedroom that she uninhibitedly shared with current boyfriends. Back when she had one of her modelling jobs, she came home with a fur coat as a bonus. Something in her demeanour made me suspect that she had slept with the owner to get a bonus like that. To sum it up, she was too casual about sex. I guess she never had all the hangups that haunted me. Up until now Nick had been wonderful and understanding about my not wanting to go all the way, but I expected he would tire of that—and of me.

By now I knew I was his only girlfriend and he gave me a key to his place so I could come and go as I pleased. I got into the habit of staying at Nick's on weekends and at Leona's on weekdays. When Nick gave me his key, I let myself really fall in love with him. How much in love? Deeply. That's when I gave myself to him completely. And that's when, I think, I got pregnant.

Of course, I didn't know the exact moment of conception because I was only thinking that sex was overrated. It was not at all what I imagined. It hurt. I'd once overheard Leona and her girlfriends talking and they all liked it. But me, I had to be different. I didn't like sex at all, but to please Nick I pretended I did.

One night when I was in Nick's bed I dreamt I was on the toilet. I immediately woke up because the sheets were warm and wet. Horror of horrors: all the humiliations of my childhood years of bed-wetting came flooding over me. I lay there very still, not wanting to wake Nick up. Sometimes during the night Nick would turn over and hug me close to him and put his leg across me. If he did that now, boy, would he be surprised. Finally I eased out of bed, got a towel, and spread it to cover the sheet where it was wet. In the morning I waited for him to go to work before I got out of bed. I missed that day of work and worried about not phoning in, but I had a covert operation here to perform. Before I took the bedding to the laundromat a few blocks away, I washed the mattress. When I was done, I left Nick a note that I would see him on Saturday night. I would no longer be able to stay overnight at his place.

At our apartment I continued to have a bed-wetting problem—not every night, but I never knew when it would happen. So every night I had towels nearby. Nick couldn't understand why I would no longer stay at his place overnight, and I was sure he was going to break up with me. Instead, he asked me to marry him. Thinking he was joking, I asked, "Why?"

"Why? Because we love each other. Don't we? And I want to spend the rest of my life with you."

Secrets. All my life I had kept secrets. Well, no more. "Nick, I have to tell you something. And if you want to break up with me, I'll understand." I took a deep breath, briefly thought about lying, and then blurted out, "Nick, I peed in your bed." I said it quickly, but clearly, because I did not want to have to repeat it.

He started laughing and laughing and I started getting kind of offended. "Why are you laughing?"

"I thought from the way you looked you were going to say you met someone else," he said.

"But Nick, I just told you that I wet your bed. I'm a bed-wetter."

"Hey, I'll marry a bed-wetter any time, as long as it's you. Besides, you can see a doctor about that. Okay? Problem solved. Now will you marry me?"

"Yes! A thousand yeses." I smiled. Inside I was so elated.

He even came up with a plan to help me try to control the bed-wetting problem. If I wet the bed, I was to note the time so we could set the alarm clock for those times and get to the washroom before any accident happened. This worked fine, and I began to feel I would not be spending the rest of my life washing bedding.

At the end of June Leona arranged a special party for my nineteenth birthday. She had friends who had friends with a cabin at Winnipeg Beach and, because it was a long weekend, a group of us would go up and spend the whole weekend there. Having resigned myself to the fact that Nick was going to have to meet Leona some day, I decided they should meet beforehand at our place. Nick came for supper on a Thursday night. I watched closely for signs of fireworks between them and was relieved when they both seemed normal.

The Winnipeg Beach weekend was great. Nick took off that whole weekend to be with me. Still, I was again watchful because Leona was the centre of attention and Nick couldn't help being drawn in by her incredible charisma. Knowing by now I didn't have a father of any kind, Nick jokingly asked Leona for my hand in marriage. The way he asked, and the way everyone else laughed, made me feel that I was back at family visits where Mom and Leona talked and laughed and excluded me. I was also sure that some of Leona's girlfriends were wondering why Nick was with me and not with Leona.

Later that month on a Tuesday morning, I woke to the sound of heavy rain pelting at the window. I was at Leona's place, having maintained the habit of staying at Leona's for the week and Nick's for the weekend. At work, thunder was still crashing overhead in the early part of the afternoon and we could see constant flashes of lightning. After an especially loud crash, the fluorescent lights stopped humming and the machinery went dead. Some of the workers started joking as we waited to see if the blackout was temporary. After about fifteen minutes, the manager came out to tell us we could all go home. Sarah, the lady with whom I worked and who lived a few blocks from me, asked if she could use my car to get groceries and to pick up her kids. She dropped me off at my place first, saying she'd see me later. I walked up to our side entrance, thinking of the long lukewarm bath I was going to have as soon as I got inside. The heat and dampness made me feel all sticky.

What I noticed first as I entered our apartment was a pair of men's sneakers, because I almost stepped on them, and the first thing I heard was the radio coming from Leona's bedroom, meaning she had company. Remembering now that she had the day off, I wished that she would at least have closed her door. The bath was out because I couldn't pass by her open door. Not wanting to go back out in the rain, I went quietly into the living room to read and wait, regretting that I was home early each time I heard her bed squeak. She didn't have a current boyfriend, so I wondered who was in there with her. I also thought about tiptoeing back into the hallway and reading and waiting there, or making some kind of noise, because they'd be so surprised to find me here when they came out. Finally, I came up with a solution. I'd go back out, return, and yell, "Hi Leona, you home?" Yeah, that would be the proper thing. I put my book down beside me, put my keys in the pocket of my jeans, and got up to sneak outside. That's when, above the sound of the radio and the droning rain, I heard quite distinctly a voice ask, "Wanna smoke?" And something inside me turned upside down.

In the next instant, Nick's voice came again: "You got the lighter on your side?"

Whoosh! A rage washed over me and, irrationally, I marched right into her doorway. Nick was in the act of lighting up a smoke and, although a sheet covered them, they were obviously naked underneath. My mouth opened and closed much as theirs did. I stepped back out, shutting the door as I did so. They both called to me simultaneously. I grabbed my damp sweater and went out the door. Outside, I walked and walked and walked. Having left my purse behind, I had no money, no place to go, and I was shivering. As I walked, I squeezed my keys in my hand as though they were Leona's neck, and I finally thought, "Why the hell am I out here in the rain? Damn them. They can leave."

I got back just as Sarah pulled up in front of our place, and I watched her and her two boys get out. "What are you doing out in the rain?" she asked. "You're all soaked. I wouldn't have used your car if you needed it."

"It's okay. Something came up unexpectedly," I said, controlling my voice. She must have sensed I didn't want to talk and, after she handed me my keys, she opened her umbrella and ushered her boys down the street.

Back at the door to Leona's apartment, I paused before I stormed in. Leona was now dressed in jeans and a T-shirt. I didn't look her in the eye, I felt so much contempt for her.

As soon as she saw me, she said, "Oh, Chris ... I'm so sorry."

"Get lost, Leona," I growled as I went into the bathroom, slamming the door in her face. Because I was shivering now, I ran hot water for my bath. For what must have been hours, I soaked in that bathtub, thinking and planning for my future. Emily, at work, had been asking around if anyone wanted to drive to Vancouver in the near future. We had never talked to each other very much, but now she might be my ticket out of this hellhole. When I finally got out of the tub, I realized I'd forgotten to get fresh clothing. I dressed in my damp clothing and immediately started shivering again.

Leona, sitting at the table across the room, jumped up as soon as I opened the door. "Chris, we've got to talk. You have to understand we didn't mean to. It just happened."

Brushing past her, though I really wanted to shove her out of my way, I flopped down on the couch and pulled a cover over me. I sighed and said, "Leona, just leave me alone, okay? I don't want to hear how you didn't mean to and all that shit."

Digging out my book from under me, because I had just sat on it, I pretended to read. The words were blurred because tears were brimming at my eyes.

*

In spite of my warm clothing I was shivering now, not because of Leona but because of Todd's blood-soaked running shoe. Heedless of my pain, the waters of the Peace River drifted by in silence, with only the occasional sound of water slapping at rocks. Being here brought no soulful connection to Peter and Todd, and, in spite of Todd's running shoe, I could not, did not, believe they were somewhere in this river. If they weren't, I wondered what Peter was doing right now. Perhaps he was with her, making love to her, while I sat on this cold rock. If that were the case, I deserved it. I deserved it because of the bad things I'd done in my own past, and I deserved it for having allowed Leona back into my life. Reminding myself of my blame made the pain just a little easier to bear.

My trembling and the darkness impeded the climb back up the steep embankment. That I might slip and fall, hit my head, and die from a head injury or hypothermia was a tempting thought. Then all the pain and the guilt would end here tonight. But I was Christine, the coward, and I made sure I got back to the truck safely.

3

ack in my truck, I turned the heater and the fan to their highest settings so I could warm up quickly. Unable to accept the idea that Todd and Peter were dead, I could only surmise that Peter and Leona were together. They had to be. As much as the picture of them together hurt, they just had to be. The alternative meant that there would be no relief from that kind of pain—ever. And so, as I began to drive away, I focused my thoughts on Leona. Almost a year ago I had allowed Peter to talk me into inviting her back into my life, into our sanctuary. I had challenged the fates, knowing I would always lose. I knew that then, but I had trusted Peter.

*

In the spring of 1982 a letter came, through my publisher, and I saw it as a foreboding of things to come. My period of tranquillity had been too short. That day, Peter had gone to Dodging and, when he gave me the envelope from my publisher, I was merely curious. I opened it to find another envelope and, when I saw the name in the return address, my stomach turned over. My first thought was to just put it in the stove with the rest of the junk mail to burn, but I put it aside to read later in private. Peter, snoopy as always, looked up from his mail to ask, "A fan letter?"

"No, I don't think so," I went to Todd's bedroom to sit for a while and watch him sleep, but, mostly, I went there to avoid further questions from Peter. I tried, unsuccessfully, not to think about the letter.

Later that day I went down to sit at the lake so I could read the letter from Leona Pelletier. Not Leona Scarlos, but Leona Pelletier. So they didn't get married after all. I turned the envelope over, looked at the postmark, and saw it had been mailed from Winnipeg. I studied the handwriting that I had once wanted to imitate, figuring that if I could write like her, I could be more like her. As long as I had concentrated, I could imitate her style, but I had soon reverted to my squiggly little introverted style. Why did she have to go and write to me? Why couldn't she just leave me alone? I could flip this envelope into the lake and just let it go. But if I didn't read it, I would always wonder. Maybe it was about our mother being dead. So what? I wouldn't go to her funeral anyways. I smelled the envelope, expecting to get a whiff of perfume. Nothing. Finally, I tore the end open and pulled out a pink sheet of paper. That figured—nothing common for the queen.

April 25, 1982

Dear Chrissy,

How are you? Bet your surprised to hear from me, eh? A voice from the past. I only recently got the bright idea of writing to you through your publisher. I need your help but if you can't, that's ok. I can do something else.

I have to have an operation soon, nothing serious, just a gallbladder operation. So I won't be able to work for a while. I'm a waitress and they won't be able to keep my job open for me. Before I go on I have to tell you I have a son. Michael's 11 years old and he's the most important person in my life. I guess that means we haven't seen each other for around 13 years. I've got a friend he can stay with while I'm in the hospital. But the doc says I need 2, 3 weeks after to recuperate. There's not enough room at my friend's for both of us.

I'm holding off on this operation till July. That way, Michael will be on summer holidays. So if you have the room and its not a problem, I'd like to visit with you. But it wouldn't be a big deal if its not a good idea.

Not a day's gone by that I havent' thought of you. About a month ago I was talking about you to one of the women at work and she asked if I was related to you because she had a children's book written by Christine Pelletier Webster. She brought it in the next day and after reading about the author, I knew it was you.

Chrissy, I have so much to tell you. I really hope we can visit with each other. To be honest, its hard writing this letter after all this time, and here I am, asking for your help. Time flies!

You can write to me at the return address until the end of June. Thanks no matter what you decide. Bye for now.

All my love to you and yours.

Leona

My impression that Leona had done well in school, as she had in everything else, underwent a bit of a change and I subconsciously gloated over her mistakes. The twelve years could have been fifty, and my feelings about her would still be the same. By my calculation, Nick was probably the father, and a wave of jealousy washed over me, not because of Nick but because she had kept her child. Why was I letting a simple letter control my emotions? The solution to the problem of this letter would be simply not to answer. I heard Peter and Todd behind me about the same time that Lady came and put her wet nose into my hand, the one holding the letter.

"Bad news?" Peter asked, sensing my distress.

"No," I answered and tried to hide the letter. I didn't want to have to explain Leona to him. All he knew about my past was that I'd grown up in foster homes in Winnipeg and that I had a half-sister I didn't know well.

He tilted his head, focused on the letter in my hand, and asked, "Want to share?"

To say no was not an option, so I handed him the letter and stooped down to adjust the hood on Todd's jacket. His instant smile restored the good feelings in me.

"Thirteen years since you last saw each other?" From his perspective, this letter should have been an exciting moment for me.

"Something like that," I answered. "But we weren't close or anything. She was only a half-sister."

"Yeah, but now you'd have a chance to get to know each other. Family is family. And she has a son. Wow!"

"Wow, wow," Todd piped up. We both looked at him and laughed. Simply watching Todd, and Lady too, could usually put a smile on my face, no matter what else was happening.

"You have to write back and tell her they should come as soon as they can."

I felt myself being backed into a corner from which only the belated truth could rescue me, but for some reason I couldn't bring myself to tell Peter I had been wronged by my own sister. "For some reason"— who was I kidding? Telling him about that meant telling him more belated truths.

"Yeah, write back and offer to send them plane tickets," Peter said, looking over the letter again. "It's too bad she didn't include a phone number. We could have phoned from Kit's place tonight."

Maybe Leona had put a secret seductive scent on her letter, detectable only by men. He didn't know a thing about her, yet he wanted her here. My mind was too slow to come up with a reason why I should not invite her.

"Come on, you can write back to her right away. You must have been shocked, huh?" Grinning, Peter handed the letter back to me, took hold of Todd's hand, and led the way back. As I followed, I considered the possibility of telling him what Leona had done to me. Instead of the truth, it was a lie that came to me. Leona was an alcoholic and I didn't think it would be a good idea to have her around Todd. But he might say that was all the more reason to have her come. And if she didn't have a drinking problem, I'd look like the liar I was.

Scratch that one. She was a heavy smoker, but Kit smoked and it hadn't bothered us.

Later that night I was writing a letter, just to stop Peter from carrying on about my sister. I had said that having Leona here would arouse all the ill feelings I had towards my mother and remind me of the bad times in foster homes. That was the best I could do. Peter responded that talking to my sister might bring a different perspective to my childhood and my mother. That's when I gave up and wrote the damn letter.

Two weeks later I got another letter from Leona.

Dear Chrissy,

Thanks for your letter. I didn't know if you would answer me or not. I pictured you living in Vancouver, since thats were your publisher is. So much time has passed since we last saw each other. We have so much to talk about.

Right now, I want to congratulate you on your childrens books. They are so lovely. I did'nt know you had that in you, a talent for writing. It took me forever to compose my last letter so that it would open doors. Chrissy, I want to see you so much. Besides thinking about you, I used to worry about you.

The second thing I wanted to tell you was a confession. I don't really need an operation. I thought if I asked for your help, you might answer. If I just sent an I-want-to-make-up-with-you letter, you would probably have tossed it out, right? And of course, I wouldnt blame you. Now that you know I lied, you may not want me around so please send me a note at least telling me to stay out of your life and I will understand.

Otherwise, Michael and me will have our bags packed on June 29 for a short visit. Speaking of Mikey, you will simply love him.

If you are going to kick me out of your life, just tell me more about yourself. It said in the book that you were married to Peter Webster, a mystery novelist. That is so neat. Do you have children? Dogs? Cats? Horses? Knowing you, you probably have them all, right?

I am looking forward to hearing from you again, soon.

Love, hugs and kisses,

Leona

Darn, if I'd known she was lying, I could have told my lies. Peter was going to want to "share" in the news and would have no idea that what was being opened here was a can of worms. He had picked up the mail and made a big production of handing this letter to me, so now he would want to read it. Although he was tapping away at his typewriter when I handed the letter to him, he immediately read it as if he wasn't doing anything important. Must have been that secret scent.

"Ah, so you had a falling-out with her?" he said looking up at me.

"It seemed important at the time, but now it's nothing," I countered.

"What a waste of thirteen years. You are going to tell her they are still welcome, right?"

Sighing, I turned away and flopped down on the couch. "I've been happy without her in my life, without all the memories she would invoke. I have never missed her. It's not like we grew up together. As I told you, she was only a half-sister."

"But it's not so much about you and her. She has a son, you have a son, they're cousins, and they should at least get to meet each other, get to know that they have family."

An appeal to my softhearted side usually ended with Peter getting his way. Besides, having Leona come back into my life wasn't going to be such a big deal. Peter's commitment to me was real. And if Leona did manage to louse that up, he would never leave Todd. But then, I would never want to be with a man who wanted someone else. What to do? Well, I wasn't going to be afraid of my sister, so I retrieved the letter from Peter's desk and wrote a nice civilized letter saying we were looking forward to seeing her and Michael in June. As I wrote, I was thinking I could ride out a two-week visit.

At the end of June, Peter, Todd, and I went to the bus depot in Fort St. John to pick up Leona and Michael. She had refused my offer of plane tickets, saying she preferred to take the train and then a bus. As we waited inside our truck for the bus, my insides churned—and the churning sped up as the bus pulled in and passengers began to disembark. Was I now going to lose Peter to her? Maybe she had aged ungracefully and let herself go.... Then I saw her in the doorway of the bus. Two men got off before her and one turned to take her hand and help her down. The other handed her carry-on luggage back to her. Damn, she was even more beautiful than ever, with that feline grace in her every movement. Behind her, a miniature Nick got off and, for the moment, he was ignored as she laughingly made her goodbyes to the two men. Reluctantly, I got out of the truck and went over to the bus, where she was waiting for her other luggage. Carrying Todd, Peter joined me, and when Leona saw me, her face glowed.

We made the necessary introductions and I was relieved when she refused my offer of the front seat, beside Peter, and squeezed into the rear of the extended cab onto one of the jump seats. On the drive back she made it easy for everyone to exchange good-natured banter—everyone but me. Pretending not to care about Peter that much, I focused my attention on Todd and Leona.

That night over a supper down by the beach, Peter asked Leona how long she could stay and she jokingly replied. "The whole summer—it is so beautiful up here."

"Done," Peter said. "Right, Chris?"

Not wanting either of them to know how insecure I was, I smiled and said, "Why not? You don't have anything pressing in Winnipeg, do you?"

"Well, no, but.... Well, okay. But if we get on your nerves, you have to promise me you'll send us packing. Okay?" Leona said, smiling at both of us.

The mental picture of me kicking Peter in the butt was my only comfort, as I smiled, smiled, smiled at everyone sitting around the picnic table.

In the following weeks, Peter, Michael, and Todd went canoeing and trekking. They played hide and seek with Lady—Michael was really impressed with that—and they went over to Kit's place to visit. At night after Todd went to bed, Michael took my place at the dining-room table and played chess with Peter while Leona and I sat in the living room, talking about nothing. Mona had given me some leather hides she had tanned and, when Leona saw them, she insisted on making each of us moccasins. I had planned to make things with them, but had never gotten around to it. So she sewed while I twiddled my thumbs and wished I could lie out on the couch and read—and that I'd never let her back into my life.

One Friday night we decided to go to Dodging for supper. Friday nights were my nights off from the kitchen, and Peter, Todd, and I often ate out or he did the cooking. We were all sitting in the restaurant when I felt someone watching us. I looked around and two very good-looking men were sitting further back in the restaurant, one around our age and the other an older man with a beard. Both of them were looking elsewhere when I spotted them, but when I got the feeling of being watched again I looked in their direction quickly and, sure enough, I caught the older of the two looking at me before he turned away. Something about him seemed familiar, but I was quite sure I had never seen him around town before. The other unusual thing was that he had been staring at me and not at Leona, but then, her back was to them. I forgot about them as our food came. While we were choosing desserts, the two men suddenly appeared at our table. The younger one said to Peter, "Excuse us, we don't want to disturb you, but aren't you that mystery writer? Oxford or something?"

That made Peter laugh, as he said, "Webster, Peter Webster."

The man also laughed and said, "Yeah, there was a write up about you in the *Peace Valley Voice* a while back. I'm Colin Sayers, and this is Howard Norach."

The three men exchanged brief handshakes and Colin continued, "My sister really likes your books. Would I be disturbing you greatly if

I asked for an autograph?"

"Well, it's the fans who keep us going," Peter said, taking the paper placemat from Colin. "What's her name?"

While Peter wrote, I looked up at both men. Colin was eyeing Leona appreciatively and they smiled to each other, but the older man was looking straight at me, giving me an intense stare. Again the sensation that I knew him came to me, but I was sure we had never met. He only reminded me of someone I had once met, that was it.

"Thank you very much. Sorry again to disturb you. In return, I'd like to pay your tab," Colin said, still smiling.

"Oh, no, no, no," Peter protested. "Book sales are great thanks to people like your sister. Thanks anyways."

The men left and I thought that was that.

In the following week, Leona and I went to town while Peter took the boys fishing. We decided to have lunch before doing some grocery shopping. Colin was already there and, when he came over to our table, Leona invited him to join us. I had forgotten my grocery list, so I began to recreate it when I finished eating, leaving Leona and Colin to carry on with their own conversation. When I heard him ask if he could see her again, I was glad. So far, Peter seemed immune to Leona's many attributes and, if she got herself a man while she was up here, that would be a good thing all round.

A few days later I was in the back hanging the second load of clothes on the line when Colin came calling. Leona and he were talking for a while before I came back in.

"Colin invited Michael and me to dinner in Fort St. John tonight. Do you mind?" she asked.

"No. Not at all," I replied and carried on with my chores. I was folding clothes in my room when Leona came in and said, "You know, Colin kind of wanted tonight to be like a date. I wondered if you think Michael would mind not coming along with me."

"You'd have to ask Michael that," I said.

"I know that, but I had to run it by you first. I don't expect you to babysit for me while I run off on a date," Leona said through a smile.

"We don't mind having Michael here. I just meant as long as he doesn't mind staying behind."

Peter returned as Leona went outside to look for Michael, so I joined the men at the table for a coffee break. Colin watched as I dumped two teaspoons of sugar into my coffee. "She likes a bit of coffee with her milk and sugar," Peter joked.

Hiding my annoyance with Peter for that comment, I finished my coffee without taking part in their conversation. They went on to talk about other things and, after Colin mentioned he was an oil explorations agent, he asked Peter if he was interested in leasing some of his land. Without hesitation, Peter said we were not at all interested in that. Leona returned and she and Colin left. When we went to bed that night, Leona still had not returned. I heard her later as she settled herself on the couch, and I wondered if she was drunk.

While Michael was friendly, we had not talked to each other much and I felt awkward with him—perhaps because he reminded me so much of the man I had once loved and then detested. He had been taking karate and he showed Peter what he knew. Peter was interested in having a younger man who was an expert in the martial arts join his usual character, Gregory M. Thomas. One night when Kit and Mona came over, Leona talked Michael into performing the *katas* for us. Before he started he told us about each *kata* he would do. He also explained that he had started with a white belt, then a yellow belt, and, when he got back home, was going to get his green belt.

In the middle of August, when it was raining one day, Peter took the boys to Fort St. John to a movie and to do some shopping. Leona and I had the whole afternoon to ourselves. "I'm in love, Chrissy," she volunteered.

"The way you were with Michael's father?" The words came out so suddenly that they shocked even me.

Leona looked at me as if she had been slapped. Then she answered slowly, "Yes."

"I didn't want to talk about it back then. But I can talk about it now.

Nick stopped being important to me the moment I saw him in your bed," I said, not quite truthfully.

"Chrissy, do we have to talk about that? It's ancient history."

"It's not. You have Michael. And he's the spitting image of Nick. You asked me if you could come here, supposedly to talk things out. So what you did to me is not ancient history."

Jealousy of my sister resurfaced, but this time for a different reason. She had Nick's son and, besides being each other's best friend, Leona and Michael had a mutually respectful relationship that allowed them to be relaxed with each other, even playful. Leona was the lioness with a cub, doling out the perfect combination of affection and discipline. Peter was like that with Todd. What I did mostly was to watch, as an outsider. Since her arrival here, the wound she had inflicted was resurrected and it brought out the worst in me.

Unable to keep my jealousy at bay, but trying hard to hide it, I had been watching, watching, to see if she intended to inflict new wounds where Peter was concerned. For over a month, now, I had been on edge, trying to detect things going on that shouldn't be going on.

Leona sighed and looked at me. "After you left the way you did, I went down to your work and found out you had headed to Vancouver with another girl from the factory. And Nick, he was always asking if I'd heard from you. All we really had going for us was a desire for each other, a sexual desire. And that wears off. When I got pregnant, Nick hung around for a while, longer than he wanted to, I think."

"You never got married?" I asked, recalling the last time I had seen them.

"No. We almost did. Even got a licence." She lit one of her cigarettes, inhaled deeply, and took her time blowing the smoke out. "But Nick pined for you. You had an innocent quality about you, he would say. I was crazy in love with him, and all he wanted to do was talk about you." Leona smiled to herself. "Poetic justice, huh?"

I didn't believe for a moment that Nick had ever talked about me and I resented Leona's condescending attitude.

"I know I've said this before, but I want you to believe me when I say I'm sorry I hurt you." She took another drag of her cigarette, and it occurred to me that she was nervous.

My sister was nervous and that's why she tried to patronize me. This wicked half-smile came to my face and I said, "Yes, before I left you said that. And then you had his baby."

"I know, but I was young back then, so I was selfish and really stupid."

"And now you've changed."

She looked at me with those beautiful eyes, a silent plea in them to let it be, but I had this irrational need to get back at her. "I imagine some of these men you fell in love with along the way were married."

Just above a whisper, she said, "Oh Chrissy, how can I ever make it up to you? It's been such a long time ago and you still hate me because of Nick."

Not because of Nick, you damned fool, definitely not because of Nick.

"You're right. I should put the past behind us. I just wanted to make sure it's going to stay there."

Leona leaned towards me, took hold of my hand, unaware she was holding the hand of a liar, and said, "It will stay there. I promise."

We smiled at each other, mine being the plastic smile I had used so many times before.

"So can I tell you about Colin? And the first thing, he's not married. We've been to his place and ..." Yap, yap, yap, she went, her eyes sparkling and dancing as she told of their wonderful moments together. All I could think was that this was a woman who had watched too many soap operas and was trying to live them. Colin wouldn't last, but she'd better not try to come and cry on Peter's shoulder.

Before the end of August, Leona told me that she and Michael were going to be moving in with Colin in Fort St. John. I had been looking forward to her return to Winnipeg, a nice safe distance from us, and once she was gone I had no intention of staying in contact with her. Fort St. John—well, at least she was focused on another man. When Peter heard about her plans, he said there was something about Colin he didn't trust. So, finally, he revealed that he was concerned about Leona's welfare. A trickle of jealousy rose up in me, but I was able to dismiss it later when he told me he liked them both but was glad he could now get back to his work.

When they left, I felt the same sense of freedom as I had when I had been released from Mount Ste. Marie, and for the first few days I went around humming to myself. Not knowing the truth, Peter thought that Leona's visit had been good therapy for me.

Over the following months, Colin brought them to Shadow Lake for visits. He now seemed completely enamoured with Leona and he would say silly things to Peter, such as, "Leona did this, isn't she cute?" Peter must have noticed the cold way I treated my sister. Without knowing the full story, he must have thought I was out of line, and that was another reason why I detested her. Whenever we went to Fort St. John, Peter would ask, to my annoyance, whether I wanted to drop in and visit with Leona and Michael.

In December we went to Vancouver for three weeks and stayed with Peter's parents. For the first time I was happy to be there, and they both seemed pleased to have us with them. I went with Peter as he renewed contacts and did research, and we took Todd out with us as much as possible. A week after we celebrated Todd's third birthday, we returned to Shadow Lake. Leona and Colin never came to visit us again, and I assumed it was because Leona was fed up with my attitude. Sometimes I felt sorry that I had behaved badly, but then I'd remind myself that Leona was a woman with no scruples and should be avoided.

*

As I was driving back to the cabin, I was startled when Lady came dashing out from the north side of the road. Stopping the truck, I opened the door and she jumped in, licking my face in her excitement. I knew I had left her inside, so she wouldn't try to follow me. She didn't know how to open doors, especially locked doors, so how did she get out? She must have slipped out before me and I had locked the door on an empty house.

Yes, but I had left the kitchen light on, and now, as I drove into our yard, the cabin was sitting in darkness. Thank God that Lady was with me because, alone, I'm not sure I would have got out of the truck. Inside the porch, I had the usual trouble of unlocking the cabin door, but once inside, I flicked the light switch on as I entered the kitchen. I thought I could smell beer, and I looked through the cabin for its origins. Nothing was out of place, though, so I reckoned it was a combination of my imagination and forgetfulness.

As I prepared to go to bed on the couch, I thought of the contradiction in my feelings. Now I was scared, yet less than an hour earlier I had thought an accident that ended my life was just what I needed.

4

The next morning when I opened my eyes, the weight of depression bore down on me immediately, pinning me to the couch. I lay there, looking up at the knots and the swirls of the tongue-and-groove pine ceiling. Lady finally coaxed me into getting up and, while I moved about in slow motion, doing only what I had to, I mourned. Today I would give Lady her bath after taking one myself, and I brought out the large pots I used for boiling water. When she came back in and saw the pots boiling on the stove, she went immediately under our desks at the far end of the living room. Like Todd, she hated baths, and they both hated getting combed, too. What Todd had loved was when Peter wrapped him in a big cozy towel and lifted him high in the air as he wiped him dry—just as he did that day down at the lake.

The mirror was all steamed up and I wiped a hole clear, thinking I should cut my hair evenly. I must have picked up lengths of my hair and just cut it right off, for it was long here, shorter there—a total mess. More for something to do than out of vanity, I had begun the task when I heard the sound of a vehicle. I remembered then that Sergeant Trolley had said they'd be back and I braced myself, in case they were here to tell me they had found Todd and Peter.

Thankfully, the sound of the vehicle belonged to Kit's pickup, not the police. Kit and Mona got out as I went from the dining-room window to the door to let them in. They had brought a pot of stew with them and some pie. Mona guessed that I hadn't eaten, and she took charge of my kitchen. Despite my protests that I wasn't hungry, I found myself eating venison stew with them. Afterwards, while we were having coffee with dessert, and to distract me from my own thoughts, they told me that government people had shot and killed the wolves of Shadow Lake around the time I'd been in Norway House. At another time I might have mourned for the wolves, but right now I didn't care if wolves became extinct.

My next visitors, later that afternoon, were two other RCMP officers, Corporal Watherson and Constable Ringer. After the preliminary condolences, they began asking me something, but I interrupted and asked, "Did you find them?"

Corporal Watherson paused before answering, "No, we didn't. And Sergeant Trolley was told that, because of ice, the search will be delayed until there's warmer weather."

Until they came, I had been able to avoid thinking about Todd and Peter being dead, but now that these messengers of death were here I shivered. Shivered, in spite of the warmth of the cabin, shivered from a cold that came from somewhere inside me. I got up and went to get my jacket, feeling their eyes on me. Maybe they thought I was going to walk out and just leave them sitting there. "I'm just so cold," I explained as I returned to sit at the table.

The corporal contradicted another repeated expression of condolence by asking whether Peter and I had got along.

Immediately defensive, I murmured, "Sergeant Trolley asked me that yesterday."

"Yes, but someone came forward and told us of having seen you about to strike your husband with a rock. So I'm sorry, but it doesn't sound like you were getting along."

Outraged that someone would tell such a lie, I was about to protest that I had never, would never, hit Peter when I remembered that long ago, we had acted out a scene for his book. "Mrs. Springer told you that. We were working out a scene for Peter's book and that was back, like four years ago. The rocks were balled-up paper. Do you want to see the passage in the book? Did she tell you we had opera music play-ing loudly? It's all in the book." Watching their reaction, I could almost see them adjust their view of me, as I adjusted my view of Mrs. Springer. Before I didn't like her. Now I hated her.

"Okay, but Sergeant Trolley felt that you were holding something back," Corporal Watherson said.

"I told him what I know."

The sudden turn of their conversation took me by surprise. "We had to ask," Corporal Watherson said. "I'm sorry. Someone phoned in the sighting of your husband's truck and we'd like you to come in and listen to the tape, to see if you recognize the voice."

"Okay, but ..." It dawned on me why they wanted me to listen to the tape. "You think it might be Peter's voice!" I said incredulously.

The younger officer said, "Too many things about the accident don't look right. Besides that particular location, for instance, there were no skid marks, and ..." His voice trailed off as he caught Corporal Watherson glaring at him.

"You think Peter staged the accident? Peter would never have done something like that. He is—was—the most decent straightforward person I ever knew."

"Mrs. Webster, it's hard to ask about sensitive matters at a time like this, but is it possible he was involved with someone else?" Corporal Watherson asked.

"Another woman?" Even as I asked, I was shaking my head no. "If he had met someone else, he would have told me, and if he wanted to leave me, he would have told me."

"And what about your son? Would he have walked away from him?"

That question had me stumped momentarily. I finally answered, "We both loved Todd very much and we would have arranged some-thing that was beneficial to him. Another thing, that running shoe had blood stains on it, didn't it? Peter would never hurt Todd. Never."

For me to doubt Peter was one thing, but for these strangers to come here and bandy about suspicions was unacceptable. I was almost snarling as I continued, "Besides, the whole idea of staging an accident means he'd have to cut himself off from everything, from his parents, from his friends—and you just talk to them. They'll tell you what he's like. And like I said, he just finished another book. Writing is his life. He wouldn't abandon that. He wouldn't abandon anything here. I, I don't know how to convince you what kind of person Peter is. Was."

Before they left, Corporal Watherson told me again that the search was being delayed and that he was sorry. What he didn't say was the alternative, that they would find proof that Peter had staged the accident.

At the end of that day, I suddenly felt overwhelmingly lonely as it dawned on me once again that Peter and Todd were not coming back. Once again I sat in the darkness, Peter's and Todd's clothing on one side and Lady up on the couch on the other side. Right now she was my only friend, the only one who could try to comfort me. What was I going to do without them, without Todd? One thing I knew was that I would not leave Shadow Lake until Peter and Todd were found.

For the rest of the week I existed, performing routine duties out of habit and necessity, and I waited. When I had phoned Peter's parents again, to tell them the search was going to be delayed, they told me they were having a memorial service and I should come to Vancouver, but I said I had to wait here.

On Friday morning I woke, unable to obliterate the thoughts which had come before and which had been reinforced by the police. I finally forced myself to think through a scenario that had Peter leaving with Leona. They would have had to have planned it months ago, maybe when Peter first knew I would be away on a trip. The best time for an accident would be at night, when the risk of being seen was minimal. And icy road conditions, while handy, would not have been necessary to their plan. The spot was well chosen because a vehicle going down that embankment would certainly come to a stop only in the river. After planting Todd's running shoe inside, he would have driven the truck to the edge and jumped out, so the gear would still be in Drive. The blood on Todd's running shoe could have been from a nosebleed, or Peter could have cut himself and dabbed it on. And he could have propped the doors open, so investigators would assume their bodies were taken by the currents. All the while, Leona would be waiting nearby with another vehicle so they could drive away together.

There it was. If Peter wanted to get away from me that badly to be with my sister, and to keep Todd, he could have gone through with this plan, this elaborate plan. As a mystery writer, he knew a lot about the procedures of police investigations. If he and Leona had done this to me, it meant that Peter was evil. And Leona, well, it was already a given that she was evil.

With this scenario in mind, I was both anxious to go listen to that tape and afraid. The only comfort I could give myself was the thought that if Peter did run away with Leona, then Todd was still alive. And that would be the one good thing to come out of such evil. The police had planted the seed in my head, and I watered it well with the knowledge I had of my sister. The only thing that wasn't credible was Peter being capable of such actions. Surely there would have been indications that his commitment to me had waned. In the few months before my trip to Norway House, Peter had been the same as always, usually thoughtful unless he was focused on his writing. Okay, so sometimes he was snappy with me and I with him, but, mostly, he did those thoughtful little things that showed he cared.

That afternoon, sitting in what I imagined was their interrogation room, I waited apprehensively as they brought in a tape recorder and the tape. Sergeant Trolley mildly rebuked me for not coming sooner as he inserted the tape and pressed the play button. A man's voice, not Peter's, came on, and it was repeatedly interrupted by the operator, who was trying unsuccessfully to get his name. Some parts I couldn't understand because of the operator's interruptions.

"Uh hi. I was driving ... I was driving home last night, had a flat tire, and when I was changing it, I thought I saw something shining, down in the Peace River ... from the moon? ... binoculars, it looked like the back of a truck. You should check it out."

That was it. There was nothing distinctive about the voice, and I looked up at Sergeant Trolley and said, "I've never heard that voice before. Not that I remember."

As I drove home, I was more confused than ever. Peter would never have brought in a third party to his elaborate plan, if this was a plan. For Todd's sake, I fervently wished it was a plan.

Over the next few weeks, I went from thinking Peter and Todd had died to thinking that Peter had betrayed me and was probably with Leona. She had left Colin for Peter. But, still, that would have been in February, and Peter had not gone anywhere without me in that time. Lovers would want to be together, would have to be together, especially Leona. Still, Peter was a mystery writer, capable of plotting devious schemes.

These kinds of thoughts were interrupted when Colin, himself, came calling. He was so sympathetic and so easy to talk to that I told him almost everything that had happened so far, leaving out my suspicions about Leona and Peter. He told me they had broken up in February—his fault—and that he was surprised I hadn't heard from her at all. His last visit to us was to see if she was here. He asked me to tell him right away if I did hear from her, and I asked for the same consideration. After he left, I was disturbed that Leona and Michael had disappeared. And then again, Todd might be with them.

Some time during the night Lady woke me to go outside. I didn't want to fully wake up because I'd have a hard time going back to sleep. Heavy rain poured from black skies, and now that she had me up I almost had to force her out into the rain. I returned to the couch, just to sit for a few minutes while I waited for her.

The sounds of a dogfight woke me, and then I heard the high-pitched squeal of a wounded animal. Remembering with horror that Lady was still out there, I jumped up and raced out, thinking the wolves had gotten her. The rain had stopped and the only night sounds now were from water drops falling from leaves and from the edge of the roof.

"Lady!" I yelled out into the night. A barely audible moan came from the direction of the truck. Grabbing a flashlight, I made my way towards the truck, calling for her and listening. She walked slowly and stiffly into the beam of light, her fur matted and covered with mud mixed with blood. "Oh baby, I fell back asleep. I'm sorry. I'm sorry." Lady gave a feeble wag of her tail. I led her back inside so I could get a better look at her. She lay heavily on the floor and began trying to lick at herself. When I saw that blood was oozing out of a long gash on her side, I thought of Mona, because she knew a lot about medicines and could help Lady. I dressed quickly, wrapped a towel around Lady's middle, and got her out to the truck. At Mona's I honked the horn until I saw lights come on.

We got Lady inside to their kitchen and, after Kit took a closer look, he asked if I'd seen any stray dogs.

"You mean it wasn't a wolf?" I asked.

"Doesn't seem like it. But it's hard to tell."

Mona put the kettle on and made some kind of mixture with dried leaves and herbs before cutting away Lady's fur from around the main gash. I watched as she checked Lady for other wounds, and we were both surprised to find what looked like stitches from a recent but older wound, just behind her left ear.

"She must have been hurt while I was gone. And Peter must have taken her to the vet," I said, wondering what could have happened.

"Look at this here," Mona said, pointing to a spot just under her throat.

Looking to where she was pointing, I couldn't see much, except that her fur seemed to have been rubbed away by some kind of rope.

"It's like a rope burn. Maybe she got caught up in some barb wire, somewhere," Mona said. Lady squirmed, impatient at having to lie still.

I soothed her as Mona dipped a needle and thread in the cooling mixture and began to close the wound with stitches. Lady gave a deep, low, rumble of a growl, but didn't try to bite or anything. Afterwards, Mona coated the area and the other minor wounds with the salve. She put some gauze over the gash, wrapped Lady's body tightly with a clean towel, and pinned it.

"She was lucky. You must have scared off whatever attacked her," Kit said. "You notice any animal acting strange?"

"No, I haven't even seen any animals lately," I answered, and then realized what he was talking about. "If you mean rabies, Lady had her shot for that. But then, that was last spring. She's due for another one, I think. But maybe Peter had that done if he took her to the vet while I was gone."

"She should be okay," Kit said.

"She should stay here. I can check on her and change the dressing," Mona said, petting the now sleeping dog. "Our granddaughter, she's coming to stay with us. Kit's going to pick her up tomorrow. She can help me."

Before I left, I petted Lady's head, and thanked Mona once again. Back at the cabin, I thought about the sense of Lady's being at the cabin with me. I think that was when I realized I did have a plan for my future—and it didn't include Lady.

The next morning I returned to Mona's to see Lady before I went to Dodging. By then, Kit had gone to Hudson's Hope to pick up their granddaughter. Lady seemed much better, but Mona wanted to keep her a while longer. I told Mona I had to go to Dodging to pick up mail and get some groceries. On my way back, I stopped again to see Lady and, by now, Amber, their teenage granddaughter was there. With a brush in her hand, she was sitting on the living-room floor, petting Lady.

"Hi. I like your dog," she said to me, without an ounce of shyness.

"She seems to like you, too," I responded, bending to pet Lady, who was excited to see me.

"Yeah, I've got a way with animals," she stated.

"So, you're going to be here for a couple of weeks?" I asked, more to make conversation than to satisfy any curiosity.

"Nope, longer. Mom wanted me out of the city 'cause I got in trouble." She began brushing Lady, who, surprisingly, seemed to be enjoying it. Whenever I brushed her she always made growling noises, and if I yanked on her fur too hard she would pinch my arm with her incisor teeth, to let me know what it felt like. Still brushing my dog, Amber said, "I heard what happened. I'm sorry."

"Thanks," I said, not knowing if she was talking about Peter and Todd, or about Lady.

"You're a writer, aren't you?" she asked. "I never met a real writer before."

"Just children's books," I said, almost as if that made me not a real writer.

She seemed to agree by saying, "Oh, that's all?"

"So far. Maybe one day I'll write a novel. Peter used to write murder mysteries."

"Oh yeah? I love mysteries. I read them all the time, but I don't think I've read any of his books. But then, I never remember authors' names."

"Well, I've got all his books if you want to read them."

"Sure. I'll come out on horseback tomorrow, okay? Not tomorrow—school." Amber made a face, then continued: "On Saturday, I'll come out. You like riding?"

"Yeah."

"I'll bring Piwon along. I've already met all the horses. I love horses, don't you? We could go for a ride."

I smiled at her enthusiasm and asked, "You think that would be okay with your grandfather?"

"Call him Kit. Everyone does, except Mom and Mona. He pretends to be real mean and grumpy, but he's okay. He won't mind."

My smile this time wasn't from being polite and it felt strange to have a genuine smile on my face. Mona brought the tea in and said to Amber, "Why don't you go see to the horses?"

"That means she wants me to get lost," Amber said, giving us a mischievous grin. She took Lady's head in both her hands and said she'd brush her later. Then she left with a "See ya" to me. I could tell that Lady was tempted to follow her new friend.

"I remember when she was just a tiny little girl. They grow up so fast, 'specially in these days." Mona said, shaking her head.

"She seems really nice. She offered to bring an extra horse over on Saturday so we could go riding. I hope that's all right."

"Oh yeah, that's okay. Kit will go, too. Your dog could go home with you today."

We must have been on the same wavelength because, as I was about to ask if Lady could stay here awhile, she asked, "But do you think you might leave her here for a while? I think it would be good for Amber. Her mother, she works two jobs and Amber, she got into some trouble, eh, so she could use a friend right now." Mona paused and added, "On the other hand, you could use a friend, too. Besides us."

"Well, I was going to ask if Lady could stay here longer and you did take care of her last night. Next week, I'll take her to the vet for her shot. I should call first. Mind if I use your phone?"

When I returned from making my call, I must have had a puzzled look on my face. "What is it?" Mona asked.

"I just talked to both the receptionist and the vet and they said Peter did not take Lady in at all. So who could have stitched her up?" Sitting near Lady, I ruffled the fur on her head, feeling the small raised lip where her skin had been sewn together behind her left ear. She shook her head and I continued the previous conversation with Mona as if we hadn't left off. "Yeah, with what happened to her, it might be better for Lady to stay here. For a while."

"You feel guilt for what happened to her."

"I guess so," I answered, but that was hardly the reason.

The winter's supply of wood was down to less than a cord and, while I didn't need fires for most days, nights were still cool. A plan, if one could call it that, was beginning to take shape in my mind, but I wouldn't fulfil it until the bodies of Peter and Todd were recovered. Or perhaps the police would prove that Peter had run away. I was living in limbo. Peter had not run away—they were dead. They were not dead. He had betrayed me.

Getting the key for the ATV, I headed for the garage. The garage had been our last project and, like the cache, which was really a summer kitchen, the garage was just a large shed to house the snowmobiles and the ATV, but not the trucks. The ATV growled but refused to start. Since Peter had always changed spark plugs, I looked about for the operating manual, found some spark plugs in an unopened package, did everything I thought I had to, and tried the key again. Still no luck, so I fiddled with it some more and, when it finally started, I backed it out so I could hitch the trailer to it. A small accomplishment, but I felt good about it. I was ready to go gather wood.

Mostly, I spent the morning lugging wood. When I was back at the cabin with my last load of wood for that day, I brought out the chain saw, but I couldn't get it going. No matter how many times I pulled on the cord, rechecked the choke and gasoline, and pulled some more, it just wouldn't start. After a while, swearing and sweating, I was mindlessly yanking at the cord. I finally stood up and gave the stubborn little sucker a good vicious kick.

And then I damned Peter all to hell. "You had to have your own way, didn't you? 'I want to move up here.' Damn you!" Stomping around in a circle, I kicked the chain saw again. "If you hadn't made me come up here, our son would be alive. You took him with you in your rush to get to Leona and you killed him. Damn you, Peter!" Another kick. "And if you didn't die, you're hiding him from me and I hate you, Peter Webster. I hate you!" I stopped thinking it and yelled it out loud.

With one last kick at the chain saw, I turned and walked down to the lake. As my laborious breathing subsided, I wondered how I came to be here, in this time, in this place, in this situation. If I hadn't met Peter, where would I be now?

*

In the two years after fleeing from Winnipeg for good, I had hung around with Emily's hippie friends. No matter where I went, I was always the outsider, never really part of any group. So even though I had many one-night stands, even though I got drunk and smoked whatever they smoked, the watcher in me kept me apart. The watcher in me tried to figure out what their problems were—easier to ignore my own—that they led such hopeless lives.

I was too much the coward to get in trouble the way they did. For instance, I smoked pot if they offered it, but I stopped there, refusing the heavy-duty drugs. Most were happy to lie around all day, living off welfare, the girls turning tricks for money to buy drugs, the guys going out to score—whatever that meant. Police raids and arrests were not uncommon, and I think it was part of a game of suspense we all played. Twice I had near misses, leaving with a guy in both cases, and the cops raiding the houses we'd just left. The hippies had a language all their own which I was slow to learn and quick to forget.

Ironically, I got a job at a FabriChoice store, mostly because I knew materials, thanks to Leona. It was the last place I would have thought of, but when I saw the sign in the window, I'd gone in on a whim. After getting the job, I told myself that working in a FabriChoice store would serve to remind me that I should trust no one, ever again, thanks or no thanks to Leona.

Emily's group was forever changing—people went, people came—and I think what we all enjoyed was that we had an easy acceptance of others. Andrea was new to the group and she and I became good friends, spending Saturday afternoons together, starting with brunch, and sometimes going to movies on weeknights. She was nuts about movies, and occasionally she'd drag me to the theatre too. Sometimes she would drop in on our weekend parties, entertaining us with her lively mimicking or having us in stitches with comedy routines she'd seen somewhere else. Too soon, she had to go out on the streets, for she turned tricks for a living. She wanted to be an actress, and her weekdays were devoted to theatre school.

One Saturday, on a cold February day, she dragged me to an audition for a play at a small local theatre called Goblins. That was how I met Peter, who had been the playwright. But it wasn't love at first sight. In spite of Leona, I still had Nick on my mind. Peter and I joked our way through six months before he laughingly proposed. Appropriately, I laughingly accepted. Even when I learned he was serious, I thought I had nothing better going on in my life. Still, I couldn't help comparing him with Nick. Where Nick had been terribly handsome, wildly romantic, thoughtlessly reckless, and even arrogant, Peter was merely attractive and boringly predictable.

The play he had written, and which Andrea starred in, was called *Check and Mate,* and he was making it into a novel. When he sent it out and got all these rejection letters, I thought I was jinxing him. Most times we lived on my wage, eating Kraft dinners six times a week. We had lots of fights, some about my smoking, others because I felt he was trying to control everything. Eventually I quit smoking because I realized it was Leona's thing—and I didn't want any kind of connection to her. I let Peter think I quit for him.

There were times I packed my two suitcases and was about to walk out the door, and Peter would ask me to stay—and I stayed because I had nothing better to do. When success as an author came to him, it came in a gush. I think his passion for writing was greater than his passion for me, and he happily went to work on more novels and began to travel a lot. He was the one who talked me into trying my hand at writing books. When I came up with my first children's book, he helped me get it published. My success was nothing compared with his, but I did get asked to do talks at schools. Mostly, I ended up talking about Peter's writing rather than mine.

While I was never sure that I loved him, I was positively jealous when, at parties, all these talented, attractive females gathered around him, practically pushing me aside. Part of it was that I didn't trust him any more than I trusted anyone else. But if I didn't love him, why was I jealous?

His first book was optioned for a movie, and when he got paid for the rights, he broke the news to me that he wanted to leave the city for an isolated place in the foothills of the Rockies. He and Al Roberts, his life-long buddy, had found it when they went for their yearly hunting trip along the Alaska Highway. A hunter from another party almost shot Al, so they had taken time to find an area where they could hunt in peace. I didn't like the idea of moving, and I liked it even less when Peter confessed he had already put an offer on the cabin with its two sections of land.

As usual, I had no real say and we ended up here at Shadow Lake. Like a child in a time of upheaval, I was sullen and silent, hating everything in sight. The first time we saw Kit, he was just an old Indian man on horseback with a packed mule trailing behind. Peter stopped his truck to say hello. The man had looked over at us with piercing, cold eyes and merely nodded. Without any apparent movement, he urged his mount onwards.

"There's a taste of your new neighbourhood," I snorted. Of course, I didn't know the man on horseback was Kit.

Even though he didn't have to, Peter continued his sales pitch about the new place. "This is a great place for kids. Won't have to worry about perverts grabbing them or their getting hit by cars or any of the other things that happen in the city."

"I told you already, I don't want children," I said, irritated by the mention of kids.

Peter ignored my protest and continued. "We'll get a boat, a snowmobile, two snowmobiles, we'll get skis." He looked eastwards across to the grassy meadow between the lake and the tree line and added, "And dogs and horses. I'll build a barn and corrals ..."

"You said there'd be no distractions up here. You'd have to cut wood for the winter, lots of wood, and tend to horses after you build a barn and corrals for them. And you don't even know how to build things, or take care of horses, or even dogs for that matter."

"I had a dog when I was a kid. And I'd learn or get help from the locals. Christine, look around. This place is ideal for us. It's everything I've wanted."

Well, it wasn't as if I had anything better to do, so I finally accepted our new home.

In our very first autumn up here, Al wrote to say he couldn't come for their yearly ritual of deer hunting because he'd broken a leg. Perhaps to make up for my childish behaviour, I offered to go with Peter on his hunting trip.

Peter scoffed, saying, "You? You couldn't shoot a deer if it was looking right up your nose."

"Sure I could," I said confidently. "I took a course once."

"You took a course on how to shoot deer?" His cynicism dripped all over my confidence.

"Not on shooting deer," I responded. "At one of my foster homes, the Knights of Columbus sponsored a whole bunch of kids in town to take rifle-shooting. I used to have a certificate."

"I can't see them doing that," he replied.

"Well, maybe it was a Hunters and Anglers group. Mr. Gerard was a member of them, too. Or the Rifle Association."

"Ah-hah, another piece of your mysterious past comes to light. Anyhow, you probably used only a .22, and with deer you need a .308 or 30-30."

"What's the difference? I was a good shot." My confidence was evaporating because I didn't know anything about rifles.

Peter set some cans up for target practice and I started with the .22, pleased when I hit my targets. Then he had me try his 30-30. When the recoil hit me hard in the shoulder, he burst out laughing. I yelled at him for not warning me about it, but the more he tried to say he was sorry, the more he laughed. He helped me make a shoulder pad, and I practised until I no longer anticipated the recoil.

The very first day we went out, I saw a deer and I was the one who shot and killed it, out of pure reflex. Peter was pleased, but I felt such regret, such sorrow, for killing a living thing—for what? To show off? Yet, at the same time, I had a millisecond of vicious delight as I squeezed the trigger. As with all the other secrets of my past, I kept it to myself. After that, I never went hunting again, and I hated that Peter went, and that Al and Iris came up here in the fall for hunting season.

The buck I had killed was young and healthy. Earlier that day it had run and fed, and life for it was good. Then I came along and a beautiful living animal became just a carcass. The worst part was that I preferred eating beef, pork, and chicken to venison.

*

I shrugged myself back to the present, mildly annoyed that, even now, I could still be haunted by the vision of the animal I had killed. As with everything else that was bad in my life, I couldn't undo it. Just as I couldn't undo whatever it was that had happened to Todd and Peter. Kit had once told me that regret was useless—and, right at this moment, I could understand how true those words were.

5

Knowing that regrets were useless had not prevented me from dwelling on them. Besides, how could I not regret losing Todd and Peter? I wouldn't think of them, that's how, and with that thought I got up from sitting on the picnic table and went back to where I had left the chain saw. After I had put everything away, I went into the cabin to make a peanut-butter sandwich and coffee and returned to the lake. Memories came flooding back and, rather than fight them off, I let them take over.

When I first learned I was pregnant with Todd, I couldn't believe it. There had been no indication, not until I vaguely remembered that I must have missed my period once or twice. While this pregnancy excited Peter, it churned up turmoil in me. This was the time to confess to him, but when he came with me to the medical office and the doctor asked, "Is this your first?" I said yes, and proceeded to dig myself in deeper by being a hypocrite and saying I was hoping for a girl.

For the rest of that pregnancy I was miserable, trying to drum up the courage to tell Peter about one of my secrets at least. Peter had taken me to Vancouver in December so that we wouldn't be at the mercy of bad weather or impossible road conditions, and we stayed at his parents' place. That added to my unhappiness because I knew his mother didn't like me, and her advice sounded more like reproach.

On January 5, I was in the hospital by 4:30 p.m. and, at six o'clock that night, I gave birth. The doctor said, "I hope you wanted a boy."

"Oh, yes, I did. I did," I said.

With this baby came my first-ever mother's instincts to protect. My baby would sense the tension I felt at my in-laws, so I told Peter to get us a place of our own. He must have been aware of my feelings, because he agreed without objecting. We stayed in Vancouver until February, and my time with Todd was totally relaxed, totally enjoyable.

Totally unlike that time before.

*

The day after I found Nick in bed with Leona, I went to work and Sarah took one look at me and asked, "My God, what happened to you?"

Not wanting to tell her Nick and I were finished and why, I lied, saying I'd caught a chill from yesterday's rain. Now that wasn't a total lie.

At our morning break I went over to Emily and asked if she was still looking for a ride to Vancouver. Her face lit up and she nodded, but the bell rang and we had to go to our separate work areas. At the lunch break she found me and we talked some more. After lunch, with plans formulated, we both went into the front office and gave our two-weeks' notice. From then on we talked every chance we got, like long lost buddies, making more plans for Vancouver. I had the car and she had the gas money and knew people in Calgary, where we could stay over. When I told her I didn't really have a place to stay right now, she invited me to her place. That night I found she was staying with a group of hippies, and no one had washed the dishes that day or done any other cleaning. A pile of dirty laundry sat in one corner of the living room, which contained only mattresses on the floor. But they did give me a mattress for the night.

The next morning the smell of home-rolled cigarettes hung so heavy in the air that I felt nauseous. That day I told Emily I had to get my things from another place and, although I might stay at her place again, I wasn't sure. When I went to Leona's after work, she was already there doing her second favourite thing, sewing. She was working on a pair of bell-bottom pants for me when I walked in. She looked over at me and said, "Chris, I was so worried about you last night. I'm almost finished with these."

Unable to handle Emily's place, I intended to stay here until I left for the west, but I didn't trust myself not being coaxed into reconciling with Leona. Torn between wanting to forgive and not to forgive, I sighed and, after I made myself a coffee, settled on the couch to stare over at her. Awe had changed to jealousy. "Jealousy is red," I thought, as I watched the selfish, thoughtless, perfect bitch who had ruined my future efficiently run the material through the sewing machine. If I pretended to forgive her, she would be so relieved. Then, within two weeks, I'd disappear and she would always regret what she had done to me. She must have felt my eyes on her because she looked back at me and hope sprang to her beautiful eyes. "Can we talk, Chrissy?" she asked.

Shrugging, I said, "I guess so." This should be interesting, I thought.

Leona came to sit on the couch beside me and she covered my hand with hers. "We really didn't mean for it to happen. You must know that." She looked into my eyes, playing out her role as the older, wiser sister, and I hid my disgust. "I went to FabriChoice to look for some material. Remember we talked about that suit you liked? So I was waiting at the bus stop and it was pouring and Nick passed by. He was with a friend and they gave me a lift back here. Nick figured he'd wait for you, take you out for supper. And then, later, you could drive him home."

My, my, what a coincidence that you both had the day off.

She looked so very sincere as she waited for my response, but I remained silent, thinking about Nick's part in this fiasco. Had I not walked in on them in the act, he probably would have taken me out for supper and I would have unknowingly been trapped in an unbearable situation. The opportunity to be alone with Leona was there and he had grabbed it. That he had intended to so innocently wait for me while in her presence all afternoon was bullshit.

"Well, we had that window open, remember? But the rain started coming in from there and, while I was trying to close it, Nick came to help and ... and the next thing I knew, we were ... well, I'm sorry.

I'm just so sorry." She squeezed my hand tightly now as if she were recounting some horrible experience. "Oh God, Chris, we never meant for anything to happen. Nick loves you. He does. And so do I."

Oh, you're just breaking my heart, I thought sarcastically. Finally, I spoke. "So now I'm supposed to marry him like we planned and pretend that nothing ever happened between the two of you."

"Chris, it will never happen again. I promise. Nick would never do that to you again, either. He was so, so sorry. He loves you."

I freed my hand from her grip and leaned forward to get my cigarette package from my purse. Her touch had become repulsive. She was repulsive, but because she was sitting right beside me I offered her a cigarette and she took that as a sign that everything was back to normal.

"Chris, would you forgive me? Please?" she said, after she lit up.

"Okay," I said, flippantly. No big deal.

"Do you mean it? Really mean that?"

"Yeah, I mean it," I lied. "I will forgive and forget, okay?"

"Okay, and, remember, I promise I will never ever hurt you again. Never." She leaned over and gave me a hug. I thought I was going to puke.

"Oh, before Nick left, he said he was going to come back and make things up to you. Like I said, he really, really loves you. And when he comes, I'll just make myself scarce." Her enthusiasm was funny to watch.

I smiled at the absurdity of it all. Leona thought my smile indicated I was happy that everything had returned to normal. "Leona, you don't have to go off somewhere," I said. "Not if you mean what you said."

"Hey, when I make up with a guy, I like to clinch it in the bedroom. Know what I mean?" She winked at me and smiled. The idea that I would make up with Nick by going to bed with him shocked me. This was a side to my sister that had always disgusted me. At Quillo's Bar, which I had by now lied my way into, I had watched her in action. With a few drinks in her, she had loyalties to no one. If she saw a man she wanted, she took him, and it didn't matter if that man was with someone else. I had watched and pitied the partner, but, because she was my sister, I had said nothing. And now with me, she hadn't even needed a few drinks to take my fiancé from me.

Nick didn't come over that night. He came over two nights later on Friday, carrying a bouquet of flowers. It seemed that he and Leona had talked somehow beforehand, and I wondered if that's all they had done. They didn't look at each other and, as Leona left, she winked at me and I gave her a phoney smile.

Nick couldn't do enough for me, couldn't make enough promises. Once I appeared to be willing to forgive and forget with him, he launched into our plans for the future. To keep him going, I made the appropriate responses, pushing aside tempting thoughts that, maybe, it could work between us. But if we did get married, how many more bouquets of flowers would I get? The one thing that kept me on track was that I had made a commitment to Emily and we had given up our jobs because of that.

With my rose-coloured glasses ripped from me, I saw these two people whom I had idolized in a totally different light. Unfortunately, love doesn't get rinsed away like soap. I still loved Nick and I still loved Leona, but I hated what they had done to me. Forgive and forget? Not on your lives, you beautiful, shallow, selfish jerks.

Mending the hurt by going to bed was on Nick's mind, too, and he had the idea that I wouldn't object to using Leona's bed, of all places. I told him I had my period and that I would see him the next night. As soon as he left, I threw the bouquet in the garbage can and picked up the book I was currently reading. Those dying flowers seemed so pitiful. They weren't what hurt me and, feeling silly for having compassion for a bunch of flowers that were already dying, I retrieved them from the garbage, found an empty coffee container, filled it with water, and plopped the flowers into it. Somewhat satisfied, I returned to the couch and my book. A little later I got up and put the can of flowers on the table, because Leona was the only one who ever used that table. There, now I was fully satisfied.

The next night I went to a movie by myself. When I got back, Leona had gone out and I wondered without much caring whether she was out with Nick.

Playing out my role the following week was hard, and I pretended to be immersed in my book so I could avoid conversation with Leona. Friday came, the last day on the job, and once we got paid Emily and I cashed our cheques and got all our money out of our banks. We planned to meet later that night so she could load the car with her belongings. Early the next morning, we would be heading for Vancouver.

That night, when Nick came over and asked where I had been the previous Saturday night, I told him I had to babysit for a friend from work. The lie came so easily and I said it so casually that even I believed it. I was getting awfully good at lying. Leona came out of her room, dressed to the hilt, and we headed to Quillo's to meet up with her friends. Nick, who didn't like the bar scene, seemed to be enjoying himself very nicely, laughing and joking with all of them. Drinking my pop, I watched that night's scene unfold and, if I hadn't had my own plans, I would have been miserable. Leona came back from the dance floor with a guy who fawned all over her, but it was Nick who ordered another drink for her. In her white tight top and white bell-bottoms, she knew that most male eyes were on her, appreciating her looks and her movements. She was in her glory and, if I thought about her at all in my future, what I would remember was the way she was tonight, a woman without scruples.

One of the ironic things was that, even though I was the one who had always driven people home, everyone had always thanked Leona. Tonight, they would have to thank a cab driver. Without saying good-bye to anyone, I got up and left, because I had my packing to do. Then I would go to Emily's, where I would spend my last night in Winnipeg. As I walked away I was glad, for I had seen Nick's eyes on Leona and they betrayed everything he had said to me.

The next morning Emily had no idea there was a broken heart in the car with us. I hid it well by laughing and joking and singing along with her. She told me she had come to Winnipeg with her boyfriend and a group of their hippie friends and he had taken up with his former girlfriend, leaving her stranded. She could easily have called her mother to get home, but it was a matter of pride. I asked why she didn't just take a bus back, and, as she answered, she was rolling a home-made cigarette. "Because of this. Can't toke up in public. Want a drag?"

She gave me a brief lesson on pot and, when she said it was illegal, I immediately glanced in the rear-view mirror and all around, looking for cops. Lately, I didn't like the taste of booze, and even the smell of cigarettes in the morning gave me a headache. The first night we slept in the car just past Moose Jaw, and the next day we reached Calgary, where she had a group of hippie friends. After a few days there, we drove all the way to Vancouver, a long, tiring drive, during which I was immune to the majesty of the mountains. In Vancouver, rain greeted us late that night as she directed me to another flop-house, where she was warmly greeted by those who weren't spaced out. Someone made us a meal of scrambled eggs and toast.

The next morning, with plans for job-hunting, I went out to look for a store so I could get a paper. First thing I noticed was that my car wasn't where I had parked it, so I went back in and woke Emily to tell her. One of the other kids said the cops probably had it towed away. Another said it was probably stolen. In either case, I most likely wouldn't see it again. I knew I couldn't call the cops about it, because of the smell in this place and the residue of Emily's pot smoking in the car.

Oh well, at least now I wouldn't be able to break down and drive back to Winnipeg. And I didn't have to worry about repair bills either. The car had been on its last tire. We had had to start it up by touching a screwdriver to the solenoid switch, plus the muffler was coming off, the passenger door didn't close right, and we had tied them up with string. We were lucky the old tank even got here, so if it did get stolen, the thief was probably swearing at me by now.

Emily got up late that afternoon. My losing the car did not seem to concern her at all, and my idea of going out to look for a job right away seemed to amuse her.

"You don't just go knocking on doors," she said.

"Why not? I did in Winnipeg and it worked."

"Do you know how big Vancouver is compared to Winnipeg?"

"Then what should I do?"

"We'll go to my mother's place. She has a phone and she's usually home. I'll tell her to take messages for us."

"And she'll do that?"

"Yeah," she said, not explaining further.

Emily's mother had a large place. She was a widow and rented out the two top storeys to roomers. Within two weeks I got a job as a store clerk at Woolworth's. The job was better than the factory job, except that the smell of morning coffee also made me nauseous and its taste was horrible. I started drinking orange juice or milk, figuring that Vancouver coffee or the water was different from Winnipeg's. Worse than that, it seemed I had no control over my bladder and I spent all my breaks in the washroom. Whatever problem I had was made worse by the damp weather of Vancouver.

Emily and I went to her mother's a few times a week to eat. I suspected they must have been rich at one time. Mrs. Brett always had wine with her meals. Besides not liking its taste, I didn't want to be like Mom, so I always refused.

One night Emily said to me, "Mom asked me if you were pregnant. Are you?"

Shocked, I looked at her and said, "I don't think so. But gee, I don't really know."

"Well, do you get your periods?"

Looking at her, I realized I didn't remember having periods recently. "They've always been irregular. I read once that stress could make a woman irregular and I figured that's why."

"Well, Mom said ... God, I hate it when I do that—Mom said this, Mom said that."

"Don't you like your Mom?"

She gestured with her hand that it was so-so, then said, "You should go see a doctor."

"I can't afford that."

"Sure you can. You're covered by Manitoba insurance for three months."

"No, I mean I just started at Woolworth's. I can't take time off."

Emily shrugged, and I was left to think about the repercussions if I was pregnant. Nick's last present to me. Just great.

When I finally got around to seeing a doctor, he confirmed that I was pregnant. He made me feel embarrassed that I hadn't come sooner, telling me I was already into my fourth month. I hadn't put on any weight and I was still wearing my usual clothing, so how was I supposed to know? Since I was here, I told him about my bladder problem. He explained that the foetus was pushing down on my bladder and that, as time passed, it would probably shift and my problem would cease.

For the next four months I worked right up until my supervisor told me I had to leave, because of my pregnancy. By then, a few of my co-workers looked down their noses at me because I was going to be an unwed mother, and I got that old-time feeling I was being booted out once again. For some unknown reason, I decided I had to return to Winnipeg to give birth.

January in Winnipeg was unbearably cold. As soon as I got off the bus, I called Mr. Carruthers at Children's Aid and told him I was pregnant and had nowhere to go. When he told me he was going to come and meet me, I almost wept out of gratitude. We met in the restaurant at the bus depot and, over coffee, I learned some startling information. But first thing, I asked him not to tell Leona about my pregnancy.

At the mention of her name, he asked, "Oh, she doesn't know?"

"No, and I don't want to see her again." The way I said it implied that I didn't even want to mention her name.

He wisely didn't ask more about her and, after inquiring what I had been doing, he said, "Remember your social worker before me, Pauline Branzil?"

Nodding, I said, "Yeah, she disappeared, right? Did she come back?"

"No. Apparently, she went off with the doctor and his girls. They all went south to the Caribbean and their boat got wrecked in a storm. The authorities down there believe they all drowned. So you can put him out of your mind. And the experience you had there."

Showing no expression, I was shocked, delighted, and sad, all at the same time. Dr. Coran was gone and that was good. It was just too bad he had taken his daughters down with him.

"Well, let's get going and get you settled." He had already arranged for me to go into a home for unwed mothers, run by the Oblate Sisters.

For the following weeks I was known as Patty, since my last name started with a *P* and all the girls assumed a false first name when they came here. One Wednesday I felt no different from previous days, but, by the end of that day, I went into labour and, less than three hours later, I gave birth to a beautiful little girl.

And then I gave that beautiful little girl up for adoption.

When I was released from the hospital, Mr. Carruthers took me to a rooming house where I would share a room. Children's Aid had paid a month's room and board for me. Once when my roommate was gone and I was alone, I sat on the edge of my bed, feeling completely despondent. At the home for unwed mothers the girls had talked about getting the baby blues after giving birth, but this was more. The act of giving my baby up for adoption was an act of betrayal to her. Yet what could I offer her? I was a loser going nowhere. And I would only drag her down with me, betray her over and over again in the future. No, I'd had no choice. I was a loser, a total loser.

An idea came to me sometime during that day, and it grew over the next few days. I made an appointment to see a doctor and I told him I had trouble sleeping and it was seriously affecting my job. He gave me a prescription for Valium and a stern warning that I was to follow the directions. One night at the large kitchen table, I kind of said goodbye to the other roomers. They had all been so nice to me, and sometimes a few of them had come to my room and tried to make me laugh and talk.

My roommate, Wendy, had a record player and, among her 45s, was a favourite from when I was younger. I had made her play "Moody River" over and over again. Now, alone in the room, I played it while I swallowed pill after pill, and then I cut off all my waist-length hair. My hair had attracted Nick's attention and, if I hadn't met Nick, I wouldn't be where I was now. When I was all done, the song had ended and I replayed it one more time, hoping Wendy wouldn't be mad that I didn't turn her record player off. I lay down on the bed, listening one last time to the song—a perfect ending for an imperfect life.

When I woke up, I was in a hospital bed. My throat was dry and parched and I ached all over. There was movement all around me and I heard an impatient voice saying my name. "Christine Pelletier ..." I hated my name. It was a bad-luck name. I didn't care about anything, and didn't care to know about anything.

I think I was charged and maybe I was even arrested, because after I was out of the hospital I was in a courtroom. One of the repercussions of not having done the job right was that I had to see a psychiatrist twice a week. Since I couldn't have another go at doing myself in if I was sitting in jail, I agreed to the terms.

At my first few appointments, I refused to talk except to tell the psychiatrist that I was in his office only because I had to show up or go to jail. Gradually, the man tricked me into saying more than I intended. He already knew of my recent background and, when he asked how I felt about giving up my baby, I answered with my own question, "How would you feel?"

"So you suffered a great loss and you're mourning for her."

"Whatever," I said, and added, "but I shouldn't be mourning because this kind of stuff runs in my family. It should be natural for me."

"Natural to give up a child?"

"Yeah, like mother, like daughter. Do you know I don't even know who my father is?"

"Does that bother you a great deal?"

"No, of course not." Then I smiled and sat back.

"What is it that you find humorous?" he asked.

I looked at him and dropped the smile. "Just that if I became a hooker, I couldn't do older Indian guys because one of them might be my father. Or, for that matter, a brother. With my mother, anything's possible." I added that one to show what a contemptuous woman my mother had been—is, and I smiled again.

He didn't return the smile. "Are you afraid that will happen to your daughter?"

"My daughter isn't going to become a hooker. She's ... she's going to have good parents. And she's going to come out clean and healthy."

"And you didn't?"

"I'm shit."

"You don't really believe that, do you?"

"What does it matter? I'm here because the court says I have to be here." Shut the fuck up, I wanted to tell him.

"I understand that. But as long as you're here, why not talk to me?"

Sitting back, I said nothing. I looked around and, spotting an ashtray on his desk, I asked, "Got a cigarette?"

"I don't smoke."

"Of course not. You wouldn't have any bad habits, would you? So what would you know about shit? Nothing." I spit the words out with all the contempt I could muster.

"So why don't you tell me about that?"

"Because I'm not a teacher. And you, you can't even say the word 'shit,' can you?" The sudden taste of soap filled my mouth. Nonetheless, I enjoyed the rush of power I thought I had over this man.

The sparring continued for another three weeks before I gave it up and spilled my guts about the feelings I'd had over Nick and Leona, and the daughter I gave away. But that lasted for only an hour, and then it was time to pull myself together and walk out of his office to make an appointment for the next time. One time he gave me a book by

Dale Carnegie to read. I asked him if he gave books to all his clients and he said no, only to the ones who might benefit from them. That made me feel a little better about myself. But then, whenever I talked about trying to get my daughter back, he gave me words to live by: "Let her be, Christine. Let her be." And that told me he didn't think I was good mothering material.

I never did tell him my most private secret, the secret of the grampa-man. As low as I was, I didn't want anyone to know it had started when I was three.

During the daytime, I often went to the library downtown. One day I was walking home towards Spence Street, near Broadway, when I saw them, Leona and Nick, walking hand in hand. At first I didn't want to believe it was them coming towards me. I pulled my collar up and lowered my face, glad now that it was a cool day. I wondered if Leona would recognize my spring jacket.

I didn't have to worry, though. They had eyes only for each other as they passed right by me and I was briefly tempted to follow them, eavesdrop on their conversation, tap them on their shoulders and say hello. Ruin their intimate moment. Enjoy their shock. But I merely watched them walk by, then continued on my way, suddenly chilled not from the outside but from deep inside me. I went into the building I saw them come out of and guessed right off they had been here to get a marriage licence.

That night I coaxed the other boarders to lend me some money, telling them I probably wouldn't pay it back. With what they gave me added to the allowance from Children's Aid, I had enough to buy a one-way ticket back to Vancouver. The next day as the bus rolled out of town, I vowed I would never, ever return to Winnipeg. By the time the bus reached Portage la Prairie, I decided my vow wasn't good enough and I revised it. What I had really meant to say was that I would never ever see my sister again. I had no sister. I had no mother. I had no daughter. My life in Winnipeg ended in May, 1970.

*

I had given away one child and God had given me another one. And because I didn't deserve anything good, he had taken that child away, along with a husband who might have once loved me.

While I had considered Peter a good father, I had doubts about my own mothering instincts. In the beginning I held Todd to feed him, bathe him, and change him, but I watched Peter holding him just to enjoy the contact, and he talked to Todd the way I talked to Lady. I had a more natural rapport with Lady, and, while I often petted and stroked the dog, touching humans was something foreign to me. Thinking about that now, I realized that when I grew up, only Leona had touched me, and then Nick, and, at times, even his touch annoyed me. Gradually I had learned to demonstrate affection towards Todd from watching Peter and by responding to Todd's own needs.

Often I had wondered if I loved Todd, truly loved him, and just this past winter the answer had come in a dream. Todd and I were down by the lake and the ice was just beginning to break up. We were building a fort with wet snow. My attention was focused on building the fort and I was perfecting a comfortable seat for Todd. A small plank of wood on the seat would prevent his bottom from getting wet. As I looked around for one, I saw Todd way out on the lake, balancing himself on a rocking slab of ice. One minute he had been right beside me, and the next he was out there, helpless. I screamed at him to stay still and began running towards him, but I was still too far away when the slab of ice tilted, one edge rising above the main body of ice. Todd slid right down into the icy waters. The slab of ice levelled itself, closing the gap over my son.

I had woken then, crying and paralyzed from the horror of seeing my son swallowed by Shadow Lake. Unable to move, I wanted to go back into the dream so I could save him and, at the same time, I wanted to go to his room to reassure myself that he was all right.

Watching him sleep that night, I knew in my heart that I did love him, very much, just like a real mother.

That dream hadn't been an answer, after all. It had been a premonition. Shadow Lake had not swallowed Todd, but the Peace River had. Whatever made me think I should have had a good life?

The memories were gone for now, replaced with—nothingness. Looking out across the lake, I saw nothing, felt nothing. I don't know how much time passed, but I suddenly got this feeling that I was being watched. Turning, I looked all around, saw nothing, and looked around again—and that's when I caught the flicker of movement by the edge of the tree line to the east of the cabin. A tawny, grey wolf was standing there, watching me, its ears bent forward, its tail raised high. My first thought was that this was the wolf who had attacked Lady.

Paradoxically, seeing a wolf this close up was thrilling and I forgave it for what it might have done to Lady. We stared at each other and I wanted so much to know what it was thinking. The wolf tilted its head, gave the slightest wag of its tail, and turned to disappear into the underbrush.

6

The next morning I went out onto the porch to look at the piles of wood I'd made the previous day. I had no intention of trying the chain saw again, but I could use the shears and the axe to cut off smaller branches into kindling wood and I could begin to sort the rest into what needed cutting and what needed splitting. It was something to do, and I desperately needed something to do while I waited for more news from the police.

Later that afternoon, having abandoned the kindling to gather more wood, I unloaded this last load from the trailer and put everything away. The black flies had buzzed incessantly around my head all morning, annoying me but not biting. I thought about sorting this pile, too, but I'd had enough. It would still be there the next day and, maybe, if I was up to it, another pile would take its place. If I wasn't here to use it up, Kit could come and get it in his pickup.

Barking a greeting to me and with her tail whipping back and forth, Lady, obviously recuperated, dashed up to me, just as I was going down to the lake, and poked her nose into my hand. Amber and Kit followed in on horseback. I was expecting them only on Saturday, so I was surprised to see them now. Kit and I went into the house for some tea while Amber remained with the horses down at the lake, where she let them drink. Lady chose to stay with her. "Her and that dog of yours are like family now," Kit observed. "She even sleeps on her bed."

Peter had never allowed Lady to sleep on our beds. If I'd had my way I would have let her, especially after a bath. Smiling, I said, "I kind of told Mona it might be a good idea for Lady to stay at your place. At least, as long as Amber is here."

"It would be a good thing for Amber. Yes. Thank you."

After his tea, Kit took the canoe out to do some fishing while Amber and I went for a horseback ride. It felt great, as long as I focused on the scenery, as long as I concentrated on moving as one with the horse, as long as I did not think about Todd and Peter.

"I guess Lady's going to stay with you now, huh?" Amber said as we rode side by side.

"Kit and Mona said Lady could stay with you while you're here."

"Really? You don't mind?" Amber asked, excitement in her voice.

"No. She was attacked by something out here, maybe a wolf, and I saw one yesterday. I think she'd have more protection at your place. Kit told me once that mule of his, I-ee-mon, keeps all the predators away, even grizzlies."

"Yeah, he's crazy, that mule. Only Kit can handle him. But when Kit puts his bridle on him, he turns completely docile. Anyhow you don't have to worry about Lady. We're like glue, eh."

Later, as they were getting ready to leave, Amber asked Kit, "Did you give her that telephone message?"

Kit slapped at his shirt pocket to dig out a piece of paper. "I forgot. This was why we came here in the first place. Mona got this call earlier today. This social worker, she wants you to call her as soon as you can. That's her number, there."

I looked at the scrawled words and noted that the message was from a Betty Chartrand from Children's Aid and that the phone number had a Manitoba area code. I couldn't imagine why Children's Aid would be calling me. Before riding off, Kit said he'd help me cut the wood on Saturday, and I thanked him and told him I'd come the next day to call the woman.

They left, taking all the light-heartedness of their visit with them, and I was left feeling more lonely than I had been before they came.

By now I knew I didn't ever want to go back to Vancouver or Winnipeg, and I certainly didn't want to stay up here all by myself. I didn't want to write children's books anymore, either. What I wanted, all I wanted, was for this loneliness to stop. I went inside, into my room, took the .22 down from the wall and studied it. Could it do the job? But what if Todd's alive? Putting the rifle back on the wall, I knew I'd have to wait. If no definitive news came, then I'd just have to wait indefinitely for the rest of my life.

The next day, as I was driving to Kit's, I was suddenly curious how the woman got Kit's phone number. Very few people had it—Peter's parents, Leona, our publishers and agent—but they all knew it was only for emergency use. At Mona's I had tea with them, and then I made my phone call. The receptionist at Children's Aid put me through to Betty Chartrand.

"Hello, Betty Chartrand? This is Christine Webster from Dodging, BC. You left a message for me?"

"Oh yes, just a minute please, I've got to get the file."

While I waited, my curiosity grew. The file? This didn't sound like an invitation to do a workshop or a reading. As far as I knew, Children's Aid had never been into such things for foster kids—or for foster parents, for that matter.

She came on the phone again and said, "Hi. I'm the case worker for Michael, your nephew."

"Case worker for Michael," I repeated, slowly. My first thought was that Leona had abandoned Michael. My second thought was such a thing was not possible.

"Right now he's in foster care here. He asked me if he could live with you and your husband," she said.

"Why is he in foster care? What happened to his mother?"

"You don't know?"

A flash of anger: If I knew I wouldn't ask, would I? "We've been out of touch. We don't have a phone. What happened? Is she okay?"

"Well ..." she said, now hesitant to tell me.

"She is okay, isn't she?" I pressed, containing a sudden, strange, unreasonable rage.

"She's at Portage," she finally said.

"Portage, that's a jail for women, isn't it?"

"Yes, the Portage Correctional Institute. In March she was sentenced to eighteen months for assault."

Trying hard to digest this piece of news, I was speechless. Peter and Leona were not together, never had been. Peter and Todd were dead. Her words made me want to slam down the phone and flee. Oh God, if only they had been with her, anything, but in the Peace River.

"Hello?" Her voice brought me back to the immediate problem.

"I'm sorry, but this is really hard ... to believe," I said. She would have no idea what it was that was so hard to believe. No idea at all.

"Getting back to Michael, he asked if he could live with you. And since you're his aunt, we felt that might be a good idea. I could begin the paperwork and he could go there at the end of June. He'll be finished the school year by then. You don't have to give me an answer right now, but since you are out of province, the paperwork will take some time."

I closed my eyes and thought how ironic life was. She was asking me to take care of Nick's son, of all people, while Nick's daughter was out there somewhere, winging it alone. She was asking me to take care of his son while my own was dead. No. No, I didn't think so.

"So you'll do that? You'll get back to me?" Betty asked.

Unable to make myself say that I didn't want Nick and Leona's son anywhere near me, I simply lied, "Yes. I'll get back to you. Bye."

I returned to the cabin, having made an awkward apology to Mona for leaving so abruptly. As soon as I was inside, I went into Todd's room and, hugging his teddy bear to me, I cried. When I was all cried out, I went into my bedroom, still hugging the teddy bear to me, and as I was sitting on the edge of my bed, my eyes rested on the rifles nestled in their places on the wall. I set the stuffed toy aside and brought down the .22, cradling it in my arms.

I smiled as I thought of how life was one big joke: Leona, in jail for assault, her son asking to live with his aunt, his father's reject. But what had Michael ever done to me? He couldn't help who his parents were. Besides, he only wanted to come here because of Peter. And Peter was gone. And Peter was gone and I'd had all those horrible thoughts about him. Because I was evil, I had thought he was evil, too.

I never knew I was evil, not until I was eleven, I think. I knew I was bad, but when I was eleven I looked up the word *evil* and what stayed with me was what I had thought all along—that I was morally bad—and because of that, bad things would happen to me. The worst had happened when I was three, but ever since, what started out good came to a bad ending.

*

I was four year olds now and Mrs. Grell, the lady that made me leave my Mommy and Leona, she drived the car for a long time and then there was no more houses. Then there was some houses and a big pointed building and then the car turned and it was on a short street beside a house. Mrs. Grell got out and told me to come with her, so I did. I don't know where we are but I know we are not at Mommy's house and this is not the place where I was before to see Mommy and Leona. Some other lady came to the door and she said to me that Leona was going to be happy to see me. I don't know why she say that. I don't see Leona nowhere.

They take me to the kitchen and leave me sit at a table with some milk and cookies. I don't like cookies no more, so I just sit there all by myself. The ladies came back and sitted down with me and talked to each other. A door slam and a tall girl came into the kitchen. She looked at me and got herself some milk and cookies. The lady and the girl talked to each other and she looked at me again. Then she leaved. I hear the door slam again and then there is Leona. I am so excited to see her. We give a hug to each other. Leona got some milk and cook-ies for herself and sit down beside me.

Then Mrs. Grell said it was time to go. I don't want to go. I get up and leave the kitchen and walk down a hallway. I saw a door that was a little bit open, so I looked in. Some clothes was hanging up and some shoes and boots were on the floor. I climbed in and pulled the door shut. It was dark inside. I know I am bad to do this but I don't want to leave Leona. I don't want to go back to the Manley's. I hear the ladies calling me, calling me. I am scared. Obey? Not obey? I am scared to not obey. If they find me, they will give me heck. But if they can't find me, Mrs. Grell will leave all by herself. I stay very still.

They was calling me and Leona opened the door. She saw me right away. I looked up at her. She moved a coat so it covered me more. Then she left. I hear them ask if she knows where I am. She says no. She doesn't want me to go away.

I wait, wait. Then Leona came back and opened the door and she say, "It's okay. You can come out."

I came out and Mrs. Grell said to me, "I just wanted to say goodbye to you, Christine. You're going to stay here with Leona from now on."

The lady of this house kneeled down and make some nice talk to me, and then she gave a hug to me. She is not mad at me and I am so happy. The box with my teddy bear is near the front door and, when Mrs. Grell is gone, the lady picks it up and takes it up the stairs. Me and Leona follow her. The lady tells me that the bed in a small room is for me. She shows where me and Leona can put my clothes and then she went down the stairs.

Leona showed me her room and there are two beds in there, one for Leona and one for Grace—that is how the tall girl is called. I ask Leona what is the lady's name. I heard Leona call her Mommy, but she is not our Mommy. I want to ask Leona why she call her, that but I don't. She said the lady's name is called Mrs. Charette. I learn how to say that, Mrs. Charette. I like Mrs. Charette, but I don't want to call her Mommy. When I want to ask her something, I tell it to Leona and Leona asks for me. Only Leona knows what I say.

Leona has to go to school all the days. I told her I went to school and I know how to go to school, so could I go with her. She said no. It wasn't the same kind of school. When Leona is at school, I have to play in my room. Sometimes I go to Leona's room and play with her toys. When I am bad, I play with Grace's things. Then Grace gets mad at me and I get heck.

Every night I have to go to bed first 'cause I am just little. I don't go to sleep. I wait. When there is no more noise, I get up and look out in the hallway. It is dark there. There is the bogeymans in the dark. I have to cross the hallway to get to Leona's room, so I run as fast as I can. Then I get in bed with Leona. Sometimes Leona gets mad at me, so I lie on the top of the covers at the foot of her bed and I try not to move. Leona is not scared of the dark. In the night time she takes me down the stairs for me to go to the toilet. Every morning time I wake up in my own bed.

When the snow comes, me and Leona went to see Mommy "downtown." After Mommy gives a hug to us, I have to sit on the floor with the toys, and Leona and Mommy talk and laugh. I am too little to talk and laugh with them. Me and Leona don't make temper tantrums when we leave Mommy all alone.

Mr. Charette cuts my hair short and he shave it up the back. Leona don't have to get her hair cut 'cause it is long and curly and soft. I wish my hair was like Leona's. I like long hair. One day when I get bigger, I will have long hair too.

Leona don't have to go to school no more. It is summer holidays time. Me and her play all the days. We have fun playing with marbles and with cutouts. She tells me how to count more, and how to say the A, B, Cs. She learns me some more songs, like "Mary Had a Little Lamb," and I sing the songs that I know.

Then Leona has to go to school again and she is in Grade 2. Grace is in Grade 4. Every day I ask to go to school with her and when will she have summer holidays again. Leona told me not for a long time. Wintertime came again and we went "tobogging," far away across the river. It is so much fun. Except for when my ears get too cold. That hurts a lot.

When the snow is gone, Mrs. Charette told me I could go to school with Leona for a day. I am so excited. One day Mrs. Charette dressed me up in my good clothes. After breakfast time, Leona took my hand and we walked to the school. When the other childrens see me, they start to sing a song. "Look at the little Indian. Look at the little Indian." At first I think they be nice. Leona tells them to be quiet and she is mad. That's how I know they are mean to me. I ask Leona what is a little Indian. She told me they were just being nasty. I am scared of them.

Leona took me inside and there was a nun-lady. She is very nice and she showed Leona where I could sit. There are lots of chairs in that room and little tables on the chairs. I have to sit at the back. Leona tells me to just sit still and be quiet. When some other girls come in the room, they look at me. Leona has to sit way over by the windows. She looks back at me and smiles. I smile back and I am not so scared.

A bell rings and it is time for recess. Leona comes and gets me and we go outside. The girls right away call me some more names. I don't know what they mean. I ask Leona, but she won't say, just that the girls are mean. She tells them again to be quiet.

After recess time we go back inside. After a while I have to go to the toilet. I am too scared to ask the nun-lady to go to the toilet. I don't want the other girls to look at me. And I'm supposed to just sit still and be quiet. Leona told me so. I sit there and try to be still. Then I pee right in the chair. The pee falls on the floor—drip, drip, drip— and the girl beside me sees that and she yells to the rest of the peoples that I peed myself. Everyone laughs and makes fun of me and Leona got up and came to take me to the toilet. She tried to clean me, and the bell rings and that means it is lunchtime.

We walked home and some girls follow us and they are shouting that I am a dirty little Indian. They are shouting that I peed in my pants. I got tears in my eyes and I hold tight to Leona's hand. Leona stops and tells them all to be quiet and she even pushes one. When I get home, Mrs. Charette tells me I should have asked to go to the toilet. I don't go back to school after lunch. I never want to go back to school again.

Leona got summer holidays and I got a birthday again. This time I had seven candles on my cake. Leona told me one was for good luck and the others were for how old I am now. I liked summer more than winter. Leona and me could play all the days again. Lots of other children came and we played tag and hide-and-seek and when the older children came, we played dodge ball, and if it rained we played marbles and cut-outs. None of these kids make fun of me, so I liked all of them.

I helped Leona and Grace with their chores so they could hurry up and play with me. Leona learned me how to say prayers for real, like "Our Father Who Art in Heaven," and "Hail Mary" who was full of Grace, and "Glory Be to the Father, to the Son and to the Holy Ghost." She told me that I would have to know all these prayers when I went to school. When I said them in front of Mr. and Mrs. Charette and Grace, they all clapped.

In August time Mrs. Charette told me that I was going to start school in September and that I would be in Grade 1. I started crying right away and I told her I didn't want to go back to school. She said everyone had to go to school. That's how we learned things. I told her Leona could learn me what she learned. Mrs. Charette smiled and said everything would be okay.

One day not long after, Grace told me that Marcel, one of the altar boys, had died. He was on a tractor in a field and it tipped over and it crushed him to death. That must be awful to be crushed to death. I guess I'd rather go to school than to be crushed to death.

Me, Leona, and Grace had to go to Mrs. LaVendry, something like that, to have our tunics made. I didn't like that at all. I had to stand for long times without moving while the old lady put pins in the tunic. She would get mad if I moved and she made my tunic too long and it hung way down. Leona and Grace got tunics the same as all the other girls at school.

School time came and Leona walked me to school. The same kids that made fun of me before started to make fun of me again as soon as they saw me. This time they also made fun of the way I was dressed. My teacher was named Sister Gauthier. She was very nice. Leona told me not to pay attention to what the other girls said, only to the teacher, so that's what I tried to do. Two girls call me a papoose or a squaw or a Indian when I am all alone, so I try not to be alone. At recess time I made sure to go to the toilet, so I wouldn't pee in my pants again.

A few days after I started going to school, Mrs. Charette told us that Father Forest died. He was our parish priest and everyone liked him and they were sad. Grace took us to the church on Saturday morning to have a look at him. That's where he was laying in a coffin. No one else was in the church. We had to kneel down and say some prayers for him. I wanted to see Father Forest in his coffin. I never saw a man died before. I want to see what that looks like. So Grace takes us to stand by the coffin. I can't see in. I am too little. I ask Leona to lift me up. She helps me and then Grace helps me too. I can see the man now. His face and hands look kind of grey. And someone put some lipstick on him. I put my hand on his hand. I want to see what he feels like. Grace drops me and Leona and me fall down. Grace gets us out of the church right away and she is so mad at me, but I am pleased to touch a dead man.

On Sunday night we have to all get dressed up again and go back to another church. Grace said it was the Basilica in St. Boniface. She said that it is the home of all the priests and the nuns. They are going to have a big Mass for Father Forest. When we get there, Mr. and Mrs. Charette have to talk to some priests or something. Me, Leona, and Grace have to wait in a little room. There is a TV in there. We don't have a TV at home. A man on the TV is singing and he is wiggling his hips and all the ladies is screaming. I think they want to kiss the man wiggling his hips. Grace said his name is Elvis Pesley. I look at the door. The priests and nuns don't know what's on their TV. I think they would get mad if they knew we were watching Elvis Pesley wiggling his hips like that. That's what I think.

After a while we have to go into a big giant church. All the priests and all the nuns of the whole world are in there. I got some new shoes on. They are so pretty and shiny and they hurt. We have to stand up and kneel down and sit down. I am so, so tired, I just want to lie down on the bench and go to sleep, but I know I am not supposed to. My feet hurt so much from my brand new shoes. I think of Elvis Pesley. He was fun to watch. Mass is not fun.

At school we have to take Catechism. I like that because Sister Gauthier said we have to be nice to each other. The Catechism says so. If anyone calls me names, they are being bad. Sister Gauthier told us that in God's eyes, everyone is equal. We have to learn some more prayers because, in the springtime, we are going to have the Sacrament of Confirmation, the Sacrament of Communion, and the Sacrament of Penance. Sister Gauthier told us that after we were born, we got the Sacrament of Baptism. I don't remember that part. I ask Leona about it later and she said Mommy got us baptized so we could go to Heaven. She said only Roman Catholics go to Heaven. I wonder why that is, if everyone is equal.

In the springtime, we had to go to the church for our Catechism classes. The priest came and talked to us. The boys from the boys' school were there too. One time during class there was some noise at the back of the church. We all turned to look. A lady with three children had come in, but a nun was holding her arms out because she doesn't want to let them in. The priest asked what she wanted. She asked if her children could take the Catechism classes. I looked back at the priest and it looked as if he didn't like the lady and her children. I looked back at the lady with the children. They are dressed in old torn clothing. They must be very poor. I looked back at the priest and some of the nuns and I could tell they don't like this lady with her children. I think it must be because they are too poor. The priest told her it was too late for them and they were sent away. I felt sorry for the lady because she seemed so sad.

The priest told us that *Monseigneur* Something—I don't understand how his name is said and I am too shy to ask—is going to come and say the Mass for us to get confirmed. He said we are supposed to kneel to *Monseigneur* and kiss his ring. I think that I won't do that because everyone is supposed to be equal.

Before Confirmation day, Mrs. Charette got a box out from the attic and opened it up. Leona and me were watching her. She took out a beautiful white dress, a crinoline to make it flare out, and a see-through veil. I got some new socks and some new shoes too. On some Saturday afternoons, me, Leona, and Grace had to go to church because people were getting married and we had to go to the Mass part. This dress and veil was almost like what a bride wore, except the dress was short.

On Sunday all the boys and girls met in front of the church, and some of the girls in white dresses are acting smart, and the boys got on little man suits. Then it was time to get in line and walk one by one into the church. When I got to the top of the stairs I saw *Monseigneur* just inside the entrance. He has the tallest hat on. The boys and girls in front, they stopped and kneeled and kissed his ring. When my turn came, I kneeled down, too, and kissed his ring. I was too scared not to.

In church I am thinking that people are not really equal to each other. *Monseigneur* was more important than all the priests. The priests were more important than Sister Superior. She is more important than the rest of the nuns. The nuns are more important than Mr. and Mrs. Charette. They are more important than Grace. Grace more important than Leona. And everybody is more important than me. I'm not important at all. But yet, if Sister Gauthier told us that every-body was equal in God's eyes, then that must be true. Because Sister Gauthier would never lie to us.

Christmas time is always so much fun. Except that every Christmas times, we have to wake up during the night and go out in the cold to go to Mass. After Mass we sit in the living room and Mr. Charette hands out presents to everyone else. Then we go in the kitchen and we eat some fancy foods and I like the cinnamon bread that's made like a braid in a circle the best. Afterwards, we go back to bed. When morning comes, we play with our new toys until it's time to go to Mass again, and then we have a big turkey dinner.

A few days after that we go to another town where Mrs. Charette has her parents and there are lots of people and lots of children. That is their family reunion. I am seven years old now and Leona is going to be ten in January. All of us children have to play in the living room next to the dining room, where all the grownups are sitting at a big long table. Mrs. Charette came and got me and took me to meet a young priest. He is sitting at the head of the table because he is the guest of honour. He picks me up and sits me on his lap. I feel so special to be getting this attention. I look at the table with the fancy glasses and all the plates matching and the flowers in a vase. They are all set on a big white tablecloth.

Then, under the tablecloth, the hand of the priest moves to between my legs. And while he is doing this, he's talking to other people. I am confused because they said he was a priest, I'm sure they said he was a priest. And a priest is not supposed to do something like this. I look at Mrs. Charette, but she is at the other end talking to a lady beside her. I don't know what to do. So I slide down from the priest's lap and return to the children in the next room. I try to stay beside Leona for the rest of the time.

On our way home, I am thinking, thinking about what the priest did. Mrs. Charette tells me I was very rude to Father Bolanger. I know I can't tell her what he did. I know she would not believe me. She is too much religious.

At the end of January I woke up one morning not feeling well. At school my teacher sent for Leona to take me home. Mrs. Charette put me to bed, and by then I was hot and cold at the same time. That night when Mr. Charette got home he drove me to the hospital and I had to stay there. On Sunday afternoon Mr. and Mrs. Charette came to visit me and they brought me some candy. Leona and Grace were not allowed to visit me. After they left, the boy in the bed next to mine started crying. He was a fat little boy and no one had come to see him. I think that was why he was crying. I felt sorry for him, so I gave him my candy.

Not long after that the nurses and doctors rushed in and took him out of our room. A nurse came the next day and asked if I had given him anything to eat. I told her I gave him my candy. She gave me heck. I didn't understand why, 'cause I was only trying to be nice. I never saw that little boy again, so I thought he must have died. And I am the one who made him die.

One night back at home I was thinking about him and I was sorry and began to cry. Leona came in my room and asked me what was wrong, so I told her. I told her it was my fault. Leona tilted her head and a slight grin came to her face and she said that boy probably had dye-a-beet-us and was not supposed to eat sweets. She said the doctors probably just kept him far away from me in another room, but still, I believed I made him die.

That summer time a little boy who Mrs. Charette had babysat was killed from being hit by a car. Grace said we could die any minute, just like that. I decided I was never going to die. Other people could die, but not me. I was going to live forever. I was too scared to ever die.

That same summer we went to a camp at *Plage Albert* for two weeks. I loved it there. Our days started with Mass in a wooden chapel. Leona and I were picked to be in the choir. Then we had breakfast in a long log building. Everything smelled so good and fresh, and I liked the smell of the woods. After breakfast we had to clean our cabins. There were six of us to a cabin, and what I liked best at night was listening to the waves and the winds rustling the leaves on the trees. It was almost like sleeping right outside. Anyways, after morning clean up was crafts, and then swimming.

The counsellors gave us swimming lessons, and we were supposed to open our eyes under water. I thought that water hitting our eyeballs wasn't a good thing, so I had trouble with that. We had to learn how to tread water. I didn't understand how a body could stay on top of the water, so I always sank to the bottom. Leona learned how to swim almost right away.

After lunch we had a rest period and then we played games. Then it was swimming time again. Afterwards, we gathered in front of the big log building where they had a canteen. They played music so it came out loud on a amplifier outside, and some of the kids danced. After supper when it got dark, we did different things. If it rained, we played bingo. I got a bingo once, but I was too shy to yell it.

Sometimes they had a big bonfire, and we sat all around in a circle and the counsellors told ghost stories. Sometimes each cabin had to make up a scary story or a funny story, and one person from a cabin would tell it to the rest. Leona was our storyteller and she was so good at it. Leona was not shy like me.

After summer holidays, Leona had to go to the new school that was built further away from where we lived. Besides the school, they were doing a lot of new things in St. Albert. They dug up holes on the sides of the streets and put pipes in there. They cut down lots of trees and bush and built new houses. They put in cement sidewalks to replace the wooden ones. Even the Charettes had changes made in their house. We got a toilet and running water. A man with a big truck used to come and fill the cistern in the basement with water. Now we didn't have to use that, or a pail or the outhouse. They had a bathroom just like at the Manley's. And Mr. Charette got a new furnace, and he didn't have to get coal delivered any more. He still kept the old wood stove in the basement so some of the garbage could be burned. I liked the new toilet and the running water, but I didn't like them cutting down all the trees and the bushes.

I was always home first because I still went to school in the convent. At school there was a collie who hung around the kids at recess time. I made friends with him and he followed me home. After that he came around a lot. Rover was an old fat collie with matted hair and some bald spots on his head. Leona would never touch him because she said he had ringworm. I had been touching him a lot and nothing bad happened to me, so I wasn't scared at all to touch him. I started sneaking food out for him. I never asked permission to feed him because, if Mrs. Charette said no, I would have to obey her. Or disobey.

One day a big German Shepherd came along. I knew dogs because the Charettes had an encyclopaedia and it had all the dogs and horses of the world in it. I called to the German Shepherd and he came straight to me, jumping over a garden fence instead of going around it. So I called him Jumper. Jumper and Rover always came around at different times, but one day they both came at the same time. Jumper started a fight with Rover right away. I ran in to pull them apart because Jumper was hurting Rover. Rover finally got loose and, with his tail between his legs, and squealing, he ran off into the woods that were still there. I turned on Jumper and yelled that he was bad.

Rover didn't come around very much after that. That was too bad 'cause I really liked him better than Jumper. Rover listened when I talked to him. Jumper never seemed interested in what I had to say. He always seemed to have something on his mind.

We also had stray cats that hung around our house. When they had kittens, everyone was excited. Mrs. Charette let us take the cats inside when they had kittens. At night I used to sneak a cat upstairs to my bedroom. In the springtime Jumper killed three of the kittens that were still left. Mrs. Charette and I found them and right away I cried and cried. I had seen Jumper earlier and I was sure he was the one who had killed the kittens. When I saw him again, I told him he was bad and I didn't want to see him again. After that, I never did see him again.

I used to sneak food out to the animals by taking it from my plate and putting it in my apron pocket. Sometimes if the animals were not around, I'd forget about the food and Mrs. Charette would find it on Monday mornings. She'd get up very early while everyone was still in bed and go down to the basement to start on the laundry, soaking some clothes in bleach and washing others in the wringer washing machine. Then she'd get to my aprons, and if I left food in the pockets, she would yell, "Christine Pelletier, get down here right now!"

Her voice from all the way down in the basement would break into my sleep and, right away, I'd get scared and head for the basement. When I got down there, she would put out her hand and ask, "What's this?"

Usually it was baloney. I hated baloney, unless it was fried. Whenever we had straight baloney, I sneaked it into my apron pocket. Anyways, I'd gape at the baloney as if I never saw it before in my life and I'd look up at her face and wonder what kind of answer I could give to appease her. No answer ever came and we'd end up just standing there, staring at each other. I stared for such a long time that it seemed to me she was shrinking. When that happened I'd have to fight back a grin. I imagined that if she kept shrinking, she'd disappear, I'd be out of trouble, and I could go back to bed. She never disappeared, of course, and she'd end it all by lecturing me, "Do you know how many children are starving in this world?" She'd scold me some more and then let me leave. I'd go back to bed wondering why I couldn't remember to empty my pockets before they went down to the laundry and promising myself I would remember from now on.

When I was almost ten years old I got some stomach pains one night, not enough to complain about, but when I woke up the next morning there was blood all over the sheets and my pyjamas. I was mystified. I hadn't been stabbed or anything and I wasn't in any kind of horrible pain. When I saw that it was mostly my pyjamas bottoms that were soaked, I realized that the blood was coming from between my legs and a chill ran through me. I knew right away what was happening.

I was finally being punished by God. I had never confessed what I had done when I was three years old, or about the priest. Even though I was living in mortal sin, I had been taking communion. I had long lost count of how many mortal sins had piled up. And now God was getting around to punishing me. I couldn't tell anyone about this, not even Leona. If she knew I was a girl with mortal sins, she might not love me anymore.

That day I pretended to go to school, but I stayed home and tried to clean up. The next day was the same. I was bleeding, bleeding. It wouldn't stop. I was so sad because I was going to die. Leona came to my room after school and asked what was the matter with me. I began to cry right away, but I wouldn't tell her about the old man and the priest.

She told Mrs. Charette that something was wrong with me and Mrs. Charette came up to my room. She was so kind and gentle that I started crying right away. She felt my forehead and asked me where I was hurting. I mumbled, "Nowhere." So she asked if I was thinking of my mother, maybe because we hadn't seen her in a while, and I shook my head, no. She asked if anything bad had happened at school. Again I shook my head, and started bawling even more, because if she found out I skipped school she'd get really angry with me. She finally left and she must have sent Leona back in to figure it out. Leona asked, "Is this about Mom? Tell me, Chris, because you're really scaring me."

I just looked at her through the tears. I couldn't do it. I tried, but I just couldn't tell her about the old man and the priest. Finally she held out some tissue and said, "Here, you'd better dry your eyes and come down to supper. If you feel like talking to me later …" She shrugged and left me sitting on the edge of my bed, all alone, with my bloody bloomers and facecloths right under the bed.

Later, after supper, I washed away the evidence the best I could, then took them up to my room to hang over the railing at the foot of my bed. On the first day, I had thrown away some facecloths, but I couldn't keep on doing that. Mrs. Charette might run out of face-cloths before I died. I was about to turn off my light when Leona came in to try to talk to me again. She saw the bloomers and facecloths right away and saw that some still had pink stains. "Why didn't you tell me about this?" she asked.

Right away I turned on the tears and I babbled my confession about the priest only because that one was not really my fault. I was sniffling as I said, "I was sitting on his lap and he touched me under the table-cloth. Between my legs. Don't tell on me, please?"

"Christine, it wasn't your fault," Leona said, smoothly covering the shock she must have felt.

"Yeah, but don't tell, okay? Don't tell anyone."

"Okay, okay, I won't, but this bleeding, it's not because of that. You're just starting your periods, that's all."

"Periods? What is that?"

"Is what all girls get once a month."

"They do? Do you?"

"Yeah. But I didn't start this early."

She smiled at me and shook her head, making me feel very foolish. She got up and went downstairs, and then Mrs. Charette came in, carrying a carton box and a white elastic belt. She told me that I had started my "menstruation" and that most girls started when they were eleven or twelve. Still, I had an idea it was connected to what I'd done as a three year old.

Mrs. Charette was very understanding about it, but I didn't think she'd be understanding if I now confessed to having thrown away face-cloths and bloomers or that I had skipped two days of school. And for sure, she would never understand about the priest and the grampa-man.

When I was in Grade 5, our class was moved from the convent to the new school. At first some boys made fun of me for being an Indian, even though I wasn't really an Indian-Indian. I was a Métis, which meant I was part Indian and part white. I looked the Indian part, though, and Leona looked the white part. Mostly the kids were okay. I just wished I looked the white part too.

Sister Lord, our teacher, gave us a name so we could remember the names of the planets, starting with Mercury, which was the closest to the sun. It was Mr. VEM J. SUN and his dog, Pluto. In English, Mr. is the abbreviation for mister, and in French, M is for *monsieur*. It was a trick I tried to apply to other lessons that needed to be memorized. I was pretty good in the subjects that I could make into a game. I loved games and, even though Leona and Grace were older, I usually won at checkers.

Leona was always busy now with babysitting and she was invited a lot to her friends' homes. She had many friends and she didn't really like it when I was always hanging around. She never said so, but I knew. So I spent most of my time reading in my room, with the cats lying nearby. When Leona first started babysitting, I used to go where she was just to be with her. Then, one night, Mrs. Charette caught us coming in together and Leona took the blame and got heck, so that ended that.

One night I had a dream that made me wake up. In it, a man with a bowler hat and suspenders was approaching me and, from the look in his eyes, I knew he wanted to touch me between my legs. I was so repulsed by him and what he wanted to do that I grabbed a knife that was somehow near me and warned him I would use it. But still he kept coming and he was grinning, grinning. When he was close enough, I stabbed him. The blade sliced into his stomach—slush—and that's when I woke up. Replaying the dream, I didn't know if I was more horrified that I had stabbed him or that he was going to do something to me.

That was the first time I had such a vivid dream and I had others like it, sometimes with the same man and once with a big, square-shaped woman who kind of looked like Mrs. Manley. I stabbed her too. I always woke up right after. These dreams reinforced the idea that I was a very bad person, so I told no one about them, not even Leona.

When I was in Grade 6, I got some babysitting jobs, just like Leona. Mostly I babysat for a couple who went to Bingo every Tuesday night. One time I found a pile of magazines stacked for the garbage. Some of them were called *True Confessions* and *True Detective*. I brought them home and began to read them. Boy, they were real eye-openers. Mrs. Charette found them one day and she gave me major heck, saying that good girls don't read such trash. That reminded me of the time I had returned from the drugstore to buy some sanitary napkins and had asked her what tampons were, and she just said that good girls don't use tampons.

I had no idea that a major change in my life was about to take place. This change was caused by my confession to Leona about the priest almost a year before. After that confession, we had had a few visits with Mom. Having visits with Mom were not a big deal to me, except this one time when Leona had broken her promise and told Mom about the priest. Mom didn't believe it, and that only added to my feelings of being betrayed. For the rest of that visit I was fighting back tears and hating Leona. They didn't notice, though, because they were so busy talking and laughing with each other. I could easily have stayed home and they would never have missed me. Leona was so pretty and so outgoing and so perfect. No man would dare touch her between the legs. That only happened to people like me.

Later I felt sorry I had bad feelings towards Leona, and I just wished I could be more like her. I even forgot about her betrayal of me and everything was back to normal. And then, one day, Mrs. Grell came to visit after school. I was called into the kitchen and I sensed right away that the mood was tense. I wondered what I had done wrong now.

"What is this story about a priest?" Mrs. Grell asked.

"Father Bolanger, I believe it was?" Mrs. Charette added. Her face had an angry set to it and her eyes were cold.

"That was a long time ago," I mumbled.

"Tell us what happened," Mrs. Grell prodded.

I said nothing for a while, just stood there staring down at a spot on the table. And then in a real low voice, almost a whisper, I said, "Father Bolanger, he touched me. Between my legs."

I glanced up briefly and saw that Mrs. Charette had her lips pressed tightly together. She looked so angry that I got scared.

"When could this have happened?" she asked.

I remained silent, recalling how Mom hadn't believed me, so how was Mrs. Charette going to believe me? I knew she didn't want to hear about any of this. And the memory returned, the tablecloth—cold, crisp, starched white linen. And the hand beneath it. The hypocrisy.

"Well? When could it have happened? You met him only once. And we were all together. You were never alone with him. Not once. So when could it have happened?" Mrs. Charette's voice got louder and louder and it had a belligerent, sneering quality to it.

My mouth had gone dry. I wet my lips. "At the table."

Mrs. Charette looked at Mrs. Grell and said, "It's impossible. We were all together. All the time. I think she got the idea from some trash I found her reading."

Tears were working their way to my eyes and I worked at keeping them at bay. I felt humiliated and betrayed, all over again. They dismissed me, Mrs. Grell saying I had too much imagination for my own good. They warned me not to ever spread such filthy lies around again. I went straight up to my room to cry.

Leona tapped at my door. I was sure she and Grace had overheard everything. I didn't care. Leona started to come in and I told her to go away. I blamed her for this. She told Mom and Mom must have finally told Mrs. Grell. Right now, I hated Leona and my Mom, and Mrs. Grell and Mrs. Charette. And because everyone else would side against me, I hated everyone.

And then I thought about me. Why had that priest picked me? Because he had looked over the children and recognized something evil in me, that was why. I was like him. I knew about bad things already. I wasn't like other kids. I wasn't like Leona and I would never be like her.

For the months that followed, I was treated with contempt. Only Leona was sympathetic, but I shut her out because she was first in line for my resentment. The school year came to an end before my twelfth birthday, and so did my stay at the Charette's. In the final week Mrs. Charette told me to prepare myself for a move. Mrs. Grell came one day and drove me to another foster home. She told me I had only myself to blame. Mrs. Charette didn't want a liar in her household. I didn't cry for Leona, and she didn't beg them to give me another chance. She had been standing among them when the goodbyes were said.

*

The truth hadn't worked for me then and if truth didn't work, what else was there? I had wanted to be good, not morally bad, but, somehow, nothing had ever worked for me and I had ended up looking like what I was—evil. With a start, I saw that I was still holding the rifle and I returned it to its place on the wall, then picked up Todd's teddy bear again. Perhaps I owed it to Todd and Peter to bury them first.

Getting up reluctantly, I wandered around the cabin aimlessly. At Peter's desk I compared his desk to mine. Everything on his was so neat, and on the wall beside it were Todd's art works. Peter's last manuscript sat neatly beside his typewriter. Peter had gone to the trouble of using the hole punch so he could put his manuscript in a binder, mostly so he could work outside where the wind was constant. Once he finished his final editing, he would take it to Fort St. John to get a copy made for his agent. His organizational skills were in such contrast to mine that it had bugged me, especially when he pointed that out.

We never read each other's manuscripts until we were getting close to finishing. Out of habit I hadn't read Peter's because he hadn't given me the okay. He wouldn't be here now to give me an okay. Flooded with guilt by the thoughts I had of him and wanting to be close to him, I took his manuscript to the couch to read. His working title was *A Dick Named Tom*. Stopping only to eat some cereal for supper, I resumed reading late into the night, until I dozed off on the couch. Since learning of the accident, I had not slept in our bed.

The next morning it was sunny and warm out, so I took my coffee and Peter's binder down to the lake, where I continued reading in the hammock until I drifted off to sleep and dreamed that something scary was licking at my fingers. Some part of my dream told me it wasn't a dream and I woke with a jolt. I jerked my arm back from hanging over the side of the hammock and looked down just in time to see a little puppy streak for cover under my truck. There was another puppy already there and they looked like German Shepherd pups, but very scrawny ones. I thought these might be wolf pups, but Peter's books on wolves said they avoided people. The wolf I'd seen yesterday was probably their mother.

My freezer was packed with meat that I would never eat, so I got myself out of the hammock and headed for the summer kitchen. As I was getting a hare out of the freezer, I wondered if I should cook it. Wild animals often ate from frozen carcasses in the winters. Shrugging to myself, I carried the carcass back out into the sunshine. I hated rabbit stew, but Peter had loved it, and so he had shot them, skinned them, and they were on our menu. The pups moved to the other end of the truck as I put the hare down. Then I went to sit on the steps, wondering if the pups would dare come this close to me, now that I was awake and watching. When the larger grey pup got the scent of meat, he edged forward cautiously as the black one eyed both its sibling and me. The grey pup tugged the hare back under the truck, and I could hear the two of them make little growling noises as they chewed into the carcass.

They had the hare in pieces when their mother, the one I'd seen before, came looking for them. She could not have been a very good hunter because she had allowed hunger to make them desperate enough to come near me. She got on her belly to retrieve what she could of the hare. Perhaps her desperation had prevented her from sensing me. I remained very still and quiet because I didn't want to scare her. When she finished, she drew one pup to her and began washing it. It squealed and tried to get away and could have, too, but didn't. The other pup took the opportunity to pounce on its exposed belly. When she was done with the pups, she licked at her paws, then got up, glanced in my direction, and led them back into the bush.

7

That evening I took another hare from the freezer and carried it to the spot where the wolf and her pups had disappeared into the underbrush. The next morning I did the same thing again, before I finished reading Peter's manuscript. It was a shame it would never be published. That morning I sat on the porch steps, thinking I should have a will made. I thought of leaving the property to Michael, but the idea that Leona and Nick might benefit down the road made that idea seem stupid. I should leave it to Kit and Mona because it had belonged to her people in the first place. In the end, I just didn't care enough to do anything.

My first thought when I woke the following morning was to wish that I didn't have go through another day. And why should I wait? I now had no doubt that Peter and Todd were dead, so I didn't really have to wait for the police to find their bodies. And I had never cared for the ritual of funerals. I knew, too, that Peter's parents would claim the bodies once they were found, so they could bury them too. Inside the small enclosure of the cabin I paced restlessly, just as I had when I was younger and felt trapped and needed to be free.

That's what I needed now—to be free. I wondered what it was like to be dead. Nothing to keep me here now. Was there another world? I decided on a time. High noon. Just before noon I was again looking at the rifles, unable to decide if I should use the .22 or the .308, Peter's last acquisition. The kickback from the .308 might make me jerk my head back and I might miss, but not completely. I decided on the .22 and prepared my mind for the event. Then I heard Lady outside, sounding out an advance joyful greeting.

Shutting my bedroom door behind me, I went outside just as Amber, Mona, and Kit rode in on horseback. Mona was dressed in jeans, a sweatshirt under her denim jacket, and cowboy boots. She looked like a younger version of her usual self. Seeing the look of surprise on my face, she knew immediately it was because of the way she was dressed. Chuckling, she smoothly eased down from her horse. "I brought you some stew," she said, and indicated with her chin that Kit had it with him in his pack. "How is everything?"

"Okay," I lied.

"I made lots of stew, so I figured we'd bring some and eat it with you. Is that okay?"

Internally, I was peeved at having my plan disrupted, but I said I was glad they had come and I hoped it wasn't rabbit stew. Amber and Lady took off on their own as Kit studied the ground once he dismounted. He had spotted the wolf tracks right off. Then he took down the food cooler and carried it inside. He got wood and put on a fire in the stove while Mona messed around in my kitchen. Considering my state of mind, lunch tasted really good. Eating one last hearty meal was a fine ritual. Knowing that Kit had seen the wolf tracks, I told them about the mother wolf and her pups and said, almost defiantly, "I know it's probably not a good idea, but I fed them."

"That was Wapan you saw and those pups, they're not her pups. She was from last year's litter," Kit said. Seeing that none of this meant anything to me, he explained: "Wolves aren't like dogs. They don't breed until they're at least two years old."

That still didn't mean anything to me, but I asked, "You know the wolves around here?" Kit and Mona never ceased to amaze me.

He smiled, but it was a sad kind of smile. "I knew them. Okimaw, he was the big boss, and Neka was his wife, and the mother to Wapan and those two pups."

"What do you mean, was? Come to think of it, I haven't heard them howl since I came back from Norway House. But then I wouldn't have noticed."

"When you were away, the government people, I think that's who it was, they came and shot them all."

"Oh yeah, you told me that before. I guess I wasn't really listening, and since I hadn't met them, I didn't really care," I said, perhaps too candidly.

"I found their carcasses up in that valley," he said, showing me which direction with a tilt of his head. "They were all shot. The cattlemen must have been complaining about them. They do that, come in with their helicopters or planes and kill them, they say, to thin out the wolf population." He shook his head and said, "Yeah, they were all shot."

Thinking that they should do that to people, and I would be first in line, I asked, instead, "How many others were there?"

"Three adults, Otakosin, Kanatan, and Nimis. There were two others. Oskinikiw, he got shot last fall and Kehte-aya, her, I think she died of old age, earlier this year. She was the mother to Okimaw."

The way he talked, it seemed like he knew them all intimately, so I asked, "Did you tame them or something?"

"You don't tame wolves. They're not like dogs. Never make pets out of them."

"Yeah, but that mother—I mean, Wapan—she didn't seem scared of me. She was like, only fifty or sixty feet from me. And that one puppy, it came and licked my hand. Scared the shi—wits right out of me."

Amber contained a snicker as smiles flickered across the faces of the elders and I shrugged an apology.

"Wapan must sense you are like her," Kit said gently, and I knew instantly what he meant. We had both suffered the loss of our families and, on top of that, they were starving. "She was at the den, watching the pups when it happened. From where we are, we could hear her crying for her family. She looked for them all over the place. There were six pups, so I guess there's only the two left now."

I remembered all the sleeping I had done on my return from Norway House, and that was why I hadn't heard Wapan's cries. "One's grey and the other one's black, and all three were really scrawny-looking, which is why I fed them. Is it bad to feed them?" I asked, watching Kit's face closely for his expression.

"No, it's only bad to make them dependent on you. They hunt in packs, so that's why they're hungry," Kit said.

"I've got meat in the freezer that I won't eat. I was going to offer it to you, but now it can go to them," I said. I sensed that Kit felt we should let Nature take care of its own, no matter how harsh or tragic the results might be. But then, it wasn't Nature who had forced the loss of her family.

My question to Kit about how much to feed the wolves without making them dependent was supposed to be my last lie to him. After they left, I intended to leave more meat for the wolves and then, after that, I wouldn't care at all about the living. When Kit had told me that this wolf was looking after the young pups who weren't even her own, shame stirred inside me. Shame, because I refused to take care of my own nephew. Or my very own daughter. As I got meat out of the freezer, I had tears in my eyes. Shame, I had lived with shame all my life. After making a few trips, I was done.

I stood on the porch looking out at the tree line, hoping to get one last look at that wolf who was better than me. How pitiful that I wasn't even as good as a wolf. I was all twisted up inside and, although I knew it started when I was three, I had never known what to do about it. I had never thought about the details of that time in my life before—the beginning, but now, I had nothing to lose.

*

Mommy was pretty, 'cause lots of mans came to see her. She smelled nice and she had lots of curly black hair. Me and Leona sometimes took turns to comb it for her. And she had high heels. Leona was bigger than me and she always stayed with me. Sometimes lots of mans and lots of ladies came to our place and there was lots of noise and some music and some dancing and all the peoples was happy. And sometimes, some of the peoples, they got mad at each other and they yelled and they even pushed each other. I used to get scared of that. Mommy took us to the stores and that was fun 'cause Mommy was happy. All the peoples liked Mommy 'cause they gave food to her. And sometimes me and Leona got some candies.

Mommy sleeped in the daytimes and me and Leona got to be quiet. Me and Leona sleeped at the night times. Leona telled to me that the bogeymans comes out late, late at night and we is safe in the bed.

Leona got lots of friends, too, and we played at the park and we played where there was lots of big trains. We got on the trains and we played tag and run all over the place and we played hide-and-seek. Sometimes we played there at night times, before the bogeymans come out. Some mans came and played tag with us and chased us and played hide-and-seek with us. Leona mostly took me home to hide. Leona pretend to be scared. I'm not scared. It was lots of fun.

One day some peoples we never saw before came to our house in a car. Me and Leona have to get in that car. The man said so. I was excited to get in the car and go for a ride. The lady help me get in. Then I hear Leona scream. It was not a scream for fun time. It made me get scared. The lady leave me all alone and she walked back to Leona and that man. I slide back out of the car and fall down on the street and I hurt myself. Nobody is looking at me. I saw Leona hit at the hands of them man and the lady. Leona and Mommy want to give a hug to each other. The bad man and the bad lady don't want them to give a hug to each other. So Leona and Mommy are crying.

I start to cry. I never seen Leona and Mommy crying before. I got up and walked to that bad man and I kicked at him for him to leave Leona alone and I fall down. He hold Leona on her arms and she kick and is screaming all the time and she is trying to get herself loose from him, but he is too big. The lady is telling something to Mommy and Mommy can't help Leona to get loose and Mommy is crying, crying.

The man take Leona to the car. Leona kick and scream and she is trying to bite his hands to get loose. The lady take my hand and I let her take me to the car so I can be with Leona.

The car is moving now. Poor Mommy is all alone now and she is crying, crying. I watch her sit on the ground and I am crying. Leona stop screaming, but she is mad at that man. The car is going fast. Then the car stop. I never seen this place before. I don't know where I am. The man has to pull Leona outside of the car and the lady takes my hand.

There is a lady I never seen before at the house. Inside, the man lets go of Leona. She takes my hand and tries to get back outside. But the man put his foot on the door bottom and Leona can't open it. The ladies make some nice talk. Leona keep her hand on the door handle and she is holding my hand, too. I looked up at her and she is stopped crying, so I stop crying. The ladies keep on making nice talk and they ask Leona something, and Leona won't talk to them. She is looking at the floor. She don't want to look at their faces 'cause she don't like them. They make some nice talk to me. Leona told me not to listen to them and she hugged me harder to her side. They make some more nice talk and I hear, "milk and cookies." Maybe they was not bad peoples. I look at them from the side of my eyes. I like milk and cookies. I put my head back so I can see up to Leona. I tell her they only want us to come for milk and cookies. I say please to her with my eyes.

One of the ladies put her hand out for me to take. Leona got angry. She told them not to touch me and she hit at the hand. The ladies talk to the man. He take hold of Leona's hand and pull it from the door handle and he pull her more inside. He is bad to do that. They make Leona sit at the table. They make me sit in a baby chair, high up. They put some milk and cookies on the table. I don't know why they do that. They be bad. Then they be good.

I looked at Leona to see what to do. Leona sits there. She don't touch the milk and cookies. She don't like the peoples here, so I don't like them, too. But I like cookies and I want to have one. Just one. We sit there. The ladies come and sit at the table. One lady hold a cookie to me. She put it near my mouth. I can smell it. I look at Leona again. She don't move. I am not supposed to touch the milk and cookies. So I move my head a little bit and I bite a big piece from the cookie, but I don't touch the cookie.

The lady with the man got up and I hear them going away. Me and Leona are all by ourselves now. My cookies are all gone. Leona looked at me and shook her head. She got me down from my chair and we went to a door. She opened it and we were outside. Leona looked all around. There is a big fence all around. I am too little to climb out. She sat down on the stairs and she pull me down beside her. She start to cry again. I am sorry I ate the cookies. Pretty soon, I am crying too. We give a hug to each other and we cry, cry.

After that, Leona never wanted anyone to touch us. I ask where Mommy is and Leona say she is going to find this place and she will come and get us and take us back home. I wait, wait. But no Mommy.

One day that lady who make nice talk came back. The bad man was not with her. Mommy is in the car, I think. Oh, goodie. I run to a window to see her. The lady is putting a box in the car. The feet of my teddy bear is sticking out the top of the box. I don't see Mommy at all. Leona is up the stairs. I run to the stairs so I can tell her. But the lady from this house come and take my hand and she take me outside to the car. The other lady get in the other side. They are not going to go and get Leona. I am so scared and I scream for Leona. Leona come running out the door and she is screaming for them to leave me alone.

I am stuck in the car and I can't get out. Leona is kicking at the door, screaming. The car start to go. The other lady from the house is chasing after Leona. Leona is chasing after me in the car. I am looking, looking for a way out of the car. The car door open up and I fall outside. The lady stop the car and she looked scared. I see that. Leona got to me and she helped me get up. That other lady see that I am not hurt and she yell at me. Leona yell at her. I start to cry. The other lady from the house got to us. The first lady, she pull Leona away from me and she yell at Leona to stop her "temper tantrum," and then she shake Leona back and forth. That was the baddest thing. After that she put me back inside the car. Then the car is moving away. I see the lady with Leona say something to her. Leona wave bye-bye to me.

The car stop at a new place. I don't want to go in the house. I sit on the stairs and I am crying, crying. I try to tell them I want to be with Leona. The peoples don't know what I am telling. Leona is the only one who knows my talking. The peoples at this house make some nice talk. I think they be good. A little doggie come out from between their legs and he come right outside. He lick me on the face and he has his tail moving, moving. He is so excited to see me, so I patted him. The new lady bend down to me and say his name is Sammy and that he has to come in the house so he don't get hit by a car. My tears stop coming from my eyes and I go inside the house with Sammy.

The lady at this house is name Mrs. Manley. She is older than Mommy, so she is a little bit fat. She talk to the bad lady. I patted Sammy and we went to sleep on the floor. I woke up and the bad lady was gone now and it was suppertime. I look to see if they went to get Leona, but she is not here. Some new peoples are here now. A grampa-man, a man, and he kissed Mrs. Manley in the kitchen 'cause I saw them, and a boy-man and two girl-ladies. They was more little than Mommy and bigger than Leona.

One day Mrs. Manley got me some new clothes, some dresses, panties, and shirts and socks. She lay them out on the sofa to show me. The dresses was all stiff. I put my face in them and they smell brand new nice. The other clothes is all nice and white. I look at them and I look at my clothes from Mommy's house. Old, new. I like new. Mrs. Manley was happy that I liked them. I saw that on her face.

Mrs. Manley has a piano in the eating room. Sometimes after supper-time she would make some music on the piano. No one danced. One time when some strange peoples was there, I dance for them. They said that was a jig I did. I don't know that. It was dancing from at home.

I sleeped upstairs in a baby crib and there was two more beds there, for the girl-ladies. One girl-lady had long dark hair and the other one had light brown hair. The one with dark hair was bad 'cause one time I saw her with a knife. One night I was in the crib and she was having a fight with the other one and she had a knife and the other one screamed 'cause she was so scared and Mrs. Manley and the man came running to the room and they took the knife away. I was scared that time.

Before bedtime, Mrs. Manley gave me a bath. They had a bathroom and a bathtub and a toilet and a sink. Mommy didn't have that at home. Mommy didn't have an upstairs cause she was poor. I liked getting a bath. Mrs. Manley or one of the girl-ladies would wash me with some nice-smelling soap. They would make bubbles on my hand with the soap and rub my hand between their hands. First one hand, then the other. And there was lots of bubbles in the water. I liked that part the best.

One day Freda—she is a little girl from down the street—came and took me to Bible School. That's where I met Jesus. Jesus has a really nice voice. They showed us how he lived a long time ago on the wall. And he was kind of mixed up with his father and a bogeyman. I don't know what they meant, but Bible School was fun. We sang songs, like "Jesus Loves Me," and a man told us stories and we played with paper and paste and lots of things. Sometimes I played at Freda's house. Her house is, one, two, three houses from Mrs. Manley's house. One day I went there all by myself. No one had to take me. Mrs. Manley came and she is mad me, and she gave me heck. I am not supposed to do that.

At night times Mrs. Manley puts me in the crib and says a prayer with me: "Now I lay me down to sleep, I pray the Lord—that's another name for Jesus—my soul to keep. If I should die before I wake, I pray the Lord my soul to take." Then she leaves me all alone in the dark. I never go to sleep for a long time. I don't want to die. That is something bad that happens to peoples. The grampa-man sometimes comes to my crib. I pee in the crib now. In the morning times Mrs. Manley gives me heck and she has to wash all my crib things.

One day in the winter time Mrs. Grell—that is how the social worker is called—came to the Manley's house. She took me for a ride in her car. She told me to sit still and not move. I don't want her to yell at me and I obey her. We got to a big building and we went up some stairs. And we walked, walked down a long room and she opened a door and there was Leona and Mommy. I was so excited to see Leona. Leona asked what happened to my hair. I don't know what happened, just that one day I had to sit on a pot on a chair in the basement and then I saw my hair on the floor. But I didn't know why Mr. Manley did that. Leona and Mommy talked and laughed and I sitted on the floor with the toys and waited. I didn't know why we didn't just all go home now. I thought Leona was already back home. Maybe I was too little to be at home with Leona and Mommy.

Mrs. Grell came back and she put my coat on me. I am supposed to wave bye-bye to Leona and Mommy. I started to cry. I want to go home with them. I don't want to go back to the Manley's. Mrs. Grell told me not to make a temper tantrum. She took me by the hand and I was still crying when we got back to the Manley's.

Every day I ask Mrs. Manley if I can go be with Leona. The snow is all gone now for a long time. Mrs. Grell took me to see Leona again, and Mommy, too. But I cried to myself when Mrs. Grell took me away from them and I am so, so sad.

Now it is hot outside and inside, and up the stairs the most. One time after supper Mrs. Manley brought a cake to the table. It had four pink candles on it and one, blue. Everyone sang "Happy Birthday" to me and then Mrs. Manley told me to blow out the candles, so I did. Then we had ice cream with the cake and it was so good, and after that, I got a present, but I don't know what it is called. The grampa-man said it's for counting and he will teach me how to count with it. I don't know why everyone is so nice to me, but I am happy.

One day Mrs. Manley waked me up from a nap. She took me down the stairs and Mrs. Grell was there. This time Mrs. Manley hug me close to her and tell me from now on I got to be a good girl. Maybe she knows about my bad secret. Me and the grampa-man, we do the bad things.

All the peoples at Mrs. Manley was mostly nice to me. The grampa-man was the best one. He was the best one at the first. He read to me from books. I sit down beside him and he read and sometimes he made funny noises. Sometimes, he tickled me and he made me laugh a lot.

One day we was all alone and he was reading to me and then he tickled me and I was laughing, laughing. Then he opened his pants and he had a big thing there inside his pants and there was lots of white and grey curly hair there. I stared at it. I looked up at his face. He was watching me kind of a funny way. He told me that I could touch it. I know that I am not supposed to touch it. He is bad to show it to me. He took my hand and put it on his thing and he moved my hand along it. I let my fingers touch it. His thing was smooth and warm. It was hard and soft. It smell of something that is bad. I know what it is for. It was to put between a lady's legs. It made a lady excited. The grampa-man knew that I knew.

The grampa-man has a bed in a room up the stairs. Every day after lunch time, I have to take a nap. Mrs. Manley has something wrong with her legs. Every morning times, she has to put some grease on them and wrap bandages around them. Her legs are all white and they got some blue lumps on them. She is glad when the grampa-man takes me up the stairs for my naps. Sometimes he takes me to his bed and I am supposed to lay beside him. And then he opens his pants some more to make me touch him and he touches me between my legs. And the bad smell is always there. I know I am very, very bad to touch his thing. I don't try to stop it and I don't tell on him. That's how I know I am so, so bad.

If Mrs. Manley knew, she would be mad at me. She would not hug me. I don't know why she telled to me I should be good from now on. I start to cry. Mrs. Grell took me to her car and she told me to sit still and not to move. I am so happy to see Leona again, and Mommy. My tears are all gone now. I try hard not to move at all so Mrs. Grell don't change her mind.

*

That was where the evil had begun and today, right now, I would put an end to it. I would put an end to myself because I was the only one who should have died.

Pushing aside more thoughts, I went into the cabin, got a bullet for the .22 from the filing cabinet, and went to my bedroom to take the rifle down from the wall. I sat on the bed, positioned the rifle, and then it occurred to me that the bedding would get too messed up.

I went to the dining-room table and sat at a chair, and then I thought if I didn't get discovered for weeks, I would stink the whole cabin up. I considered hiking further into the mountains, but I wanted to get this over with right now, right this minute. The bad evil smell was all around me, the echo of a baby crying, a baby who had just come from my womb, a baby I had shunted aside. I needed all of this to stop.

I went out through the side porch and sat on the step and loaded the bullet into the chamber. Every single time I had something I valued it was taken from me—every single time. I sometimes had something good, but only for a little while, never for long. Peter and Todd, they had been the best thing in my whole life and I wanted them, how I wanted them! But they were gone. I imagined myself there with them in their last moments in the truck, wanting to experience what they might have experienced. If only I could have been there for real. If only I could have been the only one there.

Life had been cruel to me, but I was now going to put an end to it. I tilted my head and put the barrel of the rifle into my mouth. Then I put my thumb on the trigger and all I had to do was press. One ... two ... three ...

What if Kit came—no, worse—what if Amber came riding along by herself and found me here. I took my thumb off the trigger. Could I do that to a young girl—give her an ugly scene that would stay with her for the rest of her life—could I? Yes I could, because what did I care? I was a person who cared for no one. My thumb returned to the trigger. One ... two ... I did care, and so I laid the rifle aside. Damn it, I did care, I did care. What a loser I was—what a totally screwed-up loser!

Covering my face with my hands, I began to cry. At first I cried because I wasn't dead yet and I didn't even know if I could pull that trigger. A damned coward, that's what I was. More bleak thoughts and feelings whirled around inside me. Most of all I was crying over my loneliness for Peter and Todd. I was crying over the guilt I had for not having loved them enough when they were with me. Too much unbearable pain inside and I clawed at my face, wanting to replace the pain inside me with outside pain. I wanted the pain to stop. A flash of Todd, with a hurt, bewildered expression on his face because I had scolded him for nothing, for something that was trivial, minor, silly— and now I could never take it back, never undo it. "I'm sorry, Todd. I'm so, so sorry. I love you so much and now it's too late. It's too late!"

I made a high, keening sound and rocked back and forth. The ache, the pain, it was so, so bad. With my eyes shut tight, some of the pain was lost in that pitch-black space. *All I want is to be with them. That's all I want. Just to be with them. Please.*

Through the haze of my emotional turmoil came the sound of a low whimper. Lowering my hands from my face, I opened my eyes to blinding sun. A large muzzle opened and a tongue licked the tears from my face. Without thinking, I buried my face into the wolf's neck and continued wailing. The animal stood patiently, allowing me to do this, and waited until my wailing subsided into half-sobs. Finally, I straightened up and sat back. My grief was so consuming that it hadn't occurred to me that what was taking place here was unbelievable. This had to be the wolf Kit called Wapan—a wolf who had more heart than I, a wolf who took care of young ones not her own, a wolf who gave comfort to a half-crazy, totally grieving woman in the wild.

The depth of wisdom and compassion I saw in her amber eyes completely humbled me. And then ... and then, there was more. Those maggots that had wiggled and squirmed inside me were being vanquished and stilled. The emotional and spiritual viruses that had gnawed away at my heart, mind, and soul were somehow being destroyed, as if an invisible blood transfusion were infusing life-giving antibiotics into me. Wapan was sharing her power—a clean, pure, healthy power. We were not touching now, only our eyes were locked into each other's, but I had no doubt I was being empowered.

She must have sensed this new feeling in me because she released my eyes, lowered her head, and sighed, as if to say, "There, it is done." As she slowly began to turn away, she glanced at me sideways, the expression in her eyes having changed to one of humour. And now it seemed she was saying, "Get on with life, for life is sacred."

Tentatively I ran my hand along the side of her neck, and she turned back to me again. She put a paw on my leg. "I'm okay now. I'll be okay. Thank you." My voice went shaky, as though I was going to begin bawling all over again. "Thank you, Wapan." The wolf removed her paw, licked my face once more, and turned to leave. She trotted away, then stopped to look back over her shoulder. I nodded and watched her leave.

8

A strange feeling settled over me once Wapan had disappeared. Standing to go inside, I found that the invisible oppression that had been weighing me down was gone and I felt—oh, so relaxed. Looking down at the rifle, it occurred to me that maybe I had used it and maybe, right now, I was dead, and maybe the passage to the other side was the vision of a wolf. No, her paw prints were right there, my hands still had the feel of her fur, and my face still tingled from the roughness of her tongue. If I were dead, I would be in another dimension and, surely, nothing would seem the same. Bending to pick up the rifle, I noted that my body parts still operated the same. Even though a bullet was in the chamber, I still wasn't convinced I was still alive. Unloading the rifle, I walked, not floated, into the cabin to put it away and turned on the television as I was passing by. If I were a ghost, I wouldn't be able to do that either, but still I was unable to shake the strange feeling. I felt this way mostly because I knew that what happened between Wapan and me was impossible.

That feeling gradually dissipated as I searched the cabin for the phone number of the social worker who had called about Michael. I finally found it in the pocket of the jacket I had worn that day. Hoping it wasn't too late, I drove over to Mona's place.

Later, after I made the call to Betty Chartrand, I realized I had not told her, in either phone call, that Peter had died in an accident, and now I knew why. That information might have jeopardized Michael's chances of coming to live with me. Michael might change his mind once I told him, but that would be his choice. And my trip to Winnipeg would not be wasted in any event because I still needed to talk to Leona, face to face, and find out why she had someone make that fateful call that drew Peter and Todd to their deaths.

That night I went to bed, not on the sofa, but in our bed, and lay there for a long time, thinking about Wapan. She had been here, that much was certain. Granted, I might have imagined the expression in her eyes, imagined what she was thinking, imagined that she had caused the change in me. Regardless of what I had imagined and what had been real, right now I was alive and had plans, not only to exist, but to live. I now knew I had to begin a journey of self-healing, not just the healing from the deaths of Peter and Todd, but from all the negatives in my past life which had allowed those viruses inside me to fester and eat away at my soul. I had to do that for Todd and for Peter.

As little Catholic children we had been taught that man was created in the image of God and, therefore, that we were superior over all other creatures. Animals could not think or feel the emotions we did, and they acted only on instinct, always for their own benefit. While I was listening to these teachings in the classroom, outside, the animals taught me differently.

Kit had once told us that Indian people saw things differently too. Animals and all other creatures and living things did not need people and could do very well without us. We humans needed the forests and the meadows and the rocks and the animals, we could not do without them. Yet we fooled ourselves into thinking we were the superior beings. Today, Wapan had confirmed Kit's bit of wisdom. Today, Wapan had empowered me and, even if that was only my perception of what had happened, I now looked forward to all the tomorrows to come. With that, I turned over on my side and went to sleep.

Because Michael was still in school, I didn't have to leave immediately. I took the time to prepare Todd's room, packing Todd's clothing, books, and toys into boxes and taking them up to the loft to store, or putting them in my room. Maybe in a year or two I would take them somewhere so another child could use them, but right now I could not part with them.

Later that night Kit and Mona came over in their pickup and Kit had brought more meat for the wolves. While he unloaded the packages to store in the freezer, Mona and I made a tea that she had brought with her. When it was ready, Mona said, "It's nice out. Let's have a campfire tonight."

By the time we went to the lake to light a fire, the sun had gone down and dusk had turned to night. Joining us, Kit sat on a log and picked up one of the sticks we had once used for roasting wieners and marshmallows. Mona was in a chair, and I was sitting between them on the ground. We were all facing the lake. The loons' last calls of the day echoed across the lake and, when the birds had gone silent, the frogs, crickets, and the mosquitoes began their symphony. The fire, crackling, snapping, and sizzling, mesmerized us. In the sandy soil, Kit was marking a pattern of a circle divided into four parts. He murmured, "It's the Medicine Wheel. A likeness."

I looked from the circle on the ground up to his weathered face. For a moment, it seemed that a total hush descended on us, and even the crackling of the fire stopped. Then Kit's words broke the silence. "We need four basic things to be in balance for our well-being."

When I looked back at the circle, he had written four words: spirit, mind, heart, and body. I looked back up at him, for I had not seen him move to print these words.

"The spirit, that's our way of life. It's how we are all related to each other and to everything here on Mother Earth."

Gazing into the dancing flames of the fire, I waited for him to continue, then wondered why he was telling me this stuff.

As if he had read my mind, he continued in a low voice, "I tell you this because you could do more with your writing. The centre of the circle, that's where we are, each one of us. From us, our way of life spreads out from the centre and it has an effect on others. Put yourself in the centre and think about it."

Out of respect, I obeyed, imagining myself at the centre of a large circle, but at the same time I was thinking this concept was simplistic: what I did, what I wrote, could spread out and affect others. Even my death would have had an effect on others. And the actions of others could have some kind of effect on me, even if I didn't know immediately what it might be. Since I couldn't control the actions of others, what was the point of thinking about this? I looked back up to Kit's face to see if he expected a response from me and caught a movement beyond him. Wapan had joined us and was lying down in the grass, maybe one hundred feet back. The outline of her ears was barely visible, but her eyes reflected the flames of the fire. Turning to Mona to indicate the wolf's presence, I saw she was already staring at Wapan.

As if he also knew Wapan was there, Kit said, "In Cree, Wapan means 'It is dawn.' "

Looking down at my hands, gripping my cup, I told them about yesterday. "Yesterday, I was going to shoot myself. And then she came." Tears rolled down my cheeks and I moved my cup so my tears wouldn't fall into my tea.

Mona put her hand out to me. Awkwardly, I reached out to hold her hand. She said quietly, "Sometimes we have to go to the top before we can get to the bottom."

I looked up at her, puzzled. At first she had this wise, deeply serious look on her face, then a twinkle came to her eyes and a smile cracked her face and, finally, she was chuckling loudly. By now I was laughing too.

Kit was grinning and he shook his head. "She always gets those sayings wrong."

I went to bed that night feeling special because I had these special people close to me, and one very special friend from the wild. In my third foster home I had found more animal friends, but, more than that, I had been influenced by some people I'd never met who were long gone. I think that was the first time I realized I did have something good in me, something that could not be taken away from me.

*

From the Charettes and Leona, Mrs. Grell drove south just past Ste. Agathe, to a farm where she left me among strangers—not that I cared much about anything or anybody. That night I found myself sitting at a large dining-room table with Mr. and Mrs. Gerard, their two children, Denis and Claire, both older than I was, and Philip, a helper who lived with them.

In the following days I was given chores to do and, when I finished them, I went off to walk the fields and the woods that bordered the Red River. The river was my only connection to Leona and, while I was still angry at her—no, not angry—disappointed in her, I was glad to have some kind of connection. During the night when it got dark and quiet, I sneaked out of my room to go down to the river, look at the moon, and wish I were Leona instead of me. On such nights, when I wasn't wishing I were Leona, I sometimes had the sense of being totally free.

The Gerards had one horse, Chieftan, but he was too wild for riding. He was the first to rouse my interest because, every night, he would go out in the fields, round up the cows, and bring them back to the barn. One night as we were watching the horse herd the cows into the coral that surrounded the barn, Mr. Gerard told me he had trained Chieftan to do that eleven years ago. I was quite impressed that he could communicate with an animal better than I could. I wondered how he had done that, but I never asked. They didn't have any dogs, just cats who ran wild in the barn and the storage and the machinery sheds. Philip said they did have a dog, but he had died a few months back of old age and they never got another one. I made friends with the cats and called them Kitty One, Kitty Two, and so on.

One afternoon I was walking near the woods by the river close to where a dirt road ran off the highway to surround a section of land.

A car rounded a bend slowly and came to a stop. A man let a dog out and, when the dog had wandered away into the field, the car sped up and headed back towards the highway. At first the dog ran after the car, and then it sat down in the middle of the road. For the rest of the afternoon I watched from the woods as the dog remained where it was, sometimes sitting, sometimes lying down, but always watching for his owner's return. Before supper, I had to go back to do my chores. At the supper table I told the others what I had seen.

"City folk. They're always dropping animals they don't want in the country," Mr. Gerard said.

"But could it come here? Could we take care of it?" I asked.

"I don't want another dog around here," said Claire.

No one else said anything more about the dog. After my evening chores were done, I got some food and walked back out across the fields and the woods to where I had last seen the dog. It was still there. I called to it, "Here boy, come here." I didn't know whether it was male or female. It was a large mixed-breed dog with long hair. Its head turned in my direction and it bared its teeth. I sat down where I was and talked to it, asking it mindless questions. Its ears twitched and finally it got up and came towards me, cautiously. Every so often it would look back over its shoulder, still expecting the return of its owner. It came close enough that I could see it was a female, and she looked as though she had had pups recently. Maybe that was why she needed to get back to her home. I offered her some food, but she must have been too sad to eat. She lay down beside me and I continued to talk to her and pet her.

It got dark and I knew I had to get back. By now I was calling the dog Lady. Lady wouldn't come back with me. She had to stay where she was, for when her owner returned. I left, planning to come back during the night when everybody was in bed.

I slept the whole night through and, the next morning, I couldn't hurry enough to finish my chores so I could take more food to Lady. At first I didn't see her, and I thought the owner must have felt guilty and come back for her. That was good. I called her name a few times, and she came out of the ditch beside the road. She wagged her tail as she approached me. I offered her fresh food and she was happy to eat it now. When the sun got high, I told her I had to go for lunch, but I would be back. When I started walking away, she whined. She didn't want me to leave her, yet she could not leave her place either.

At suppertime I told the Gerards that the dog was still waiting. I was hoping they would say she could come to stay here. They took me in, didn't they? But, for some reason, Claire got mad and said, "I already said I don't want another dog around here." With that, she left the table without finishing her meal. I mumbled that I was sorry, thinking I would somehow take care of Lady myself.

Mrs. Gerard said, "Claire still misses Thor, that's all."

Before I went to see Lady, I went to find Claire. She was in the barn tending to her calf which she "showed." She and Denis were in a 4-H Club. I said, "I'm sorry about your dog."

She said nothing, just kept brushing her calf.

"Your Mom said you still miss him. A lot."

Thinking she was just going to keep ignoring me, I had decided to leave when she threw down her brush and said, "Okay, take me to this dog of yours."

I found myself babbling a mile a minute about how Lady was so loyal she had remained at the spot waiting for whoever had dropped her off and how sad she was for her pups and how lonely she must be. When we got to the place, I called her and she came out of her hiding place right away, but stopped dead when she saw Claire. Her head went down, the fur on her back went up, and we could hear her growling.

"That's your special dog? It's a Heinz 57," Claire scoffed, keeping her distance.

I didn't know what kind of a breed a Heinz 57 was. I just said, "Well, she growled when she first saw me too. But if you just keep talking to her she'll get used to you."

"I know how to handle dogs," Claire replied.

She bent down and baby-talked to Lady. Lady's fur went down and she tilted her head and finally went over to Claire. My hope soared when Claire ruffled Lady's fur. When we went back to the house that night, Lady followed us.

From the beginning, I had tried to make friends with Chieftan, talking to him, keeping him company, and sometimes, if he was in the mood, he would eat grasses from my hand. When I was sure we were alone, I galloped like a horse—he liked that and trotted after me. Now when I called to him, he came to me and followed me on my walks, and sometimes we ran together. Well, I ran and he trotted. Lady must have been a city dog because it took a while for her to get used to Chieftan. When she did, I'd return from the fields with both of them following along and that made me feel good. Because of them, I liked being at the Gerards. I didn't miss Leona at all. She had always made me feel like nothing, not because of anything she did, but because of the difference in the way people treated us. When people had told me I was so different from Leona, I had always taken it as an insult.

Anyways, another thing I had wanted to do from the beginning was to ride Chieftan, even though everyone said he was too wild. So after we were friends and he was used to me, I made some reins out of old nylon stockings and tied them to the halter he always wore. Then I led him to a fence and climbed aboard. He didn't buck me off, but he didn't move forward at my request. He was too busy eating grass, so I just sat on his back and waited for him to move forward. Eventually, Mr. Gerard saw me, so he dug out an old western saddle along with a bridle and showed me how to saddle a horse. I had wanted to ride Chieftan bareback, as an Indian would, but Mr. Gerard was so nice about helping me that I didn't say anything. Pretty soon, we were all riding Chieftan—at different times, of course.

Too soon, summer vacation came to an end. When school started, I had to take a school bus because school was over two miles away. The kids on the bus must never have seen an Indian before or they had heard only the worst. After the first day, I asked the Gerards if I could walk to school. I had to leave earlier than Claire. Denis had to go away because he was starting university. I was in Grade 7 and none of these teachers were nuns. What I liked about nuns was that kids were not so rude when they were around.

I got a break from school one day when my new worker, Mrs. Turner, came to pick me up for a visit with Mom and Leona. By the time I got there, they were already together and I felt like an intruder. Instead of being happy to see me, Mom looked at me with disappointment. Eventually, she said, "Christine, it's your own fault you got sent away. Lying about a priest of all things." She clicked her tongue and added, "You have too much imagination for your own good." Where had I heard that before? I looked at Leona, my defender, my protector, and she just looked back at me blankly and shrugged. For the duration of that visit, I sat there listening to them talking and laughing. Inside, I was seething with resentment, thinking I was glad we didn't all live together. Living with a mother who didn't care beans about me would have been worse than living with strangers who didn't have to care about me.

I carried the resentment back to everyone at the farm and I talked only to the animals. On rainy days I shut myself in my room and read. By now cats were allowed inside the house and they usually came scratching at my door so they could lie on my bed while I read. All the animals were fascinating, even the cows and the pigs. Back at the Charettes, we had gone to a circus and I had been the only one who hated it. Lions and tigers, which should have been wild and free and even dangerous, were made to perform by a man armed only with a whip and a chair. It just didn't seem right. Here, because of the animals, I was fairly happy with my life at the Gerards. When I grew up I was going to become a hermit with only animals around me.

Mr. and Mrs. Gerard must have thought I was miserable because I missed my mother and Leona. In the spring, Mr. Gerard took me, and some other kids from school, to a rifle range, where we were taught how to shoot .22s. From the beginning I was a natural, in that I hit mostly bull's eyes and that impressed everyone there. I was used to not being good at most things that came naturally to other kids, so I was very pleased with myself.

At school I discovered another talent. In English classes something clicked and I got A grades in spelling, grammar, and composition. One time during lunch Mr. Boissevain copied my most recent composition on the blackboard, so when we returned from lunch I was startled to find it up there for everyone else to see. During the class, he pointed out all the things that made it such a good example. I sat at my desk, trying not to squirm because I knew I was suddenly the centre of attention and I was wishing I hadn't done so well. Afterwards, Mr. Boissevain told me I had a natural talent for writing. That night I told myself I had two talents, although neither would ever amount to anything.

I didn't always have a chip on my shoulder, as Mrs. Grell had once said. If people liked me, I liked them back. I didn't like Mom at all because she didn't like me. She would not miss me at family visits and neither would Leona. When Mrs. Gerard told me I had another family visit coming up, I told her to tell Mrs. Turner I didn't want to go. I was very aware of the date of the visit, and when it came near, I was anxious that I might break down and ask to go. Then, on the actual date, I wondered if Mom and Leona even noticed I wasn't there. I guess Leona did notice because, a few weeks later, I got a letter from her.

Dear Chrissy,

I missed you at the visit. How come you never came? Did you know about it? Everything is okay here at the Charettes but I miss you a lot. I keep asking Mom if you can come back but she never really gives me an answer. Whats it like where you are now? Are they good to you?

We got a new foster kid here. Her name's Diane and she told me that in her last foster home, she used to get beatten up.

I didn't know people could be so cruel to little children. Anyways, I'm going to look out for her now.

Guess what? I'm in love. Remember Greg Monroe? We started seeing each other. I had to drop Ron, of course, but Greg is so much more mature than Ron. Greg's in Gr. 11 now. The other kids talked me into running for Snow Queen for the winter festival. Each class is supposed to pick a girl and boy. But probably one of the higher grades is going to win. Greg was chosen from his class. It would be so neat if he and I were picked for King and Queen.

Answer me back soon. I'll be watching for your letter. I have to go now. Bye. Love you.

Your sister forever,

Leona

I crumpled the paper up and thought, "Well, Leona, you can watch all you want. And if you wanted to know what it's like for me here, you could have asked at our last visit. But no, you were too busy talking to Mom."

Leona was a hypocrite. To read this letter, you would have thought she cared about me, but at the family visits they ignored me. They had always ignored me once they were together. I decided I was not going to write back. From now on, I was not going to see her or visit her and Mom ever again. With that, I threw her letter away.

Her next letter was mostly to say that she and Greg had won the titles of Snow Queen and Snow King, though she did ask why I hadn't written back. To be honest, Leona was nice to everyone and it was not surprising that she got voted to be Snow Queen. I was her opposite— not that I wasn't nice too, but I had to settle for being a loner at school. That bothered me only at social events, which I tried to avoid, but if I couldn't, then all the other loners banded together so we didn't stick out so much. It was funny how the popular kids stuck out, and how the loners stuck out almost as much.

I started skipping school for different reasons, mostly because I didn't finish homework. Reading books took priority. Although I was good in English, I was lousy at everything else. Sometimes I pretended to be sick. When I was younger I used to get excruciating stomach cramps whenever I started my period and I had been allowed to stay home. More often than not, now, I pretended to have cramps. I had been accused of lying; now I was making the accusation a reality. And I was really honing my lying skills.

In Grade 8 the vice-principal was also our history teacher. Mr. Belmont introduced us to John F. Kennedy, president of the United States of America. After that, I began clipping everything I could on all the Kennedys. I stopped wishing I was Leona and started wishing I was like John and Jacqueline Kennedy. Mostly, though, I wished I had parents like them, instead of like my mother. Leona and I had never talked about our father—or fathers. Because we looked so different, I had long ago suspected we had different fathers. I had never known how to ask Leona about that without implying that Mom was a lady who slept with different men. That would have meant that Mom was a slut, and I knew that Leona would not have liked to hear that.

November 22, 1963, was a Friday. That morning I had skipped school because we had math and science, my two worst subjects. Even though it was winter, I had gone down to the river and played with Lady. At lunchtime I made my way to school and, right away, it felt like a hush had fallen over the place. Someone told me that John F. Kennedy had been shot in the head. At one o'clock we were all back in the classrooms. Mr. Belmont didn't start class and it looked as though he had been crying. We sat at our desks, just waiting for more news. That's when I asked God for one favour. I told God that Kennedy was needed here and I wasn't. Take me instead, I begged him. Then I waited to die. Just after 1:30 the secretary's voice came through the loudspeaker, saying that the president had died. God didn't want me because I was bad. I stood up then, looked at Mr. Belmont, and walked out of the classroom.

I bawled all the way back to the farm. God should have let Kennedy live. When I got home the Gerards and Philip were watching TV, so I sat on the couch with them and watched, my tears running freely. For the rest of that weekend the whole family watched TV, skipping all the chores that were not absolutely necessary.

When Jack Ruby shot Lee Harvey Oswald, I was glad and shouted, "Good!" But Mrs. Gerard looked at me and said, "It's not good because now we'll never know what really happened."

I didn't understand what she meant. For one thing, killing another person went against the Ten Commandments, but that's not what she pointed out. Well, if the police said Oswald shot Kennedy, then that's what happened. In those days, the police were as infallible as the Pope was.

After Kennedy was buried, I decided that I was going to be good and strong and that I would care about people, just like Kennedy. Around that time on TV, we watched news about how the black people in the South were treated by some of the white people. I couldn't understand how those people could be so evil, how they didn't see the evil in themselves. When I saw Martin Luther King Jr., I wished I could be black and could somehow help. The reality was that I was a nobody and, while I wasn't as evil as those white people in the South, I was bad and therefore useless.

Over the months, Leona wrote me a few more letters, mostly asking if I was mad at her or Mom. I always threw her letters away. When I was in Grade 9, it finally occurred to me that a good, strong person would forgive. So when Mrs. Gerard told me about another family visit, I told her I would go. What I hated about myself was that I was always finding justifications to break promises to myself.

Mom was already there when I arrived and she was obviously disappointed when she realized that it was only me and not Leona. That set the tone between us. She didn't hug me, and I just sat down opposite her. She was uncomfortable with me and I decided not to make it easy for her. She asked, "So how are you?"

"Fine."

"How's your new place?"

"Fine," I said, and thought to myself I had only been living there for almost three years now.

"What are you doing these days?" she asked after a moment of silence.

"Nothing," I answered.

Leona was late because she had been to visit a friend first. Mom was obviously happy to see her and I watched them hug each other before Leona greeted me warmly. Then they settled for a good visit with each other. Leona did notice that I was being ignored and she turned to me to ask why I never answered any of her letters. I was trying to come up with a good lie, but another thought entered her head and she turned back to Mom without waiting for my answer. Fine.

I really didn't mind too much, though, because Leona looked grown up now and I was fascinated by her looks. Her hair was a lighter brown than before, with gold highlights in it, and she wore it piled high on her head. Her makeup was not overdone, like Mom's, although her eyes were outlined in black and her thick lashes had too much mascara. Wearing a pale yellow suit and high heels, she looked just like a model, sophisticated and beautiful. And to go with her looks, she had a way of expressing herself that was as fascinating as her looks. Her eyes sparkled with a mix of both humour and seriousness. Her hands moved to add emphasis to whatever she said, and she smiled and laughed a lot. She looked as if she didn't have one drop of Indian blood in her at all.

No wonder Mom preferred her. I had been told more than once that I always looked so glum. I rarely had a smile on my face when I was around people. I was two and a half years younger than Leona, but I knew I was never going to achieve her manner. Much of Leona's beauty came from her innocence. As far as I could remember, she never had any ill will towards anyone. And no one had any towards her, except me. I would never have the beauty of innocence. I was bad. I left that visit knowing I was never going to be a good, strong person, so why try?

When I was almost fifteen, I met a boy. Larry was new in town and

I guess he didn't know that boys shouldn't go out with one of the loners, especially if she was Indian. He wasn't a real boyfriend and we never really went out on dates. He was friends with Aaron, who had a car, and we would drive around town and sometimes we'd stop for ice cream or something like that. Even though I was with them, they'd stop to talk to girls from town who were taking evening walks. One Saturday afternoon, without telling me where they were going, they drove to Winnipeg to visit one of Larry's former school friends. They started drinking beer and, when more people came to the apartment, it turned into a drinking party. Aaron passed out on top of a pile of dirty laundry in the bedroom early in the evening. I didn't know what to do. I didn't want to call Mrs. Gerard because I would have to talk to her in front of everybody and they would all know I was getting heck.

The only thing I could do was not to drink beer. That night people either left or passed out. Larry and I ended up on the couch and he tried to fondle me, so I spent the rest of that night talking him out of it. The next morning, one of the girls made breakfast for everyone. Then we headed back for Ste. Agathe. I was miserable.

The Gerards were furious when I got home. They had called Children's Aid and even the police. The more they got angry, the more I got defiant. Under the circumstances, I had done nothing wrong—unless my silence was the culprit. When they told me I was not to see Larry again, I balked. While I had resisted his advances the night before, I now had a huge desire to see him again, the sooner the better.

On Monday morning, I was approaching the school entrance when I saw Ned and his group of friends, smoking near the bottom of the steps. Inwardly, I groaned. Ned and his gang had always called me a squaw. Of all the names I'd been called, I hated that name the most, and I was intimidated by them. Ned leered at me as I passed by and he said, "Hey squaw, want to suck my dick for a change?" The others laughed and I felt myself flush with embarrassment. They followed me inside, almost stepping on my heels.

Larry was already inside near the lockers and I was relieved to see him. As soon as he noticed me, he came strutting over and bent to kiss me in front of everybody. Shocked, I backed away. This was a Catholic school and a teacher could have come around the corner and seen us. By the end of that day I had a reputation and it wasn't good. I suspected that Larry had lied about me—us.

Whatever rumours were going around must have made their way to the principal because, the next day, I was called to the office and saw that Mrs. Gerard was there. Gulping back my fear, I went in to face the music. The principal addressed Mrs. Gerard but looked at me: "We've been hearing some very disturbing things about Christine and I thought you ought to know. It seems that Christine has been, uh, intimate with the boys here. And now, apparently, she's carrying on right here in school, in front of the others. We simply can't have that. We have standards here and we simply cannot tolerate immoral behaviour."

When I heard that, tears jumped to my eyes. I had never been intimate with anyone. Well, not anyone here at school. Well, not the way he made it sound. He made this episode sound disgusting.

"Christine!" Mrs. Gerard exclaimed in a soft, reproachful tone. She shook her head and said, "Christine, I'm ..." Her sigh said it all. "What is going on with you? I'm shocked."

Equally shocked, I looked at her. Surely she knew me well enough by now, didn't she? Surely she would know I wouldn't behave immorally. Then again, Saturday night would be fresh on her mind.

The principal said, "I wouldn't be too hard on her, Mrs. Gerard. In my opinion, they're not quite like others. They want attention, and usually it's easiest to find that from the boys."

My mind blocked out the rest of their exchange as I stopped my tears from spilling over by thinking I deserved this. I was evil and people, although they didn't know why, would always pick up on it. That was why the priest had picked me out of the crowd of children. No matter where I went, people would sense I was evil.

By the time I left the office I had decided one thing. I was never going to come back to this school. Instead of going back to class, I followed

Mrs. Gerard towards the front entrance. She stopped and said in an icy tone: "You had better go back to your class. And try to behave yourself."

"I'm leaving. I'm moving somewhere else."

"Fine. But right now you have to go to class." She began walking away from me and then she stopped and looked back. "I'll call your social worker."

I watched her leave, and then I went back to my locker to get my things. From there, I headed east, crossed the highway, and went down to the Red River. I sat there and cried and cried. Maybe I had hoped she would talk me out of leaving. Maybe I had hoped that somehow everything could be made better. But just like that, she was booting me out of her home.

In the following days I waited for the social worker to come and get me and, instead of going to school, I went down to the river. I didn't want to leave the Gerards at all. I loved it here and I had thought they were decent people. But Mrs. Gerard had been so quick to arrange my departure. It wasn't that I had expected them to love me or anything like that. I was not loveable like Leona. I was a foster kid and, on top of that, I looked Indian. Recalling the principal's words, I wondered what he meant when he said they're not like us. Did he mean foster kids or did he mean Indians? Well, it didn't make any difference. If my own mother didn't love me, why should anyone else?

Just then, Lady, who had been sniffing around behind me, came up and licked me on the face, as if to say she loved me. That made me cry. Anytime now I was going to leave and I would never see her again. I would never see Chieftan again. I would never see all the Kittys again. I wished with all my might that I had never been born. "Why do I have to be alive? Why?" One answer that came to me was that I didn't know how to kill myself, painlessly.

On my last night at the Gerards, I was on my way to the stairs off the living room when I heard a documentary about the Negro struggle for equality. Not wanting to talk to Mr. and Mrs. Gerard, who were already watching, I stopped at the doorway. The special told of how

KKK members committed rapes, arsons, and even murders against the Negro people and anyone who worked on their behalf. Three civil rights activists had already been murdered. At the end, Martin Luther King Jr. gave a moving speech, "I Have a Dream." That's when I went in to sit down on the couch, next to Mrs. Gerard.

After the documentary, I silently went up to my room with tears in my eyes. What people did to each other could be so, so cruel. Lying in the safety of my bed, I wondered what it must feel like to always be in fear, never knowing when a bunch of crazy men in white sheets would come to rape you, beat you, burn you out, or even murder you. Being an activist took courage and strength and belief. I had none of that. I was a coward, happy that Indian people in Canada didn't have to go through those things. And if it ever happened to me, I would run. In my own dreams I stabbed people simply because I thought they were going to harm me.

Yet King's words made me want to do something for others—to go south and stand up to the bullies. But besides being a coward, I was only fourteen. I would never be a great person. I would surround myself with no one, no people, no animals, nothing. If I didn't care about anything, I could never be hurt again. Still, underneath it all, I had this idea that some day I was going to do something meaningful.

*

Kit's words came back to me, and I kind of knew what he meant when he said that what you do spreads out from your centre. Martin Luther King Jr., the Kennedys, all those others who fought for or who gave up their lives to achieve civil rights, they did it because they cared. They had compassion. What I had in common with them was that I cared, too. I just tried to ignore it back then. What I also realized now was that having compassion was no good to me if I didn't use it. While I had no lofty ambition to join a civil rights movement, I did have a nephew who could use some compassion. Once again, Kit's words now made perfect sense to me.

"Yo baby, what's up? Ya want some of this black beauty? They say once ya go black, ya nevah go back." The hooker recoiled when the john flashed a badge at her. She didn't wait around to hear what he had to say, but crossed to the other side so he would have to follow her on foot. When she sensed she was not being followed, she breathed a sigh of relief and walked towards Hastings. She had heard that's where the action was and was heading that way anyway when she spotted the potential trick.

Black Beauty—when Dory, her former pimp in Seattle, had laid that name on her, she had resented it, railed against it, until he persuaded her with a hard backslap to accept it. She came not only to accept it but to relish it. After all, she was long and sleek and black and beautiful, so gloriously beautiful. She could have been a model, for Christ's sake, except that no one had discovered her when it counted. Then Dory came along when she was still in high school and he had rescued her from a strict, religious home. He introduced her to the good life of parties and drugs and booze. And he introduced her not much later to johns and tricks and a lifestyle that would have made her mother triple her prayers.

Everything had been going just fine until Danny, her younger brother, came looking for her. He didn't understand that she could never go back to Mama. She was beyond saving. But Danny hadn't given up and his interference cost her business. Dory's patience ran out and he threatened to have Danny taken care of if she didn't get rid of him. At that, Black Beauty walked out and never went back.

As she walked towards Hastings, she thought about her Mama and Danny and about what Danny had said. For a young punk, he was sure smart. Maybe he was right, maybe she could change her life around, begin fresh, finish high school, take a course, a secretarial course, and maybe later she'd ...

She realized someone was honking a car horn and saw a white utility van parked in the driveway she had just passed. The driver was waving her over. Oh well, she could do the daydream thing later and, putting all thoughts of a lifestyle turnaround away, she sauntered over, assuming a coy, sexy attitude. Yeah, attitude counted for everything in this business, and, damn, if she wasn't going to make it work this time, one way or another.

She reached the passenger side and, through the open window, the driver asked if she was available. She began her spiel, "So ya want some of this black beauty? They say once ya go black, ya nevah go ..."

Startled, she watched as the van's side door suddenly slid open. Two men jumped out and forced her into the back of the van. And Black Beauty never did get to see the action on Hastings.

9

The next morning I loaded the truck for my trip and headed out on my journey east, feeling a bit like an adventurer. Now that I had shaken off the self-pity, I focused my thoughts on Leona, what she had done and why, until it occurred to me that it was futile to speculate. Being in a generous mood right now, in an I-love-every-body-in-the-whole-wide-world mood, I even considered a visit with Mom while I was in Winnipeg, if Leona had her address.

Edmonton was my first overnight stop, Regina was the next, and, finally, I was driving into Winnipeg. Traumatic memories came flooding back, washing away my generosity. Foremost was the thought I might see my daughter and not know her, and I could not drive away these feelings of guilt. Rain greeted me, and I checked into a motel on the outskirts, then found a restaurant where I feasted on pork roast.

The next morning, intending to take Michael with me to visit his mother, I went to see Betty Chartrand. She told me that Michael refused to see his mother. I drove to Portage la Prairie alone, stopping only for lunch before I went to the women's jail.

Waiting in a small box-like room reminded me of my childhood years, of family visits at the Children's Aid on Garry Street, of unbearable loneliness, but, mostly, of the time I had been in a place like this.

*

I thought Mount Ste. Marie, a reform school for girls, was to be my final destination as a foster kid. I was sixteen, in Grade 11, when I graced the place with my presence. On my very first night there, two girls got into a fight in the hallway outside the recreation room, and one of them was so vicious I was shocked. After Dr. Coran, I should have been used to violence, but I would never accept it as the norm. Thankfully, for the loser and for my sensitivity, the fight was broken up quickly. The loser turned out to be one of my roommates and she was angry at everyone, including me. That kind of set the tone of how it was going to be in here.

Within days, I was shocked again as I read and half listened to my roommates gossip about others. Just about every other word was a swear word: "Janine had fuckin' slashed herself with a razor blade, again." "Thelma had fuckin' knifed Lynn for looking at her funny."

Even later came the stories about them before they came here, stories that made my own pale in comparison. One fifteen year old had been sexually abused, or "fucking raped," for the seven years that she'd been in one foster home and she was here now because she had run away once too often. Another had been locked up in a basement room when she wasn't at school or doing housework. Not all the girls had hard-luck stories and most of them were here through their own fault, or for following the lead of their boyfriends.

I soon learned that one of my roommates, Wanda, was one of the most feared girls in there. On the outside, she ran with the North Enders, a tough Winnipeg biker gang. Once when I was in line at the food counter, three bullies from a competitive biker gang lined up behind me. They began picking on me, telling me to "get my fuckin' ass in gear." Wanda was serving us and, when she heard them, she growled at them, "Quit the fuckin' shit or you'll have to fuckin' deal with us later."

That took the heat off me as they exchanged barbs with each other, but Wanda was the one who had the upper hand. I sensed that the three girls just wanted to preserve their status in front of everyone else.

Wanda and I were alone in our room one day and she started a conversation with me, without peppering it with all the swear words. "Hey kid, what are you in for?"

"They said I knifed the man in my last foster home."

"And you didn't, right?"

"Well, no one's done what they've been charged with, right?"

For some reason that sent her into a fit of laughter, and she dug out her cigarettes and lit one, even though we weren't supposed to smoke in our rooms. "What you got going for you, kid, but not in here, is that you really do seem innocent. I can't see you spitting at someone, let alone knifing 'em."

"They said I had a history of creating problems. If a person really, really is innocent, how can they convince others?"

Wanda blew smoke out and said, "Sorry kid, you don't. You just make peace with yourself about that and you don't care what anyone else thinks." She handed me the cigarette and asked, "You scared in here?"

"Sometimes."

"See? That's what I mean. The others, they always say no. Give you some advice, kid. Best way to deal with this place is to mind your own business."

It was advice I didn't need because I had already been minding my own business. After I was finished with the chores assigned to me, I came to our room and did my homework or read. I never watched TV because that meant having to go to the recreation room where the other girls were gathered.

One thing I learned in there was that no one ever cried, because it was a sign of weakness. But one night I couldn't help it, I was feeling so sorry for myself. Tears started rolling down the sides of my face, dripping onto my ears, and, when I began thinking of all the bad things that happened to some of the others, I cried even more, as quietly as I could.

"Hey kid, what's up?" Wanda's loud whisper and sudden appearance beside me startled me and made us both laugh. She pressed some tissue into my hand.

"I was just lonely and then I started thinking about the bad stuff that happened to some of the other girls. It kind of piled up, I guess."

"Well, kid, as long as you're in here, you got to put your heart away."

That was Wanda's last piece of advice to me. The next day she was released and, two weeks later, the school's grapevine brought the news that she had been murdered by her boyfriend. We were in the dining room when I heard it and I left to go back to my room to sit on my bed. I tried to cry, but the tears wouldn't come. By then, I guess, I had put my heart away.

To my great surprise, Leona and Mom came to visit me around Christmas time. In spite of myself, I was so happy to see them—they were like the first bit of sunshine to come into my life. After we hugged and were seated at the table, Leona said, "I don't believe a single word they told us." She took a cigarette out, lit it, and offered it to me. Some of the other inmates and their visitors were watching us, no doubt because of Leona. I took the cigarette, but said nothing. The last thing I wanted to do was to try to convince Mom I was innocent.

"I take that back. The only true thing they said was that you were here. Otherwise, we wouldn't all be here," Leona corrected.

"Are they treating you okay, Christine?" Mom asked.

"Oh yeah, everyone's okay here," I answered.

"We only found out you were here last week," Leona said. "All this time I thought, we both thought, you didn't want to see us again for some reason. When I found out you weren't at the Trunce's anymore, they said you were moved to West St. Paul. And when I tried to set up a visit, your worker said you didn't want to see us."

"You mean Miss Branzil," I said, as I concentrated on not going into a coughing fit from inhaling cigarette smoke.

"So what did happen, Christine?" Leona asked. "No, don't answer.

I didn't come here to grill you. I just want to see you, make sure you're okay." She waited for me to say something and, when I didn't, she continued: "When I couldn't get anywhere on the phone, I took a day off work, went down to Children's Aid and told them I wouldn't leave until they told me where you were. The supervisor came out and sounded surprised that we hadn't been told you were here. All that wasted time! Can you imagine that?"

"Oh yeah, I can imagine that very well," I said.

"So when he told me why you were in here, I told him you would never do something like that, unless you had a damn good reason." Leona blew smoke out angrily. "So what did happen? Sorry, but if you had a good reason, then you shouldn't be in here."

"I can't tell you anything."

"What do you mean you can't? Of course you can. Or is it that you just won't?"

I eyed her, recalling how telling her about the priest a long time ago had gotten us separated. Telling her anything wouldn't solve problems, only create new ones. But more than that, I truly believed that if Children's Aid went to see the doctor because of me, he would do more outrageous things. And get away with it because he was a doctor and a real smooth talker. He was going to keep his daughters living at home forever, and no one would ever know what was happening to the women in that family. But then the idea of them living there like that just didn't seem fair, either. Damn it, what did I care? That they were prisoners was their own doing.

"Chrissy, this stuff is going to go on your record. You must have had a reason for taking a knife to that woman and for slashing that man."

I did cough then—and not from the cigarette. "If you really think that I did that, that's your problem." I was angry with Dr. Coran and Miss Branzil and even Mrs. Coran, not at Leona, but she was the one here in front of me.

"I'll go get us some coffee," Mom said. Incorrectly, she thought I would spill my guts if she left us alone. At the counter where tea and coffee were available, she began talking to one of the other visitors, whom she seemed to know well.

Leona leaned forward and said, "Chris, tell me what happened. I won't tell anyone else if you don't want me to. But tell me, okay?"

I stared at her long and hard, and then I said: "You won't believe any of it. It's all too unbelievable."

"Try me."

Exhaling my cigarette smoke, I relived the six months that resulted in my being sent here.

When I finished, Leona whispered, "Oh my God!"

Seeing Mom approaching, I hurried to tell of the doctor's final threat to me.

"Oh, Christine! That's just horrible!" Leona exclaimed.

Mom was at the table now and, as she set the coffee cups on the table, she asked, "What? What is it?"

Leona looked at me, silently asking permission to tell her. Shrugging, I suddenly felt tired, worn out. After Leona told the story, Mom turned to me and said flat out, "I can't believe any of that. Not after the time I went out on a limb for you about your priest and it turned out you were lying."

Her words stung.

"Mom, she's not lying. Christine does not lie." Leona looked at me apologetically and said, "I'm sorry. I should have known." She had put her hand on mine.

I smiled to my mother, but it was not a nice smile. "Mom, do me a favour. Leave and don't come back." With that, I stood up to head back to my room.

"Chrissy, don't go. Please." That came from Leona, but I ignored her.

The next time I saw Leona was around Easter time. She had come many times before, but I had always refused to see her. This time she had been adamant in seeing me, relaying a message that she had something urgent to tell me. I had been so happy to see them last time, but when Mom had turned on me, it was as if they had both turned on me. Maybe that was because I was jealous of Leona. If she had been the one in my predicament, Mom would have gone to her grave believing every word she spoke. But, of course, women like Leona never got into predicaments the way I did. Because I was so lonely, and now curious, I relented, but first I made sure that Mom wasn't with her. We exchanged greetings and lit up smokes. This time I was mentally prepared for more betrayal.

"Chrissy, you're going to hate me more than you do already," she said.

"I don't hate you, Leona. I love you. I hate Mom."

"Then why wouldn't you see me when I've come before?"

"'Cause I was angry with Mom, and I guess I thought you would eventually side with her."

"Mom's brainwashed by them. You must know that by now. And I said I believed you, always have, always will, so I don't think it's fair of you to ... oh, never mind."

"Mom's brainwashed by who?" I asked.

"By anyone in authority, like the social workers. She believes whatever they say."

For a minute I thought about that and then decided I didn't care. To avoid further talk of Mom, I asked, "So why am I going to hate you?"

"Because I told your new worker and his supervisor what you told me, and ..."

"You told me you wouldn't!" I shouted, standing up and making everyone look at me for a change.

"I know," Leona said, completely unflustered by my outburst. "Unlike you, I do lie."

Her calm reaction made me feel foolish and curious at the same time, and I sat back down. "Well, it's not that I haven't lied, myself," I mumbled. That was off the topic, but her demeanour told me she had something good to tell me.

"Yes, well, now that we're clear about that, the important thing

here is that it would have been a crime not to tell the proper authorities. You see that, don't you?"

"Coming from your side of the table, I guess I can see how you
would see that."

She got a serious look then, took hold of my hand, and said,
"Chrissy, you couldn't let that man get away with what he had done."

"So? Please continue." I said.

A smile replaced the serious look, her eyes dancing and sparkling
with merriment: "So you're getting out of here and you're going to
come and live with me. Darn, I wanted to say that at the end."

I sat there, stunned by this news.

"Chrissy, I thought you'd be happy about that."

"I am," I whispered. "I'm thrilled." When I had recovered my voice,
I asked, "So what happened with Dr. Coran?"

"Well, first thing I did … well, that's not the first thing because I
did argue with myself, having promised you I wouldn't tell anyone
else, but, finally, common sense prevailed and I went to your worker,
Miss Branzil, and her supervisor."

Sceptical that Miss Branzil would have listened to the story, I raised
my eyebrows. Leona's next words told me I was right. "Afterwards,
Miss Branzil said you had a history of problems and that lying was one
of your bad habits. When the supervisor seemed like he was going to
believe her, I threatened to go to a reporter—and that wouldn't look
good for Children's Aid. That Miss Branzil, what's with her, she
seemed so uptight about it, like it was her fault."

"I think she was having a thing with the doctor."

"Oh, so that's probably how he knew they were coming."

I was somewhat surprised she wasn't shocked by their committing
adultery, but asked: "What do you mean? Who was coming?"

"The supervisor, Mr. Bancoates, he finally decided to get a court
order or something. Mr. Carruthers, your new worker now, since
Miss Branzil so conveniently disappeared, well, he told me they called
in the cops, got a court order, and went to visit the Corans."

"How come they never came to me?"

"I don't know. Mr. Carruthers did say that you would have to testify against the doctor. You are up to that, right?"

"Damn right, I'm up to that," I said, relishing the thought. "Did they arrest him?"

"From what I last heard, no. He wasn't at his office, him or his daughters, so maybe Miss Branzil warned him. Mrs. Coran broke down and she's been placed in care. She ended up in a mental institution. And the other thing they found ..." Her voice trailed off and she said, "I don't know if I should tell you this."

"You can't just stop now."

"You had a bathroom to yourself, right? Downstairs, next to his office?"

"Yeah. So?"

"Leona sighed and said, "They found a peephole into the bathroom."

The picture on the wall, hanging at an odd angle, now made sense, and also the reason why only Darcy was suppose to clean the bathroom. I might have discovered the peephole. "What a pervert," I said, without much force. Imaginary worms crawled over my skin and I shuddered. "So he and his daughters disappeared?"

"And Miss Branzil, too. According to Mr. Carruthers, she walked away from everything she owned. Imagine having an affair with a foster father—too much!"

"And poor Mrs. Coran went crazy, so he got away."

"I'm sure they'll catch him. And even if they don't he's lost everything—his house, his practice—everything. So that's justice."

Sighing, I said, "I suppose so." But I would have been happier if he was the one who ended up in jail.

Leona dug in her purse and brought out a newspaper clipping. "Now, I didn't go to them. Mr. Carruthers sent them to me. I think he likes me. Anyhow, look at this."

Taking the clipping from her, I noted her picture first and read how she had helped expose the doctor. The reporter and Mr. Carruthers gave Leona all the credit. I gave no indication of the chagrin I felt. I was the one who had lived the nightmare, and Leona was the one who got all the glory. What a life!

*

Now the tables had turned: Leona was in jail while I was the one to come to the rescue. Not of her but of her son, so that was almost the same. The doorknob turned and I watched it open. Leona, devoid of makeup but still beautiful, walked in. I smiled, stood up, and we embraced each other.

She looked at me, shaking her head, "You should never have cut your hair."

"I know," was all I said.

We sat in our corners and a kind of wall came up between us. A heavy, tense silence ensued as I watched Leona stare at her hands in her lap, glance up at me once, and stare back down into her lap—as if cornered. Finally, moving nervously in her chair, she cleared her throat and asked, "Do you know what happened? Why I'm here?"

"Assault."

"Well, that's straight to the point. My lawyer figured I could get off, but I didn't want to go to trial. A plea-bargain got me eighteen months. Simple."

"For you, maybe, but what about Michael?"

Her shoulders sagged and she pulled out her cigarette package from the pocket of her sweater. "I heard he asked to live with you. That's why you're here, right?" Taking a minute to light her smoke and inhale, she continued, "I did everything I could to provide for him, to keep him with me, to keep him from going through what we did, but I guess it wasn't meant to be."

"Hey, I just stopped with the self-pity crap, so don't you start." I looked around the room and said, "On the other hand, this place doesn't induce much else, huh?" We smiled and the feeling of awe I once had of her surfaced. To see her in here now, the way she was, made me want to cry for her. "What about Nick? How come you couldn't call on him?"

"Nick's long gone. We never kept in touch. By now, he's probably married with three children."

"And he knew you were going to have his baby. What a jerk."

"Now are you happy you didn't end up with him?"

"Not with the way it happened." I winked at her and we smiled. That part of my life I could now accept, except for the part of having lost my own child by him. "So how come you assaulted a man?"

"I had to and that's all I can say about that, so don't ask for details, okay?"

"That's not okay, but I can't force you to tell me. Michael's social worker told me he doesn't want to see you. Did you know that? Is that acceptable to you?" I asked with a forced sarcastic edge to my voice. Leona seemed just too passive, and my attempt to nudge her out of it had no effect.

"Of course not, but I can't do anything about it. I'm just glad he's going to live with you." She exhaled smoke.

Briefly, I wondered if she was really glad, but then it was time to get to the other reason why I was here. "I do need to know some things. You left Colin in February, right? So, at least tell me what you did then."

"I left him 'cause he slapped me. I packed our bags and we took a bus back to Winnipeg. We stayed at Mom's for a while and then I took up with this man, the one I was accused of assaulting."

"But you got someone to phone Kit's place and ask for us to come to Fort St. John. In the middle of April."

A confused, surprised expression appeared on her face. "In the middle of April I was sitting in jail here."

"You never got anyone to leave a message for us at Kit's place?"

"No, I didn't, and I wouldn't have, because I knew that you didn't want me around. It was in your attitude, the expression on your face, the tone of your voice, the way you ..."

"Okay, okay, I get the picture. It's true, because I didn't trust you," I said.

"From the way you acted, I thought you hated me. Did you?"

"I didn't hate you, but I didn't trust you either," I said, toying with the idea of telling her about my suspicions of her and Peter being together.

Thankfully, she stopped me by saying, "So I didn't even want to go back to visit you after last summer, but Colin dragged me there. I think he wanted us to make up, and that was one thing I found endearing about him. Bottom line is I had nothing to do with a phone call. Why? It's sounds important."

Something crawled up my arms and the back of my neck. Kit and Mona would not have been mistaken about a call, and if Leona hadn't asked someone to make that call that took Peter and Todd to their deaths, then who had made it? Studying Leona, I wondered how I could get her to tell me everything that happened to her so I could decide for myself whether she somehow inadvertently had something to do with Peter's accident. Again that question: If Leona didn't have someone make the call, who had? Me? Impossible. I would remember something. But then another angle of what happened to Todd and Peter began to formulate in my mind.

Leona was staring at me curiously: "What's so important about a phone call?"

I shook my head that it wasn't important and, going back to that Sunday at Shadow Lake, I tried to remember my every movement after I landed in Fort St. John. All I could recall was that I had been happy that day, not freaked out.

Leona was talking and I missed the first part of what she was saying, " ... and Michael, well, I just don't know what to do for him."

"He has to be really confused." Having no solutions for her, and with my mind focused now on a new ominous possibility, one that I had previously rejected, all I could do was offer the usual words of comfort. And hide my need to leave immediately.

"He'll be happy with you guys up there. He should be with family."
Her voice caught and she turned away.

That's when I told her about Todd and Peter. "There's just me left."
She stopped, turned back, and asked, "What?"

I swallowed, "There's just me up there. Michael doesn't know yet."

Leona stared at me and asked, "What happened?"

"Peter's truck ended up in the Peace River and Todd was with him.
They still haven't recovered … their bodies." As I said this, I began to
tremble.

Leona leaned down to hug me. "Oh God, I'm sorry, sis. I'm so
sorry."

"I, uh, didn't tell Michael's worker. She might not have let me take
him back with me."

"How are you feeling, though?"

"I'm okay now and time's going to help, I guess. But I feel like I've
been to hell and back." Hesitating briefly, I went on to tell her about
almost being a suicide statistic and about my incredible meeting with
Wapan. "I wanted you to know all about that before I took Michael, so
if you don't want me to, I won't take him. And I still have to tell him
about Todd and Peter. He might change his mind, once he knows."

"Don't let Michael change his mind. He really does need to be with
family."

On the drive back to Winnipeg, I thought about that word, family.

Leona had given me Mom's address and, before our visit, I had
every intention of going to see her. But now I had these other thoughts
to sort out—the one ominous possibility that came from eliminating
other possibilities. And I knew I couldn't add to my distress by going
to see Mom.

I O

As I drove back to the hotel, I tried to figure out if I was crazy. Peter had a collection of psychology books and, during my years with him, I had read books about kids who had been sexually molested or abused. In later years, some of them had developed split or multiple personalities. Some had become schizophrenic or psychopathic, but, for the most part, it seemed that these adults had endured incestuous deviousness, not molestation from outside parties. Then, again, as a three year old, I could have considered a man who at first seemed to care about me to be a surrogate father and a friend.

The other thing was that in families where sexual deviations occurred, a history of mental illness was evident. As far as I knew, my mother was an alcoholic, but she wasn't mentally ill. On top of that, Leona showed no signs of being mentally ill, except for her promiscuity, and, okay, she was in jail for assault. Maybe I had inherited something from my father.

Since I could account for all my waking moments on that Sunday, I could only have done something when I was sleeping. Perhaps I'd gone into a fugue state and snapped, from being so emotionally stressed when I found that Peter was gone, presumably to race to Leona's side. And that Sunday night, when I had woken up in the truck, it was not parked in its usual place, so I must have driven it somewhere. And I had cut off my hair with no memory of doing that, so maybe I was crazy. Maybe I had harmed my own son, just as I had my firstborn by abandoning her.

Somebody called Kit's place and, since it wasn't Leona, that left only me. Maybe I had made it through the emergence of another personality, to test Peter. Maybe I had always had another personality. Truth was that ever since Leona had reappeared on the scene, I was reminded of what happened with Nick. While Nick no longer mattered, Leona's betrayal did. More than that, I was reminded that I had given up his daughter. Some things could happen all over again, and the threat could have triggered another part of me into action. Maybe I resented Peter because he could hurt me, but, again, I couldn't imagine that any part of me would harm Todd. This healing journey of mine was not going well. One step forward, two steps back.

At my motel room, I looked in the yellow pages and phoned a doctor's office. Getting straight to the point with the lady who answered the phone, I said: "I think I have a split personality and I would like to talk to a psychiatrist. Do I have to be referred by a family doctor?"

"Is this a joke?" she asked.

"No, it's no joke. It's urgent that I know how ..."

"Okay, yes, you would have to see your family doctor first. Have you seen Doctor Langdon before?"

"No. I was just phoning to find out what the procedure was. If I came in, how long do you think it would be before I could see a psychiatrist?"

"You would have to see the doctor first and he would let you know. I really can't answer that."

"Okay, thanks." I hung up, chagrined that I could not get a quick analysis.

Later, after supper, I took a long hot bath, trying to analyze myself some more. The source of my problems had been my sexual deviation as a three year old and, then again, my part in what the priest had done when I was seven. Leona had never been victimized that way and yet, as an adult, she had been sexually amoral and I was the one who had become something of a puritan. That was the only abuse I really had, plus what had happened at that doctor's place. But there, I had finally fought back. The bottom line was that my childhood experiences would not have caused me to have a split personality or any other uncontrollable mental disorder. True, I had a tendency to succumb to self-pity, but that was more of a bad habit and I could work on that by myself.

The experience with Nick and Leona, and subsequent actions such as the first suicide attempt, those were things that happened in my adulthood. While that had been one hell of a traumatic time, it would not have caused me to flip out now. By the time I got out of the tub, I had reassured myself that I had nothing to do with harming Todd and Peter. Someone else had made the phone call that had led to the accident. Someone else was involved, or it was a horrible accident.

The next day I was sitting in a restaurant across from Michael. Betty had brought him here, straight from his foster home, and at my request had left us alone. When he had come in with her, he had slid into the booth across from me without a word. Alone with him now, I had no idea of what I should say to him. So I tried this out, "Mrs. Chartrand says you're looking forward to coming to live with ... uh, up at Shadow Lake."

"Better than being shoved from one place to another."

We sat there silently, until a waitress came to take our order, then resumed our awkward silence. I had talked to hundreds of kids, well at least a dozen, who were Michael's age, but I couldn't find any words for this troubled, moody twelve-year-old boy in front of me. He had changed so much in the short time since I had last seen him.

Service was fast and our meals came quickly. Our utensils hitting our plates were the only sounds from our booth. When I was finished, I wiped my mouth with a napkin and said, trying to drum up a casual conversational tone, "I'm really happy you're going to come with me, Michael." Sounded pretty phoney to me.

"But?"

"No buts on my part. But ... okay, except for one. A major one. That you should know about before we leave."

"Peter doesn't really want me to come? Because of what my mother did?"

I paused, surprised at the depth of his wound. I wished fervently that I could relieve him of his pain.

"Or is it just me?"

"It's nothing like that at all." With effort, I kept control of my voice. "Michael, Peter and Todd, they're gone."

Michael looked up at me puzzled, perhaps wondering if we had split up.

"They both died in an accident. Peter's truck went off the highway into the Peace River."

"I'm sorry," he mumbled, no doubt feeling awkward about giving sympathy. "I'm real sorry." He blinked quickly a few times and I turned to look elsewhere. If he showed tears, I knew I would cry too.

When I regained my composure, I said, "I wanted you to know that in case you wished to change your mind about coming to live with me."

"Would you mind if I still came?"

"I'd like it very much if you did."

"Mrs. Chartrand made it sound like it was the both of you."

"She doesn't know about Peter and Todd. I wanted you to have the choice of coming or not."

Michael gave a sad smile and vaguely nodded his approval. I had no idea whether I was doing right or wrong, but I would not risk a decision that came from the outside. "So when do we leave?" he asked.

"This afternoon. Mrs. Chartrand is taking us to see a judge so I can sign some papers and become your legal guardian. Then tomorrow, on our way back, we can stop in Portage so you can see your Mom—"

"I don't want to see her. Could we just leave tomorrow?"

"Sure. But Shadow Lake's such a long ways away and you should really take this chance to see her before we go."

"What for? I got nothing to say to her."

"Then just listen to her side of the story."

"I know all about her side of the story. And if she wasn't a slut, she wouldn't be in jail."

His anger towards Leona startled me.

"I know enough and I don't ever want to see her again." He had a contemptuous look in his eyes. Then he asked, as an afterthought, "So do I still get to go with you?"

"Of course," I said immediately.

Still wearing a defiant look, he took a single cigarette from his shirt pocket and lit it. Fully aware that this action was a display of petulance, I bit back the expected objection. Plus, a single cigarette in a pocket showed that he wasn't a regular smoker, and, maybe, he was even hoping I'd stop him before he gagged on the cigarette.

Unfortunately, the well-dressed middle-aged busybody sitting across the aisle with three other women didn't understand any of this. Glaring at me, she said, "You're not supposed to let him smoke, you know." Then she turned on Michael and demanded he tell her his age.

In a low voice, I said to Michael, "So we'll probably be heading west tomorrow after lunch, so just ignore her and she'll go away."

The lady refused to be ignored. "Well, how old are you!" she demanded, still glaring at Michael. That rankled. If I had been a cat, my tail would have been swishing back and forth. Not being a cat, all I could do was drum my fingers on the table, but this was a lady who did not read body language. So I said through gritted teeth, "Lady, mind your own business."

"It is my business when I see youngsters smoking underage. You people let your young run wild and do anything they want and we're the ones who have to clean up after you."

"Lady, I'll give you five seconds to shut up and then I'll dump that plate of spaghetti on your head so you'll know what cleaning up after us really is. Okay?" I turned to give her back a taste of her glare. Peter had once told me that when I got angry, my eyes turned black with rage and, if looks could kill, mine would. It was all a bluff, of course.

I had heard that nowadays, if you even poked someone, you could be charged with assault.

The busybody looked away and grumbled in a low voice to her buddies, but said no more to us. One of them who had been smoking did butt out. They were frightened of me, and that amused me. Self-righteous people pissed me off—reminded me of myself in the old days.

Michael put his cigarette out, saying, "Sorry, I didn't mean to start a hassle."

Later, when the ladies got up to leave, the mouthpiece looked at me and shook her head in disgust.

Michael leaned forward and asked, "Would you really have dumped that spaghetti on her head?"

Smiling at the image, I said, "And get arrested? Good grief, no! I just wanted her to back off. She was right about the smoking, though, and that's the really annoying part."

"Well, sorry. But don't bug me about Mom—I mean, my mother."

I looked at my watch. I was expecting Betty back any minute now, so we didn't have time to deal with his decision to reject his mother. Suddenly, I was very anxious to be on my way back to Shadow Lake.

Assuming legal guardianship over Michael was accomplished when Betty Chartrand took us to the law courts building, where a family court judge presided over the signing of guardianship papers. Afterwards, we drove back to my truck on Garry Street and transferred Michael's belongings from Betty's car to the truck. When Betty cheerfully asked Michael if he would be seeing his mother before we left, Michael rudely turned away from her, flashing me a warning glance. As soon as I began driving, he brought out his Walkman and put on his headphones. After about an hour, I thought I might as well have been driving alone, except that I couldn't sing to the songs on the radio anymore or play my own tapes.

In Portage la Prairie we found a motel and, leaving Michael to sulk in his room, I drove to the women's jail to visit Leona. She tried to make me feel guilty for not having taken time to visit Mom, I tried to coax from her the cause of her being incarcerated, and neither of us succeeded. Knowing that Michael was just ten minutes away was disturbing, until Leona began telling me about funny things he had done and about his likes and dislikes.

Driving back to the motel, I was one minute furious with his attitude and, the next, full of sympathetic understanding. He maintained his sullen disposition throughout supper, then mumbled something that I took to be goodnight and stalked off to his room. As I waited for the bill, I was questioning the wisdom of my decision to take responsibility for him because I had nothing to guide me, no person, no experience, nothing. In raising Todd, I had trusted Peter completely to know the correct things to do, and parenting a happy three-year-old child was much easier than parenting a teenager, especially one in a dysfunctional state. I questioned the wisdom of taking Michael to the isolation of Shadow Lake, then decided it was too late to be asking these questions now. The disturbing change in Michael was making me panic.

As soon as we drove out of Portage la Prairie, Michael took his Walkman out again. Perhaps he was angry with me because I had gone to see his mother or because I hadn't forced him to come with me. Late afternoon, the sun was setting and, for much of the time, I had to drive right into it. Tomorrow I would get an earlier start so we'd reach Edmonton before the sun's rays slanted into my eyes. We had almost reached Saskatoon when Michael decided to talk. "Don't you like any music?" he asked.

"Sure, I like all kinds."

"Well, then, how come the radio's off and you didn't play any of those tapes?" He gestured towards a stack of tapes in an open container.

"I thought it would interfere with your music. Won't it?"

"No. When I got these on, I don't hear nothing else."

"Now you tell me."

"Sorry. Wanna hear some of mine?"

"Okay." I was just so glad he was finished sulking that I was willing to listen to whatever he had.

He inserted a tape in the truck cassette and sat back. All of a sudden the sound of screaming electric guitars screeched throughout the confines of the cab. I reached out and shut it off. "Sorry. I like all kinds of music, but not that," I said, glancing over at him. When I saw him grinning, I said, "You did that on purpose."

"Yeah. At the foster homes, I'd listen to my tapes and, like I said, with these headphones on I can't hear anything else. If they called me and I didn't hear, they'd get real mad and they said I couldn't use them anymore. I got this tape and played it and, pretty soon, I got to use my headphones again. So what are you into? Opera? Classical?"

"Don't like opera and some classics are okay, except that I can never remember the titles. Come to think of it, I can never remember most titles of any songs. I've got a lot of tapes there I don't even like, but I thought they had songs I did like."

"What do you like the most?"

"I guess rock, from the sixties and seventies."

"Like Elvis?"

"Some of his songs, but more like the Rolling Stones, Rod Stewart—that kind of stuff. And Disco, I like the beat. I remember the first time I saw Elvis."

"In person?"

"No, on TV. I was around five or six. The parish priest died and was being buried at the St. Boniface Basilica and we went to the funeral. The Charettes left us kids in a reception room where they had a TV, and *The Ed Sullivan Show* came on and Elvis sang "Jailhouse Rock" and another song. I wondered how come they let us watch something like that in a church, with priests and nuns all around. It was just so ironic to see Elvis before a funeral—of a priest." I glanced over to see if that put a smile on his face. It hadn't, but he looked through his tapes, inserted an Elvis tape, turned up the volume, and sat back to the sound of "Burning Love."

When we started out, I had wondered what we could talk about. Unlike Peter, I had never had the knack for easy conversation. Part of it was that Peter genuinely liked people, whereas I was distrustful and suspicious, and part was that I'd find myself racking my brain for something appropriate to say, always without success. Peter told me I should try to think of common interests. Michael and I had only his mother in common, and talking about her was off limits. Now music had broken the ice and seemed to soothe him. We drove on, listening to the tapes, and sometimes Michael would tell me things about the singer or the band before he played them.

That night in Saskatoon, over supper, Michael was the one who raised the subject of his mother. Perhaps he felt safe because we were far enough away from her, or perhaps because we were far away, he was missing her now. "So you and Mom grew up together, huh?"

"Part of the time. Then I went to live on a farm with the Gerards and your Mom stayed at the Charettes."

"How come?" he asked.

Listen, kid, you're asking one too many questions, I thought. Tell a truth or a lie? I compromised. "I guess I was harder to get along with."

"You don't seem hard to get along with," he said.

Smiling, I thanked him for his kind observation.

"So how come you and Mom didn't see each other for, what was it, twelve years or something?" he asked.

"Well, we grew apart and just went our own ways. Strange family life, huh? I hope you don't go the way we did."

"I'm an only kid," Michael pointed out needlessly.

"I meant when you have your own family."

"Anyhow, it can't be such a bad thing. You don't have to worry about anyone else's problems."

"It's a lonely way to live, Michael. Safe but lonely. I used to think that exact same thing. But then, if Leona, your Mom, hadn't contacted me, I never would have met you."

"But that's what I mean. You wouldn't have the problem of having to know about our problems."

"Yeah? So I'd live an isolated life at Shadow Lake or, for that matter, in the heart of Vancouver—big deal."

"But you're a writer, published, and you've got fans, don't you? And Mom said you travel and meet lots of people."

"Yes—and they have their own friends and families. My books might be in their houses, but I'm not. You know the sunset we saw earlier? It was beautiful, wasn't it?"

"It was okay. Blinding."

"Not quite the response I wanted. But at the lake it would have been awesome and it would have given the observer a good feeling inside. And that's a feeling you could share with someone close to you, not something I could share with readers. For one thing, I'm not that good a writer and, for another, you would have to have been there. How I feel about your Mom, the different feelings I've had, I can't share that with my readers because it's personal. I could share it with you—" Michael began to protest, but I continued "—maybe not right now, but some day, okay? And if there's someone else to share the responsibility of having problems, then the problems don't seem so big."

"I don't know, it still seems better to have to worry only about my own problems."

I watched him walk off and ordered a coffee to go. In my room, I turned on the TV, but I began thinking that I was like Michael. He had not gone to see his mother, and I had not gone to see mine. He was angry with his mother, and that's where we split. I wasn't angry with my mother, even though she had helped make my childhood miserable. I simply had no feelings about her anymore. On the other hand, if I could figure out my relationship with my mother, maybe I could help Michael reconcile with Leona.

Because of Mom, I had lived at the Manley's, the Charette's, the Gerard's, the Trunce's, the Coran's, Mount Ste. Marie, and, finally, at home with Leona. I had been at the Trunce's when I got my first realistic picture of my mother, and I let my mind drift back to that time.

*

With Martin Luther King Jr.'s speech still ringing in my ears, I watched through the rear window as the Gerards' farmhouse and buildings became smaller and smaller. Earlier that morning, before anyone else was up, I had gone outside to spend what little time I had left with Chieftan and Lady.

I was taken to the north end of Winnipeg, far away from the Red River, to an area where most of the houses were enclosed by white picket fences. The Trunce family lived in a bungalow on a treeless street. I finished Grade 9 at a school where I was surprised to find others like me, Métis and Indian students. Since I had nothing in common with them, I made friends with no one. I took long walks, particularly at night after it got dark, but walking on cement sidewalks was not the same as walking in the countryside along the river. Mostly I thought about the animals I had left behind, and I had no real plans for the future except to go with the flow and try to see that the flow went smoothly.

Occasionally, I would get so lonely, so bored, that I'd forget the promise to myself to avoid relationships and consider writing to Leona. Phoning her meant I might have to talk to Mrs. Charette. One Friday night I couldn't stand it anymore and I did phone her. When the phone rang at the other end, I got nervous and almost hung up. No one could hurt me again, I told myself, no one. As I had expected, Mrs. Charette answered and I asked for Leona. Mrs. Charette asked right away, "Is that you, Christine?"

Lie or not lie? "Yes, it is," I answered.

Leona's worker had probably told her that I had moved again and why. Add the priest affair to that, and her low opinion of me must have sunk even lower. Nonetheless, she sounded friendly and full of concern for me as she asked her questions. I kept my answers brief and she finally called Leona to the phone. "Chrissy! I'm so happy that you called me. But listen, give me your phone number, okay? I was just getting ready to go out and I'm already behind. I'll call you tomorrow, okay? And then we'll talk all day."

I smiled to myself. What else should I have expected? So I gave her a wrong number and said goodbye, meaning it to be permanent.

The following week Mrs. Trunce called me to the phone, saying I should hurry because she was expecting a call. No one had ever phoned me before, so I wasn't all that surprised to hear Leona's voice. "Chrissy, you gave me a wrong number, so I had to call my worker to get your number."

"Oh, did I?" I asked innocently, and added, "I wondered why you didn't call."

"Do you know that you're not that far from Mom? You should go and see her," she said.

"Why?" I asked, instantly spiteful.

"Why? Because you haven't seen her for a while. I know, let's meet this Saturday, okay?"

"I don't know. I'll have to get permission."

"Permission? We'll just meet in a restaurant."

Evasively, I said, "I'll see. I have to get off the phone. Mrs. Trunce is expecting a call."

"Chris, I'll come over on Saturday, okay?" Leona persisted.

Unable to think of an excuse why she shouldn't, I just said okay and told her I had to go. As we exchanged goodbyes, I noted she didn't ask for my address or set a time, so, most likely, that had just been talk.

Saturday came and, had I been a happy person, I would have said it was a glorious sunny day. As it was, such days made me feel more bored and depressed than usual. I found relief only in reading. That's what I was doing when I heard the doorbell ring, followed by Mrs. Trunce's loud voice calling me.

Instantly, I thought of Leona and that we were going to go to a restaurant. I grabbed my money off the dresser and stuffed it into the pocket of my jeans. Suddenly, I was so excited. For one thing, I had never been in a restaurant before. When I got to the front door, Leona was telling Mrs. Trunce that she was going to take me out for the afternoon—not asking, telling. And Mrs. Trunce was being very agreeable. When Mrs. Trunce saw me, she said, "Oh, you should go change."

I was wearing my usual jeans, an oversized T-shirt, and sneakers. In contrast, Leona seemed to be all dressed up, and I suspected she always dressed that way. Suddenly stubborn, I told them I was fine the way I was and we left. Leona had made quite an impression on Mrs. Trunce. She had been beautiful the last time I saw her, but today she was stunning. Walking along beside her made me feel short and frumpy, and I wished I had changed into something more appropriate. Although she was also wearing some sort of T-shirt, hers was colourful and hugged her figure. With it, she wore a scarf and beige slacks with matching beige heels. It wasn't her clothes that gave her beauty and class, but her natural flair for style. Her beauty started from her eyes, always dancing with a sense of excitement. Inside the house, she had put her sunglasses up on her head the way movie stars did in magazines. Now, although they covered her eyes, the rest of her face was perfect, with a mouth that always seemed on the verge of a smile. And her hair! How could we be sisters? While my hair was long, straight, coarse, and black, hers was soft, fluffy, and light-brown, streaked with blond highlights, and today she wore it loose and bouncy.

Her every movement was graceful. I turned my attention to the way she walked and tried to copy it. Moving her legs from her hips, she almost glided along, with no up-and-down movements. In comparison, I felt I was racing along to keep up as she took her long, sure forward strides. Her head was held high, and the overall impression was that of a lion. Cat-like, yeah, that's what she was like. She had a feline grace, and it suddenly hit me that her name was Leona. Leona the lioness, queen of—well, not Africa, queen of North America.

We got to the bus stop just as a bus was pulling away. The driver must have seen Leona because the bus screeched to a stop and, as we got on, he couldn't resist flirting with her. I was invisible to the men in their seats, some of whom turned to stare at the cat-queen in front of me. Pride swelled up in me as I saw that people appreciated Leona's mere presence. We sat at the back and some guys started a conversation with her. I got to thinking they must be wondering why this beautiful woman was with this little Indian girl.

The Main Street bus driver was dour and would not have cared if Elizabeth Taylor got on his bus. Finally we got off near Portage and Main and walked to a restaurant. Once we were seated in a booth, Leona dug out a package of cigarettes and asked, "Want one?"

"Okay," I said, and clumsily took one out of her package. She lit it for me with a gold lighter and I inhaled cautiously, for I had never tried smoking before. A lot of kids at school had smoked, but I was always an outsider. Right away I got dizzy and had to hold back a cough. She was watching me with amusement, so I confessed, "I never smoked before."

"I can see that. You're supposed to inhale, like this." She took my cigarette and inhaled deeply, then blew smoke out with the greatest of sophistication. I tried it and did end up coughing and choking. Boy, this was going to take a lot of practice.

The man who had been behind the counter came to our table and said with some sort of accent, "Ladies, what can I get for you?" His eyes were on Leona.

Leona looked at me and asked, "Are you hungry?"

I didn't know how much food cost, so I shook my head, no, even though it must have been lunchtime. I had two dollars and thirty-one cents in my pocket.

She told him to bring us menus, and he couldn't race away fast enough to do her bidding. I saw that I could afford a few cups of coffee and, when I looked up at the man to give my order, I saw he was watching Leona intently. When she pushed her hair back casually, I thought he was going to swoon. I was amused. Leona looked up at him, straight into his eyes, and fluttered her mascara-thick lashes. "Hmn, I can't decide right now. Just bring us some coffee. Coffee's okay, Chrissy?"

I nodded.

The man, anxious to please her, said, "Okay. Just take your time. I make whatever you want, special, just for you." He raced back to the coffee pots and poured coffee with quick efficient movements. He returned to our table with the coffee cups, lingered for a moment, and returned to his post behind the counter, staring at Leona whenever he could. He didn't care that I was watching him watch her. To him, I didn't even exist.

Leona said, "Mom's going to meet us here."

"Do you and Mom go to restaurants often?"

"Yeah. We never meet at Children's Aid anymore. We can wait for her before we eat. How's that?"

Shrugging, I said, "Doesn't matter. I'm not hungry at all." And I tried hard not to stare at her. What impressed me was the way other people treated her, as if they were as awed by her as I was. If I were to be an invisible attachment to her, I was prepared to take that role just to be around her.

"So what's new in St. Albert?" I asked, just for something to say. I took my cigarette from the ash tray and carefully inhaled. Again, I got dizzy as she told me what was happening with different kids I had known. When she got out a cigarette for herself, the waiter was right beside her, holding a light for her. I wondered if he knew how foolish he looked.

About three cups of coffee later, Mom walked in. She was dressed in a colourful summer dress and high heels. She wasn't as tall or as magnificent as Leona, but in that restaurant she was second. Her skin colouring in winter was almost fair, but now both she and Leona had healthy-looking tans. Her hair was blue-black, but, unlike mine, it was a mass of curls.

By now I figured that the man behind the counter was the boss and he had overridden his waitress by serving our table himself. He was back at our table before Mom was even settled in beside me, delaying her greeting to us. As he put a menu down in front of her, he said,

"I hope you don't mind my saying so, but you are the two most beautiful ladies ever to come into my restaurant."

That made me wish I wasn't here, and my amusement at watching him fawn over Leona evaporated. Mom thanked him and asked for tea. Once he was gone, she turned to look at me. "Christine, it's been such a long time. How are you?"

"Okay." I had never been able to talk to Mom with ease, and found myself uncomfortable once again. One of the reasons, I figured, was that I wanted to ask personal questions, such as why Leona and I looked so different. How come I looked like an Indian? Were Leona and I half-sisters? And who was my father? I wished for the millionth time that I was fair-skinned. I sat a bit sideways so I could watch Mom and Leona interact. I wanted to learn what they talked about. Mom took her cigarette package out, and the boss-man was right there again with a light.

I was resigned to the fact that I was, and always would be, an outsider, beginning with my own real family, so I sat back to listen and to watch. And to learn. Somewhere in their exchange I realized that another reason why I couldn't take part in any casual conversation was because I had too many secrets. That's what it was. On top of that, my interests in animals and reading were too boring to talk about. Leona was now telling Mom that she was still earning some money as a model for a hair stylist, and that's why her hair looked better than average. She was also into sewing her own clothes. Her home economics teacher had been a fashion model and she was urging Leona to try that out, even giving her a contact. Leona had told me none of this, but now she was telling it all to Mom.

They were ready to order, so Mom signalled to the boss-man, ordered their food, and asked me what I wanted. I could afford only one more coffee. "Just another coffee," I said.

"You have to eat something," Mom said. "You're so skinny." She turned back and ordered a hamburger and fries for me.

After the man left, I whispered anxiously to Mom, "Mom, I've only got a dollar thirty-one now."

She looked at me, looked at Leona, and they both started laughing. Mom turned back to me and said, "Christine, I'm your mother. I'm paying for this."

I had been so worried about not having enough money that I was filled with gratitude. "Oh, thank you," I said gratefully. Mom turned back to Leona, shook her head, and they both laughed again. I got kind of mad that they were laughing at me. By the time our food came, I was famished and tore into my hamburger with enthusiasm. Mom told me not to eat so fast, and I sensed I was a source of embarrassment to her. They had both ordered meals that needed forks and knives. They cut their food into tiny little pieces and managed to look sophisticated even as they ate. When we had all finished eating and our dirty dishes had been taken away, Mom turned to me and said, "So Mrs. Turner told me why you had to leave the Gerards."

I didn't want to talk to her about that in front of Leona. I had already told Leona that the Gerards couldn't afford to keep me anymore. That they could not afford to keep me because of my bad reputation was something I had kept to myself. I just looked down at the table.

"Christine, I know it wasn't your fault," she said. Surprised by her unexpected support, I looked up at her, again grateful. After lighting up a cigarette, she continued, "But you shouldn't let boys take advantage of you." Poof, my gratitude vanished and the usual resentment settled in its place. Mom's voice marched on. "They only want one thing from you and then, once they get it, they throw you away."

"And that goes only for me, right?" I asked sarcastically. She would never say such a thing to Leona because boys, and men, could love Leona, but they would only ever use me. That's what she really meant. I hated my mother. Hated her! Thanks to her, I wasn't in awe of Leona as much as I had been. "I have to go now." Mom stood to let me out, rather than risk my making a scene by pushing her out. I was so angry and I wanted to show it. The only petty thing I could think of was to put all my money on the table and say, "That's all I've got. I'll pay you the rest later."

Leona reached out, putting her hand on mine. In a soft tone of voice she said, "Chrissy, don't be like that."

I stalked out of the restaurant, thinking of how nicely manicured her fingernails were, long and coated with a glossy beige polish. At the bus stop, I suddenly realized I had no money for bus fare. I had two choices: one was to go back into the restaurant and ask Mom for some of the money back ... No, that wasn't an option. I started walking.

When I got home, Mrs. Trunce scolded me mildly for being so late and for not being there to help with supper. Everyone else had gone out and I started washing the supper dishes. Mrs. Trunce dried and asked me about Leona. She thought I had had a happy visit.

Gee, how could I not have a happy visit when I had such an over-whelmingly wonderful sister? Just throw in a mother who wished I wasn't her daughter, a mother who was always willing to believe the worst of me, and that would turn a visit into a—a what?

"If you scrub that pot anymore, you'll make a hole in it," Mrs. Trunce was saying when I finally came back to the present.

Suddenly, I smiled and said, "I was thinking of Mom. She has a way of pissing me off." Mrs. Trunce wasn't at all like Mrs. Gerard and Mrs. Charette, and worse swear words were part of her everyday speech.

"Oh? You saw your mother?" Mrs. Trunce asked.

Oops, I wasn't sure if I was supposed to get permission first from Children's Aid to see my mother, so I said, "Yeah, we ran into her. That's how come she pissed me off."

"She made you angry. She didn't piss you off," Mrs. Trunce said.

"Actually, she did both," I said. I looked at Mrs. Trunce as I dried my hands and grinned. She just shook her head. I had never really said more than two words to her before, so that exchange made me feel a bit better. In my room I tried to concentrate on my book and forget about the "family" visit.

As I lay in bed, my mind drifted, recalling the day's events, and now I was thinking about Mrs. Trunce. She had a rough edge to her. She smoked and swore, and whenever she got angry, there was hell on earth. Here we didn't have to go to Mass if we didn't want to, and the school wasn't a Catholic school either. Not going to Sunday Mass was supposed to be a mortal sin, but I had long ago given up on counting my mortal sins. At least, here, I was among others who had mortal sins. I kind of wished Leona was bad because I was sure going to miss her after we both died. Leona with her life of purity at the Charette's became Lovely Leona, and I dubbed myself Christine, the Corrupted. Didn't really match, but I was too sleepy to think of something better.

Leona and I got into the habit of seeing each other more often, and she never urged me to see Mom again. She told me that Mrs. Charette wanted me to come for supper, but I flatly refused to go back there. Whenever she told me personal things, I was all ears, hoping to spot a mortal sin. Going to bed with a boy would be a mortal sin, but she never went that far.

One evening after supper we were walking down Main Street, intending to walk all the way to Graham, where she would get a bus to go back to St. Albert. I would then get a bus to return this way and go back to the Trunce's. Suddenly, Mom came out of a hotel with an ugly old man. She was giggling and talking in a high-pitched screech, her makeup was smeared, and her hair was all frizzed out in different directions. The man had an arm around her waist, and I didn't know if they were walking funny because of him or because of her. Shocked by this sight, I stopped, but Leona stepped forward with a greeting. Mom, seeing her, said, "My baby! Whacha doing here? Oh, this is my baby girl."

"Your baby? Looks all woman to me," the old man said as he leered at Leona. "Where you been hiding this little honey of yours?" he asked Mom, but his eyes remained on Leona. Both Mom and the old man swayed from side to side, unable to stand still in one place. "Yeah, you a real honey, eh?" The old man's arm went from Mom's waist to reach out for Leona. Because he was so unsteady on his feet, his hand missed her arm and landed on her breast. To my surprise, Leona was not at all revolted, but Mom yelled at him to keep his paws off her baby. I didn't know if she was really angry or just pretending to be.

Remaining ten feet back, I took in the whole scene. My mother was drunk enough to cozy up to the foul-looking old man. And what was with Leona that she let his hand linger on her breast a touch too long? As for him, the one word that described him was pervert, and there he was, laughing at himself for his obvious clumsiness. Mom was still screeching when our eyes met. That stopped her for the moment: she could tell that I was judging her and, for one brief moment, she seemed embarrassed.

The old man was saying to Leona, "Come on with us. We're going to get some beer and go to your mother's place. We're going to have us a party." Then he was rubbing Leona's arm up and down while using her as a leaning post at the same time.

Leona disentangled herself from him and said she had to go home. She told Mom she'd see her later.

We continued walking in silence, then Leona said, "I'm sorry you saw her that way."

"Have you seen her like that before?"

"Yeah, lots of times. She changes as soon as she starts on even one beer."

"Well, what about that man?" I had imagined Mom would have had good taste in men. With her looks, I thought she would go only for good-looking men.

"What about him?" she asked.

"Is he her steady or something?" I couldn't imagine that, but anything was possible.

Leona laughed. "Chris, when you live to drink, you don't really care who you're drinking with."

"Or who's buying the drinks?"

"I guess," Leona responded. We walked a ways before she spoke again. "Don't judge her, though. She doesn't have any reason not to drink."

I never replied to that. Having seen my mother as she really was brought satisfaction that I had been right about her all along. At last I could feel superior to someone else, and I silently relished the feeling.

Winter came and, in January 1966, Leona turned eighteen. She was still living at the Charette's and would be until she found herself a place. She had a job as a waitress and was doing some part-time modelling for a catalogue. One Saturday we got together and she told me about a plan she had which made every one of my resentments towards her disappear. She wanted me to move in with her. We talked about our futures. I would go on to university, because Children's Aid would pay for that. I didn't know yet what I wanted to be, but Leona said I could be whatever I wanted. Then we'd both have jobs and we'd buy a house together. Right on the Red River I said, and she agreed. We would buy brand new furniture and we'd get our drivers' licences and we'd each have our own car. I asked if I could have a dog and some cats, and she said I could. Life was going to be absolutely wonderful.

We went to my new worker, Miss Branzil, with the idea, and Miss Branzil went to her supervisor. A few weeks later she told Leona that Children's Aid felt I needed more supervision than what Leona could provide. When Leona told me about it, an anger settled over me. She tried to appease me by saying that we'd live together as soon as I was out of Children's Aid, but nothing she said could make me feel better. I wanted to live with her now and not have to wait another two and a half years. Leona suggested that Mom could maybe take me back, but I said no to that right off. I'd rather live in foster homes than with my mother.

My anger was with Children's Aid, but I could only exhibit it at the Trunce's. I stopped doing my chores, I talked back to Mrs. Trunce or didn't talk at all, and I did a whole lot of other little annoying things. At school I made friends so I would have places to go, people to see, and things to do. Weekend parties were the norm and, once I started going to them, I never worried if I was out too late. Then the late nights became whole nights and, sometimes, I didn't return to the

Trunce's until Sundays. Mrs. Trunce's fury was hard to take, but I managed to shut most of it out by simply not caring. She never beat me up but she would call me a slut, to which I would say, "Like mother, like daughter." That wasn't to imply I was her daughter, but for some reason that infuriated her more.

Finally, she told me what I wanted to hear: she was going to get Miss Branzil to move me the hell out. I hadn't planned out the strategy, but when she said that, I was elated. Children's Aid had to give in and let me move in with Leona at last. I had won!

*

Moving in with Leona hadn't happened, of course. I had jumped from the frying pan into the fire, right into the hellhole that was Dr. Coran's home. No one, not even Leona, had known then how devastating it had been when Children's Aid refused to let me live with my sister. Michael should not be in foster homes and I knew now, without a doubt, that taking Michael to live with me at Shadow Lake was absolutely the right thing to do.

I I

On Sunday night we stayed in Edmonton and the next day I was impatient to be on our way because, tonight, I would be sleeping in the comfort of my own bed. When we arrived in Fort St. John we stopped to eat a light supper and, lacking the energy to do more, we picked up only a few groceries. By the time we were ready to leave, the skies had become overcast and I hoped it wouldn't rain. Luck was with us and, late that evening, we were finally driving into the yard—and that's when my luck ran out.

The cloud covering made it very black outside and I pointed the head-lights of the truck towards the porch, so we could see our way in. Intending to go straight to bed and planning to unload the truck the next day, I carried only the groceries in. Inside, with Michael right behind me, I flicked on the light switch and discovered a mess of major propor-tions. Something had been inside and had ransacked the cupboards, and flour, sugar, molasses, syrup, and other torn packaging lay scattered across the floor. "Damn—I mean darn—racoons must have gotten in."

Michael, still behind me, tapped me on the shoulder and I turned to look at him. "Is that your idea of a bear rug?" he asked in a low voice, pointing towards the darkness of the living room.

Puzzled, I turned to look in that direction, and there lay a choco-late-brown mass of a nightmare. The grizzly looked kind of groggy, or maybe that was my impression because it hadn't come charging right at us—yet. I dropped the bag of groceries and we both dashed for the truck. I drove to the front, where I could aim the headlights at the front door, and, yes, it was wide open and very inviting. Nothing happened when I honked the horn, tentatively at first. So I pressed again with a bit more authority. When the bear still didn't bolt out the door, I pressed again, long, hard, and demanding. I wanted to go to bed. But the bear remained inside. Honking the horn like that, I was probably scaring it and preventing it from leaving the way it came. I backed the truck to its original spot.

"Maybe it doesn't remember how to get out," Michael whispered.

"Maybe it knows the laws of homesteading," I said, "and I'm not going to serve it an eviction notice right now." The idea of stretching out in the luxury of my own bed had invited drowsiness on the last leg of our journey. Now I was fully awake, and all we could do was sit in the cold, uncomfortable, cramped cab and wait.

"I think it's moving," Michael said, breaking the silence. Rolling down my window a bit, I could also hear movement inside. "Oh shoot, I should have brought those groceries back out," I said with regret.

"Yeah, and some pillows and blankets while you were at it." Michael reached for our jackets from the back, handed me mine, then tilted his seat all the way back and covered himself with his jacket. I put mine on backwards and kept my eyes on the door. "I'd hate to be a cop. They do this all the time on stakeouts."

In the morning I awoke because Michael was poking at me. He was anxiously pointing outside my window, so I looked to my left and all I could see was blue sky with puffs of white lazily drifting eastwards. Just as I was about to sit up and pull my seat forward, the bear's head popped into view. All that separated us was a glass window. Right away I told myself, "I'm not scared, I'm not scared, it's only Lady looking in," so it wouldn't get a fear scent and try to bully us. Did I say bully us? Make that tear us to shreds. The bear plopped down on all fours and casually sauntered away.

"He just wanted to thank us for supper." Michael's sense of humour eased my fear and we both went inside.

"Yeah, well, do drop in again, but not in our lifetime," I said, trying to match him. "How long was it there?"

"It was there when I woke up. Maybe Winnipeg wasn't such a bad place after all." Michael unloaded our luggage while I looked around and tried to decide where to start.

Showing him to his room was easy, so that's where I started. At least I had closed the bedroom doors to keep the mosquitoes out—if only I had made sure that the front door had been locked. Looking at the good side, I was thankful that the bear hadn't relieved itself before it left. Returning to the kitchen to start a fire and heat up some water, I noticed through the foliage the flash of sunlight against glass, and then Kit's old truck rolled into sight. Not wanting them to see the mess inside, I went outside to greet them. Kit, Mona, and Amber all got out and we stood outside making small talk.

When it didn't look like I was going to invite them in, Kit asked, "Coffee on?"

"Um, I can make some. Come in, and I'll see if I can find some." I led the way back in, embarrassed to let them know that a bear had breached security.

All four of us silently took stock of the chaos, with me almost acting like this was the first time I saw it. Amber walked around, taking care to step only in the clean spots. "Boy, you must have thrown one heck of a welcome-home party."

Michael came out of his room and said hello to Kit and Mona.

Amber paused to look at him. "Hi. My name's Amber." She continued stepping around, looking at the mess. "Either that, or you are one lousy housekeeper, Mrs. Webster."

"It's good that you can joke about it, 'cause, as a good neighbour, you won't mind helping to clean it up," Kit said with a mischievous twinkle in his eyes.

"Well, on the other hand, it doesn't look half bad in here after all," Amber shot back immediately.

"Too late," Kit said, then turned to me. "We thought we heard you go by last night, so we came to tell you to be careful. A grizzly's been sniffing around nearby."

"Well, it sniffed its way right inside here."

"Most likely the meat I left for the wolves," Kit responded. "But don't worry, you're back now so he'll stay away."

"We should call him Stay-Away Joe," Michael piped up. He and Amber exchanged smiles, but we only looked at him, blankly.

"That door was locked," I said out loud to myself.

"And I'm sure I locked it, too." Amber said.

We all turned to stare at her.

"On Friday. I came over here, checked everything out, and looked to see if you had any dog food left because we ran out of the proper food." She walked over to the kitchen door to have a closer look at the lock.

"That's not the door that was open," I said.

"But it's the only door I used," she said.

"Then it is very strange because I know the front one was definitely locked."

Kit walked over to the front door and checked. "It wasn't forced open."

"Did you hear anyone drive by?"

"No, and we didn't go anywhere. But we don't always notice, either."

Kit went outside and studied the ground as we started cleaning up. When he returned, he said, "Can't tell if there are strange tire tracks. It rained yesterday, on and off."

Now apprehensive, I looked everywhere to see if anything was missing. Looking over our desks, I didn't miss it at first, but the second time, it registered. Peter's manuscript had been on the top right-hand corner of his desk. Now, the binder was gone. "Peter's manuscript is missing and I know I put it there."

"I didn't take it. Honest. I wouldn't do that without asking," Amber said.

"Oh, I believe you, don't worry. They didn't take the rifles or anything else that was valuable. But someone else was in here. Someone else with a key."

My words as I said them sent chills up my spine. Peter? Had Peter staged the accident? But how could Peter move around out there without being recognized? Still, they hadn't found their bodies and, by now, their search should have come up with something. To take my mind off Todd and Peter, I began to clean up. Unable to stop myself, my thoughts returned to the mystery of the missing manuscript.

By the end of that day, everything was pretty much back in order and I'd restocked the supplies after a trip to Dodging. Amber insisted on coming with us, and I suspected an intense curiosity about Michael was the reason. On our way back from town, I dropped Amber off and Lady came happily to the truck. For now she belonged to Amber, so I thought of ignoring her but I couldn't. I missed her so much, but I couldn't think of a way to ask if she could come back home.

That night I looked everywhere very carefully, but the only thing missing was Peter's manuscript. This time I knew that I had not done something with it in my sleep because, when I left, I had taken one last look at the interior. I remembered clearly the binder being on his desk, because I had considered taking it with me. This was more than mystifying; it was downright creepy.

Within a week of Michael's arrival, we had a system going. Morning times, we gathered and cut wood, and afternoons, Michael went canoeing or fishing or hiking through the woods, often with Amber and Lady, while I read books. On nice days, we ate our meals down at the lake, sometimes with the company of Kit's family. It was a relaxing atmosphere and I was sure Michael had to force himself to be moody.

Amber came over one day, towing a saddled horse behind her, and asked Michael if he wanted to go for a ride. Michael, agreeing immediately, went to mount from the right side as Amber and I watched. She rolled her eyes upwards and said, "Don't tell me you've never ridden a horse before."

"Oh sure." He stopped, looked at me, and added, "Not really."

"Well, around here, we mount on the left side."

"What's the big deal?"

"The big deal is that a horse gets used to it and knows if you know how to handle it. Otherwise, he'll try to be the boss."

As if to support her theory, when they started off, Michael's horse began backing up. A surprised look appeared on his face and he yelled, "Hey, it's stuck in reverse. It won't go forward."

Amber stopped and looked back at them. "Don't be pulling on his reins so hard. That's what makes him back up."

After that day, Amber came over more often to give Michael riding lessons. They usually stuck to our road, as it made a really nice riding trail, and they rode back and forth between our place and hers. When Michael got better at it, Kit took them up into the mountainous region to the west. Afterwards, Amber and Michael were able to follow Kit's trails.

On one such day, Colin and the tall bearded stranger from the restaurant came to visit. Putting my book aside, I offered them coffee, but they declined, saying they were in the area and thought they'd just drop by to see how I was doing. Although introductions had been made before in the restaurant, Colin introduced us again: "Chris, this is Howard Norach."

Because of Howard's presence, I didn't tell Colin that Michael was living with me now and that Leona was in jail. Colin asked me all the usual questions appropriate for my circumstances and again offered any help he could give. They left, leaving me to wonder why they had stopped by in the first place. Colin had probably wanted to know if I'd heard from Leona and, if so, he should have come alone.

In the following days, whenever I was alone, I went for walks on what I now thought of as the wolf trails, hoping to see some signs of the wolves. I worried because I had not seen any tracks. One day a soft rustling of leaves alerted me that I was being followed, and a feeling of dread wiggled up my front, over my forehead, and down the back of my neck. I sent a prayer upwards that it please not be the grizzly, knowing I had to turn to see, but not wanting to. We had seen no bear tracks anywhere in the vicinity for the last couple of weeks, which made us think the bear had been as traumatized as we had been and had taken up residence in the next county. Ready to accept my fate, I turned quickly and was relieved to see only the wolf pups.

The black one, with a look of surprise on its face, was on the trail, having stopped as soon as I turned. I caught a glimpse of the grey one disappearing into the underbrush. The black pup was much larger now and had lost its scrawny look. Wapan did not seem to be around. I continued my walk, ignoring the young ones, but wanting more than anything to try to make friends with them. For their sakes, I knew I couldn't. Continuing my walk, I glanced back to see if they were still following and was relieved to find they had both disappeared.

One night I woke, alarmed, and wondered what it was that had roused me. I got out of bed to check the front rooms. The doors were locked, but that didn't mean much now. I had been meaning to ask Kit if he could change the locks, but forgot. Returning to my room, I heard groaning sounds come from Michael's room. Listening closer, I thought I could hear him pleading, "No, no, no, get it off me. Get it off."

When I asked him about it the next morning, he said he couldn't remember having any kind of dream. I didn't believe him, but I didn't pressure him for more.

A few weeks after I saw the pups, Michael and I were piling wood when a feeling of being watched came over me. Scanning the area, I saw Wapan, sitting near the edge of the woods, and I swear she had a smile on her face. When I called to her, I was amazed that she came trotting towards us. I dropped to my knees and let her make the first move. After she had nuzzled my hands and sniffed at me all over, I ran my hands over her rough fur and noticed Michael staring at us with an open mouth.

"That's a wolf!" he finally exclaimed in a low voice.

"It's Wapan, the mystical, magical wolf of Shadow Lake. Kit named her Wapan. That means 'It is dawn.'"

"You guys have tame wolves around here? What about Stay-Away-Joe? Is he tame, too?"

"No. They're all wild and free. Come over and introduce yourself."

"Won't it be scared of me?"

"I don't know, and it's a she." Wapan's head turned to Michael and her tail-wagging paused, then continued. "Don't be scared."

"I'm not scared," Michael said.

"No, what I mean is that wild animals can scent fear."

"Well, I'm really not scared." Like me, Michael dropped to his knees so he was face to face with Wapan. She went over to him, licked his face, and behaved as if they were good friends. "This is neat," Michael said, more to himself than to me. The little black one came galloping along but stopped about eighty feet from us, sitting there with a quizzical tilt to its head.

"That's one of the pups she looks after. I never touch them because they should be afraid of us. There's another one, a grey one. It licked my hand once."

Michael was grinning from ear to ear as he marvelled, "She likes me!"

When Wapan decided to finish her brief visit, she headed towards the black pup, boxed its ears, making it squeal, and they vanished into the woods. Unlike Lady's bouncy gait, Wapan seemed to travel on air with her long loose strides.

"I think she just scolded it for coming out in the open," I said.

"I read that wolves always avoid people," Michael remarked, staring at the now vacant tree line.

"Wapan's special, unique. And she took to you, just like that. Now, that was amazing."

"Yeah, but how come? How come she came when you called her?"

"Because I'm special and unique," I said, jokingly. "No, I fed her before I went to Winnipeg to get you and I guess she remembers that."

"So all you did was feed her?"

"Yeah, but we're not really supposed to."

"How come?"

"Cause if they think we can feed them, they'd always come around and then, some day, they might hurt us."

"Like Lady."

"Yeah, but I can't see Wapan doing that to Lady. I don't know. Even if she did, her family lived here long before we came, so we're the trespassers. See, we're supposed to let nature takes its course, meaning that I was supposed to let them starve to death. I couldn't do that. If Todd were still here, I would still have fed them, but we would have taken the food into the mountains, much further away from here. Kit already started doing that, so I'm surprised they're still around here."

"Why couldn't they hunt on their own?"

"They hunt in packs. And Kit thinks government people killed her family. So if they overrule nature that way, than I don't feel so bad about having fed them. Besides, she helped me a lot more than I helped her ..."

"Is that why Amber has Lady now?"

"Yeah, partly that, and I didn't think I'd be staying here for long."

"But how could you be friends with an animal that tried to kill your dog?"

"Like I said, it might not have been Wapan. It could have been a coyote, a stray dog, or even another wolf. And even if it was Wapan, wild animals have their reasons for doing things and we don't know what they are most of the time. And we should either accept that or get out, I guess."

Fortunately, Michael did not ask how Wapan had helped me, and I turned the conversation to the pups. "Those pups, I hope they learn to hide from us, or hunters will get them for sure. Kit hasn't named them, so I'm going to call the black one Midnight. And the grey one I'll call Shadow. What do you think?"

Michael shrugged. "Sounds okay. Yeah, I like the name, Shadow."

I watched him return to work and, for a change, he was smiling to himself. Wapan had worked her magic, once again.

He rummaged around feverishly in the bin and was delighted when he pulled out a half-eaten pizza loaded with everything. Oh yummy. He hadn't eaten since yesterday morning—or was it the morning before? He couldn't quite remember—only knew he was so hungry that his stomach was gnawing on itself. He took a big bite, curled it over, and put it in his jacket pocket, so he could savour the feast later. Best time of day to go digging through the bins for food was after lunch and dinner. Jake didn't realize that it was Sunday and that the pizza had been discarded on Friday. So, to him, after lunch was the best time 'cause all those snots threw food away. Didn't know a good thing when they had it.

Jake had it once, the good thing—a wife, two children, a job, two cars, smart clothes, the whole enchilada. Then, at a stag party, when he was feeling no pain, he'd tried heroin. From that point, the road downhill was quick and painful. He lost his wife and children, his cars, everything—and now he lived on the streets of Vancouver.

He was making his way down the alley when the sun's rays reflected back from a large broken wall mirror leaning against a building. He approached it for a closer inspection, speculating whether it was salvage material or not. Abruptly he stopped, startled, when he saw his reflection. Although he was only forty-two, it was a man who appeared to be in his sixties who squinted back at him.

From behind, a white utility van rolled into view and stopped, and

Jake turned as a younger man came around from the passenger side. "Hey man, this is your lucky day. We got a little job for you, if you want it."

Jake became suspicious. No one did good deeds for street people. "What do you want?" he asked, his gruff voice not used to much conversation.

"We're doing research. Just want maybe an hour of your time. To answer some questions. Pay you twenty bucks," the man said, grinning.

Jake didn't like the grin. It reminded him of a shark's grin—not that he'd ever seen that, but he could sure use a twenty. "Okay. But make it quick."

The young man led Jake back around the van to where he said they kept their recording equipment. He opened the sliding door and helped Jake climb in. The piece of pizza fell to the ground before Jake could catch it, and he thought, "Ah, it was rotten anyhow. I'll buy me a fresh one after this."

The van began moving, and Jake never did get a chance to buy himself that pizza.

12

To stock up on firewood, we went further into the woods north of the cabin. About a mile and a half north, a deep gorge that might once have been a stream ran from west to east, and Peter had said it was the boundary of our property. Since I wanted deadwood or freshly fallen trees, we cleared and widened the deer trails for the ATV and trailer, and towed load after load back to the cabin. When Amber and Lady came with us, the work got disrupted as Michael and Amber played hide and seek with Lady and drew me into their games. Along the sides of the gorge they found small caves formed by tree roots and rock formations, and Michael found a large one well hidden by bushes. I would never have known it was there, but Lady sniffed him out as soon as I let go of her.

Back at the cabin, all the logs had to be cut to size and split, the fresher wood going into one pile, the dead wood into another, and kindling wood into a third. Cutting wood was hard, sweaty work, made worse by the swarm of mosquitoes that kept us company.

Nagging at me while I worked was my financial situation. Our royalties had come in March, and Peter had always made sure they carried the basics through the year. Earnings above that would be limited from now on because organizations had generally wanted him, not me. The motel rooms, gas, and food had not been in the budget, neither was getting the road ploughed. I could get a sleigh to attach to one of the snowmobiles to bring in supplies and ask Kit if I could park at his place. Other than that, all I could do was carry on with Peter's budget.

In the third week of July I received a visit from Howard Norach and, this time, he came without Colin. Michael was on the lake, fishing, while I was in the hammock, reading and half-listening to the radio. When he said, "Hello there," I was so startled that the book jumped out of my hands.

Embarrassed, I grinned at him as I sat up, took the book he had retrieved, and said, "You must think I'm always lying around, reading."

Returning my smile, he said, "If you can do it, why not?"

He asked how I was and said he hoped I didn't mind his dropping in like this. As he spoke, he moved a lawn chair around so he could face me as I sat on the edge of the hammock. At first our conversation was one between strangers first meeting, but he worked it in that he found me fascinating. He had even read all he could about me and had bought all my books—all three of them.

"So you have children?" I asked. His children were grown and he was a widower. While his hair showed no signs of greying and his face was mostly unlined, I guessed he was older than he looked. Not liking where he was heading, I started talking about Todd, how I had tried to write for his enjoyment—even though he loved rhymes more—and then about Peter.

"You must miss them very much," he said.

"I do. Every single day. It'll probably take me a lifetime before I ever stop thinking about them and missing them."

"I believe you," he said, taking hold of my hand. He sighed and added, "I wish I could do something to take away your pain. But I know I can't, so if I can do anything else for you, anything at all, let me know."

You can let go of my hand, I thought, and I withdrew my hand as politely as I could. As replacement, all I could think of was to ask whether he wanted a coffee or tea and hope he'd say no.

"Coffee would be nice," he said.

He followed me up to the cabin and, not wanting him to come in, I pointed to the table and bench in the porch and said, "We can have it out here. I'll be back in a minute."

He was the kind of person who would look at everything inside, making me more uncomfortable than I presently was. Plugging in my new electric kettle, I returned to the porch and slid onto the bench opposite him. "Peter built this, isn't it nice?"

"Yes, it is. So he was a carpenter, too?"

"Yeah, once we moved up here, he got into it. He built the garage and the summer kitchen."

"Very impressive."

"I helped," I said, to fill in the awkward moment of silence.

"Even more impressive," he said, smiling.

More small talk, and then I heard the kettle whistling. Over coffee, he asked me about my childhood. He had read that I lived in foster homes, and now I was writing such wonderful stories for children. I began to talk about my animal stories, but he seemed more interested in what my foster families had been like. To avoid details, I just said that they were okay, but I really didn't like thinking about them.

Again, he reached out to me and covered my hand with his own. "It sounds like they were not all okay."

And, again, I removed my hand and covered the awkwardness by offering him some oatmeal cookies. He accepted, and I could have kicked myself. When I returned, I worked at keeping our conversation impersonal, wishing he would just leave. When he finally did, I realized that I had learned nothing about him, except that he was a widower and he was now alone. Okay, he was just a lonely old man looking for some company.

At the end of July we celebrated Michael's thirteenth birthday. I invited Kit, Mona, and Amber to a bonfire. We had baked potatoes with onions and carrots, and hot dogs and hamburgers made from deer meat. With the music blasting, Amber made a reluctant Michael dance and, later, I put on some tapes of jigs and polkas so Kit and

Mona could dance too. The sounds of human laughter combined with music were sounds I hadn't heard for a long time.

In August Wapan came to visit, but this time she seemed nervous. Approaching us, she stopped to sniff the scents to the north of us, retreated, returned towards us, and finally retreated to the cover of the underbrush. Michael and I walked towards the bushes and stopped on the edge. Wapan came out again and greeted us. As I was kneeling, I was surprised to see further back through the foliage another large tan and grey adult wolf, watching us anxiously. Movement of foliage behind him meant that the pups were also back in there. Michael's attention was on Wapan and he missed the sighting. Not even considering that the strange wolf might have been a female, I was excited that Wapan had found a mate. With another adult wolf, it would be easier for her to hunt.

Leona had sent two letters to me so far, mostly just to ask how everything was. Michael received weekly letters from her which he silently took to his room as soon as I handed them to him. Once I had asked what she wrote about, and he said nothing important. She was still a taboo subject, and he had never written back to her. I'd heard him groaning through the night again a few times and tried to talk to him about it, but that seemed to be another subject he didn't want to discuss. His good moods came only because of Amber or Wapan.

Over the past couple of months I had noticed a change in some of the people in Dodging. They had spoken to me, even joked with me, when Peter was around. Their vocal sympathy right after Todd and Peter's accident had now become silent hostility. Mrs. Martens, who owned the grocery store, gave me back all my books, which were there on consignment. I looked down at the top book and saw it looked well used. She explained that a few people had returned their books and she'd had no choice but to refund their money.

Michael, Kit, Mona, and Amber went to the Fall Festival in Fort St. John one Saturday. Wanting to avoid anyone who might eye me with suspicion, I chose to remain behind. After lunch, I imagined everyone

else was having fun at the festival and, to break the boredom, I drove
to town to check the mail.

One of the few people who did want to talk to me was Mrs. Springer,
the local reporter. For the past few months I'd been avoiding her because
she had gone to the RCMP about me. Even though it may have been for a
good reason, I still resented it. She must have believed what she thought
she saw because she didn't want to see me enough to drive out to
Shadow Lake, as if she was scared of me. Now she had left another message in my mailbox, and I promptly dropped it into the garbage bin.

The return address on one of the envelopes showed Al and Iris
Roberts' names. That set me to thinking about them on my drive
home. They no doubt wanted an update on Peter and Todd. Al was one
of Peter's flaws—a misplaced loyalty. Peter and Al had grown up in
West Vancouver together. Iris had delighted in flirting with Peter, first
when we'd lived in Vancouver and saw too much of them, and later
after we moved up here and Al brought her along for his two-week
hunting trips.

Behind their backs, Peter and I had fights over both of them, but
that was a long time ago. To be honest, I think I was mostly jealous
because they were part of Peter's history, but I also disliked them
because I thought they had racist tendencies. In addition, Iris didn't
even like animals. When we first got Lady and they had come up, she
wanted us to keep Lady outside. "Animals don't belong in the house,"
she claimed. I had given Peter my warning look, and he distracted her
on to something else. But throughout their visit she complained of all
the doggie hair and the doggie smell, until I shut her up by complaining about all the tobacco smell. Both she and Al were chain smokers.

I recalled one time when they were visiting and Peter and Al had
been out all day, hunting. That night, as we were playing cards and Al
was drinking too much beer, he said that the smell of gunpowder was
like looking at girlie magazines. Iris chimed in, "Oh yeah? Maybe I'd
better go out with you boys tomorrow. Wouldn't want you messing
with some squaws."

A moment of tense silence followed and, realizing her gaff, she looked at me and said, "Would we?"

Staring back at her, I replied, "I really don't care what Al does." That was the best return volley I could think of.

But then Kit got them good. One evening he had come over to bring a part for Peter's truck and Peter had invited him in. Since Kit never drank alcohol, I made him tea. Peter went to put the part in the garage, leaving the four of us alone. Al cleared his throat and, with a slow pronunciation, he leaned towards Kit and asked, "Good hunting up here, chief?"

Kit slowly shook his head. My impression was that he was shaking his head in disgust. Like me, I think Kit couldn't believe this guy was Peter's friend.

"Al ..." I began, but I caught a look from Kit and could see he didn't want me to say anything.

Kit looked thoughtful for a minute and then he began gesturing with his head and arms, pointing to the southwest. In a deep low voice, he spoke: "Good hunting that way. But first, must go this way. Then that, around big mountains." He paused, as if trying to remember the directions. Peter had come in and, hearing Kit speaking like that, he looked at me. I silently told him to stay quiet. Kit resumed. "You stay on trail, fourteen, maybe fifteen hours. Hard to get lost if you stay on trail. Then you see sign. Much good hunting there. Much good hunting for you."

Still articulating his words, Al pushed on, now also gesturing like Kit. "What kind of game? Moose? Deer? Elk? What kind of game? Me look for deer. Good deer-hunting there?"

My initial outrage had turned to amusement and I had to keep a grin off my face. Kit frowned, thoughtfully, "No. No deer. Maybe a few. Me go now." Kit noisily slurped up the last of his tea and stood up. He nodded to both of them and said, "Chow!"

I almost did laugh out loud then, but I was able to keep a straight face as I looked at Kit and echoed, "Chow." So Iris and Al said, "Chow," too. Al never realized that Kit had given him directions for Vancouver.

When I got home, I tore the envelope open and read the two notes inside. They each offered me help: from Iris, come on down and stay with us a while; and from Al, if you're ever strapped for cash, let me know, we'll wire it to you. It was their sincerity that struck me, and that brought tears to my eyes. Peter had always known this side to them. Peter would never have done anything evil. He was not the one who had taken the manuscript. He was dead. They were both dead.

No, I was not going to tumble down into that hole of self-pity. Slipping my favourite Rolling Stones tape into the cassette, I turned up the volume and went outside to chop wood. Exercise would drive away the blues or, at least, keep them in check. I soon got into a rhythm: set up the log on a base log, raise the axe, and slam it into the centre to split the log in half. My concentration was focused on the aim.

A man's voice came from right behind, startling me, and the blade of the axe thudded into the ground. Three men, wearing plaid shirts opened over T-shirts, work pants, baseball-type caps, and work boots, had formed a semicircle around me.

"Didn't mean to scare you. You know where the Rutlands live? We're kind of lost."

He scanned the area, maybe to check that I was alone. One of the others asked, "You got a phone? Maybe we could phone them."

"I'm only the help. I'll go ask," I said, backing away towards the porch.

"The help? No, you're that writer, I saw your mug shot in the papers," one of them said, almost scornfully.

"The writer? Oh, yeah, people are always telling me that," I said, trying to keep the fear I felt under wraps.

"Yeah, you squaws do all look alike, but we know it's you. Nice try." The guy who seemed to be the leader grinned, showing nice white even teeth. His eyes were what scared me. His eyelids were kind of pink, with a fringe of blond lashes, and the blue of his eyes was a dead, pale blue—or maybe that was his soul I glimpsed.

"Michael!" I yelled, above the music. They stopped closing in on me, as they looked towards the porch area, warily. If I ran inside, they'd kick the door in before I got a chance to lock it.

So I took that second to bolt around to the front of the cabin, then to the west side, then towards the back and into the forest, northwest of the cabin. My preference would have been to go east to the well-worn deer trails, but I didn't want one of those men throwing the axe into my back. With their heavy boots on, they sounded like a herd of elephants stomping, stomping behind me.

A plan came to me. Get a good lead on them, circle the area so I could get back to the cabin, back to where the rifles were. I ran, jumping over fallen trees, driven onward by terror, but a small part of me knew I was heading east as planned. Then one of them tackled me from behind, pitching me forward under his weight. The thistles of the briar bush I'd landed on prickled painfully into my flesh. The others caught up and the first stood up, grabbing a handful of my hair to force me to stand. We stood there, breathing hard, and I saw my future—a brutal rape and then death. A shudder ran through me as I tried to think of a way to escape. And then I had help.

To our north, a low growl drew our attention. Wapan was about seventy feet away, her head lowered, the fur on her neck and back ruffled, making her appear larger than she normally was. Further behind her, shaded by the foliage, two more wolves were barely visible.

"Let go of me or I tell them to attack," I said in a low voice. The grip on my hair loosened and the leader's arm went down to his side. Backing away from them, I said, "Lie down—on your stomachs."

"They'll attack," one of them grumbled.

"No, they'll only attack if you don't do what I say."

The three men sank to their knees and did as they were told. When I looked to the north, the wolves had disappeared, so I turned and ran back towards the cabin. Once I was at my road, I increased my speed, fearing they might cut across and stop me from getting to the cabin. Because I was concentrating on the area to the north to my right, I didn't see the man come rushing at me from my left. Suddenly, an arm went across my midriff, stopping me from running. Yelping once in terror, I punched wildly at the body now blocking my way. A voice I recognized was asking, "Hey, hey, hey, what's going on?"

"Howard!" I stopped to catch my breath, then said, "Three men, they … I've got to get to the cabin." With that, I ran ahead and he followed. "What is it?" he called after me.

At the cabin I ran into my bedroom, then to the filing cabinet to get some bullets, loaded the rifle, checked that the safety catch was on, and went back out, ready to face my attackers. Howard followed me around, trying to find out what was going on. While I looked towards the woods north of my driveway, I told him of the three men chasing me and began to tremble. Seeing me tremble like that, he took the rifle, hugged me, and led me back inside.

"It's okay. It's okay. You've had quite a fright, but I'm here now and everything's going to be okay," he said soothingly. "I'll go out and take a look."

"Be careful," I said, and then I moved to the dining-room window where I could see to the north.

He returned a while later, saying he couldn't find anyone or anything, and then he plugged in the kettle to make us coffee. Once he joined me at the table, he spooned two teaspoons of sugar and lots of milk into my coffee as he asked again exactly what had happened. When I finished with my brief account, he said, "I didn't see any vehicles along the road when I came in."

"Maybe they hid it or something. But they were here."

"Oh, I believe you. I'm just wondering why they would have taken the trouble to walk in. That's what they must have done, because there's not too many places to hide a vehicle on your road. How'd you get away from them?"

"A distraction," I said, not wanting to tell him about Wapan. "I should go to town to phone the police. But I don't want to leave here. Michael might come back while I'm gone. And those men might return, too."

"Michael?" he asked.

"My nephew. He's staying with me. He and Kit's family went to the Fall Festival in Fort St. John. I don't expect them back until late, but they might come back early. I don't know." The clock on the wall showed that it was only around 4:00. "Could you go phone the police for me?"

"Of course. Are you going to be okay, here, alone?" he asked, as he got up.

"Yes, I'll be fine."

"Okay. Because . . ." he looked at his own watch and said, "I did have a five o'clock appointment in the area, but I can cancel it and come back."

"That's okay, you don't have to come back. I'll be okay."

"You're sure?" He took hold of my hand and, this time, I found his touch comforting.

I nodded and he walked to the door, pausing once more to say, "You lock these doors and close those shutters."

As he drove away, I locked the doors, closed all the shutters, and moved a chair up to the dining-room window to the east, so I could sit there and watch the driveway and woods to the north. The rifle on my lap gave me a small sense of security. Now that I was alone, I could replay the event in my mind. Wapan had saved my life. Without her intervention, nothing would have stopped those men from raping me. And because they were not wearing any kind of disguise, that meant they intended to kill me once they were done raping me. They might not have been armed, but they could have strangled me. Yes, Wapan had saved my life, once again.

Because of their suspicious ways, I was not looking forward to talking to the police again. By 7:00 p.m. I was beginning to suspect that Howard was a part of what happened, but all my scenarios did not include a motivation for him.

Half an hour later I mentally apologized to Howard when a police car drove into my driveway. I unloaded my rifle and carried it back to my bedroom, throwing the bullets onto my night table. Then I went to unlock the front door, where they were knocking.

13

entally, I prepared for their scepticism as I opened the door to let them in, recognizing Corporal Watherson immediately. He walked in first, followed by an Indian man in uniform who looked a lot like Billy Jack from the movies, but was darker skinned. He was introduced as Special Constable Cormier. At their prompting, I recounted everything that had happened, except that I didn't want to tell them that wolves helped me get away.

"Where did these stray dogs come from?" asked Corporal Watherson.

"I don't know," I said. "See, I fed them before because they looked scrawny and I had meat in the freezer that I wasn't going to eat. And one of them was friendly."

"Can you show us where everything happened?" Constable Cormier asked, pausing from writing in a small notebook.

Corporal Watherson apparently wasn't ready for that yet, so he said, "Before we do that, there are a few more questions I have. I wonder if you had any other thoughts about your husband's disappearance."

Noting his use of that word, instead of "accident," I bristled. "Look, you've implied that he might have run off, but I know he and Todd drowned in the Peace River. I know that and I can't understand why they haven't been found yet." Because I began to tremble, I dropped that subject. "Sorry, the only thing new is that when I was away in June, someone broke in here and the only thing missing was Peter's manuscript."

"You never reported this before?"

"No because it was valuable only to Peter." I swallowed and added, "And you might think he took it and concentrate on that and not look for their bodies, but he didn't take it. He is ... gone. Him and Todd."

Corporal Waterson looked away for a minute and then he said, "I understand how you feel, but there were questions about the accident, so anything to do with him should have been reported to us, right away."

A spark of anger sizzled and I said tight-lipped, "Well, I didn't know that."

Constable Cormier was watching me, and I sensed sympathy and a real understanding in his eyes. "Perhaps we can look over the area before it gets too dark," he suggested. With that he stood up, so I stood up too. If the corporal wanted to ask me any more questions, he could do it outside.

We went out through the side door and I asked, "Do you need to see where I ran, exactly?"

Constable Cormier, nodding, said, "They might have dropped something."

Retracing the route I'd taken, I answered more questions from Corporal Watherson. Then we came to the spot where they had caught up with me. Constable Cormier examined the area thoroughly while I speculated on whether he was part-Indian. Having seen a few Billy Jack movies, I'd always wondered whether that actor was part-Indian or whether he just empathized with Indians. Distracting myself with such speculations allowed me to escape the recent feelings of terror I had experienced. Once he satisfied himself, we continued on to where I had run into Howard.

Just then we heard the rumble of a vehicle coming up the road and, soon, Kit's pickup rolled into view. Seeing us on the road, Kit slowed and came to a stop. Michael jumped from the passenger side and Kit got out as well.

"What happened?" Michael asked, rushing to us.

"Three men came here and they were, um, bad guys," I said, not wanting to mention the word "rape" to a kid his age.

Kit came up to us and said, "Hi, Bob. What's going on?"

Before Constable Cormier could answer, Michael asked me, "Do you think it was the same ones who let the grizzly in our cabin?"

"The grizzly?" This came from Corporal Watherson.

Michael explained, "Yeah, when I first came here. Someone with a key left the front door open and a grizzly got in. I had to spend my first night here sleeping in the truck."

Needless to say, I was no longer trembling. Instead I was feeling great discomfort, even though I had not lied. As far as I was concerned, I had given them all the information they needed, and now Michael was complicating matters for me.

"I didn't want to bore you with all the details, but that was when Peter's manuscript disappeared," I said to the older officer, whose eyes were boring right through me. Wanting them to leave now, I asked, "Do you think those men will come back?"

"From what you've told us," Corporal Watherson emphasized this phrase, "it's hard to determine what their motive was. They knew who you were. If I were you, I would seriously consider staying at the motel in town for a while. Without a phone, you're really isolated out here."

"I can't afford to stay in a motel," I said, more to myself than to him. Besides that, I thought, rapes and murders did occur in motels too. From now on, I'd be on guard. No one was going to drive us out of here.

"Could you come in tomorrow to look at pictures?" he asked.

"I'll come in as soon as I can," I said, still miffed at him for his attitude. I should have told them this, I should be doing that—easy for him to say.

Before they left, both Kit and Constable Cormier said they would come out to check on us more frequently.

Very early next morning Howard was back, saying he'd wanted to return last night but thought it was too late by the time his meeting ended. He wanted to know exactly what happened with the police.

Because I was still feeling apologetic towards him, I told him almost everything I had told them, except the part about Peter's manuscript and the wolves.

Michael came out on the porch, and Howard turned his attention to him, almost as if he wanted to ingratiate himself with Michael. Having just got up, Michael was unresponsive, almost impolite, towards Howard. After telling me he was going to go over to help Amber clean out the horse shed, he went back inside.

Shortly after that, Howard said he had to leave, and I walked him to his van. There he gave me an unnecessary hug, promising he would try to look in on me more often. Withdrawing from the hug as politely as I could, I told him that was really not necessary. Until this moment, he had been more likeable than when he'd first come here, but I was still uncomfortable with his possible attraction to me.

After he left, I returned to my coffee and spent some time thinking about Peter, back to when he'd proposed marriage to me. Although I had never been in love with him the way I had been with Nick, I had never cheated on him. In the beginning there had been temptations, and one time I had seriously considered it, only as an act of revenge against Peter. What I thought was jealousy in the beginning was most likely only my insecurities. I had wanted Peter to love me in a way he loved no one else, but he had never been passionately in love with me and I had never figured out why he married me. We had probably wisecracked our way into it.

Now he was dead, I missed him terribly, I missed our intimate moments, our humorous moments, even our spats. No, the spats we could have done without. Right now, I wished he could be alive, even if it meant he was with someone else. And the wish now was not just for Todd's sake. I felt it in my heart. I hadn't loved him enough. I hadn't trusted him enough. He had never known me, the real me, and so I hadn't given him much of a choice.

Thinking about Peter washed away the discomfort I felt from Howard's interest in me. And then I switched gears and pictured Todd with his father. I thought of Todd, running down to the lake to greet Peter, back from a fishing trip, a big grin on his face.

"What's so funny?" Michael asked, interrupting my thoughts.

"I was just thinking of Todd. He had a way of making me smile even if I was down."

"You must miss them a lot."

"I sure do."

Michael sat across from me at the table and, not wanting me to get morbid on him, he asked, "You know that manuscript that went missing?"

"Yeah?"

"Did you read it?"

"Yeah, I did," I answered.

"What was it about?"

"Well, you know Gregory M. Thomas, right?"

"Yeah, the old detective."

"Right. Well, in this book, *A Dick Named Tom,* Mr. Thomas learns he has a son by an Indian woman way up north, from the fishing trips he took twenty-five years earlier. He's investigating a murder case in Vancouver, gets wounded in action, and spends the remainder of the book in a coma. Meanwhile his good friend and lawyer finds the son, Tom Keesik, as instructed, and eventually Tom learns something about running the detective agency his father owns. Then he takes over his father's last murder case, which leads him back to the north where there's a secret compound of white supremacist maniacs, and, of course, they're involved with the murder."

"Sounds pretty neat. But now that he's gone, it's not going to get published?" Michael asked.

"No, because I don't know what happens in a case like this. Only Peter would be able to make the changes a publisher would want."

"That's too bad, I guess. Well, I better get going or Amber will finish cleaning the shed without me and I'll never hear the end of it."

"I'll drive you. Those three men, you know."

"Does this mean I can't walk this road alone anymore?"

"Only until they catch them."

"That sucks."

"I have to go to Fort. St. John anyway, to look through some family albums. May as well get that over with."

At the detachment, Constable Ringer took me into the same room as before and brought out binders containing pictures. While I was leafing through them, trying to hold pictures of the three men in mind with which to compare, Sergeant Trolley came in carrying a thick file, which he set down on the table.

"Hello again. Are you all right?" he asked, cordially.

"Hello. I'm okay."

"According to Corporal Watherson's report, those three men seem to have come to your place looking for you specifically."

"It seemed that way."

"So you must have some idea of what's going on."

By the thickness of the file, I figured he was including Peter's accident. "I've thought about everything," I replied, "but we kept to ourselves a lot. We couldn't have offended anyone in any way."

He pulled out a clipping from the file and asked, "Have you read this?"

The clipping was a half-page taken from the June issue of the *Peace Valley Voice*, with the continuation stapled to it. The article was by Mrs. Springer, who reported her own speculation as fact, including the point that she had saved Peter from my murderous intentions. I shook my head in disgust as I read on. Her words kicked at me like a mule—no, make that a jackass of the human variety. It explained the hostility I'd been getting.

Handing the clipping back to the sergeant, I said, "I hadn't seen this before."

"I can talk with her if you like," he offered, and that really surprised me.

"No, the damage is done," I said, thinking that someone from here had already done some talking to her about the idea that Peter's accident might not have been an accident.

He told me the usual—that if I thought of anything, to let him know—and then he left me alone with the binders. Speeding up my pace, I finished going through the pictures without coming across any of the three men. If they had had long hair once, and beards, I would not have recognized them anyways. As I retreated back to Shadow Lake, Mrs. Springer's article was foremost on my mind.

I stopped by at Mona's to pick Michael up, but he, Kit, and Amber were out riding in the back 40. Wanting to lick my wounds in private, I declined an offer of tea from Mona and returned home alone.

Later that afternoon, Special Constable Cormier returned with Michael and Amber in his jeep and Kit and Mona following in their pickup. Kit and Mona seemed to know the officer really well, and Kit had told him all about Wapan. One of Constable Cormier's first questions to me was to ask why I had said stray dogs instead of wolves. I told him that if any of this became public, I didn't want people knowing there was a wolf pack in my area. Instead of asking me more questions about the three men as I expected, we talked about Wapan and wolves in general. And he became simply Bob, instead of Special Constable Robert Cormier.

Michael had taken an immediate liking to Bob and they learned they shared a common interest. Bob helped teach karate in Fort St. John and, because that was too far away for me to take Michael, he offered to give Michael some lessons here. Michael looked over at me and said, "You should take some lessons, too, Auntie Chris. You're the one who needs them."

That led to a discussion of what to do in case we needed help, and the talk finally distracted me completely from Mrs. Springer's article. In addition to Kit and Bob coming over at different times of the day, Kit suggested that, if we needed him, we signal by shooting the .22, count to five, and fire again.

That night we tested the plan to see if the sounds could be heard from Kit's place. The next day, when we learned they had, I felt a whole lot better.

Bob came over as often as he could to give us karate lessons. On my own, I would have felt silly, but watching Michael do his *katas* gave me the incentive to learn as much as I could. When Bob wasn't around, Michael coached me so I could stay in shape.

At the end of August, Mona and I had to go to the school to register Amber and Michael. While I was surprised Amber would be staying here longer, I didn't ask why. Preoccupying my thoughts more and more these days was how I was going to earn a living without Peter. Once Michael was in school, I would force myself to write.

In the first few days that Michael was away at school, I did sit down in front of my typewriter, but my mind was a complete blank. On Wednesday night I had woken up, most likely from Michael's nightly moaning, and got up to check the locks. Just before I returned to my bedroom I looked out a front-room window. The moon was high and full, and lit the landscape with a silvery brightness. Staring beyond the moon, I wondered about life on the other planets. We learned and believed that, on most of the planets, life was not possible, but who was to say that life, not as we know, did or did not exist?

Now at my desk, I thought of Mr. VEM J. SUN and his dog Pluto. What if the man from Mars came calling on Earth and found us to be the only racist beings in our solar system, and what if each planet had a turn to send someone to different parts of our planet?

My stomach started growling and I was surprised to find it was already after two. A peanut butter sandwich would be quick, and then I could lose myself in space. What I needed, I was thinking as I spread peanut butter on my bread, were books on the planets, and that meant making a trip to Fort St. John.

I took a bite of my sandwich and was about to clean up when I heard the distinct sound of a man's cough outside. I walked over to the dining-room window to look out. No vehicle was in sight and a prickly sensation came over me as I thought of those three men.

Although panicked, I was able to think through what I ought to do—check the locks, close the shutters, get the rifle, some bullets. Kit and Mona had gone to Halfway River today, so I couldn't signal to them.

Eating my sandwich, I sat on the floor, hidden in a corner of my bedroom. From there I could watch for a reflection of a person in the mirror, if he came around to the west side. No more sounds out of the ordinary came to me, no one trying the door, no footsteps on the porch, nothing except the monotonous ticking of the wall clock in the living room. Finally, I had enough, and I cautiously moved back into the living room. I had waited for over two hours in my corner and, by now, my initial panic was replaced with practical thoughts.

Michael would be on his way to Kit's from school and I had to go to pick him up. Before that, I wanted to make sure there'd be no surprises for us when we got home. Outside, I couldn't find any signs that someone had been here, so I finally conceded that the man's cough had been either my imagination or a passing animal. Because Kit and Bob had made their many sudden appearances, both Michael and Amber were bugging us to let them use the road alone again. After today, I decided, I would still have to keep driving Michael to and from Kit's and they'd have to do their horseback riding around Kit's place.

Since Kit and Mona might still be away, I went over to their place to meet the kids when they got off the school bus. I hung around until Kit and Mona got back, and I told Kit what I thought I had heard. He came over later and checked for tracks, but found none.

On Monday, in spite of his protests, I drove Michael to Kit's for the school bus, and I picked him up in the afternoon. Later, Amber defeated my whole purpose by coming over on horseback, bringing her homework with her. But, at least, she had Lady with her.

They sat at the dining-room table while I baked a lemon meringue pie. Lady was lying at Amber's feet and I thought, "What a lovely domestic scene they make."

Michael looked over at Amber and said, "That Warner, he's pretty friendly, eh?"

"Yeah, he is. Just like Marla, huh?" Amber responded, without even glancing up at him.

Michael grinned. "So you did notice."

"Okay. You got me on that one." Amber smiled to herself. She finally looked up, still smiling. With the sunlight shining on her face from the west, Amber's greenish, tawnyish eyes sparkled and her face seemed lit up from inside. I thought to myself, "My, my, I think that girl's got a major crush."

Whoa, they're only kids, so I cleared my throat to break the magic of the moment and was pleased to see the normal, sassy, impish look return to Amber's face. Feeling better, I snickered to myself silently.

Amber said to me, "All the guys at school are crazy about this Marla." She pronounced the name with emphasis. "She's new in town, just moved here. Real hot stuff. Right, Mikey?"

"I wouldn't know," Michael said, glancing down at his books. He looked up again and said with a mischievous grin, "But I could find out."

Amber made a face at him and said, "Up yours."

Kit had told us that wolves had a larger winter territory that they roamed, beginning in August and September. This was when the younger ones began to learn how to hunt. So, when I heard the sounds of distant rifle shots the following Friday, I was glad that Wapan and her family were probably far away and safe. The other reason why I didn't give those sounds much thought, considering the jumpy state I was in, was that hunting season had started. I was also enjoying the story I was writing. The previous Saturday Michael, Amber, and I had gone to Fort St. John, where I left Michael and Amber in the mall to look for cassette tapes while I hit the book stores and the library.

On Saturday morning Michael went outside to get some wood for the fireplace. His scream sent shivers down my spine. When I got outside, I groaned. On the ground at the foot of the steps lay Wapan. Her beautiful rich grey and tan coat had been soaked in spots with blood and mud, now dried. Michael was standing at the top of the steps, staring down wide-eyed, but tears rolled down his cheeks. Even though I knew she was dead, I jumped to ground level and leaned over her, calling her name. I put her head onto my lap. Wapan, the beautiful, mystical wolf of Shadow Lake, was dead and I wept. Michael finally came down and we both stroked her body, even though we knew she couldn't feel anything anymore.

14

apan's eyes were glazed and her body was stiff, almost flattened. In death, she hardly looked like herself, except for her tan and grey coat. Simultaneously, I was filled with grief and rage. Whoever had brought her here might still be out there, and perhaps we were in their sights, right now. Gently, I eased out away from Wapan, saying, "Michael, I'm going for the rifle. You should come inside. They may still be out there."

Michael shook his head, no, and said, "Let them shoot me. I don't care."

I put my hand on his shoulder to comfort him as I passed by him and hurried in, grabbing the rifle, some bullets, the keys to the truck, and a bath towel. Back outside, I moved the truck so it blocked the view of Michael from the north. I went back inside to get the binoculars, so I could scan the area all around us. Michael was crying, crying. All the while I could barely breathe. Suddenly the rage inside me burst and I kicked out in helpless frustration. I knew Wapan's death was my fault.

But it was not the time for grief or rage. Returning to Michael's side, I said, "Michael, we have to take her to Kit's and we need to call Bob."

Michael didn't budge, as I thought out the drive to Kit's place. They could be anywhere out there, waiting for us. "You'll have to stay low, in the back of the truck, with the rifle. I'm going to turn the truck around."

With that, I got in the truck and turned it so the back was close to

Michael and Wapan. Then I got out and opened the back. "Come on, Michael. Let's go."

Michael looked up at me with a tear-streaked face. "It's your fault."

"I know," I said, as I began to wrap the towel around Wapan's body. Michael didn't need to see the caked blood all over her. Looking at his face, I repeated my words: "I know."

He looked back down at her, ran his hand along her side, and he helped me finish wrapping the towel around her. Then we lifted her into the back of the truck and he climbed in after her. Handing him the rifle, I explained. "They might still be around, so this is to scare them off only."

As I drove to Kit's, watching both the road and the sides, tears ran down my face. With my horn blasting, I drove into their driveway and the noise drew them all out immediately. Jumping out of the truck, I told them that Wapan had been killed and I rushed in with Mona to phone Bob. As soon as I told him what had happened, he said he was on his way. We went back outside and both Kit and Amber were comforting Michael. As soon as he saw me, Michael said, "I'm sorry for what I said."

"It's okay, Michael."

"No. Wapan was a great wolf. She wouldn't go around blaming anybody else for bad things."

Kit glanced into the back of the truck and, turning to me, he said, "I'm going to go see if any more of the wolves were shot." I was surprised to see tears in his eyes.

Less than an hour later, Bob drove into the driveway. He came over to the back of our truck and said just the right words to Michael and me, then motioned for me to come with him. We went inside to the kitchen, and he asked exactly what had happened. When I finished, he said he was going to take Wapan with him, as I had expected, because they would need the slugs. He asked me if I remembered anything more about those three men. Towards the end of our conversation, he said: "Listen Christine. Those men are dangerous. It's not safe for you and Michael to stay way out here alone."

"They're not going to drive me away. Shadow Lake is my home."

"Think about Michael."

"I'll ask Kit if he can stay here. But don't you have any idea of who those men are?"

"We've got nothing. No sighting of any vehicle, no tire tracks, and you couldn't pick anyone out. Someone even went to NAK-WAN, and the director there said they have no personnel fitting the description of any of the three men you described." Bob shook his head, then, with a nod towards the truck, he added, "But now we'll at least have bullets." With that, he got up and phoned his superior, and I left to return to Wapan.

He and Mona joined us a short time later and he said, "I made the arrangements." He opened the back of his jeep and returned to take Wapan.

Michael looked at him and asked, "You're taking her?"

"He needs to take her, Michael. For the bullets."

"But I want her buried at Shadow Lake," he said, alarmed.

"I'll bring her back, Michael." Bob put a hand on Michael's shoulder, and Michael slowly nodded. At Bob's silent gesture to me, I followed him to the driver's side of his jeep and he asked, "Are you going back there now?"

"Yeah."

"I'll go back with you and look around. Some other officers are going to be coming and I'll try to be back later. If not today, first thing tomorrow."

"Okay. I just have to go say bye to Mona."

"Don't forget to ask them about Michael."

Nodding, I watched Bob get in, then drive towards our place before I went in to talk to Mona, briefly, and then Michael and I drove home. Mona had said both Michael and I were welcome to stay at their place, but I made no commitment.

By the time we got there, Bob was looking over the area around our cabin and then further back in the woods to the north of us. Michael went inside while I watched, until Bob returned to his jeep. Shaking his head, Bob said he couldn't find anything out of the ordinary. Because Amber, Michael, Lady, and I had often gone into those woods, it would have been hard to tell who broke what branch or trampled on which leaves. If others had been there, they were long gone now, and that was all that mattered to me right now.

As Bob was getting into his jeep, I asked, "Could you ask them not to cut her up too badly?"

"Sure, of course. You take care, eh. And the others should be here within an hour."

After he was gone from view, I went inside. Michael was sitting at Peter's desk and he asked: "How could anyone do something like that—how?"

Having no answer, I gave none. The shutters were still closed and the front rooms were dark. We sat there in silence for over an hour and I got up only when I heard the sound of tires on gravel. These other police officers who had arrived were all new to me and no introductions were exchanged. They must have seen the grief on my face, because they spoke quietly and were sympathetic. This is how it should have been when Todd and Peter died. I should have been able to mourn from the very beginning, and the officers should have been sympathetic instead of suspicious. I told these officers what I had already told Bob, and they walked off to look around.

Sitting on the porch step, I waited for them, anxious for them to leave. They finally returned and asked more repetitious questions about who would do this to me. I wanted to scream that I didn't know, but of course I didn't. I was polite and I came up with a spontaneous answer that must have sounded far-fetched to the officers because it sounded far-fetched to me as I was saying it. In Mrs. Springer's article, she had reported that I was being questioned in Todd and Peter's disappearance. The implication was that I had something to do with it. Maybe one of Peter's fans believed that and was looking for revenge. And maybe it was just racism, I added, to show that I had racked my brains for an answer.

Back inside, Michael was still at Peter's desk, his thoughts most likely filled with the memory of Wapan. I returned to the couch and sat there in silence again, trying to figure out why all this was happening.

It would have been so much easier to shoot me than to shoot a wolf. How did they manage to get her? Kit had once told Peter and me that guides had baited black bears so they got used to a feeding spot. That way, when hunting season opened, the hunters could easily shoot them as they came to their feeding spots—great sportsmanship there. Maybe they had done that with the wolves, baited them, and, if so, I was the one who had made Wapan less cautious than she might have been.

If I had wanted to shock someone with a terrible sight, I would be around to see the reaction. They must have planted her during the night, or very early that morning, and they must have been waiting out there when we came out. Not wanting to dwell on the memory of Michael's horrible scream at the sight of Wapan's body, I moved on and that brought me to Bob's advice. "Michael, Bob thinks it's too danger-ous for us to stay here right now and Mona said you could stay with them for a while."

"What about you?" he asked, after a few minutes.

"I'm staying here. No one's going to drive me away."

"Then I'm staying, too."

"Michael, you can't. Bob's right, it's too dangerous," I said, without much punch.

The next time I spoke, it was to ask if he wanted anything to eat. Rain began to fall and the cabin grew chilly. More for his sake than mine, I finally got up to put a fire on, then returned to the couch.

Later, I began to talk about Wapan and how we first met, face to face, back on that day when I was going to shoot myself. I told Michael that shooting myself had taken priority over everything else, even though I had received the first message from his social worker.

"You mean, you weren't going to come and get me?" he asked a low voice.

"Michael, at that time in my life I couldn't have sunk any lower. Without Todd and Peter, I just didn't want to live. And there was so much more, so many reasons for all the guilt I felt."

I hesitated, briefly wondered if Michael were old enough, and decided, today, he was old enough. "When I was nineteen, I gave birth to a daughter. And then I gave her up for adoption. And right after that, I went into psychiatric care because I had tried to kill myself. I never told Peter any of this because I never got the courage to tell him. And then I never had the chance."

Blinking back tears, I stopped long enough to regain control of my voice, then continued: "So you see, leaving you alone to exist in foster homes, that's what I was all about. That's the kind of person I was. When I was growing up, I had developed a strategy for coping. Let no one get close to me and I would never get hurt. So now, even with Lady, she was a part of our family, but then she became a constant reminder of Todd and I pushed her away. All that was before Wapan. She made me think of so many important things, all in the blink of an eye, like how precious you were. It was too late for my own daughter, but I could give you a home."

Prepared to receive his anger, his contempt, even a thought that he might be sitting in a dark room with a crazy woman, I waited for him to say something, anything. The silence was deafening. Then I heard him sniffling, and I went over to him and gave him a hug. He seemed to accept it gratefully.

For the rest of the afternoon we sat in the darkness of the cabin, and my offer to make something to eat was again declined. A while after that, he started talking. "Those dreams I have, well, this man is leaning over me. And all of a sudden blood is pouring from his ears and his mouth, and his eyes, and he's bleeding all over me." His chair creaked as he moved to get some tissue. In a stronger voice, he continued, "He was touching me. Rubbing me, you know. And I was ..." I heard him swallow.

While I was trying to think of comforting but honest words, we heard tires on gravel and I remembered that Bob said he would try to come back. Annoyed at the disruption, and wondering why Michael would have such dreams, I got up to go to talk to Bob. Michael stood up, too, and said he was going to bed now.

Expecting to see Bob, I was even more annoyed at seeing Howard, but politeness made me offer him coffee. With Michael having gone to bed, I could at least try to get another opinion of why all this was happening. He came in and sat at the table, saying that something told him he had to drive out here and he came as soon as he could. He watched me closely, full of concern, as I moved around to make the coffee. Finally, I settled at the table and he asked if the three men had returned.

"Yeah, they did. They killed Wapan."

"Wapan?"

"A wolf. A friend. She was the distraction I told you about before, remember? That's how I got away from them."

"And so they shot her." Taking hold of my hand, he said, "You must have felt awful."

"Why are they doing all this?"

"Did you ever cross anyone?"

"Not that I know of. It's like they want to drive me away from here."

"Maybe they want your land," he suggested. I looked up at him because I hadn't thought of that before. He continued, "Colin might know if seismic tests have ever been done here before, for an oil company, and, if so, what the results were."

"So that means those three men could be working for someone else."

"Not necessarily. One of them or all of them could have an interest in an oil explorations company."

We continued talking quietly over more coffee and, after mentioning Michael's pain, I found myself telling him about Leona being in jail.

Howard leaned forward and said: "You know, Colin's always talking about her. He misses her so much. You know what would be a good idea? If Colin could write to her. She could use another friend, right?"

"To be honest, she said he abused her, physically."

"That doesn't sound like Colin, but she would know better. Well, regardless, he could still write to her. And if she didn't want to answer, it would be up to her."

"I guess," I said, and I went to copy Leona's address, not sure whether I was doing the right thing.

Before he drove off, Howard hugged me to him again, which made my gratitude for his opinions turn to irritation.

Midmorning the next day, Bob returned with Wapan's body and he told me they had recovered nine bullets. She was still wrapped in the towel and I was glad to see there was no fresh blood on it. Bob told me to make sure the towel stayed on her. Michael came out, looked in on Wapan's body in the back of Bob's jeep, and went to get a shovel from the garage. Bob carried Wapan as we followed Michael to the last place we had both seen her alive, east of the cabin. Bob placed her in the shallow hole that Michael dug, then returned to his jeep so we could be alone. As I watched Michael shovel the earth back on top of her, tears came to my eyes and I sent a thought to the other wolves out there: *Always be afraid of us, my friends, because we cannot be trusted.*

Fifteen-year-old Vivian had spent the last two days hanging around the bus depot because Chad had said he would meet her here. To avoid intimidating icy stares, she quickly learned that she had to keep moving, from the coffee shop to the washroom to the waiting areas to taking short walks, but keeping the main entrance to the bus depot in sight. When she got on the bus the morning before, she thought that she and Chad would find a place to live together and they'd get some kind of jobs. Simple, and so much better than staying with her Mom. She'd been in foster care as long as she could remember, and then they gave her back to her Mom a couple of months ago. But her Mom was a drunk most of the time and, fortunately, she'd met Chad.

Chad was from Camrose, too, except he wanted to live in Edmonton. Before he left, they made plans that she was going to join him. And here she was, but no Chad. Something must have happened to him. Without him, she had no idea what to do, so all she could do was wait.

She was taking one of her short walks when a white van pulled up beside her. The driver called through the open passenger side window, "Hey, I know you, don't I? From, um ..."

"Camrose," Vivian said shyly. She was trying hard to remember where she knew him from so he wouldn't be insulted that she didn't remember him. "Do you know Chad, too?"

"Yeah, good old Chad. How's he doing?"

"I don't know. We were supposed to meet here yesterday."

"Oh yeah? Well, you know how he is. He probably got his days mixed up, right?"

"I don't know," she said in her soft, quiet voice.

"Well, come on, jump in. I know where he lives and I'll take you there. There's pimps and perverts and all sorts of low lifes around here. You shouldn't be alone." Smiling, the guy leaned over and opened the door for her.

Vivian hesitated, but he seemed nice and didn't mind that she was an Indian. Plus, he knew Chad and was going to take her to him, so she climbed in. The van pulled away from the curb to make the long trip northwest. Vivian would never know that Chad had no intention of meeting up with her again.

15

Later, when I relayed Howard's theory to Bob, he asked if anyone had approached me about leasing my land or offering to
buy it outright. Replying that only Colin had asked, more with
passing politeness than genuine interest, I added: "But what if someone else had approached Peter and he refused, so they made the accident happen? Without him, I probably wouldn't stay here, right? I'd
move back to Vancouver or something."

"I think you're stretching, but still, it is something to consider. I'll
see if any seismic permits were issued for your land. Who owned it
before you?"

"Wayne Schumack, but he died in a plane crash. I guess you must
know about that, though. And the land was up for sale for a few years,
so if someone wanted the land he would have had lots of time to buy
it before we did. So it can't be the land. Anyways, Howard said he'd
get Colin to check whether there were any seismic permits."

"Okay, but I'll check it out for myself. Is Michael going to stay at
Kit's place?"

Embarrassed to say I wasn't going to take his advice, I said, "I suggested it to him, but he wants to stay here with me."

Bob shook his head, looking very much like a cop. "Christine, if
anything happens ..."

"I know, I know. I'll keep trying to convince him."

"You shouldn't be staying out here alone, either."

"I'm not leaving. Everything has always been taken away from me. When I move out of here, it will be because I'm good and ready to, not because someone else is trying to scare me away."

As it turned out, I would not have a say in this matter, either, but I didn't know that as I watched Bob drive away.

The next few days passed with no dramatic incidents. Howard was now stopping by almost every other day and I had no idea how to tell him he really wasn't welcome, but at the same time he was. That was the problem. I liked the man as a friend, but I think he wanted to be more than just a friend. And there was something else about him, perhaps some instinct on my part, which made me suspicious of him. That's what it was—I was suspicious.

The rain began on Monday morning and all day, off and on, it drizzled heavily at times, then softly, as if some unearthly conductor were leading a melodramatic opera called the *Symphony of Showers*—at least that's what it sounded like inside the cabin. By nightfall the dripping of water outside competed with the crackling of fire in our stoves, and it was actually a soothing sound. Michael and I retired early that night.

In the early hours of Tuesday morning I woke to the howling of a wolf. At first I thought I had been dreaming, but when I heard it again, it sounded as if came from right outside my window. Donning my robe as I looked out, I saw only blackness because the clouds had not yet moved eastwards. From my doorway I called softly towards Michael's room, "Michael, are you awake?"

He said, "Yeah, I heard it."

"It sounded like it was right under my window, but I can't see anything."

We hurried to the living room to look out the front-room windows and right away, I noticed through the slits of the closed shutters of the dining-room window that a bright moving light was coming from beyond.

Seeing it too, and interpreting its meaning immediately, Michael grabbed me and pulled me towards the front door, saying, "We have to get out."

When he opened the door, a wall of flames and the smell of gasoline greeted us and he slammed it shut. I wanted to get the fire extinguisher, but he pulled me towards Peter's desk, to the west window, the only window that opened for cross breezes. Just as he was opening those shutters, another fire flared up, blocking our way out.

Leaving me, Michael raced into my bedroom, came out carrying the .22, and got bullets from the filing cabinet. Seeing him do that, I yelled, "Michael, forget the rifles! We have to get out!"

A picture of Peter and Todd hung on the wall next to where he was standing and, while he raced to the front corner window behind my desk, I grabbed the picture frame, intending to take it with me. The smoke alarm at the east end of the cabin went off, joined a few seconds later by the other one at our end. By now, I thought a forest fire was about to engulf us, but I was confused because of the smell of gasoline.

Michael was trying to move my desk closer to the window and I hurried to help. When it was close enough, he lay on it and kicked out at the window panes, breaking only glass. Like me, he wore running shoes, not very effective for breaking through fir. The windows that must have been designed to keep bears out were now keeping us in. As he kicked again, more glass panes broke, sending pieces flying about. While he carried on, I ran to the kitchen to soak some dishtowels, but the water ran out too soon and I only got one towel dampened. Michael tied it to cover his mouth and nose and then lifted my chair onto the desk. Standing up on the desk, he slammed the chair against the wooden frames. I sat on the floor, out of his way, clutching the picture close to me. Little by little, the wood splintered and gave. By now, more smoke was swirling around, and I remembered reading that most people who died in house fires were killed by smoke. Although I was sitting on the floor, I was finding it difficult to breathe. I couldn't imagine what Michael must be going through. He was amazing. The fire was inside now, lighting up the interior. Embers of burning paper and cloth floated about the room, riding on the draft from the broken window.

Trying to keep the smoke out of my lungs, I covered my nose and mouth with my hands. Then I felt a stinging sensation on my back. Panicked, I lay back and wiggled to squelch out the fire. That's when the acrid smell of singed hair came to me and, looking up at Michael, I knew I couldn't afford to panic. My eyes and my throat stung from the smoke, and my ears were ringing from the high-pitched screech from the smoke alarms. I didn't want to turn to see how far the fire had advanced because I didn't want to know. Shutting my eyes to keep the smoke out, I heard Michael hitting at the frame, again and again. He jumped down from the desk and crouched down beside me. "Someone's out there. When you get out, get down and take the rifle. Ready?"

Nodding, I climbed up on the desk and put the picture frame down so I could slide backwards. Feet first, I went downwards and out through the small hole. One jagged end of the wooden frame scratched along my back and snagged in the collar of my robe. Michael disentangled me and handed me the rifle. Crouching down immediately, I turned to give him cover if anyone began shooting—not that I could have seen anything, I was blinking so much. The smoke alarms went silent, but the ringing in my ears continued. Michael was taking too long and, looking around one last time, I was about to go back in when his foot poked at my head. My heartbeat started again as he slid out. Taking the rifle from me, he signalled for me to follow him towards the darkness of the lake. A loud explosion came from behind us and I turned to look. The garage for the ATV and snowmobiles had become a huge bonfire. Michael grabbed at my wrist and we kept going.

At the edge of the lake, we took cover in the tall damp grasses, then crawled over to an outcrop of boulders. Watching the flames shoot out from the windows of the cabin, I realized only then that I had forgotten the picture on the desk. Inside the burning cabin were all my memories of Todd and Peter. Gone. All my things. All of Michael's possessions. Gone. Tears ran down my face, but I didn't openly weep. Michael tapped me on my shoulder and pointed in the direction where we had parked the truck. A man, dressed in fatigues, was putting a torch to a rag stuck in the gas nozzle and he raced for cover up the road, where two others were waiting at the back of their own pickup.

Michael aimed the rifle at them, but I stopped him.

Michael yelled back, "They tried to kill us!"

"But we're not in danger right now," I said calmly. "Besides, they're probably more armed than we are."

Michael lowered the rifle, just as our truck burst into flames. When I looked back to where the pickup was, I saw its tail-lights come on and disappear around the first bend. Through the branches, I thought I saw another set of tail-lights come on as well.

Turning my gaze back to where thick black smoke curled up from my truck, then to the cabin that was now beginning to cave in on itself, I said, "On the other hand, I should have shot them myself."

"No. You were right. They must have had rifles. And they must have seen that we got out, so why didn't they try to finish us off?"

All I could say was that I didn't know. Everything that had happened so far was incomprehensible.

A soft low whine came from the nearby bushes and we both raised our heads to look in that direction. We saw eyes reflected in the light of the fires, then I could make out a dark outline, and then there was nothing. Michael moved to wash the smoke out of his eyes and I thought of doing the same, but I had no energy to budge, and certainly no inclination to touch icy cold water.

Afterwards, Michael said, "I should signal Kit."

"You think they've passed by his place yet? We don't want Kit running smack dab into them."

We waited an eternity, well, twenty minutes at least, and then Michael shot into the air, counted to five, then shot once again. He suggested we begin walking to Kit's in case they hadn't heard.

"I don't want to leave here," I said.

"There's nothing we can do here. We'll come back tomorrow if you want. Come on." He stood up and held a hand out towards me.

"Let's wait until the last embers die," I said, not moving.

"But Auntie Chris, that might not happen until tomorrow. Late."

"Oh." I smiled at the tone of his voice and reached for his hand, saying, "Okay. Let's go."

My body was stiff, my back stung, my throat was sore, and I was cold. Other than that, I was okay. Michael helped me until I could get some of the stiffness out of my joints and legs. Sitting on damp earth and grasses hadn't helped my aging bones. As we headed for Kit's place, the smell of burned wood mixed with the smell of gasoline stayed with us, even when we were a ways down the road.

Sniffing, I said, "I can still smell the smoke."

"That's because it's on our clothes and in our hair," Michael said casually.

His matter-of-fact tone made me smile. "You were right on, Michael. The way you reacted and everything. How did you know it wasn't a forest fire?"

"When I looked out, I saw a man run towards the back after the fire started. We were lucky they didn't shoot at us."

"I wonder why."

"Probably busy carrying cans of gasoline. If the wolf hadn't howled, we'd most likely be burnt to a crisp now."

"Wapan would have warned us, but I can't think which other wolf would have done that. That's what's so incredible," I said, as we walked on towards Kit's place.

Suddenly we saw two lights bobbing in the distance and we stopped. "They're coming back!" I whispered.

"Get in the bush!"

We dove into the underbrush at the side of the road, getting scratched by branches and thorns in the process, and Michael was about to put the rifle in position.

"Give me the rifle, Michael. I don't want you killing another person. You're too young."

"I won't aim to kill. Just to wound."

"No. Even that is bad enough. Besides you might not just wound. I'm a good shot. Give it to me."

"You might freeze. You're not into shooting living things."

"I can so. I shot a deer once."

"And probably cried over it."

That silenced me for a moment. "Why would they come back?"

"Maybe they forgot something, something incriminating. Hey, look. It doesn't look like headlights. More like two people walking. See how the lights move differently. Like they're carrying flashlights."

Innately suspicious, I watched as the lights approached. Even after we heard the sounds of horses snorting and treading over the ground, I had a hand on Michael's arm to hold him back. If the riders were Kit and Amber, they would have had Lady with them. When their identities were unmistakable, I sighed with relief, jumped up, and ran over to them, yelling "Kit!"

That must have given Kit quite a shock, for he dropped his flashlight. I had startled the horses, too, and they almost bolted, but their riders got them under control. Amber was able to hold onto her flashlight and her reins.

"Sorry, she didn't mean to startle the horses," Michael said.

"You okay?" Kit asked, with a testy edge to his voice.

"Yeah," Michael answered simultaneously as I said "No."

I babbled on: "Those three men came back and this time they burnt us out. Even the truck. We were coming to your place. Where's Lady?"

Amber was the one who answered. "I thought I heard your signal, so I woke them up. And the truck's not working, so we had to get the horses saddled up. And Kit said to keep Lady in the house."

"Didn't want her saying hello to strangers," Kit explained. "Get on."

Michael got up behind Amber and Kit helped me get up behind him. Now that I was safe, I began to tremble. Forcing myself to relax,

I'd stop for a while, but then the tremors would come again and again, until I could no longer get them under control. By the time we rode into their yard I was really having the shakes. While I couldn't control the shakes, my mind remained vaguely aware.

Kit stopped in front of the house and helped me off. Amber and Michael headed for the horse shed, but Kit called them back. Both of them dismounted and ran back to us. I still had the presence of mind to be amazed that Amber had just left her horse untied in the yard. Michael looked stricken when he saw how violently I was trembling. His eyes moistened, and I was moved by his concern.

"Get a blanket, Amber," Kit said, as he asked Michael to help me inside. "Don't look so worried, it's just a delayed reaction. Shock. But we have to get her warmed up, quickly."

Mona appeared at the door, and Amber came running back out with a blanket. They put it around me and I tried to walk on my own legs, but I really just wanted to lie down. In the light of the living room, Amber's mouth opened as she looked at me, horrified. She later told me that a few burns had gone right through my robe and pyjama top, that blood from a long gash down the right side of my back had seeped through the material, and a lot my hair had been singed. She imagined I must be in great pain. Some soot had blackened parts of my face and she thought they were burns too. Looking much worse than I really was, my concern was for Michael and I told them so.

Assuring me that she would take care of Michael, Mona left for the kitchen and returned with some tea. I tried to drink, but I couldn't keep my hands steady and it slopped over. Amber held the cup so I could drink from it. When I was done, Mona helped me out of the robe and pyjama top so she could work her medicinal magic on my back. But first, air hitting the exposed wounds sent a shock of excruciating pain through me and I cringed. Mona said in a quiet, calming voice, "It's okay. We have to get these off."

In the kitchen, Kit was telling Michael that they had called Bob and he was on his way. Then Mona was washing my back with a nice warm watery solution that muted the pain, and I began to relax. Amber left and returned with a clean pair of pyjamas. Finally I was lying down under some warm blankets, the tremors gone. Unable to sleep, I listened to the others in the kitchen. Lady came over to me and licked me a few times on my face, just as in the old days. Then she lay down beside the couch, and I put my arm down so I could pet her.

In the kitchen, Mona ordered Michael to take off his shirt, and Kit said, most likely to Amber, "Come on, we'll go and put the horses away."

For some reason, that phrase, put the horses away, struck me as funny.

Mona said, "Don't pull away. You got glass in there."

A little later I heard her say, "I can't get it."

Michael said, "I can get it out later."

"No, it will go deeper in."

Amber and Kit returned and Mona said, "Amber, go get me your tweezers."

Amber said, "Why? You giving him a facial?"

That too made me smile.

By the time Bob came, I was sound asleep and no one disturbed me. When we were having breakfast the next morning, Michael told me everything that had happened. Bob had come first, later followed by more cops, and he and Kit had gone with them to the remains of the cabin. They had taken pictures of almost everything. "Want to know what they didn't burn? The outhouse. Bob said they had a really warped sense of humour."

I began to laugh, a mirthless laugh.

"What?" he asked.

"Next time, I'll know where to put my valuables." My own sense of humour could be pretty warped.

"They found their footprints all around the buildings. And they found the wolf's tracks too. It was right outside your bedroom window, Auntie Chris." He took a big bite of his toast and continued, "Oh yeah, and they found some matchbook covers. The other cop, he's the one who found the wolf's prints first. I told him they would be look-ing for murderers right now if the wolf hadn't woken us up."

"What did he say?"

"He asked if it was a pet."

That cracked me up too. "No, I mean, did he believe you that they tried to kill us?"

From the look that Michael gave me, I knew he thought I was act-ing very strangely, but I couldn't help myself. He shrugged and said, "He didn't say anything about that. Just asked if the wolf was a pet."

"How are you feeling?" asked Kit.

"Much better, physically. I want to go to the cabin," I said. Kit and Mona looked at each other and I guess they figured there was no sense trying to talk me out of it. I looked to Michael to continue.

"So this cop asked if the wolf was going to be a problem for when the others came. And Kit told him they would never see it."

"What others?" I asked.

"The fire inspector or something. Oh yeah, and Bob said you should call your insurance agent."

When we finished breakfast, I stood up, thinking I should go and get dressed. Looking down at the strange pyjamas and robe I was wearing, I realized I didn't have any clothes to wear. I noticed only then that Michael was already dressed in some of Kit's things. Kit, with Michael following, went out to work on his truck. Mona and Amber took me upstairs to pick out some things to wear. Amber was too slim for me to wear any of her jeans, so I had to tie a belt around a pair of Mona's. I was taller than Mona, so the short pant legs made me feel awkward. When I came back down, I heard another man's voice in the kitchen.

Corporal Watherson stood up when I entered and he pulled his chair back for me to sit in. "Your son told us about last night. How are you feeling today?"

"Fine." I exchanged a look with Michael and smiled.

Amber was the one who corrected the officer. "She's his aunt, not his Mom."

"Auntie Chris is like a Mom," Michael explained, shrugging.

Last night when we had still been in the cabin trying to get out, he had called me "Christine" once. He had been in the driver's seat then. Now I was back to being Auntie Chris.

"Oh, so your name's not Michael Webster?" Corporal Watherson asked.

"It's Michael Pelletier."

The officer looked at me and said, "Mrs. Webster, I know we're beginning to sound like a broken record, but by now you must have some idea of what's going on."

"I don't. Only that they must have been those same three men I told you about before."

"Yes, well, unfortunately, we haven't found anything new on them. What about a grudge, maybe against your husband?"

"I guess I'm going to sound like a broken record, too, but people liked Peter. Everyone did." Repetition seemed to be what they wanted, so I repeated my speculation from before. "What was in the papers, maybe someone believed it and thought I should pay. Or maybe it's just racism. Or maybe someone wants my land, I don't know. I don't know and I don't understand why all this is happening."

"Whatever this started out as, it looks as if they want to kill you now. You be extra careful from now on. We found a matchbook, but that isn't going to tell us anything, so there's still nothing much to go on."

Later we drove out to Shadow Lake, where Sergeant Trolley and Constable Ringer were already poking around and another man was photographing this and that. With all these strangers, I contained my emotions by not thinking about my losses. They didn't want us creating new footsteps before they had taken more pictures in the daylight, so we went down to the lake to wait. Another police car drove in and Bob, in uniform, got out from the passenger side and came directly towards us to offer me his sympathy. At this point, that was all he could offer.

On Monday, after Michael and Amber had gone off to school, I asked Kit if he could drive me back to the cabin. We all went over and, when we got there, I imagined Lady must have been really puzzled by the change that had taken place. She jumped out of the back and ran around the truck towards the cabin, where she came to a dead stop. Mona and I had remained in the truck to watch her. Lady sat down, as if puzzled, looked back at us, and then went to work sorting out the new scents. She moved in and out of the rubble that was scattered on the ground, sniffing and blowing, sniffing and blowing. We finally got out and walked around, looking at the ash-laden debris that had once been a comfortable safe home to my family and me. Now it was all gone, including the mementoes of Peter and Todd.

As if reading my mind, Kit said from behind me, "They're still with you."

"But ..." When Michael was away, I had lain across my bed, looking at their pictures in the albums. I blinked rapidly a few times to hold back tears that threatened to come. How could I have forgotten their picture? And now I was scared that a day would come when I would forget what they looked like. The photographs on Peter's books and the one of Todd in the paper were not what they really looked like. The photograph I'd forgotten showed how very special they were to each other.

Later that day, Kit and Mona drove me into town and left me at the Castaway Motel while they went on to do some shopping. The woman who ran the motel told me she had heard about the fire and how sorry she was. She said I could have two rooms at half-price and, to my embarrassment, her unexpected kindness made me cry. She looked at me in alarm, wondering what she had said to make me cry. When I went to pay, that's when I realized I didn't have any money, no charge cards, no records of the paper trail we create and need for our existence. After the offer she had just made, that discovery was even more embarrassing. I stopped crying and told her I couldn't pay right now, and she said not to worry about it. That made me want to cry some more, so I quickly left to go up to my new room.

Dropping off the care bag Mona had put together for us, I hurried over to the grocery store. I didn't want to go in there now where I had experienced months of cold hostility, so I waited near the truck. When Mona and Kit came out, they were surprised to see me there already.

"You know what? I forgot I don't have any money or charge cards. And my bank's in Hudson's Hope. Um, I was wondering if you could lend me some."

Kit took out a wallet and gave me sixty dollars, just like that. "We should have thought of it. Tomorrow, we'll make a trip down there. We'll meet you at ten?"

Overwhelmed by their generosity, I nodded, then walked back to the motel, where I sat in my room for a long time, wondering how to tackle the immediate problems. We'd need a lot of money for clothing and things and I'd need another vehicle, too, because I couldn't expect Kit to drive us around. With that thought, I decided to call the insurance company. Fortunately, I didn't need the policy number, and I told the agent that the police probably had more details of the fire than I did. Next, I called the vehicle insurance company and gave them what information I could. They wanted details I didn't have, and I got so flustered I even forgot what my licence plate number had been. By the time I hung up, I had learned that I'd have to rent a car on my own. That reminded me that the police still had Peter's truck. Although I didn't want anything to do with it, I wondered why they hadn't mentioned it.

To put all the distress aside, I decided to watch TV for the rest of the afternoon. Michael was supposed to meet me here and I was watching the time so I could go down to the lobby. At 3:45 Michael knocked at my door to pick up his key and went to his room, but he returned a little while later, saying he was bored. Bored out of my mind, too, I took him down to the restaurant to play some pool. A few of his school friends were already there, playing, so I left him there while I reluctantly went to the grocery store to get some books.

Later that night, Michael came to my room, flopped down on one of the chairs, and asked, "So what are we going to do?"

"I don't know. We'll have to be careful with our money. Right now, it's Kit's money. I'm going to Hudson's Hope tomorrow. Maybe I'll have a car tomorrow night."

"No, I meant how long are we going to stay here? Are you going to rebuild? We can't stay here."

"Oh, well, I haven't thought that far ahead. What do you think?"

"You should rebuild." Michael looked at me, hopefully.

"You mean stay here?" I was surprised he'd want to remain here.

"Yeah. At the lake," he said.

Unable to commit myself, I merely sighed. In the back of my mind I had thought we would be moving back to Winnipeg. No matter what we did, the land would be here for the wolves, and Mona and Kit could continue using it too.

Still later that evening, Howard called from the lobby and, not wanting him alone in my room with me, I told him I would meet him in the coffee shop. He said all the appropriate things again, wanting to know how I was reacting. Further prodding from him made me realize that he wanted to know how I felt as we were trapped in the cabin with the fire all around us. After he was gone, I thought how peculiar his questions had been. Previously he had asked how I felt when I first saw Wapan's lifeless body, and focused in on that, as a psychiatrist would. Maybe he thought that was therapeutic for me. And yet, there was something kind of unnatural about his train of thought. Not wanting to think any more about him, I flicked the channels on the television set, trying to find something that would hold my attention.

The next morning, when Michael was at school, my phone rang. Bob was in the lobby and wondered if I might join him for a coffee in the restaurant. The first thing he told me was that no one had ever been issued a permit on my land to test for oil. Although it had nothing to do with the investigation, he said that oil exploration seemed to have priority over private land ownership. If they wanted a seismic permit for your land and you objected, then you could go to the arbitration board and all they would do was ensure fair payment.

To use Michael's words, I said, "That sucks."

The other matter Bob mentioned was Wayne Schumack's accident. The plane crash had been considered no more than an accident and no intensive investigation had been done.

"So?"

"So that has nothing to do with what's happening with you. The only other reason why I can see someone wanting your land is for the lumber. But no one's ever approached you to lease or sell?"

"No, and now I wouldn't. For one thing, Mona owns a trapline that runs over that land, a traditional trapline. And if those oil companies want to drill for oil on my land, I'll run to Greenpeace and those groups before I give in."

Bob merely smiled.

"The other reason why I wouldn't sell the land now is that the wolves live there. Two sections isn't a lot for them, but it's something, so even if we move, I won't sell." As I was saying those words, I recalled my words to Bob from before, that no one was going to drive me away from my home. And now here we were, living in a motel.

Michael wanted to return to Shadow Lake, so, although I'd seen enough of the burnt rubble, I drove him out there on Saturday afternoon. He seemed to be fighting off a melancholic state recently, and most likely it was because he didn't know what our futures would hold. When we got there, he walked around, looking at the rubble, much as I had done, while I went to sit at the picnic table, to look out at the lake.

He came to sit beside me and, after a spell of silence, he surprised me by talking about his mother.

"My Mom—I miss her," he said, looking down at the ground.

I glanced over at him and had to remind myself again that, even though he was tall for his age and had exhibited a maturity in the past few weeks, he was still just a kid, and right now he probably needed a guidance I couldn't honestly offer.

"Those letters she sent me—they're gone, all gone," he sniffled. "I never even read them, not one."

I had been so engrossed in my own losses that it never occurred to me that Michael had suffered losses too. Perhaps he was afraid that I might now send him back to Winnipeg, alone, where he would go back into strange foster homes.

"Michael, those letters, well, you can ask your Mom what she wrote. Why don't you do that? I can arrange for you to go visit her."

"I don't know." Now that he had the opportunity to see her, he was perhaps not sure that he wanted to take it. "The funny thing is I'm still angry with her. For lots of stuff."

"For being in jail?"

"For lots of stuff," he repeated. "Yeah, that, too. It was her fault."

There was nothing I could say to that. Leona wouldn't talk about why she went to jail and neither would Michael, although I suspected he knew more than he realized. All I could do was to encourage him to talk to his mother, and to assure him that he would never again go into foster homes.

16

In late September the chill in the morning air reminded me that winter was coming, and I didn't know if I had the fortitude to face it. While the townspeople were still snuggled in their beds, I would go for one of my long walks and, later, join Michael for breakfast in the restaurant. Alone at that time of the morning, I felt an intimate connection with Mother Earth. That was also when my mind seemed the clearest and I could think about all that had happened and wonder why, but so far I had come away blank. So much for clarity. Today I was thinking about Dr. Coran, and dwelling on him disconnected me from Mother Earth. Perhaps it was blasphemous to think of them both at the same time.

*

I thought I was going to live with Leona at last, but Miss Branzil told me she was taking me to a doctor's home and, one Friday afternoon, drove me north on Main Street towards West St. Paul. It was only when we turned down a treeless cul-de-sac surrounded by large split-level homes that curiosity replaced my anger.

Inside, while introductions were being made, I took in the view of the interior from the foyer as if I would be leaving right away. A short staircase went down and the other went up. The living-room ceiling slanted up to meet the second floor ceiling, giving the impression of spatial grandeur. In the other foster homes, mothers had greeted us while fathers had been away at work, but here the doctor had made the time to welcome me. He showed us in through the living room to the dining room off the kitchen.

Thick hardcover books were lined up in a long low bookcase spanning the length of the living-room picture window. Heavy beige and gold drapes were tied back, with their folds on each side perfectly even. Sheer lacy curtains hung loose, softening the view of the weedless front lawn and the other driveways and houses beyond. A cream-coloured sofa between glass end tables faced two matching high-back chairs. A large rolltop desk occupied the wall that separated the kitchen from the living room.

As the doctor talked about their concern for children who were abandoned by parents, I studied him, his wife, and their two daughters. He sat at one end of the table, his wife at the other end, and the two girls across from Miss Branzil and me. The doctor was a tall, handsome man, even though he wore thick black-rimmed glasses and had a prominent hooked nose. His wife and daughters were pretty, but would have been prettier if they had better hairstyles and wore makeup. First thing I noticed was that he did all the talking, while his wife only nodded whenever he silently prompted her.

The girls were introduced to us as Queenie and Darcy. My eyes settled on Queenie's hand and I saw that her baby finger was missing. She must have realized I was looking because she put her hands in her lap. My ears picked up when Miss Branzil said, "Christine is a wilful teenager so she'll need a strong hand."

Wilful? Me? Miss Branzil hadn't meant to compliment me, but saying I was wilful meant that I had a mind of my own, something I had never realized before. The doctor assured her that they strongly believed in discipline, tempered with understanding. As he was saying this, our eyes met and he winked at me. Miss Branzil, placed between the doctor and me, missed that, she was so busy being charmed by him and no doubt dazzled by his looks.

From where we were sitting, I could see the kitchen, with its white décor, and, again, everything was spotless. Coming from the Trunce's home, when the only major cleaning happened before important visitors arrived, I could sense this cleanliness was a permanent state. Sterile was the word that came to mind. The doctor and Miss Branzil were standing up, so I did to. The others remained seated and silent.

We followed the doctor to the staircase going down. At the end was a bathroom and, on the right, my bedroom. The doctor told Miss Branzil that the family bedrooms and bathroom were upstairs. This meant I would have a bathroom all to myself. Living here might not be so bad after all. Across the hall from the door to my bedroom was another door, but it was closed and the doctor said it was his study. Next to my room was a laundry room and it was nicely finished, unlike at the Trunce's, where the washer and dryer sat on cold cement flooring in the corner of the basement. Another short set of stairs led down to the basement under the living room and kitchen area.

Miss Branzil left after that, and Dr. Coran invited me to return to the dining room, where the others still waited. He gave me a list of the household chores I could do, saying I would know what was expected of me to help the household run smoothly. When he casually mentioned that I would not need to go upstairs to where their bedrooms were, I got the impression that he did not want me up there at all. If he had just showed me around up there, my curiosity would have been satisfied, but when he subtly told me not to go up there, of course I wanted to see what it was like.

After I unpacked, I went upstairs to the living room to take a closer look at the books. By now I could see there was no television, and not even a radio. Only religious books and medical books occupied the two shelves in the living room. I was looking through one to see if it was readable when Mrs. Coran said, "Dr. Coran would not want you touching his books."

I put it back, mumbling, "Sorry. Are there any books we can read?"

"There's one in your night table," Mrs. Coran said, as she glided back into the kitchen. I wondered where everyone else had gone as I went downstairs. The book in my night table was a Bible. "Great," I thought. What I needed were some babysitting jobs so I could buy my own books.

That night, after cleaning away the supper dishes—and that meant washing the kitchen floor too—we had to gather in the living room. Dr. Coran, sitting up straight and stiff in one of the fancy high-back chairs, read from a religious book. So this was our evening entertainment. Sighing under my breath, I looked around at the others. Mrs. Coran sat in the other chair and, in my mind, I put some makeup on her, pulled her hair loose from the bun she was wearing, and already she was looking much better. Queenie was sitting to my right on the sofa and, again, my eyes were drawn to her hand with the missing finger. She immediately covered her left hand with her right one.

"When I'm reading, Christine, you are to look down and think of the words I am saying," Dr. Coran said gently.

His reading seemed to go on for hours and it was worse than church. Afterwards, we gathered at the dining-room table and he went into the kitchen to make us some warm milk. What a strange but thoughtful thing for a man to do, I thought. Mrs. Coran helped bring the cups of milk to the table, followed by Dr. Coran. "Warm milk before bedtime is healthy," he said. "It makes you sleep better and feel refreshed in the morning."

The taste of boiled milk was disgusting, but I drank it because, although he seemed kind and gentle, the doctor intimidated me. I was the last to finish, and no one left until my cup was empty. My first scheme would be to figure out how to avoid drinking this milk. We each had to rinse our cups, then Darcy had to remain behind to wash and dry them, along with the saucepan. Already I knew that Dr. Coran didn't like anything out of place for long. He was right about one thing: the milk seemed to put me to sleep right away. I even slept through the whole night and that had never happened before. But he was wrong about the other: instead of feeling refreshed, I felt drowsy and sluggish for most of the next morning.

On Sunday mornings Mrs. Coran and Darcy went to the early Mass so they could prepare dinner. In all my other foster homes, only the man had a car or a truck, but the Corans were so rich they had two shiny new cars. Dr. Coran, Queenie, and I attended the 11:00 Mass. Many of the people we met going into the church knew the doctor and seemed to respect him. Watching him talk to them, I noted how popular he was—so charming and concerned, saying just the right things. If anyone noticed me, he would introduce me as their new foster child, another unfortunate abandoned child sent to them through God's will.

While I liked the doctor, I resented his saying that. It made me want to roll my eyes and say it wasn't God who sent me here, it was Children's Aid, and since I was going to be sixteen at the end of June, I wasn't a child. In church, I wondered why his wife and daughters hardly spoke at home and never laughed.

Ironically, school gave me a sense of release from my first weekend of constant silence in the house. Not that I was fun person, myself, but I did like some noise. And I liked having access to all the books in the school library. In addition to my homework, Dr. Coran took an interest in the books I brought home and criticized my choices, so I started bringing ones I didn't like, just to show them to him. Doing homework was preferable to reading the Bible and the religious books, so my grades were suddenly much better than they had been when I was at the Trunce's. And here, I didn't dare skip school.

At the doctor's place, I completed my chores without a fuss, since we each had our specific jobs. Every night Dr. Coran made us the hot milk and he sat there watching like a hawk, almost as if he knew my intentions. One time he and Mrs. Coran went out for the evening, and she looked totally different once she was all dressed up. She even wore makeup and her hair-do was older chic. She looked better than I had imagined she could. But even that night we had to have our milk before they left. Dr. Coran looked totally out of place as he prepared our milk in a tuxedo kind of suit.

At the end of June Miss Branzil returned for a visit and was impressed that the Corans had made such a positive influence on me. For the first time in my life the average of my marks was ninety, so that made me an A-student. Wanting to brag to Leona about my grades, I asked Miss Branzil if she could arrange a visit. She said she would, but she seemed preoccupied with other thoughts.

It dawned on me that she really did have a crush on Dr. Coran. Without appearing to do so, I watched for signs that I was right. By the time Miss Branzil got ready to leave, I still wasn't positive, but with Mrs. Coran in the room with us there wasn't too much they could have done. Mrs. Coran took the coffee tray into the kitchen while Dr. Coran walked Miss Branzil out to her car, where they stopped to talk. I was watching through the sheer curtains—okay, I was spying. Miss Branzil dropped her pen and Dr. Coran stooped to retrieve it for her. As he straightened up, he touched his fingers to the inside of her ankle and ran his hand right up her leg a little past where her skirt ended. I jumped back because Dr. Coran had turned to stare directly in my direction. When he came back in, he didn't say anything or act differently, and I never knew whether he had seen me or not.

In all my foster homes, starting with the Charettes, I had periods of being deeply suspicious of foster parents, mostly because I didn't know why they had taken me in. They had to have had a motive. My suspicion flared up again one night as I was sipping my milk and wondering why a man, especially one like Dr. Coran, would make hot milk for us. But I quelled the suspicion by thinking he was a doctor and must know what was best for us.

My sixteenth birthday passed without notice and summer holidays had just begun when I saw another side to Dr. Coran. We had just returned from church, and Queenie and I were about to set the table. Darcy and her mother were still preparing a roast beef dinner that sent waves of mouth-watering aromas through the house. Dr. Coran called to Darcy in a chilling tone of voice that I had never heard before: "Darcy, come down here right now."

Darcy went down the stairs and, curious, I followed her. Except for the bathroom, I was supposed to clean my room, the laundry room, and the basement where he kept exercise equipment. Somehow he had discovered that my toilet wasn't clean enough. It beat me as to why he was even looking in there. After berating Darcy, he grabbed the back of her head and made her kneel in front of the toilet.

"You don't see that filth? Look at it. Take a good look at it." And saying this, he shoved her head right into the toilet bowl.

By this time I was at the bathroom door and I wanted him to stop, so I said, hesitantly, "I made that dirty."

Still bent to hold her head down, he turned to me, and gone was all the pretence of being a kind and caring man. "You. You had your own duties to fulfil. This bathroom is Darcy's job. She is responsible. Not you. From now on, you will all do the duties I have assigned to you, is that clear?" His voice rose, so by the end he was shouting. He released Darcy's head as I nodded meekly.

"Clean that up," he snarled at her. When she came up, the top of her head was wet and her hair looked funny, so a smile flashed across my face. Dr. Coran turned to me and maybe he caught the smile. Approaching me, he growled: "And you," he stopped in front of the sink to pick up the bar of soap, "you wash your mouth out."

Having backed out of the doorway to let him pass, I looked from the bar of soap up to his eyes, shocked by the change in him, and I saw that he was serious. "You think I don't know you just lied? You wash your mouth out now or I will wash it out for you."

He was crazy if he thought I was going to wash out my mouth with soap and I said so: "You're crazy."

Darcy gasped, as I turned to walk away. His hand grabbed me just under my mouth and he yanked me back, close to the sink. He turned on the tap, wet the soap, and shoved it into my mouth. I struggled to get free, trying to keep my mouth closed, but he was too strong. When he was finished with me, I stomped up the stairs and marched towards the front door. More with astonishment than shock, I felt him grab my arm and yank me back. "Where do you think you're going?"

"I'm getting out of here. And when I do, I'm telling what you did."
As soon as I said that, I wished I hadn't because it sounded so babyish.

"Telling what? That you lied and I had to clean out your mouth? It's done all the time."

"I'm telling what you just did to Darcy."

"Darcy, come up here," he said.

Darcy came up the stairs quickly. He said to her, "Darcy, did I mistreat you in any way?"

"No, father. I disobeyed you. I'm sorry. I should have been more responsible."

He looked at me, a gleam of triumph in his eyes. "I want to show you something." He latched on to my arm again and dragged me towards the rolltop desk, letting go of me to dig some keys from his pocket to open a drawer. He brought out a case, opened it and removed a kind of knife with a sharp, shiny blade. Since he was a doctor, it must have been a scalpel. Suddenly afraid, I took a step back, wondering if I could somehow get outside before he stopped me.

As if reading my mind, he said, "Oh don't worry. I'm not going to use this on you." Raising his voice slightly, he said, "Queenie, come here. You too, Mother."

When Queenie and Mrs. Coran came into the living room, fear jumped to Queenie's eyes as soon as she saw the blade. Taking a small stainless steel tray from the case, the doctor placed it on the desk and said in a low chilling voice, "Come here, Queenie."

Incredibly, she obeyed, advancing until she stood at the other side of the desk.

"Put your right hand on there." Queenie looked at me with terror in her eyes but she placed her right hand on the tray.

"Spread your fingers apart," he said. Something in his voice reminded me of the old man and his thing, a perverted kind of excitement, and it was in his eyes too. Queenie's hand was shaking so much she could barely keep her fingers flat on the tray.

Relenting, I said, "Okay, okay, stop. Don't hurt her. I'll do whatever you say. I won't tell anyone anything."

Trance-like, he touched the blade to her finger, very slowly, very deliberately.

"I said stop. Please stop. Please don't hurt her." My voice sounded hysterical with panic.

Despite my pleadings, blood began to ooze from a cut.

"I promise. Whatever you want."

He looked up at me and said, "You made me cut her. You see that? You made me do that."

I started breathing again only when he had removed the blade from her finger. He looked at it and said, "This is dirty." He handed it to Queenie and said, "Go clean this up. Sterilize it."

To his wife, he asked, "Is dinner ready?"

She nodded right away.

To me, he said, "Go set the table. We're going to eat now."

Eat? The only thing I wanted to do right now was puke. But that would get Darcy into trouble again. Swallowing bile back a few times, I joined Mrs. Coran in the kitchen, wondering why she hadn't even said anything to protect her daughters.

On rainy Sunday afternoons, after the dinner dishes were done, I went straight to my room, where I tried to preoccupy myself with reading and drawing. I began writing a diary, but when I finished for the day I ripped the papers into tiny pieces and sneaked it into the kitchen garbage. I wouldn't put it past Dr. Coran to check my garbage can to see if I was up to anything.

Whenever the Corans had visitors, the parish priest being one of them, I made sure to eavesdrop on their conversations. Mostly, I was fascinated by the contrast between the doctor's private self and his public self, but I was also hoping to pick up on something I could use later. If only those visitors knew how hypocritical he was they wouldn't just sit there, talking and laughing it up with him.

One afternoon, as I was listening to the murmur of voices from the living room, something I had read came to me. A character had said,

"Know your enemy." Then he was killed, but the hero to whom he had said this learned about his enemy and, in the end, he outwitted the bad guy. Okay, that meant I had to get into the locked room across the hall, and see the upstairs while I was at it. Another saying came to mind: "You have to fight fire with fire," but in my case I would fight evil with evil. To begin with, I decided to play his game. He had turned the others into zombies by terrorizing them. It seemed that he wanted zombies around him. Well, from now on, I would be a zombie too.

The long hot summer passed slowly, and the physical and emotional abuse from Dr. Coran continued, erratically. Sometimes I thought it was because of the weather and sometimes I thought he was testing me, in particular. While I played the role of the zombie, superbly I thought, the temptation to talk back was always there.

One day Mrs. Coran and Queenie went shopping for school supplies and Dr. Coran and Darcy were at his office. For the first time, I was alone in the house. Taking some cleaning supplies from the kitchen, I went upstairs. If anyone came home unexpectedly, I would say that I only wanted to surprise them with some extra cleaning, a feeble excuse since everything was meticulously cleaned every morning. The two doors on my right led to bedrooms slightly larger than mine, and the door on the left was to a very large bedroom. On one of the nightstands was a phone. All this time I had thought there was no phone in the house, for I had never heard it ring. I had no idea what to look for, but maybe I would find something that was incriminating. Maybe I would know what it was if I saw it. I started walking into the large bedroom towards a dresser when I heard the sound of a car in the driveway. A chill ran up and down my spine and I raced back out, glad that I hadn't touched anything, shut the door, and ran down the stairs back to my room.

When the front door opened, I was trembling and wondering who had come in. The doctor or the others? I went to my doorway and saw the doctor's trousered legs as he passed by. I heard him move around in the kitchen. He rarely came home during the day, and then only for lunch, but it wasn't lunchtime. Suddenly I remembered I had left the cleaning supplies in the upstairs bathroom. Oh my God! I had to get them or there would be hell to pay. Slowly, I ventured down the hallway, testing the floor and the stairs for squeaks and staying close to the walls. The sound of the kettle whistling made me jump, but I was quick enough to move with its sound and I was able to get to the cleaning supplies. Should I go into one of the bedrooms or try to make it back to my room? I didn't know, I didn't know. Mrs. Coran and Queenie might come back and I could be caught in one of the girls' bedrooms. Then I would be the one to lose a finger. Swallowing, I decided to go for the safety of my own room.

I was just starting back down the hall when Dr. Coran passed right in front of me, carrying his cup of tea. Had he been looking up, he would have seen me. As it was, he was looking down at his cup and he went down the stairs. I heard the sound of keys, then a door opened and closed. He had gone into his study, and I moved forward. I put the cleaning supplies away under the sink in the kitchen, and then indecision set in again. Should I go downstairs to my room or outside for a walk? The doors had automatic locks, so I wouldn't be able to get back in. I decided to get back to my room and, should I be discovered, pretend I had been sleeping.

At first my feet didn't want to move, but once I forced myself to take the first step I gritted my teeth and kept moving. As I was passing the closed door on my left, I heard some noises. It sounded as if the doctor was having sex or something. Maybe he had brought a nurse home. No, I would have seen her or heard her. I made it to my room, closed the door quietly, and lay down on my bed. My shakes stopped only after I heard the doctor leave. As soon as I was sure he was gone, I got up and went to the door across the hall to try it, but it was locked again. Didn't matter. Elation hit me as I thought I was one up on the doctor.

But then that night during supper, the doctor asked his wife, "How did your shopping go? Did you have enough money?"

"Yes," Mrs. Coran answered.

"And did you get everything you needed?"

"Yes," Mrs. Coran answered.

"And Christine, you got some things, too?" His eyes were on me.

"No."

"Why not?"

Mrs. Coran was going to tell him I hadn't been with them and he was going to cut my finger off. I froze.

Thankfully, Mrs. Coran cut in and said, nervously, "You didn't give me money from Children's Aid."

"You could have bought her something. We're not poor, you know."

"I'm sorry."

"Don't say you're sorry to me. Say it to Christine."

Mrs. Coran looked at me and said, "I'm sorry, Christine."

Dr. Coran's chair scraped the oak flooring as he got up, walked over to her side, and said: "Being sorry means nothing. Poor Christine. How do you think she felt watching you shop for yourselves and getting nothing?"

Mrs. Coran had put her fork down and was now looking down at the table. She said, "I really thought you wouldn't want me to."

"I would appreciate it if you look at me when you talk to me."

She looked up at him and was about to repeat what she had said when—whack—he slapped her hard across the face, leaving a bright red impression on her smooth white cheek. I opened my mouth to confess, but her eyes met mine for just an instant and I got the impression she wanted me to stay silent. What was the point? Somehow, he knew I had not gone with them. I must have left some evidence that I was here today, alone.

He returned to his chair and began eating again as if nothing had happened. The other four of us had stopped eating and resumed only after he ordered us to eat our food. When we finished, he thanked God for the food we had eaten.

I wanted to say I was sorry to Mrs. Coran, but the look in her eyes told me not to say anything at all. We cleaned up the kitchen in silence and then went into the living room for his reading. For a few days after that we were jumpy, because we didn't know if he was going to pursue the shopping trip further. It occurred to me that the doctor slapped Mrs. Coran for not buying me anything. But he would have slapped her if she had bought me something. By now I had learned it was part of a game he liked to play, putting us in positions we couldn't win.

The new school year provided relief from the daily boredom and evening tension. But even then the doctor managed to invade my domain. At the supper table one night he said the school had called and complained about lice in my hair, and he threatened to cut my hair off. I pretended I didn't care what happened to my hair by playing the zombie, and he never did carry out his threat.

Gradually, he relaxed his guard against me and, at night, I managed to spill half the milk into the sink as I was rinsing out my cup. One night I was running water and pouring the milk down the drain when I heard a sharp intake of breath right behind me. I turned and there was Queenie, towering behind me, shocked by what I was doing. Her mouth was open and, when our eyes met, I saw just a tiny flicker of life in them. But we both knew she had to tell on me.

For weeks after, I waited for Dr. Coran to confront me. By now I was also aware that he liked to rage over an offence we might have committed long before. One time I was walking home from school and a boy in my class was telling me how he liked this other girl in our class. No problem with that, except that he was walking down the sidewalk beside me, and Dr. Coran happened to drive by and see us. He didn't say anything about it for a few weeks and then, suddenly, I was the slut of sluts. That was one of the times he yanked my hair and slapped me around.

His waiting games were intended to make us spend days or weeks living with fear. Mostly, we never even knew that we had committed offences, and his rage came out as surprise attacks. I think we were always supposed to be on edge. Whenever the others got beaten up,

I blamed myself. If only I had just minded my own business when he stuck Darcy's head in the toilet, he never would have behaved this way in front of me.

Well, if he thought I was just going to hold my finger out for him to cut off, he had another think coming. Again, I thought how pathetic the female contingent in this household was. There were four of us and one of him. I daydreamed that we ganged up on him, tied him down, and strapped his hand to his desk so we could cut off one of his fingers. See how he liked that. But that daydream always ended with us being unable to decide who would do the cutting.

Mrs. Coran: Well, Queenie, you do it. He did it to you.

Queenie: I can't do it. I hate the sight of blood. You do it, Darcy.

Darcy: Ugh, not me. I'll get sick. You do it, Christine.

Christine: No. I don't have it in me. You do it, Mrs. Coran. He's your husband. Besides, this is my daydream.

In reality, I was so petrified of a potential onslaught from him that I had been drinking all of my milk at night. Finally, I couldn't stand it anymore and, when Queenie and I were all alone, I asked her, "Did you tell your father about the milk?"

After staring at me for a moment with her doleful eyes, she shook her head, no. Sighing with relief, I said, "Thanks."

Almost immediately, I took to dumping my milk again. In the past when I had been dumping most of it, I began waking up during the nights more often. I think it was because of noises upstairs, like doors opening and closing and the shower running. The water and drain pipes ran close to my room, so I knew when someone upstairs took a shower or bath or flushed the toilet.

One night I woke up and thought it must have been from some noise, perhaps a door closing. After lying in bed for a while listening and hearing what sounded like a bed squeaking, I finally got out of bed to investigate. I sneaked up to the living-room level and everything was dark, no lights coming from under the cracks of doors. A door on the right side opened and I guessed Queenie or Darcy was going to the bathroom. Suddenly, the bathroom light went on and I saw Dr. Coran. He was completely naked! He closed the door and I was in darkness again. The shower water was turned on and I waited, replaying in my mind what I thought I had just seen. The doctor, naked, had come out of one of his daughters' bedrooms and now he was taking a shower. The water stopped running and, after a while, the door opened again and, in the light, I saw he now had pyjamas on. He shut the light off and I heard the door on the left open and close.

Stunned by the obscene implication, I returned to my bed. What do I do now? What I did was try to convince myself I had been mistaken, because this was too much to deal with. But I couldn't just let it go like that. More than ever, I needed to get into the room across the hallway. I tried to figure out how I could get the key to the room, but was getting drowsy because I had no good solutions. Another thought hit me and my eyes popped right open. All this time I had thought the doctor was showing a kind streak when he prepared our hot milk at night. He was not capable of kindness. He was evil. So he was drugging us, that's what he was doing. That's why he didn't care about the sounds he made in the night.

Turning onto my side, I plotted how I could use that against him too. I had to get the key to his study. Maybe I could switch cups with him, since he obviously wasn't drugging himself. Would he know, though? In my mind, I replayed the nightly routine. He was alone in the kitchen while we four dummies sat at the table, waiting. When he was done, he'd call Mrs. Coran to get our cups. She'd bring Darcy and Queenie their cups, then go back and get ours. That's where I hit a wall. She would never have the guts to switch cups. More than that, I couldn't even see myself explaining why she should switch cups.

Maybe he was a heavy sleeper. A warm shower at night might make him a heavy sleeper and I could sneak into their bedroom and take his keys. I wondered if he believed in sleepwalkers. If I were caught I could pretend I was sleepwalking—yeah, right. I turned over again and tried to think of a better way, with no success.

The next day I watched all of them closely, wondering if they knew what was going on and liked it that way. Because none of them acted strangely, I suspected that the doctor had been in his daughters' beds before. I also found myself wondering how far he went with them. Did he touch them or did he go all the way? It was too hard to believe a father would do that to a daughter, so I convinced myself I'd made a mistake. I just wanted to believe the worst in him, that's what it was.

Not long after that I had a really yucky dream. In it, the doctor was kissing me and touching me. But what made it truly yucky was that, in my dream, I liked it! For days afterward, that dream haunted me and reminded me of what I was. Of all the people I should have stabbed, he was the one. It made me wonder if I had a secret crush on him, something my sane mind wouldn't allow.

As it happened, the opportunity to get his keys came in a completely unexpected way. As was their habit, the doctor and Mrs. Coran went out a few times a month—after we had our milk, of course. Besides hitting us, he liked to throw things at us, anything that was within his reach—hardcover books, potted plants, cups, glasses, forks, plates, anything. Once he had thrown a glass at Darcy and it had cut her quite badly. Mind you, the cut came when she was picking up the pieces, but she wouldn't have gotten cut if he hadn't thrown it in the first place. Anyways, being a doctor, he just stitched her up, telling her it was all her fault. Another time he had tossed food from a hot casserole right in Mrs. Coran's direction, saying it wasn't hot enough. Yet he had used the oven mitts to hold the casserole dish. Always, his outbursts were our fault.

This one night they went out to a fancy place, all dressed up, and Mrs. Coran looked quite stunning in her pale-blue evening gown. After they left, we each went to our rooms. Later, I awakened when the front door slammed shut. The Corans were back and the doctor was in a foul mood. Usually he used a cold, quiet, eerie voice when he was angry with us, but this time he was yelling at Mrs. Coran that she was a disgusting whore and then he must have pushed her or slapped her, because I heard thumping noises. "I saw the way you looked at him, you filthy whore. Didn't give a damn about how that made me feel. Or what others thought."

By now I had opened my door a crack to see what I could see. He yelled that she was all kinds of different whores, and I saw him shove her by the top of the stairs towards the kitchen. Surprisingly, she must have got loose and headed for the stairs, because something went flying by and made a clanging noise when it landed on the tiles in the front foyer. Then he stomped up the stairs after her, yelling that he was not finished with her and how dare she turn away from him. His voice was muted once their bedroom door was slammed shut, and I went up the stairs to see what he had thrown this time. The moonlight came through the windows above and beside the door and I could see his keys clearly, lying in a pathetic little heap.

Here was my opportunity, but I was suddenly too petrified to move. He might have been yelling at her, but his rage scared the wits out of me. I looked upward, back over my shoulder to where only an ominous silence now hovered in the darkness. Maybe he had planned this. Maybe he had quietly come out and was standing there in the dark, watching for me. I wouldn't put that past him, so I went back down and waited and listened and waited some more.

Setup or not, I finally decided to go up and get those keys. Once upstairs, I also checked the kitchen and dining room to make sure he wasn't lurking about, and, if he were, I would just say I thought I heard a noise. Returning to the keys, I made sure they didn't jingle when I picked them up. Downstairs, I tried one key at a time, and it was the last key on the chain that made the lock click.

My eyes had to adjust to the darkness and, when they did, I crossed to the window and pulled open the curtains. The moonlight flooded the room and that was good, because if I turned on a light he might have seen it from his bedroom window above. Some kind of medals and framed pictures of what looked like army people hung on one wall. A framed photograph sat on his desk, and I took it closer to the window where the lighting from the full moon was better. It was a wedding picture of him and his wife, only they were younger and she was smiling up at him with adulation in her eyes. It occurred to me, once again, that I had not once seen Mrs. Coran smile with pleasure, not her or her girls. When that picture had been taken, she must have thought he was quite a catch. The other thing that struck me, as I returned the photograph to the desk, was how much her daughters looked like her.

Opening the drawers to the desk, I found nothing of importance in them, and in the top three filing cabinet drawers there were only file folders—old medical files, I guessed. But the bottom one contained magazines and I took one back to the window and discovered it had pictures of naked women. Some of it had half-naked men doing it to naked women, who were tied or blindfolded. One big picture in the middle showed a naked blindfolded woman, with her legs and arms handcuffed to four bed posts. A naked man was shoving some sort of stick between her legs and she looked as though she was screaming in pain. Sickened, I closed the magazine and put it back where I found it. The doctor was a pig, a sick, disgusting pig. Sorry, pigs. I mean he was a pervert, a monster, a mean, slimy, evil monster. Well, this was no time to stop and think of more adjectives. I eased the drawer of the filing cabinet closed, with hands that were now trembling. I wanted to get out of this room, yet I had to do some more snooping. Up on the shelves behind his desk chair were more books, and then I spotted a jar. I reached for it, took it to the window, and almost dropped it when I realized what was in it. A finger bounced around in some liquid. Queenie's baby finger!

My jitters increased tenfold as I put the jar back on the shelf. Anxious to get out of there, I made sure that all the drawers were closed securely. At the doorway, I spotted a garbage can at the other end of a leather couch, but when I checked, it had only used tissue paper. Just above the couch a picture of more army people was hanging at an odd angle. That was unusual, because the doctor liked everything just so. He had once beaten Mrs. Coran because the living-room drapes weren't pleated evenly on both sides. Leaning over, I went to straighten it, when I realized what I was doing. Dumb or what? I walked back to the door, wondering who cleaned up in here. The key turning in the lock now seemed so loud. I tested the door to make sure it was locked. Then I went up the stairs to the front entrance and placed the keys as I found them. Once I was back in the "safety" of my own bed, my breathing gradually returned to normal, but the shivers stayed with me.

Sitting cross-legged on my bed, I wondered what I should do next. If I told anyone and the doctor found out, he would cut off another finger, probably one of mine. I could run away, instead of going to school, but then one of the others would get her fingers sliced off. So I couldn't do that, either. And who could I tell? I'd been here for six months now and had heard no word from my social worker about a family visit. Miss Branzil and Dr. Coran were most likely committing adultery together, so she was out. Leona, being on her own, was probably too busy for me, and Mom was not going out of her way to ask for a visit with me. Even if they thought of me, I had a history of avoiding visits with them, so they would think I was in one of my miserable moods. Everything comes back to haunt.

Unable to resolve the problem, I lay down and tried hard not to think of dirty magazines, jars with baby fingers, stupid yucky dreams, or anything else like that. I thought of Lady and riding Chieftan, his mane and my long hair flowing back in the wind. I must have been on the verge of sleep when a thought jumped out at me. If that shelf had been dusty, the doctor was tall enough to see that the jar had been moved, and same with the wedding picture on the desk. In bright daylight, he would immediately see disturbed dust. His keys had been out in the open, so he might check around in his office just because he was by nature an extremely suspicious man.

Unsuccessfully, I tried to convince myself that he wouldn't put up with dust, gave up, and got out of bed once again. Up the stairs I trudged, looked up the other staircase, and then around the corner to the foyer. I blinked. The keys were no longer there. I looked again. Still no keys. A line of panic surged through my centre. It had been a setup. I tiptoed back down the stairs and paused at the door to his study, but I couldn't hear anything. I returned to my bedroom, wondering if Dr. Coran was somewhere behind me, in the basement, perhaps, watching me.

The next morning I went upstairs and played the innocent, trying hard not to think of my nocturnal activities. It seemed that whenever I was trying to hide something, it was right up front on my mind and someone else always picked up on it. One time, I was convinced that everyone around me could read my mind. Mrs. Coran was wearing a bruise on her cheek. She was the only one who got decked in the face.

Dr. Coran was reading the morning paper as he ate. Without looking at me, he said, "I think it's about time you had a checkup, Christine."

The basement, I thought. I hadn't checked the basement, and that's where he had been, watching me and waiting. Plotting. That's why the keys weren't there the second time. His way of letting me know that he knew what I was doing. And now began another game of cat and mouse. That was the moment I remembered I hadn't closed the curtains, and I felt like throwing up.

When we ate, we made sure our cutlery didn't hit the plates, because that disturbed him. I had once gotten a fork thrown at me because I forgot. Now the silence grew, if that was possible. That was when I knew the girls were aware of what their father was doing to them. They knew. A tremor came to my hands and I put down my fork and knife. I said, "I had a checkup before I came here. Just before I came here." The lie was said in a calm voice that hid how I really felt inside.

"Oh? And who was your doctor?" he asked, not lifting his eyes from the paper.

"I don't remember. Dr. Erinburg, I think," saying the first name that came to mind. Last time I had seen a real doctor was when I was in the hospital and the boy died.

"I'll check with your worker. They'll be happy if I give you a checkup," he said, sipping his coffee and finally looking at me. In his eyes I saw something sexual and malevolent.

Trying not to overstep my bounds, I said as forcefully as I dared, "I don't want a checkup." The girls looked up at me, in spite of their not wanting to get involved.

"We won't discuss this anymore. You'll do what I say. Is that understood? I'll call your worker today." He eyed me coldly but knowingly, that gleam still in his eyes. As I stared back, his gaze shifted from me to rest on Queenie's hand, which I took as a subtle warning.

Dr. Coran must have been in his element, for he let me brood for the next two weeks. The day after he told me he would give me a checkup, he brought home some needles and vials and took blood samples from all of us. My dream about him had been a crock and I knew I had no desire to be touched by him, not even medically. But I couldn't let him cut off another finger. I didn't know what to do, had no one to turn to, and so, cornered, all I could do was wait.

Then one night he announced as we were drinking our milk that I was to wash the saucepan and cups. That meant everyone else had to go to bed, leaving me alone in the kitchen. Queenie gave me a look I couldn't decipher.

As I was scrubbing the milk from the bottom of the saucepan, Dr. Coran came up behind me, put his arms around me, and whispered that we were alike and he knew exactly what I wanted. Hiding my apprehension, I said, "Get your filthy, dirty hands off me."

In response, he turned me to face him and hit me hard across the face. I tried to race for the front door, but he easily caught me there and was kissing at me, groping at me, and hitting at me. Squirming free from his hold, I raced for the back door, even though I knew I wouldn't get out. He caught me again and gave me quick hard jabs to the stomach that brought tears to my eyes and made me want to puke. When he got me back in the living room, he threw me forward and, tripping on the leg of the chair at the rolltop desk, I landed hard. He was down on top of me right away, with a crazy lunatic look in his eyes.

I thrashed around trying to avoid his punches, hoping to get free. When the fight had gone out of me and I lay still, he kissed me hard on my mouth. Just before I squeezed my eyes shut, I saw Mrs. Coran at the top of the stairs with Darcy and Queenie looking over her shoulders.

The thought that they might help me made me renew my efforts, and I squirmed some more until my head was under the rolltop desk, which would prevent him from kissing me again. But that was right where it seemed he wanted me. With his weight holding me down, he got his keys from his pocket and unlocked the drawer where the black case was stored. With one hand he fiddled with the lock and, with his other, he gripped me by the neck, choking me. My alarm at seeing his intent gave me strength I didn't know I had and I bucked, making him lose both his grip on my neck and his balance. Instead of trying to flee again, I tried to scratch and bite at him, so he found it hard to get another good grip on me and get at his case. I yelled at those women to help me. The doctor now had the case on the desktop, but he stopped trying to get his scalpel out as he again focused his attention on getting a firm grip on me. Repeatedly, he hit me across my head, back and forth, and he said, "You think I don't know you went into my study?" And then he was tearing at my clothing and suddenly his hand grabbed at me between my legs.

"You like that, you little whore? Oh yes, I know all about you. You squaws like to play so, so coy, don't you? And what you really like is for us whites to jam it into you. Isn't that what you want, my little brown whore?" He didn't say these words all at once. He said them between gasps and hard breathing. And the hard breathing didn't come from him exerting himself as he beat me. It came because he was sexually aroused. Instinctively, I knew nothing would stop him from raping me.

He stood up, forcing me to my feet, and headed for the stairs, dragging me along as if I was a child's rag doll. When he noticed his wife and daughters at the top of the stairs, he hissed, "Go to your rooms. Right now."

When they didn't move, he yelled, "You want to watch? Huh? Is that what you want?" In a lower tone, he said, "Filthy whores, that's what they are. Filthy, filthy whores."

Then he was dragging me down the stairs, down the hallway to my bedroom, inside my bedroom, and my bed loomed larger. He threw me on the bed and, as he started to undo his buttons, I tried to get out. He easily pushed me back, taking the time to give another hard slap. The doorbell buzzed and, in quick succession, it was followed by the sounds of someone pounding on the door and a muffled voice saying, "Police. Open up."

A stricken look came over Dr. Coran's face, but he quickly recovered and hissed at me, "All five fingers."

He raced back upstairs, rebuttoning his shirt. I followed right behind, because I wasn't going to stay here tonight or ever again. If I had to attack a policeman to make them take me with them, I would. Before he went to the front door, he glanced around, saw the case on his desk, took the scalpel from the case, slashed himself on the arm, and tossed it on the floor nearby. After that, he went to the front door. Two policemen barged in, and the first thing they saw was the blood running down Dr. Coran's arm, dripping crimson onto the beige carpet. Their hands went down to their holsters as their suspicious eyes fell on me. By this time Dr. Coran was saying: "I'm glad to see you. You've got to take this girl away. She went after my wife with that." He pointed over to the scalpel lying on the living-room carpet and continued his spiel: "She went completely berserk on us. Just like that."

While he was talking, I was thinking with delicious satisfaction that since Mrs. Coran must have called the police, she and her daughters would tell the truth. I was about to get another surprise.

He turned to his wife and gently asked, "Are you all right, dear? Did she cut you anywhere?" He looked up at her, full of loving concern. To the police, he said, "I'm Dr. Coran. I have a medical practice in town."

One of the policemen looked up at Mrs. Coran and asked, "Is that right, ma'am? Did she take that knife to you?"

We all looked up at her. She very deliberately took hold of Darcy's hand, held it tightly, and looked straight at me. She wet her lips and then she nodded, yes.

The policeman next to me said, "You'd better come with us. Nice and easy, now. Could you get her coat?"

Dr. Coran got my coat from the back closet and, as he was handing it to the officer, he said to me: "We went out of our way for you. And this is our reward." To the officer he said: "Don't be too hard on her. She's had a difficult life, going from foster home to foster home and she's told us some fairly strange tales. I'm not a psychiatrist, but I would diagnose her to be schizophrenic."

While he was saying this, I put on my coat. They handcuffed me and one of the officers led me outside to a police car, with its lights still flashing. Large lazy snowflakes were falling and I turned my face upward. They felt so good, so fresh, so pure. While Dr. Coran was still talking to the other policeman, neighbours gathered, wondering why a police car was at the Coran house. I heard one asking the doctor if everything was okay, and I'm sure another one of them said something about crazy squaws and how you couldn't trust them. None of that mattered. Although I was in a lot of pain, I was just so happy to be getting out of that madhouse. I bet not many people thought that getting arrested was akin to getting their freedom.

The police took me downtown to Winnipeg, to a police station on Rupert Street, and once I was inside the handcuff was released from one wrist so they could handcuff me to a bench. I had to wait a long time before a social worker I had never seen before came along and the first thing she said to me was, "You've really gone and done it this time."

She set down her large purse, retrieved a notebook from it, and, with her pen poised above the paper, she asked, "What on earth got into you to pull a knife on Mrs. Coran? My God, that poor woman. The doctor says she almost had to be hospitalized, you traumatized her so much. And slashing the doctor, that's a very serious matter. What happened? What set you off?"

Thinking of Mrs. Coran's last silent plea to me, combined with the doctor's last threat to me, I knew I could say nothing. Could I ever convince anyone of what was going on in the Coran house? I didn't think so. No one had ever believed me before. I had been booted out of all my foster homes so far because they believed I was a liar. No one who counted was going to believe this story especially. So I kept my silence about the night's events and all I said was, "I really need to take a bath."

*

Way back then was when I first got the idea that one had to fight evil with evil, and now, maybe, that's what I had to do again. Not that I had won anything back then, not until Leona got involved and we made that doctor lose everything he had. What was happening now was as though someone was playing games with me all over again. Evil twisted games that had resulted in the deaths of Peter and Todd. But who around me would be doing such a thing?

Maybe I could make them show themselves if I spread the word that Shadow Lake was for sale. Whoever came forward might have something to do with these games. I'd tell Howard first. While there was something about him I didn't trust, he wasn't evil, not the way Dr. Coran had been. Maybe Colin. But then, who were those three men, and would they surface once they knew I was willing to sell?

My walk had brought me back to the motel and restaurant, and I went in to join Michael. As I said good morning to Michael, the waitress brought me my coffee, with lots of milk in a creamer. She knew my ways well by now.

I was spooning sugar into my cup, when a thought hit me. After those three men had come, Howard had made me coffee. Without asking, he had spooned two sugars into it. How did he know to do that? I had noticed at the time, but I was too busy thinking about the three men to correct him. After he left, I had dumped the coffee because it was too sweet.

Ever since Peter had made that comment to Colin a year ago about my liking for sugar, I had fixed my coffee in private. I had been cutting back on the sugar, so now I was down to only one teaspoon. Why did Howard add two teaspoons? Such a little thing, but it bugged me, long after Michael had left for school.

17

I finally got rid of that bug in my head, mostly because I really couldn't see Howard having anything to do with what was happening to us. He simply had no reason, and he was just a pathetic lonely old man. Bob was to meet us at four o'clock and we were going to Mona and Kit's for dinner. Michael really liked Bob and, on my good days, their friendship was a pleasure to watch because it reminded me of what Peter and Todd would have had in their future. On the days when I was hurting, I tried not to think of Peter and Todd and the future they would never have. Every night, in the privacy of my bedroom, that's when I let the pain out.

Tonight I would tell Michael that I had decided to move back to Winnipeg. The insurance money would not cover a winter here in the motel, and I couldn't expect the special rate to continue. Besides, the insurance on the cabin would give us a down-payment on a house in Winnipeg. If I wanted to save that down-payment, we would have to move soon. Most regrettably, I would not be able to wait for the police to find the bodies of Todd and Peter. Waiting for that to happen over these past months had been an agony I had suppressed. It was just not possible to rebuild at Shadow Lake with those three men lurking out there somewhere, wanting to kill us. The decision brought both relief and a deep regret. Now that I had come to a decision to leave, I realized how much I really wanted to stay.

The day progressed slowly, and the morning clouds moved on without dampening my spirits unduly. With the sun shining so brightly it was hard for me to remain in a dismal mood. When I finished the book I was reading, just before lunchtime, I decided to go to the grocery store. Mrs. Martens was so much kinder since she had heard of our latest misfortune, and I had forgiven her for the way she had treated me.

After lunch around 1:30, a knock came at my door. When I opened it, Howard was standing there and he invited himself into my room. His advances lately were getting just a little too persistent, and I was uncomfortable that he had come into my room.

"I've got a surprise for you at Shadow Lake. Want to take a drive with me?" he asked enthusiastically, after the preliminary greeting.

"What kind of surprise?"

"If I told you that, it wouldn't be a surprise," he replied, a mischievous grin on his face.

"How long would we be?" I asked.

"We won't be long," he said, smiling at me with what he probably thought was boyish charm.

I didn't want to go, because of the two teaspoons of sugar, but that incident seemed ridiculous at the moment and I was also curious. If I sent him away for good, I would never know if he had a part in recent events and, this way, I could eliminate him completely. Maybe he wasn't the lonesome old man I thought he was. We seemed to be studying each other more closely and, to hide my suspicion of him and be polite, I said, "Okay, I'll meet you down in the lobby."

Howard took hold of my hand and said, "You will love the surprise. I guarantee it." To withdraw from his touch, I pretended I had an itch on my cheek. To me, that would have been an obvious tip, but Howard chose to ignore it, just as he had ignored all my previous signals.

After I closed the door on him, I sat on the edge of the bed to put my sneakers on and scribble a note to Michael, in case I was late in returning. In the hallway, I shoved the note under Michael's door and, as I went to meet Howard in the lobby, I thought that since we were moving away, I didn't really have to be polite to him anymore.

On our drive to Shadow Lake, Howard tried to make conversation, but I wasn't in the mood. His sympathies were mildly annoying and I wondered why I had put up with him. We drove into my driveway, and everything looked the same as when I had last been here—piles of burnt rubble that had been the cabin, the summer kitchen, and the garage. Lording over it all was the outhouse.

Once Howard parked, he made no move to get out, but glanced in his rearview mirror as if he was expecting someone else. He turned to me and said, "I am going to have your cabin rebuilt for you. What do you think of that?"

This was his surprise? I could have arranged for that myself. "Howard, don't bother with it," I replied. "Remember how I said I was thinking of returning to Winnipeg? Well, I made up my mind. I'm selling this place because I definitely have to get Michael away from here. Whoever burned us out intended to kill us. And I can't risk Michael's life just because I would like to stay here." I watched him closely for a reaction.

A horn sounded from behind us and Howard smiled. "I thought you might say something like that, so that wasn't really the surprise, I was just buying time." He rolled down his window and motioned the other vehicle forward. Curious, I turned to see who was coming, and Colin's van appeared. Before getting out, Howard told me to come around to his side. Annoyed, I did so, and reached Howard's side just as Colin's van stopped. When I saw who the passenger was, I was shocked and delighted. Leona and I ran to each other and embraced.

"You're out early?" I exclaimed, looking at her.

"That's a question and, no, I didn't escape. Colin, here, helped me. We started writing to each other and I finally told him what really happened." The look she gave him said that she was in love with him all over again. "And, now, he just picked me up at the airport and brought me straight out here. He told me what happened—the fire— and Chrissy, I'm so sorry."

Turning to look at Howard, I said, "This is a great surprise. Thank you, thank you so much." My gaze returned to Leona, and I wondered how Michael was going to react when he saw her.

"No need to thank me," Howard muttered. "Getting her out wasn't for you. It was for me. Since I could see I wasn't going to get everything I wanted, I decided to end the games." Behind me, Howard had opened his van and I had no idea what he was yapping about. I was wondering why Leona had confided in Colin and not in me, especially since I thought we had made up.

The look on Leona's face changed as she looked over my shoulder. A wide-eyed, open-mouthed look of horror replaced the sparkling eyes and dazzling smile, and she pulled me towards her. I turned in time to see Howard advancing on us with a scalpel in his hand. He raised his arm, as if he intended to slice open Leona's neck.

"What the hell are you doing?" Colin uttered, but he made no move to stop Howard.

Wishing now that I had taken the karate lessons more seriously, I used what I knew and jabbed at Howard's wrist to block his aim. Before he could react, I followed this with two quick jabs, one to his windpipe, the other to his midriff. His reaction could have been faked, but he grabbed at his throat. "Let's go. Let's get out of here," Leona said to Colin.

To our amazement, Colin shook his head, no. To my left, Howard suddenly lunged towards me with the scalpel. I jumped back, but I saw blood spurt onto the ground between us. One of the karate lessons was to always be in a state of awareness. Having forgotten it, I now felt a stinging pain at the tip of my left middle finger. Colin was the enemy, too, and Leona and I had to get away from both of them. Grabbing her arm, I raced for the safety of the forest.

As we crashed and stumbled through the underbrush, I realized that I wasn't completely surprised by the sudden change in Howard. It was so similar to how Dr. Coran had changed, and, as with Dr. Coran, I didn't know why. The finger on my left hand was sending pain messages to my brain. "Leona, slow down," I whispered, loudly. In her panic, she had raced ahead of me and we were going nowhere fast.

"Why are they doing this? It doesn't make sense," she whispered, studying the landscape to our south. I wrapped my bleeding finger with tissue I had in my pocket. The pain was excruciating and I tried to concentrate on answering Leona. "Howard said the games had ended. Something like that. Maybe this is all part of a plan. Anyways, we don't have time to talk about it right now."

"What are we going to do?"

"I know a place, but we have to move quietly. We're making too much noise. Come on."

We listened for a moment and there were no other sounds. Scanning my surroundings, I picked out landmarks and, once I knew where I was, we moved forward carefully. A little map came into my head: "You are here," followed by a dotted zigzag line, leading down into the gorge up ahead, east along its basin, to the spot marked X, our destination. When we got to the place where I thought X should be, we stopped to listen again. I studied the southern wall of the gorge until I recognized the rock on which Lady had stood to bark out that she had found Michael's hiding place. The sounds of birds going on with their usual business resumed, and that meant we were probably alone in the gorge. The mouth of the cave was five feet up from the ground level, and getting to it meant a few seconds of exposure. If we were seen, it meant we would be trapped in a hole. I braced myself, then clambered up into the hole. Turning, I studied the surrounding area closely, then signalled for Leona to follow. The mouth of our cave was well hidden by bushes.

At first, we just breathed heavily. "Michael found this cave," I whispered.

"Michael. I'm never going to see him again."

"Of course you will. Just not when he gets out of school. We were all supposed to have dinner together at Mona and Kit's. Not you, but this Constable Cormier. He's been helping me and ..."

Howard's voice rang out and it had a madman's sing-song quality to it. "Christine, where are you? You know we're going to find you. It's just a matter of time. My men are going to track you down. So come out of whichever hole you've crawled into."

Leona and I looked at each other silently and we both must have had the same thought: we were not going to get out of this alive. Howard had just said his men were going to track us down and, now, another piece of the puzzle fell into place. Besides Colin, those three men had been working for Howard all along, and Howard was the one who ordered them to attack me, kill Wapan, and burn us out.

Time passed while I tried to figure out why, gave up, and turned to projecting the near future. Michael would get out of school at three-thirty and he would see my note. Howard didn't know about that, nor did he know that Bob would also be looking for me. As I thought about the advantage we had, I smiled, but it quickly faded as I wondered how they would find us here in this place.

Leona whispered very softly to me, "Look!"

Leaning forward over her shoulder, I saw a man in fatigues, poking a long stick in among the bushes on the other side. Then we heard the sound of rustling leaves as someone approached us. When the man on our side came into view, I recognized him as the leader of the three men, but, of course, he was not really the leader. Howard was. Leona flattened herself on the ground and I leaned back against the wall, wanting to watch but not wanting to be seen. He paused right in front of our hideout to study the embankment. Muttering to himself, he moved on.

The cave was barely big enough for the two of us, as long as one of us sat up. Changing position, I bumped my wounded hand and fresh pain shot up my arm. The tissue was soaked with blood, so I raised my arm, hoping that would slow the bleeding. My heart was racing again, and common sense told me that meant more blood was being pumped into the rest of my body. I tried to have calming thoughts—Peter and Todd out on the lake; Peter fishing, Todd napping, while I read. That wasn't a good memory, though, because they had died. Something nagged in my mind, but I left it and tried to have another calming thought. Wapan's visits to us, but she, too, had died a violent unde-serving death. More thoughts, but I rejected them because all the good times in my life really had come to abrupt disastrous endings. The thoughts took me far back in time and perhaps now I should con-fess my sins. What good it would do I wasn't sure, because I had long ago put Catholic beliefs behind me.

Lowering my arm, I wrapped the bottom of my sweatshirt around my hand and I whispered, "Leona, I want to tell you some things."

"What?" she asked.

"Like a confession," I replied.

Having resumed her watch position, she now turned over to face me and whispered, "You mean like a last confession." By the light fil-tering through the bushes, she spotted the blood on my shirt and exclaimed in a loud whisper, "Holy Christ, what's that on your shirt? That's blood! He stabbed you!"

Her concern was obvious, and I wondered if she would still have it after I told her my confession.

"No. Just my finger, but I'll live. I think."

"Let's see."

"No. I don't want to look at it."

"So don't. Let me look."

"No. I just wanted to tell you my confession."

"Okay, go ahead."

Now that I had the floor, so to speak, I was suddenly shy and I didn't know how to begin. "Um, well, uh, okay, when I was three, I was molested. Sexually molested. At the Manley's place. By an old man who lived there. I think he was Mrs. Manley's father."

"Oh Chrissy, that's awful."

"I know. And then again when I was seven, and that was by a priest. But he just touched me between my legs. Remember? I told you about him when I was ten."

"Yeah, I remember now. But if the priest just touched you there, what the hell did the first one do?"

"He made me touch him." It had started out that way. Swallowing, I continued. "And then I let him make me touch him—more." The scenes of that time came to me—the smell, vile and putrid—and I tried to force the rest of the words out.

Leona put a halt to my confession by whispering, "But Chrissy, if you were only three, you couldn't possibly know about sex."

In other words, she didn't believe me and, in a way, I was glad because I should not have unloaded my perversion onto her shoulders at a time like this. If I were going to go to my grave soon, I ought to take my secret with me. I could at least tell her about the effect. "I never told because I knew what we were doing was wrong. It was evil. I was evil." By now I was shivering from that chill that came from inside.

Leona reached out and put a hand on my forearm and I could feel her love. "Oh, Chrissy, you were never evil."

We smiled at each other and, while I was sincere, I hadn't told her everything I should have. For what seemed a very long time we were silent and she turned over again to watch the outside. I wondered what Howard and his men were doing out there. Why did he want to kill us, not just me but Leona too? Leona must have been on the same wavelength because she turned back to me and whispered, "Who the hell is that man?"

"With that scalpel, he reminds me of that Dr. Coran."

"Who's he?" she asked.

I quietly giggled. "From that one foster home I was in. You're the one who got in the papers about it."

"So I did." Casually she asked, "Did he have a brother?"

"That's it! That's got to be it. Howard always reminded me of someone else. He's not as tall as Dr. Coran and he doesn't have that hooked nose, and Dr. Coran had these thick glasses. But his eyes, they seem familiar. The last name's not the same, either."

"Could have changed it. Lots of women in jail had aliases," Leona suggested.

"Dr. Coran died a long time ago, so, yeah, maybe Howard is his brother, looking for revenge."

More silence as Leona turned to look out again. I raised my arm, and we each had our thoughts about Howard and his motivation. That nagging thought returned and it hit me: maybe Howard and his men had killed Peter and Todd. Outside, the late afternoon sunlight brightened as clouds lolled by and the sun's slanting rays from the west lit up our interior.

Leona turned back to me again and said, "It's my turn for a confession. Why I went to jail."

I nodded and whispered, "And why you told Colin and not me."

"You were too close. I didn't want you knowing what might have happened to Michael. And I didn't want it in the papers, that's for sure. Anyhow, after Colin and me broke up, I went to Winnipeg. That fight had been about you. Remember I told you that Nick was always talking about you? Well, Colin was always asking questions about you too. And of course, that made me jealous after a while. After today, I know he was fishing for information to pass on to Howard. That was another thing, he was always with Howard.

"So we went back to Winnipeg and I picked up where I had left off. I partied with this guy, Frank, and this one night we were at my place, so Michael was sleeping in my bed instead of on the couch. Tim and Lola were there too. Lola I knew from a long time ago, so we were celebrating our reunion. To be honest, we were just getting drunk, and any excuse was a good reason for drinking. Like Mom, you know? Anyhow, Lola and Tim went out to get more beer and I passed out. When I came to, Frank wasn't with me, so I grabbed my beer and went looking for him. I found him in my bedroom, leaning over Michael. He was ... going to touch Michael, or maybe he had already touched him, I don't know. I flipped out and broke my beer bottle on the door frame or something and I plunged it into his back, more than once."

"Michael was having nightmares about a man bleeding all over him."

Leona bit her lower lip, but said nothing. So I continued. "I don't think he really knew what it was about. And then again, maybe he did."

After giving that some thought, Leona continued. "I got Mikey out of there, washed him—he did have some blood on him, but only a few spots—and while he dressed, I called a cab and we went over to Mom's place. When the others came back, they found the bastard on the floor where he belonged. He was more passed out from drinking than badly hurt. The police came later to Mom's place and I confessed, because I didn't want it coming out what he'd done to Mikey."

Again, I whispered, "You were protecting him from a pervert. If he does know what happened, why is he so angry with you?"

Leona gave me a wry smile and whispered, "Because he would blame me for what happened to him. My lifestyle. I should have prevented anything like that from ever happening. So he's right to blame me."

A piece of another puzzle that had nothing to do with our present situation clicked into place and I whispered, mostly to myself: "So that's why I hated Mom. I blamed her for what happened to me."

"Mom told me once that she never knew how to deal with you. You always looked at her with accusation in your eyes."

"That's because she loved you more than she loved me." I smiled as I whispered this other bit of truth, disguised now as a joke.

Leona returned my smile and whispered, "That was because I was easier to get along with. She said that right from our first family visit: you ran to me and hugged me, but you only seemed to put up with it when she hugged you. And, later, I noticed the cool reception you always gave her. You never talked with us."

"That's because I always felt excluded."

"If I had known that, I wouldn't have babbled on and on to her. I was trying to make up for your silence."

I was amazed at how different our perspective had been and another confession came to me. "When we were growing up, I was always jealous of you. Because you didn't have any mortal sins like

I did. I never told anyone about the man at the Manley's before, not even in the confessional. So I lost count of how many mortal sins I had. But the worst thing now is that I never even told Peter."

Again, Leona reached out to comfort me. Then she said, "When I was fourteen and babysitting for the Camerstons, I had an affair with Mr. Camerston—Joe. For a year."

"Holy, you really mortal sinned!" I whispered in astonishment. "So, if you were only fourteen, he could have been charged with rape. What if you got pregnant?"

"We made sure that wouldn't happen. Anyhow, he got tired of me, or maybe his wife suspected something, 'cause next thing I knew, Gillian Thatcher was babysitting for them." She glanced outside, saying, "I never could keep men."

"Well, maybe you gave men only what you thought they wanted from you—and what they thought they wanted from you."

"Now that's confusing, but somehow it makes sense," Leona whispered.

"So how did Colin get you out?"

"Well, let's see, we wrote to each other and then I told him what really happened. So he hired another lawyer—paid for him, too—and then I had a meeting with a prosecutor. Frank was already on record for having molested another child, so that helped. Next thing I knew, I was released. Colin sent a ticket for me so I could come back to Fort St. John. Now I'm wondering why he went to all that trouble if he knew it was going to end up this way."

"Maybe it was all part of a greater plan on Howard's part, but Colin didn't know what the whole plan was," I suggested. By now my middle finger had gone into *rigor mortis* and I couldn't bend it, but at least the bleeding seemed to have stopped. In spite of the intensity of the throbbing pain, I focused my thoughts on Howard and why he was doing this, trying to figure out whether he was capable of murdering Todd and Peter. Colin had gone to a lot of trouble to get Leona's sentence waived, or whatever the legal term was. Then he brought her here to be killed by Howard. That didn't make sense, and he had seemed too surprised by Howard's actions to have known what was going to happen. Yet Howard had moved in on us with his scalpel as if he had known Colin wouldn't do a damn thing about it. Furthermore, Colin had refused to drive us to safety, when we'd had the chance. Now they were all hunting for us and, if they found us, Howard would finish what he had begun. We might never know why—and that sucked.

Just then, three things happened around the same time. I glanced out, over Leona's form, shocked to see Howard's grinning face at the entrance; I heard a dog barking in the far distance, and, although faint, it sounded like Lady's bark; and I heard gunfire coming from the far west.

"Come out, ladies. I don't think I have much time, so move it."

Leona and I looked at each other one more time and, before she could move, I crawled over her to climb out of the cave first. I realized that Howard had a pistol in his hand just as Leona was coming out of our hiding place. Suddenly Howard took quick aim in Leona's direction and fired. Colin deflected his aim, shouting "No!" But Leona grunted and fell over.

While the two men struggled with each other, I looked around and found a short, solid branch nearby. Having seen Leona fall back, I knew she had been hit and I wanted to see how badly. Priorities, my subconscious screamed, and I watched the men, hoping for a way to get that gun, hoping Colin would wrestle it from Howard, because he was the lesser of two evils. The gun went off again and Colin went down, a pained, surprised look on his face. Howard stepped back. The circumference of the blood stain on his shirt expanded, spreading across his midriff. "You think I don't know you saw them come here?" Howard snarled. "You wasted all this time for me. Your usefulness to me has just come to an end."

As he aimed the pistol once again, I forced myself to ram the end of the branch full force into Howard's face, then slammed it down hard on his gun hand. The pistol fell to the ground as he automatically raised a hand to his face. I bent down to grab the pistol and he kicked at me, catching me in the side. Undaunted, and now in a kneeling position, I jabbed him again with my branch, aiming for his crotch but getting him in his leg. Then I dove to the ground, grabbed the pistol, and rolled away from another kick.

As I quickly stood and backed away from him, we heard more gunshots, some sounding like a succession of quick snaps and some booming like shotgun blasts. Glaring at me, he pressed his hand to his bleeding right cheek and, after a quick downward glance at Colin, he smiled. "He's dead. And you, I was not finished with you. I still had the best surprise in store for you. But now?" Still smiling, he clicked his tongue and shrugged.

The smile turned to a sneer and he glanced to the west of us, where gunfire continued sporadically. He turned and began to walk away from me, following the gorge eastward. He knew I wouldn't shoot him in the back. Leona was still and I needed to have a look at her, but I couldn't just let him leave. Colin was on his back, his eyes open to the sky above, but Howard was right. I didn't think Colin saw that sky.

Lady pranced up to me, her tail flying high. She saw Colin and bypassed me to go sniff at him. "Leave it," I said, and she returned to my side.

As I watched Howard arrogantly walk away, frustration and anger washed over me. I wanted him away from Leona, but I didn't want him getting away completely, so I lined up the sight on the pistol and, when I squeezed the trigger, I knew I'd crossed the line. A red spot appeared on Howard's leg and, at the same time, he stumbled and fell forward. Satisfied that his progress would be reduced or maybe even stopped, I climbed up the embankment to help Leona. She had fallen back onto her side and blood stained the front of her blouse and jacket. But she was breathing.

"Leona, can you hear me? You're going to be okay, you hear?"

Her eyes fluttered open and she moaned, "It hurts."

"I know. Lady's here. The others must be here, too. I'm going to get help. Okay?" I removed my jacket so I could cover her. Her eyes closed. Because of the blood all over her front, I didn't know where, exactly, she was hit, but all I could do was to get help. Then again, I couldn't just leave her here by herself, because Howard might come back and finish her off.

Lady whined anxiously from below and, when I called for her to come to me, she had to circle around the area before she found a place where she could climb up. As soon as she reached me, she wanted to lick my face. She must have smelled the blood and sensed how desperate we were, because when I told her to stay, she settled right down beside Leona.

Holding back my repulsion, I went to Colin's body after I climbed back down and rummaged in his pockets until I found the keys to his van.

As I left, Lady whined, but didn't attempt to follow me. Wanting to get an immediate overview of what was going on, I climbed straight up the south side of the gorge I was in. The gunfire was still coming from the west, but I couldn't see anyone. When I got to the very top, I looked out over the gorge again. Howard had gotten up and, with the help of a stick, he seemed to be dragging his leg behind him. I was relieved to see that he was still going east and that he was not making progress quickly. The sun would go down soon, so there was no time to linger. Still wondering what all the gunfire was about, I headed for the road. I was almost there when Michael's voice came to me. "Auntie Chris! What's going on?"

"Michael! I need help. Your mother's been shot. Here's the keys to Colin's van. Call for an ambulance and the cops. We're near that cave you found."

"My mother?"

"Yes. She's here, but Howard Norach shot her. And he killed Colin."

"Colin? What's going on? Mom is here?"

"No time to explain. Hurry. I've got to get back to your mother."

Taking one step, I paused and called back to Michael, "Who's doing all that shooting?" After all the whispering Leona and I had done, my voice sounded unnaturally loud.

"Kit and Bob. We were looking for you when someone shot at us. Bob shot back and Kit got some rifles from Bob's jeep. I just came back from calling for more cops."

"Okay. Call for an ambulance and tell them your Mom was shot in the chest and she's bleeding really bad." I said that part so that the medics would hurry, but Michael's jaw dropped and tears came into his eyes. "Michael, I think she'll be okay, but tell them that so they'll hurry. Okay?"

After a brief nod, he ran off and I hurried back to Leona. When I got there, I called Lady back down so I would have room. Once by Leona's side, I looked for the wound that was spitting out so much blood and found the entry hole about two inches down from her collar bone on her right side. Because she had fallen over onto her left side, the blood had oozed downwards, soaking her across the chest. I placed the flat of my right hand so it covered the wound and pressed hard. Leona groaned and I began talking to her, telling her that Michael was going for help and that everything was going to be okay.

Dusk was upon us now and soon it would be dark. The shooting was still sporadic, and then came the welcoming sounds of sirens. I'd had to change hands to keep the pressure on Leona's wound, and that had renewed the pain in my left hand. Silly thoughts about why all this was happening had gone through my mind, but one remained with me. As soon as Leona was in the ambulance, I was going to go to that laboratory, or whatever it was, to the northeast of us, because I was sure Howard was heading in that direction. Having read Peter's manuscript, I was thinking now that maybe it was a militia training compound. Maybe it was heavily equipped with guns, and Howard was planning to make his last stand there. The gunfire here had now been replaced with men shouting, and the shouting had that authoritative tone that cops used. A new sound, the whirling sound of a helicopter, drowned out the voices.

A little while later, from my vantage point, I saw flashlight beams, like search lights, criss-crossing the gorge. Michael called out and I answered, so they could locate us quickly. A man carrying a black bag was the first to climb halfway up to us. After a series of quick questions, he asked if she had been conscious. That she had was a good sign, he said. I had to climb down to make room for him. Once he had stabilized her, they lifted a stretcher up, and another man climbed as far as he could. Then they placed Leona onto it, secured her, and, with the help of the other men who had gathered, they brought her down. Michael led the way as others with flashlights lit a pathway up the steep slope. By now it was completely dark and much colder.

Some of the men remained behind with Colin's body, and I saw flashes from the photographer's camera. Sergeant Trolley's voice came from right behind me, asking his incessant questions. So far they had done nothing for me, and I decided I was going to be in charge for myself from now on. Besides, I was desperate to talk only to Bob, so I ignored the questions and asked where Constable Cormier was.

"He's with the prisoners. Now, could you please tell me exactly what went on here?" Sergeant Trolley demanded, arousing only hostility in me.

"I need to talk to Constable Cormier. He's not leaving, is he?" He might have to take the prisoners to Fort St. John, and he was the only one to whom I could explain quickly what we had to do. Besides, I was already huffing and puffing, and had no voice or time left to give Sergeant Trolley the detailed explanations he required.

"They should still be there when we get back. Shit." That last word meant he had tripped and I turned to offer assistance, thinking that was unbecoming language for an officer. He got up on his own and, right away, resumed the questions.

Annoyed, I blocked his path and said, "Okay, Howard Norach shot Leona, then he shot Colin Sayers and he headed to the east." I was about to say that I shot Howard in the leg, but stopped, because I might get arrested on the spot. This officer wouldn't know that one had to fight evil with evil. "Like I said, he was heading east and then I think he'll go north, because I think he has some kind of place out there—that laboratory. That's all I know. Now I'm going after him." With that, I turned and hurried on as fast as I could.

Sergeant Trolley caught up to me again when we were on level ground and said: "You must have the eyes of a cat. You know you can't go after him. That's what we're here for."

"Well, I won't stop you. He shot my sister, killed Colin, and he had his men shoot Wapan and probably her family, and he—"

"Who's Wapan?" he interrupted.

"She was a good friend. But she was a wolf, so that wouldn't matter to you guys."

"Hey, slow down, Mrs. Webster, I'm not your enemy. I just want to help, but I have to get an idea of what's going on."

"You're right, I'm sorry. But I don't want you stopping me from going after him."

"You should be going to the hospital with your sister. We'll handle everything here."

Either he didn't understand any of what I had said or he thought little of it, so I stopped trying to explain further. Besides, if he ordered me away, I would have to obey. Or disobey. Actually, I'd broken one law already when I shot Howard in the leg, so disobeying would be nothing.

We finally came out on the road near my driveway, and the sound of the nearby helicopter drowned out further conversation. Michael and Kit were over by Kit's pickup, talking to Bob, and I rushed over to them. Seeing me, Michael shouted above the noise, "I can't go with her, so Kit's going to drive us there."

I took hold of Michael's hand to pull him aside and said into his ear, "You love your mother, right?"

His lips quivered as if he was on the verge of crying, and he nodded.

"So tell her that, first chance you get. Even if she's sleeping, tell her." He bit his lip and nodded again.

"I'm going to come up there later, as soon as I can. But I have to do something first." He looked at me, his eyes curious, but he didn't say anything as he got into Kit's pickup.

18

I returned to Bob and said loudly, "Bob, you know that place that's north of us? That place with the NAK-WAN sign? We have to go there. Right now."

"But I have to go back to the detachment now."

"No! It's not finished!"

"What do you mean?"

"Howard was going there, I'm sure of it." He followed me as I unthinkingly headed for Colin's van. "You can't go in that. Come to my jeep and you can explain on the way."

Following him, I climbed into his jeep just as Sergeant Trolley caught up to me again. Before he could say anything, I looked at him and asked, "Are you coming?" And then I slammed the door and we took off.

Two kilometres past Kit's driveway, we turned north onto the road that had a sign posted:

NAK-WAN LTD.

PRIVATE ROAD—KEEP OUT

TRESPASSERS WILL BE PROSECUTED

The last warning had always made me think that the place was legitimate.

Along the way, I explained what I knew and what I suspected as Bob focused on the winding road ahead. In turn, he told me why they had begun to look for me, and how Michael and Amber had thought of using Lady to find me. The mention of her name made me wonder where she had gone. She had disappeared into the dark when all those strangers had come down. I hoped she had made her way back to Kit's.

Not a moment passed before we saw her up ahead, at the side of the road, and she seemed to be tracking something. Bob slowed and then stopped, and we watched her raise her head to look at us, then lower it, as she continued in a zigzag fashion. I called to her and she reluctantly obeyed. She jumped into the rear and Bob drove on very slowly. Then he got out and studied the side of the road. When he returned, he said, "An ATV passed here, and take a look at this."

He poked a finger at me and, in the dim interior light, I saw some reddish guck on the tip of his finger. "It's blood. Your dog must have been tracking Howard."

"Let's hurry," I said, having only an inconclusive idea of why I felt this urgent need to find Howard. Earlier this afternoon, he said he'd had a surprise, and Leona showed up with Colin. Tonight he had said something about the best surprise to come. Yet I didn't dare raise my hopes about what the best surprise might be.

Bob spoke, cutting into my thoughts. "My boss has just joined us."

In the side mirror, I noticed the reflection of another vehicle's headlights appear after rounding a bend, as it caught up to us. Like the road to my place, this road curved according to the landscape and, about fifteen minutes later, we came to two six-foot gates, one side still open. A winding driveway led about two kilometres further in.

Bob parked and we looked at our surroundings. Yard lights illuminated buildings of different sizes, one to the left and some set further back. A large bungalow, with lighting coming from almost all the front windows, sat on higher ground to the right. A couple of white utility vans were parked over by one of the buildings, but the ATV was nowhere in sight. Neither was a man dragging his leg. I hoped I hadn't made a mistake.

Telling me to stay in the jeep, Bob got out to join Sergeant Trolley. One of them shouted "Over there!" and they both raced towards the

buildings on the left as if they had seen someone. Watching them disappear around a corner of a building, I wondered why I should obey
Bob's order. As I was arguing with myself, my peripheral vision caught
sight of movement at the side of the house, where the shadows were
the darkest. It had been like a flash of light, like someone with a flashlight. Staring hard, I couldn't make anything out. Perhaps I should just
go check it out, and look in the windows while I was at it. Yes, that's
what I'd do. I got out, telling Lady to stay and be quiet, because she
had begun growling, a deep low rumble in her throat.

Like Bob, I didn't slam the door shut, even though anyone around
would have seen our headlights as we drove in. The wind had picked
up and, without my jacket, I began to shiver again. I was halfway
across the lawn when I saw a shape move out of the shadows and then
the shape came into the lighted area. A huge black Rottweiler came
right at me and there was no time to run back to the jeep. Behind me,
Lady was barking and growling, trying desperately to get out of the
jeep. The Rottweiler ran past me to attack the jeep, trying to get at
Lady. Praying that neither dog would break a window, since a collie
was no match for a Rottweiler, and wishing I could stick around to
help Lady, I ran towards the house. Instinct told me that the answers I
needed were in that house. Someone must have opened a door back
there to let the Rottweiler out, and who else but Howard would have
done that?

From the veranda, I peered into windows, some covered with lace
curtains and others with the drapes drawn, but I could see that the
large front rooms were empty. Back at the front door, I tried the knob
and, since it wasn't locked, I entered. A hallway led into the depths of
the house. A floorboard creaked under me, so I stopped, then continued, keeping as close to the wall as I could.

"In here, Christine. I'm surprised Adolph didn't get you. Come and
see what the best surprise was. Don't be afraid. Come on."

Howard's voice sent chills through me, but I walked forward to the
first open doorway. He was sitting in a leather swivel chair, turned

away from a large mahogany desk, to face the doorway. Although I already had an idea of what the surprise might be, I was still shocked. On his left leg, his good leg, Howard was holding my son. Todd's legs dangled limply between Howard's legs. Recovering from my shock, I whispered, "You murdered him!"

His eyes took in the blood on my sweatshirt and he smiled. "Oh, he's not dead. I just gave him a little something so he wouldn't come to. And when he does, you're the one who's going to be dead."

My eyes focused on Todd's face, as I looked for signs of life. Yes, he was breathing, very softly.

Howard's crazy voice penetrated through the moment. "Oh my, what am I saying? No, no, no, the reason why I didn't kill you before was that I wanted to see your face when I slit the throat of your baby."

His words brought me back to the present, and that's when I saw the scalpel in his right hand. As I had in Peter's murder scenes, I play-acted and asked, with no hint of emotion, "And then you'll kill me and what good will all this do you?" I had to convince him that I really didn't care what he did. "I've already accepted Todd's death, so you can't hurt me anymore."

"I don't believe you. I saw your eyes. I see them now the way you look at your child." That was true, so I turned my gaze up to his face. He looked at the wall behind me on my left, studying it for a minute. Curious as to what he was staring at, I glanced back.

A bank of black-and-white monitors took up the wall space on one side of the door and one of them showed the two officers ushering some men out of a building. Another showed the front of the house, so that's how he knew exactly what I was doing.

When I turned back to him, I noticed a handgun, a stainless steel tray, and a coffee mug on the desk beside him. On the wall behind him were pictures of people, one of them of Hitler, a poster of a swastika, and one of some kind of emblem I'd never seen before. Howard was part of a white supremacist group, yet he had touched me, a lowly Métis woman—the supreme hypocrite. What was it he wanted from me? And then the answer came when one of the pictures caught my eye, a wedding picture of Dr. Coran and his wife.

"You are Doctor Coran," I gasped. I had grown a few inches since I was sixteen, so he wasn't shorter. I was taller.

"And you never once suspected who I was. You are such an imbecile. A little plastic surgery, a beard, contact lenses—that's all. I, on the other hand, recognized you as soon as I saw your picture in the paper. Because of you and your sister, I lost everything. Everything!" His voice rose at the end so that he almost screamed the last word, and he moved the scalpel close to Todd's exposed throat. But he got his anger under control and continued, "You were unfinished business for seventeen years. And tonight, I'll finish with you. By the way, how is your sister?"

My breathing began again and, trying hard to hide my contempt, I stared at him, impassively. Somehow, I had to get Todd away from him. I had noticed that Todd had been slipping downwards.

The doctor put the scalpel on the desk so he could adjust his grip on Todd. He talked on as he did so: "No more confiding in me? Too bad. I think I enjoyed that the most. That and the time you almost shot yourself on your porch there." He waited for my expression of surprise, but I remained silently emotionless, so he went on, not bothering to pick up the scalpel again. "Yes, that would have ended my game very nicely. But that wolf—it was the only time it wasn't scared of us. And I was greedy and wanted your sister to pay too. My mistake is that I should have handled her the same way I handled that wolf of yours. And that Colin," he made a scoffing noise before continuing. "He betrayed me. He stupidly fell in love with your sister and he betrayed me. But enough of all this, I think it's time I took another little keepsake from you. Come here. Put your hand on the tray here. You remember the routine?"

Without a word or show of fear, I walked over and placed my hand on the tray, mere inches from the gun. I had been wondering how I could get closer to the doctor and my child and, having made a quick plan, I had been about to throw myself at him. He was in a swivel chair and he had a serious leg wound, so that made him vulnerable.

A woman's voice came from behind me. "Father, what are you doing? You don't love her. Do you?"

Howard/Dr. Coran leaned over a bit to look past me and issue an order. "Queenie, go back to bed."

That second of distraction allowed me to grab the handgun. I pretended to check the safety catch with my other hand, as if I knew what I was doing, and pointed it at the doctor's head. With my free hand I gingerly picked up the scalpel and tossed it across the room, out of reach to both him and his daughter. As I leaned in close, I said just loud enough so only he could hear, "You know I'm going to shoot if I have to."

Very carefully, I removed my son from his lap and backed away from him. He made a movement as if to lunge for me, so I squeezed the trigger, aiming for the wall beyond. He'd had the safety off, because the gun fired and he sank back into his chair. Still this had all seemed too easy—anti-climactic was the word that came to mind. The sound of this shot would bring Bob or Sergeant Trolley in here, and soon everything would be okay. But right now I continued backing away, keeping an eye on him. Knowing it was Queenie who was behind me was of small comfort because she was most likely as mad as her father and therefore unpredictable.

At a safe distance from the doctor, I half-turned to Queenie to make eye contact, to show her I was harmless. Although she was only a few years older than I was, she had not aged well. In her nightgown and robe, she looked plump and matronly. I began speaking to her, "Queenie, I have to take Todd to bed now."

"Don't let her pass," Dr. Coran warned his daughter. She's going to take your son away from you."

"Todd? He's my son, you know." After she eyed Todd tenderly, she looked at me to see what my intentions were, and said, almost petulantly, "Let me take him."

"Okay, we'll just put him on the couch in the living room, okay? You can watch over him," I said, without relinquishing my son to her.

"Queenie, it's a trick. Don't let her go." I was at the doorway now, waiting to pass by her, but I didn't want to force my way. "He really needs to go back to bed, Queenie," I said, changing tactics. "Could you show me where he sleeps?"

"You're not going to take him away from me, are you?"

"We'll just put him back to bed," I said, reluctant to use an outright lie on the girl-woman.

She turned and I followed her. Behind me, I heard the springs of his chair and a drawer being pulled open, just as the front door burst open behind me and Bob came in. Startled, I turned and signalled for him to stop, so he wouldn't walk into the line of fire if Dr. Coran had got himself another gun. Bob came forward and, indicating direction with a nod of my head, I said, "In there. He's got monitors and maybe another gun."

"Is he alone?"

"Yeah." With that, I followed Queenie further down the hall to a small bedroom and I laid Todd down on the bed, pulled the covers over him, and, as Queenie leaned over and kissed his forehead, I noticed five capsules on the nightstand beside Todd's bed.

"What are these, Queenie?"

Her eyes widened in fright and she tried to grab them from my hand. "Don't tell father, please?"

"I won't, but what are they?"

"Father told me to put them in the milk, but I forgot. I put one in and then he came back from putting Adolph outside."

"The milk was for Todd?" I asked.

"And for me." She looked almost insulted.

"Did Todd drink his milk?"

"Maybe. Father took the milk. And I had to take Todd to him. Todd doesn't like his milk and he was already sleeping. I drank all my milk." She was looking from the door, to me, and back to the door, perhaps nervous that she was talking to me.

"All of it?"

She nodded solemnly, and it didn't look as though she was at all sleepy.

"Okay. We should go now," I whispered, wanting to draw her out of the room, away from Todd. That the doctor had attempted to give his own daughter, along with my son, an overdose of sleeping pills did not surprise me, nor did the fact that he had tried to use his daughter to do it.

Outside the now closed door, she turned to smile at me. "Isn't he precious?"

I nodded, looked down the hall to Bob, and then turned to Queenie. "You should go back to bed too. I'm going to leave now." As soon as she was gone, I intended to ask Bob if they had found Peter.

"I have to go say goodnight to Father first," Queenie said. With that, she slipped by me before I could stop her and stood in the doorway. I expected a shot to ring out and to see her fall, but nothing happened. "Oh, he's not here," she said, and turned and walked by me.

Bob and I both rushed to the doorway and, sure enough, the doctor had disappeared. Seeing the coffee mug on the desk, I took a closer look at it and was relieved to see that it was still full. I felt the milk and it was warm. Todd would be okay until we learned what had happened to Peter, and then we could all get out of here.

A small noise came from an area to the right of the doorway, behind a bookcase. Pressing himself against the wall, Bob cautiously yanked the bookcase door and when it swung open, he stepped back. But he didn't step back quickly enough. A loud sound snapped, making Bob spin back against the wall as blood bubbled out from his shoulder through his jacket. He immediately pushed me back out into the hallway.

"Oh man, you've been hit."

"I know." Bob grimaced and, seeing the alarm on my face, said, "It's okay, it's just a nick."

"Those are the worst kinds," I quipped, as my warped sense of humour came into play.

"Looked like he was about to climb a ladder in there. We've got him cornered." Bob pressed his hand onto his wound and said, "Damn, this hurts." He spotted the blood on my sweatshirt then and, concerned, asked, "Did you get shot?"

"No, he cut my finger and, if I don't talk about it, it doesn't hurt. Did you find Peter out there?"

"No, only one guy going into this room with enough of an arsenal to equip an army, and five more sleeping in a dorm. There's like twenty, thirty cots in there, so we don't know where the rest are. I'm sorry we didn't find Peter. The little one, was that your son?"

"Yes. He tried to drug him, but he didn't have enough time."

"I know you must want to leave …"

"Not without Peter," I said.

We stared at each other for a second. "Sergeant Trolley radioed for more backup and they're on their way," Bob said. "We'll keep looking for Peter, so don't worry about that. Right now, we don't have enough handcuffs for them out there and I should get back to help. Howard is pinned in there. Do you think you can keep him in there?"

After giving me some advice and checking the pistol I was holding, Bob left. Knowing Dr. Coran, I had to face the fact that he had probably killed Peter a long time ago.

Impatience and curiosity made me enter the office quietly to take a quick look in the storage room. The doctor, breathing heavily and grunting, was still climbing the ladder, using his wounded leg just enough to hop on his good leg upwards.

Where he thought he was going, I didn't know, but it suddenly occurred to me that if there was an arsenal of weapons in one of the other buildings, maybe there were some more up there in the attic. Bob had told me to stop him from coming out, but Bob didn't have my imagination. The doctor was at the top now and both his hands were occupied, one hanging on to the rung of the ladder and the other pushing open the trap door. His weight was on his good leg. All I had to do was shoot that one and he wouldn't be going anywhere. I tried, but I couldn't make myself squeeze the trigger.

"Get down from there," I said.

His left side was to me and the gun was in his right hand, the one pushing open the trap door. He tried to aim it at me, over his left arm, but in his rush he lost his grip and tumbled to the floor.

He pulled himself into something of a sitting position, looked up at me, and hissed, "Go ahead, shoot."

"What kind of drug did you use on my son?"

The doctor gave me a nasty grin and said, "If he's not already dead, he will be soon. So go ahead, shoot me."

The gun in my hand was shaking, or rather it was my hand that was shaking as I tried to squeeze the trigger. He had murdered my husband, he had taken my son from me, he deserved to die! But something inside me just wouldn't let me kill a human being in cold blood, not even this ... thing. Tears came to my eyes as I fought with myself, one part telling me I was bad, so what did it matter, and the other part telling me what I already knew.

"We're alike, you know," he whispered. Trying to provoke me, he added, "You and me. I saw that when you were sweet sixteen. So sweet, so ripe."

To shut him up, I said, "Shooting you would be too easy. I'd rather see you rot in prison."

The doctor shifted and brought his arm up from beside him, having gotten hold of his gun again. He lowered his arm to his side, since it was obvious to both of us that I could shoot him before he could shoot me. It appeared that the fight had gone out of him, but just to add to his misery, I said, "My son is going to be fine. You're the one who stopped Queenie from putting all those capsules into the milk. You."

Suddenly he screamed, "Damn you!" And he pointed the gun at his head and fired.

I stood there, shocked.

What brought me out of my trance was a thumping noise from above. Crossing the small space, I stepped over the corpse and began to climb up the ladder. Pushing open the trap door, I looked into a pitch-black darkness.

It seemed dumb, but I said "Hello?"

"Mmm-mmmm-mmm" came a sound from a corner, along with the squeaking of bedsprings. The light from below barely lit up the area around the trap door, but as I moved further into the blackness, my eyes gradually adjusted to the dark. On my hands and knees I felt along where two-foot-wide plywood had been placed over the joists. At one point they seemed to split off in different directions, so I stopped to ask, "Where are you?"

The "Mmm-mmmm-mmm" came again and I got excited, because it really did sound like Peter! He wasn't dead!

Inching my way forward again, I bumped into a metal rail. Running my hands along it, then upwards to a thin mattress, then higher, I felt a warm human body. Down along the form I touched ropes that seemed to be wrapped around ankles and then down to the legs of the cot. Moving my hands along, I found that the man's hands were taped together with heavy-duty tape, like duct tape. Further towards the face, more rope wound around the man's neck, securing him tightly to the cot, and it felt as though tape was wrapped all the way around his head. With my hand on the side of his head, I asked, "Peter?"

And I felt him give a slight nod! I tried to loosen the tape around his wrists, but the tape wouldn't give.

"I have to get scissors. Don't worry, I'll be back as soon as I can."

Before I got back to the trap door, I heard Bob calling me.

"I'm up here. Peter's up here." I answered, emotion making my voice quiver.

When I got to the bottom, Bob asked, "What happened?"

"He shot himself. I wanted to do it, but I couldn't. I need some scissors." Then I spotted the scalpel on the carpeted floor. Déjà vu. Only this time it would be put to good use.

As I picked it up, I asked, "Did the others get here yet?"

"Just Ringer and Boutlane. But we can hear the sirens now." Bob sank down into the leather chair and a show of pain flashed across his face.

Back in the attic, I hurried over to Peter and began freeing him, beginning with his hands so he could pull the tape from his face. Finally he was able to sit up and stretch.

"Tell me I'm not hallucinating," he said.

"You're not hallucinating," I said. As with Todd, I held back the urge to hug like crazy. "How long have you been up here?"

"He had me brought up here … I don't know. It was morning when I was brought up here."

We crawled back over to the trap door and I asked, "Can you make it down the ladder?"

"You bet."

"I'll go first."

"To catch me if I slip?"

"You bet."

At the bottom, he stepped over the doctor and stopped to look at the corpse. "Bastard!" he snarled.

"He won't hurt anyone else now," I said.

"He killed Todd. He almost made you kill yourself."

"He didn't kill Todd. Todd's sleeping. He tried to give him some kind of drug."

Looking at me with surprise, Peter noticed the blood on me. Before he could ask, I said, "I'm okay."

Tears came to his eyes as he asked, "And Todd's really alive?"

I nodded, tears in my own eyes too.

"Well, let's get him out of here," Peter said, looking around.

Turning to leave, I spotted something familiar on the bookcase. "Hey, isn't that your manuscript?" I asked.

"Yeah, it was part of his game. Where's Todd?"

I led the way to the bedroom, and Bob was already there, wrapping a blanket around Todd. Queenie was asleep in a rocking chair and it alarmed me that she didn't wake up as we moved about, but then I remembered that she had drunk all her milk.

As Peter lifted Todd from the bed, I said to Bob, "Wait. There's a Rottweiler at your jeep."

"So that's what that ruckus is out there," Bob said. "We'll have to get rid of it."

"You mean, shoot it?" I asked, as we followed each other down the hallway.

"We have to get out of here."

"We don't even know if it's vicious. I'll go call it from the side door. Wait here." Before they could veto me, I left, racing towards the back of the house, opening and closing doors along the way. The door at the end of the hall led into a bright, gleaming white kitchen, and I saw the side door at the east. I made sure the kitchen door was securely shut to the rest of the house. The name Adolph had been mentioned twice, so I stepped outside and yelled, "Adolph! Come!"

From where I was standing, I could hear the dogs in the distance, but not see them. Their sudden silence meant that Adolph was obediently coming. That was good, but once he got here, I had no real plan to deal with him. That was bad.

I stood behind the door and he tap-danced into the kitchen and turned to face me right away. As I took a few slow, cautious steps so I could back out of the door he'd just come in, I saw his eyes as he processed information: This human knows my name. This human is a stranger. Attack!

By then, I had swung the door closed, but had to do so with my left hand. He lunged at the door, the door slammed shut, and the knob banged into my middle finger. Daggers of pain shot through my whole body, right up into my head. Gritting my teeth, I ran around to the front, where Bob was the first to come out.

Police car sirens were shutting off as they rolled in, one after another, and their headlights and flashing beacons lit up the yard. Two police officers came around the side of the house and I saw that one was Constable Ringer. Following behind were two girls and a man, all with blankets over their shoulders. Constable Ringer said, "This is Vivian, Jake, and—"

"Bob was shot," I interrupted. Could you drive us to the hospital?"

After getting a nod from Bob, Constable Ringer said he'd be right back from letting Sergeant Trolley know.

At Bob's jeep, Peter and I got in the back with Todd, while Bob sat in the front passenger seat. Lady could not stop wiggling her rear, as she tried to plant her kisses on our faces. Her mood was infectious and, as Peter stared into his son's face, nothing could have wiped the smile off his face. Constable Ringer jumped in the driver's seat and we were out of there.

19

On the drive to Fort St. John, Todd began to stir and then he awoke. His eyes focused on Peter, but, in the shadows, he didn't recognize him and he became alarmed. Peter murmured his name, and that's when Todd hugged him. Then Peter moved so that Todd could see me, too, and, right away, he put his arms out and we hugged. A distressing thought broke through my happiness, but I kept it to myself, not wanting to burden Peter with it.

When we arrived at the hospital, Bob had weakened considerably and Constable Ringer had to help him in. Constable Ringer made the explanations at the admittance desk, and Bob was taken away in a wheelchair. Todd was next and, while Peter stayed with him, my turn came. While skin was being grafted from my arm to cover the missing tip of my finger, I told the doctor about Dr. Coran and what he had done years before, and now I was very concerned that he might have molested Todd. The doctor assured me he would examine Todd again more closely. He said, as far as he knew, paedophiles didn't usually switch genders. When he was done with me, he gave me a business card for a child psychologist, Dr. Angeline Laboucane. He recommended that we take Todd to her, regardless, and I was already thinking she might do some good for Michael. After Peter was examined and Todd re-examined, we went to see Leona.

Michael and Kit were sitting in a small waiting room and, when they saw Peter and Todd, they both jumped up, their faces a mixture of shock, then puzzlement, and then wide grins as they welcomed them back to the land of the living. Michael took the time to say, "Mom's going to be fine," then they carried on with their reunion.

A doctor interrupted to tell us that Leona was sedated, and that only Michael and I could go in to see her. Leona looked beautiful and peaceful, her colouring back to normal. Michael said he wanted to stay the night at her side. Back in the hallway, only Peter and Todd were there now. Noticing Todd's drooping eyelids, I said, "We should get a hotel room, get him to bed."

"Okay. Kit went down to see how Bob is doing. Let's stop there first."

Kit was now waiting patiently in another area enclosed on three sides, and he told us that Bob was still in the operating room. We told him we were going to find a hotel room nearby, but we'd call in later. Kit gave us the keys to Bob's jeep, saying that Officer Ringer had had to leave. Before we were almost out the doors down the hall, I remembered to tell him that we had Lady with us.

Later that night, Todd was peacefully asleep in the extra double bed. Peter had showered and shaved, and he looked like a new man—or the old one I was used to. Afterwards, I took a long, luxurious bath to wash away the aches I had accumulated from that day. While I bathed, Peter went out to find us coffee. After my bath, I phoned to check on Bob's condition. Everything fell nicely into place when they told me he was going to be fine.

Lady came over to me, wagging her tail, and then she jumped onto Todd's bed. She made me think of Wapan, and the one major regret I had was that Wapan had been killed and nothing would bring her back. Ruffling Lady's fur, I whispered, "Lady, you are one heck of a little trooper, you know that?" She wagged her tail and moved to make herself more comfortable.

Peter returned with two large coffees and some milk and sugar for me. He spotted Lady on Todd's bed right away and I said, "Aren't they a beautiful sight?"

That stopped him from ordering Lady off the bed. "Yes, they are," he grinned, "and so are you."

Setting the Styrofoam coffee cups down, he came over for a hug. "I didn't think I'd see you again," he murmured.

"I know. Once I finally believed you and Todd were gone, I ... I didn't want to go on living."

"He showed me the tape."

"He showed you a tape? Of the time ... I was on the porch?" I asked, embarrassed that I was even seen, let alone taped.

Nodding, Peter continued. "His men were spying on you, sometimes taping you. Not too long ago he showed me a tape of you and him, trying to imply that he was carrying on with you. But I saw your body language. You acted the same way with him the way you do with Al and Iris—grudgingly polite. He said that you ruined his whole life, you and Leona, and he never forgot."

"He should never have taken on the Pelletier sisters. Anyways, he ruined his own life. I'm just so sorry you and Todd were the ones to pay." I took a sip of my coffee before I continued. "Peter, Dr. Coran once committed incest with his daughters, or at least I'm pretty sure he did. And he tried to rape me. So I talked to the doctor about Todd, and he said perverts don't usually switch genders. Anyways, he gave me a card for this doctor, here, and he said we ought to take Todd to see her. I'm sorry. I feel so responsible."

"Chris, the man was crazy, so don't put this on your shoulders. We'll come through, no matter what. When did he try to rape you?"

"When I was a foster kid in his house. But, thank god, I got arrested."

"You got arrested? My goodness, you do have a past, don't you?" he smiled.

"I've got a lot of secrets from my past. And I have to tell you about them. I should have already told you, and I'm sorry I didn't. But first, you have to tell me what happened to you and Todd."

We rehashed everything from the beginning. On the day I was

expected back from Norway House, Kit had come to give him a message that a man had made a call for Leona saying that she wanted us to come to her place in Fort St. John and that it was urgent. Expecting me home soon, he intended to wait, but right after Kit was gone, Howard came with another man for what Peter had thought was a social call. When he answered another knock at the door, two of them grabbed him and Howard brought out a pistol.

Lady attacked, and one of the men hit her with the edge of our cast-iron frying pan, making her bleed. Howard had to stitch it up so I wouldn't know anything had happened. He had his medical bag with him because part of his plan was to add a powdered sedative to my sugar. After that, Howard brought out a syringe and gave Peter a shot and that was all he remembered.

I interrupted to tell him that when I got back from my trip, Lady was at Mona's place and she wanted me to go north into the woods. Now I knew why, and we both acknowledged that she was one smart dog.

Then Peter continued with his narration. When he awoke, he was in a small dark room and he didn't know what had happened to Todd or me. But over the days, then the weeks, then the months, he heard sounds out there that made him think he was in an active militia compound.

"Your manuscript was about something like that," I interrupted.

"Yeah, remember, a couple of years ago, on one of my walks in the woods, I came across that place, so my imagination kicked in and the manuscript was supposed to be based on imagination, not reality. Anyhow, since that very first day, I never saw Todd again, until tonight. Howard used to tell me that if I tried to escape, he'd kill Todd."

"What a nightmare for you."

"One morning he would tell me that he accidentally gave Todd an overdose and that Todd was dead. The next day he'd tell me that Todd was alive, so I'd better not try anything. He was totally insane and, while he terrorized you, I had to sit by and do nothing. He's the one who cut your hair, gave me some as a keepsake."

"He did that? I thought I did it, in my sleep. I thought I was going crazy. I thought …" I stopped, embarrassed by what I had almost said. Well, if I was going to come clean with other things, I may as well start here, so I said, quietly, "At first, I thought you had run off with Leona."

Peter tilted his head and said, just as quietly, "Chris, I would never do something like that. I like your sister just fine, but it's you I love."

We looked at each other and something inside clicked and I knew, *I knew,* that I loved this man and, maybe just as important, I trusted him.

Peter picked up from where he had left off. "So, sitting by helplessly, that was frustrating as hell, and it almost drove me crazy. Maybe that was part of his game plan too. After he got tapes of you, he'd have me taken to his house and make me watch them. And when he showed me my manuscript, he said he could come and go inside our cabin anytime he wanted. The last tape was of the cabin burning."

"So you know we don't have the cabin anymore."

"Yeah, but I've got something better, now." Saying that, Peter reached over and squeezed my good hand.

He resumed the account of what he knew. "This morning, he came in and said he could kill two birds with one stone, but, before that, the first to go would be Todd. By then he had drugged me, and I felt myself going under. I thought I was dying. But then I woke up and found myself roped down and gagged and, after the second gunshot, I gambled and started bucking as much as I could. And then I heard your voice and I thought I was hallucinating. Or that my mind had finally snapped. You of all people. Imagine that."

Taking a sip of my coffee, I said, "So much has happened, and I have a lot to tell you. But I'm just glad we all got out of this alive. Except for Wapan, that is. Peter, I wish you knew her. She was—wow!"

"Wow-wow," Todd's sleepy voice came from the other bed and, when we looked over, he was sitting up, rubbing his eyes. Peter and I went over and lay on either side of him, whispering soothing nothings. Todd lay back down on his side and moved the satin ribbing on the edge of the blanket into his mouth. After I moved away, Lady inched up to take my place beside him, licked his face a few times, and Todd put an arm on her shoulder.

The next day, when we walked into Leona's room, she and Michael were holding each other's hands and laughing. Wonderful to see, wonderful to hear. She was as surprised as everyone else had been to see Peter and Todd, even though Michael had already told her what he knew. As Leona and I silently looked at each other, I knew that the bond between us would never be broken again.

From Leona's room we went to see Bob. Kit, Mona, and Amber were already there, visiting. Kit looked over at us and said, "We didn't look at that wolf close enough."

"What do you mean?"

"Bob was just telling me that the wolf they looked at was a young male."

"But I always thought Wapan was a female," I said, confused.

"She was," Kit replied. "She is."

And when it dawned on me, I asked, "She wasn't killed?"

"No. The wolf that was shot was probably a littermate to her. But she must be alive."

"Yes! Yes, she is. She's the one who woke us when the cabin burned." I was just starting to get excited when I paused. "A wolf still lost its life because of me."

"Chris, that wasn't because of you," Peter chided me gently. "It was because a man was insane, and you can't hold yourself responsible for his illness."

"You're absolutely right," I agreed.

Amber turned to me and said, "I guess, um, Lady's been real good for me, it was great having her around. But I think she should be with Todd now. Don't you?"

"Are you sure, Amber?" I asked.

She nodded, and I was so moved by her generosity that I went over and hugged her.

Later that night, Peter and I talked for hours—that is, I talked and he listened. I began with the grampa-man, telling how the touching had begun, and the progressive steps that had led to my culpability, my deviance, until I came to the point where I had left off with Leona in the cave.

"Before you say I couldn't possibly know sexual feelings at the age of three, I'm telling you now that I was there and I remember everything as it was. Not the number of times, because I didn't know how to count back then. But Peter . . ." I swallowed and looked away, not at Todd, but somewhere to a distant past, and then I continued. "Besides going to his room on my own, I *wanted* him to put his thing between my legs." Wiping away tears that had spilled over, I stared down at the floor as I finished. "I became a willing partner, even though I knew it was wrong."

"Christine, look at me." Peter's voice was quiet, full of compassion instead of contempt. "I can understand how you would have felt after that. Children tend to blame themselves first, partly because they are the centre of their small worlds. But you are the most loving and love-able person I know. Your only competition is our little guy over there."

"No, you're wrong. I'm not competition to him because there's more."

"More?"

"Yes," and with that, I skipped ahead to tell him about my daughter, ending with a truth I had been unwilling to face until that moment. "You see, the other girls in the home for unwed mothers, my room-mates, they were giving their babies up out of love for the babies. But me, I gave up my child as an act of revenge. I had in mind that, some day, I'd run into Nick and I'd tell him I gave his daughter away to strangers."

By then I was unable to stop my weeping, and he held me close to him. When I finally stopped, he said: "This daughter of yours, let's see if we can find her. If everything's good in her life, we'll leave her alone. But if she's in and out of foster homes or something like that, let's reclaim her."

I don't know if it was his forgiveness or his ready acceptance that made me start crying all over again, but this time it was with happiness. I loved this man and I was grateful to God for having allowed me to redeem him and Todd from the evil insanity of the doctor. With the help of my friends and family, I knew that at this moment I had found redemption for myself.

Three weeks later, we were all at Shadow Lake. The latest edition of the *Peace Valley Voice* had just come out and, on the front page, Mrs. Springer pronounced me a heroine—and that made me squirm. The news story attracted media to the area, and we were soon all ducking reporters.

Mrs. Springer's column was a summary of what had happened, but we learned the details from Bob. The three kidnap victims provided the initial information, and that made Archie Brighton talk, in an attempt to get himself a better deal. Archie was one of the three men who worked for Howard and he provided shocking revelations about NAK-WAN, the North American Klan of the White Aryan Nations. Every year four or five people were kidnapped—homeless people, street prostitutes, anyone they figured would never be missed. Then, after hunting season began, special guests who had paid a fortune were brought in one at a time for a hunt of human prey. The militia operation was on hiatus by then, so only a handful of men remained at NAK-WAN. Over the years, this handful of insiders had each had to murder one of the kidnapped victims. That way no undercover cop could ever penetrate the inner circle.

Long before we had moved to Shadow Lake, Howard had befriended, drugged, and caused Wayne Schumack to crash. Howard/ Dr. Coran knew that Mr. Schumack had flown over the compound and might have seen one of the hunters in pursuit of his human prey. What really gave me the willies was that Dr. Coran had such a hunt in mind as Peter's fate.

The evil of this man was especially evident when the police viewed a tape of him killing his other daughter, Darcy, by beating her and strangling her to death with his bare hands. In the video, Howard explained afterward that he had done so to purge his daughter from having defiled herself with a black man. The video was made to show other leaders that, in the new order, Howard Norach would never put anything ahead of the movement. According to Bob, Darcy looked to be about eighteen, and the doctor looked like a completely different man in his forties. I added the information that that Dr. Coran had taken his daughters and Miss Branzil to the Caribbeans, where they were all supposed to have drowned.

Our greatest concern now was Todd, and we took him to see Dr. Laboucane. She reported that he showed no signs of having been molested and that he was recovering well from his separation from us. Michael had also been to see her and he, too, seemed to have benefited.

Leona and Bob had been meeting with people at the Friendship Centre about organizing a life-skills program for women coming out of jail. While Leona had been recuperating, she had given a lot of thought to her former roommates. Because many of them had been institutionalized in some way for most of their lives, one of the fears they had was of living on the outside.

As soon as the townspeople knew Peter and Todd were alive, attitudes towards me changed dramatically, making me almost as uncomfortable as when I'd been under suspicion. They offered to help us rebuild and they called on others, and, before we knew it, they were coming from as far away as Hudson's Hope and Fort St. John. The new cabin was similar to the old one, but with a usable upper loft.

Once we moved in, we invited everyone to return for a barbecue. After the last of our guests had gone, we sat around a fire down at the lake, eating some of that day's leftovers. Another car drove in and Mrs. Springer got out. Walking over to us, she apologized to me for the earlier columns and, because she had tears in her eyes, I accepted her apology. Then she opened the bag hanging from her shoulder and brought out an envelope containing enlarged photographs she had taken of us.

After she was gone, Michael helped us take the plates and cups back to the cabin, and he and Peter cleaned up in the kitchen while I put Todd to bed, upstairs. From the window in his room I saw Leona and Bob down by the lake, holding hands. They were both healing nicely, together.

Somewhere out there, Wapan was running wild and free. Her clan would grow, and they would be healthy and strong.

During the night I woke up, sure I had heard the wolves. A full moon flooded our bedroom with its silvery light and I got up to look outside. Oh, to be a wolf. If I were a wolf, I'd be out there, running and playing and hunting, living life as it was meant to be lived. Peter's touch startled me and, as we both stood there, looking out, I realized I was happy just being me.

Thank you, Paul Seesequasis, for your notes on one of my first drafts. Thank you, Arlene LaBoucane, for sharing your home, your time, and your knowledge. I am also indebted to Mary Schendlinger, senior editor of *Geist,* who encouraged me when I really, really needed it and who put me on the right track. And to Rosemary Shipton, who made the editing process a delight. Any errors in this book will be my own and may be intentional—or not. Florene Belmore and Greg Young-Ing at Theytus Books, thank you.

I gratefully acknowledge the Canada Council for its grant.

Many thanks to all those, like L. David Mech, who have listened carefully to what the wolves are telling us. Your books have been invaluable to me.

And, finally, thanks to my own family, especially Debbie and George—hey, at last I'm done!

Beatrice Culleton Mosionier was born in St. Boniface, Manitoba, in 1949. She was the youngest of four children born to Mary Clara and Louis Mosionier. From the age of three to seventeen, she lived in different foster homes. In 1980, after a second suicide in her family, Beatrice decided to write a book. Her first novel, *In Search of April Raintree,* was published in 1983, and she has since written other books, a play, and a short filmscript for the National Film Board. She now lives in Toronto and in Bracebridge, Ontario.

MEMBER OF THE SCABRINI GROUP

Quebec, Canada
2000